Whispers on the Wind

ALSO BY CAROLINE FYFFE

Prairie Hearts Series

Logan Meadows, Wyoming Territory, 1878

Where the Wind Blows
Before the Larkspur Blooms
West Winds of Wyoming
Under a Falling Star
Whispers on the Wind
Where Wind Meets Wave

The McCutcheon Family Series

Y Knot, Montana Territory, 1883

Montana Dawn
Texas Twilight
Mail-Order Brides of the West: Evie
Mail-Order Brides of the West: Heather
Moon Over Montana
Mail-Order Brides of the West: Kathryn
Montana Snowfall
Texas Lonesome

Whispers on the Wind

Caroline Fyffe

A Prairie Hearts Novel

To Cheryl, a dear, dear girl friend from the very start! Love, Caroline

Montlake Romance

This is a work of fiction. Names, characters, organizations, places, events, and incidents are either products of the author's imagination or are used fictitiously.

Published by Montlake Romance, Seattle

www.apub.com

ISBN-13: 9781503939059
ISBN-10: 1503939057

Cover design by Anna Curtis

Printed in the United States of America

Dedicated to our beautiful granddaughter,
Evelyn Chanel.
We never knew how bright the stars could shine until
the day that you were born.

PROLOGUE

Soda Springs, Idaho Territory, 1883

A biting north wind cut through the thick layers of Hunter Wade's clothing as he reined to a halt in the yard. He paused to look around. Quincy Malone's usual hired gunman was nowhere to be seen. Dismounting, Hunter flipped his reins over the hitching rail and climbed the steps of the large Victorian home so unlike the rest of the structures of Soda Springs. Trail weary and tired, he rubbed his left leg. The usual throb had grown more intense over the long ride.

Raising a fisted hand, he rapped his knuckles loudly on the front door. Hard to believe more than a year had come and gone since he'd set off from Soda Springs. Once he collected what was owed him, Hunter planned to spend a few weeks relaxing in town—*doing nothing*. He'd earned a rest—and the money from Quincy would keep him fat and happy for a good long time. First thing he'd do was visit Ned, who poured the worst whiskey in the Americas, and take in a show or two of his favorite singer, Dichelle Bastianelli. But only after he'd consumed three portions of Sherman's beef stew at the café.

When no one answered, he knocked again. Quincy hadn't spared any expense when he'd built this place fifteen years ago, off the profits he'd acquired by owning a good portion of the town. The man, only five foot one, with the face of a schoolboy even though he was over fifty years old, was a black-hearted snake. Just as soon sell out his mother if a profit could be turned. Hunter hadn't gone looking for the contract Quincy hired him for, but he'd been in between jobs awhile, and hunger can make a man do almost anything. As long as he wasn't breaking any laws, he'd hold back his judgment on any man.

He rapped again—harder—anger igniting his belly. Maybe Quincy had gotten word that Hunter had returned, that he'd soon be in for his recompense, and the man didn't want to hand over the substantial amount of money. Who would?

If Quincy thinks I'm leaving without my pay, he has another think coming.

He waited a half a second more, then grasped the doorknob. The gun resting on his thigh was good and loaded. Pushing open the thick oak door, Hunter stepped into the quiet entry and looked around.

"Quincy! It's Wade. I know you're here."

A noise upstairs drew his gaze to the stairway. "Quincy," he called again. Getting caught on the staircase would give Malone the advantage. He glanced around again, taking stock of the two open doors on opposite sides of the room. "I hear you up there. Come down so we can talk."

He silently backed out the front door, careful not to let the lock click, and circled around to the back of the house, but found the rear door locked. Extracting his pocketknife, Hunter made fast work of getting in. He glanced around. He'd been in the house only a handful of times, but it had never been this quiet. He wondered where the cook and other servants were.

Finding the back stairwell, he proceeded up. Not taking any chances, he drew his revolver. At the top, five doors lined a long hallway. Because it would afford more privacy, he guessed, the master suite would be at the end. Moving forward, he kept his body out of the line of fire. He nudged the door open with his shoulder and found the businessman slouched in a corner chair, his bloodshot eyes wide with fear. The room reeked of whiskey.

"Don't shoot!"

"I'm not here to kill you, Malone, so just relax." Hunter's reputation as a gunman was much exaggerated. But, in his line of business, he guessed that wasn't such a bad thing. He'd killed a few men, but always in self-defense, which wasn't against the law. Still, he didn't holster his weapon. "I'm here to collect what you owe me. Nothing more. I'll be out of your hair just that quick."

"Can't do that, Wade."

Now what? And why hadn't he found Malone in his office in town, with a handful of others scuttling around doing his bidding? "I've just spent a year delivering your precious sister and her family safely to the other side of the country. I took outdated routes like you wanted, which added hardships and time. I've done *my* job, now you'll pay up the other half of what I'm owed."

The small man raised his hands in submission. "It's all gone. My money, my businesses, everything. Won't be long before I'm forced to leave this house."

Disbelief rippled through Hunter, followed by anger. "I don't believe you! You've hidden your assets so your debtors won't be able to collect. And shielded your family by moving them east. All because you knew this was going to happen." He stepped forward, lifting his gun. "You'll pay up, Malone, or you won't see the light of another day."

CHAPTER ONE

Logan Meadows, Wyoming Territory, October 1883

Wielding a hammer, Tabitha Canterbury pried at the wooden lid of a container with the claw end of the tool. It slipped and clattered to the floor, missing her toe by an inch. Determined to open the crate on her own, she hefted the weighty hammer once again and wedged the iron prongs under the lid, pressing down with as much force as she could muster.

Stubborn thing won't budge!

Exasperated after fifteen minutes of fruitless labor, she let an uncharacteristic curse whisper through her lips—just as the front door opened. Silver bells jingled in announcement.

Her forehead warm and sticky, Tabitha glanced up. Jessie Logan, who Tabitha had met upon moving to Logan Meadows almost a year ago, stood in the doorway, her son balanced on her hip and a teasing smile on her face.

"Tabitha, you've scalded my ears. I've never heard you curse before." Jessie laughed and set Shane on the wooden floor, keeping ahold of his hand. In a swish of fabric, she came forward, looking curiously at the good-sized crate. "Books, I presume?"

Tabitha sighed, and then nodded. "Exactly. I'd like to get them on the shelves that look so empty, but I'm ashamed to say this crate has gotten the better of me. I swear!" She gave the sturdy wooden box a disgruntled glare. "One would think it had a mind of its own."

"Let me fetch Chase. He's just a couple of doors down at the bank speaking with your uncle. He'll have the top off in a jiffy."

Jessie was almost to the door when Tabitha caught her arm.

Startled, Shane frowned as if she'd just struck his mother. "Stop!" he cried. "Let go my ma!" His back straightened as he prepared for a fight.

"I'm sorry, Shane," Tabitha said. "I didn't mean to startle you." She crouched to his level, and a wary look slowly replaced his frown. A deep longing grasped her heart and squeezed with a vengeance as she looked into his inquisitive eyes. Reaching out, she pushed back a hank of hair that drooped over his forehead. What would her child look like? At nearly twenty-nine, marriage may have passed her by, but she'd make sure her life didn't. She'd traveled west without a man and built this store. That was a huge accomplishment. How many single women could claim the same? Her parents would hold the feat in high esteem once they finally forgave her for the bold move. Marriage and motherhood weren't the only paths that made life worth living.

"Can you forgive me, sweetie?" she implored, gazing into the child's large blue eyes. She cupped his cheek, made pink by the light wind blowing outside. "I just didn't want your mommy fetching your pa. He's a very busy man and has better things to do. With your aid, I'm sure we can get this done on our own. Will you help?"

Shane glanced up at his ma, still holding his hand, and Jessie nodded, then crooked her brow as Tabitha stood. "You're one stubborn woman, Tabitha Canterbury. It wouldn't hurt to let Chase pop that off. *However,* I guess I understand. You want to prove to everyone in Logan Meadows that you're capable of doing for yourself." She wagged her head from side to side.

"It's not quite like that." *I need to prove to myself I can provide as I grow old—alone. I can't scurry off in search of a man each time I run into an obstacle.*

"No? I think you're trying to convince yourself more than anyone else. We all see what you've achieved in the short time you've been in Logan Meadows."

Her admiring glance around Storybook Lodge, at the different sections of books, even in their meager state, warmed Tabitha.

"I love spending time in your cute little shop," Jessie continued. "Reminds me of a dollhouse. It's my favorite place to visit."

They'd had this conversation before. Everyone and their brother had turned out to help the new "town spinster." She shivered. How she hated that title! Why was a man handsomer and more respected as he grew older, even if he chose to remain a bachelor forever, but a woman was just an old maid? Past her prime? Only good for baking for church socials or mending old socks?

It wasn't fair!

She was the same woman she'd been at nineteen, only wiser by a country mile. *What about that gray hair you pulled from your temple this morning?*

"Tabitha?"

"I'm sorry. I got lost . . ."

"In your thoughts? I know. I guess that's normal for a bookstore owner with all the places you can read about every single day, since you don't have a family to do for, or suppers to cook . . ."

Pain sliced Tabitha, but she didn't look away.

Jessie quickly reached for Tabitha's arm. "I'm so sorry! That didn't come out the way I'd intended. I just meant—"

"I understand. I'm sure most married women dream of time to do as they please. By the time chores are complete, nighttime has fallen and the day is over." *Then, once in bed, lying next to their husbands . . . no, I won't go there.*

Jessie Logan was a dear friend. She'd been Tabitha's first customer on the day the shop had opened. Her husband, Chase, had learned to read in the last few years and seemed to be making up for lost time. After the Logans' costly purchase of several books, Tabitha had offered to lend them some from her personal shelf upstairs. No one here in Wyoming Territory had pockets filled with gold, unless you counted family love as such. The Logans had gladly accepted her offer, but only if they could pay a fee when they returned the copy.

One book turned into three, and then five, and before she knew what had transpired, she had her own small lending library in the corner of the store. That was fine. Tabitha wasn't trying to earn a fortune. Only enough to get by and pay her monthly loan to Uncle Frank. Just because her uncle was the owner of the town bank, she didn't expect special treatment. She'd make her own way without his help, too. For now, she was paying off her debt with the savings she'd earned while assisting at the library back home. She looked forward to the day the shop would pay for itself.

"Now, back to the problem at hand," she said. "If the two of us push down at the same time, maybe we can pry off the lid together."

"So you'll accept *my* help."

"Of course. I'm not stupid, Jessie, just stubborn. You're a woman, I'm a woman. I welcome a hand from you."

She winked, and then went back to the crate. Seesawing the claw prongs under the well-constructed lid, she beckoned her friend over.

"Now, you hold here and I'll take it here. One, two, three . . ."

They both heaved down. The corner lifted in a crackling of splintering wood, but the loud crash that followed wasn't the lid coming off. Both women spun around.

Shane stood next to the window, a shattered water glass at his feet.

"Shane!" Jessie let go of the hammer and rushed to her son, hefting Shane into her arms.

The door opened and Chase Logan stepped in. At thirty-one, Jessie's husband was a man who drew attention. The few lines fanning from his eyes, and his tanned face from working out in the elements, actually added to his appeal. Wide-set shoulders and strong arms offset his trim waist. He would catch any woman's eye, and Tabitha was no exception.

"What's going on?" he asked, his gaze taking in the mess. "I saw Shane in the window." His gaze rose from the shards on the floor to Tabitha, who still held the hammer attached to the crate, and he assessed the situation instantly.

Without asking, he extracted the hammer from Tabitha's grip, and had the lid off in seconds. Smiling, he handed back her tool, then strode over to Jessie and lifted Shane from his wife's arms. "I can see a whole lot of trouble is going on in here." He ruffled Shane's hair. "What did I tell you, son, about not touching things that aren't yours?" Shane ducked his head into his pa's shoulder. "Sorry about your glassware, Tabitha. We'll replace it."

"No need." Tabitha hurried for her broom and dustpan in the storage closet. "I shouldn't have left it on the windowsill where little hands could reach." Shane's earnest expression brought a smile.

With a few sweeps, she had the mess in a pile, and Jessie held the dustpan to make the cleanup faster. Finished, she took the remnants and put them into her trash barrel out back, only to return quickly. "Now that Chase has victoriously beaten the book crate and my dilemma is over, how can I help you?" She glanced at the small table by the door where Jessie had set her reticule, to see if she was returning books. "Or did you just stop by to visit? That's more than welcome on these slow days."

"I came to browse while Chase was at the bank. See if you'd acquired anything new since last week." Jessie glanced longingly at the crate. "I'm pleased to see that you have."

"Yes. I've been waiting on this order for over a month." It took a great deal of inventory to fill the amount of space she'd built. Perhaps she'd been overzealous in her thinking. Even with hundreds of volumes, the area would still look like she'd just opened. The sight of Chase reminded her she was waiting on an important decision. "Chase, any news from the town council about the saloon?"

Chase shook his head. "You're fighting a losing battle, Tabitha. There's not a man in this town that will agree that the saloon should close at midnight. I'm sorry to disappoint you, but you may as well give up now."

"It's not in me to give up, Chase, no matter how much Kendall or the other men dislike me. Every night, shop owners try to sleep, and drunken yelling and gunshots make that impossible. Besides, think about all their hard-earned pay they're wasting."

Chase chuckled. "It's not all that bad. You make our sleepy little town sound like the stockyards in Kansas City."

"Close enough."

Jessie nodded. "I agree with Tabitha. How many hours do the ranch hands need to carry on anyway? You'd think they'd want to get some sleep."

Chase turned for the door, clearly sensing he was in a losing fight. "How about I take this little cowboy with me? I still have beef to drop off at the restaurant. I'm not ready to head back to the ranch just yet."

"Thank you, Chase, if you're sure you don't mind." Jessie was already eyeing the books packed in the crate.

"'Course I don't."

"You'll know where to find her when you're finished with business, Chase. I appreciate your help." She turned in time to see Jessie's smile and raised eyebrows. "Be sure and tell Hannah I said hello." She and her younger cousin got along like sisters. Since the moment Tabitha had arrived in Logan Meadows, her cousin and aunt had lovingly taken her under their wings. Introduced her to the townsfolk, acquainted her with where the best bargains were to be had, extended dinner invitations every so often. Aunt Roberta had been as generous as Uncle Frank in her way. Both siblings were so different from Tabitha's mother, and she didn't want to let them down, too. Their approval felt good after the condemnation and disappointment she'd suffered from her parents. "Oh, and please remind Hannah she promised to stop by this afternoon when she gets off at the restaurant."

"Will do."

Tabitha and Jessie waited as father and son exited through the door.

"Just let me retrieve my order sheet from my desk so we can mark off the volumes as we unpack. But before I do that, I'll put on some water so we can have a cup of tea while we work."

Tabitha turned to go into the small kitchen in the corner of her store sectioned off with two drapes, but something outside winked in the sunlight. She stopped to glance out. A stranger was riding down the middle of the street. He had one hand on his horse's reins, the other holding the lead rope to a mule who followed a half a length behind. He was dressed in a fringed buckskin shirt. Tall black boots hugged his muscular calves. With his brimmed black hat, he reminded her of a character from the Wild West stories she was so fond of reading. His sandy-brown hair hung loose, brushing the tops of his extremely wide shoulders.

"Who's that?" she asked, intrigued by the newcomer.

Jessie came to her side and looked out. "I don't know. I've never seen him before. He looks very—windblown though."

More like untamed.

The two women stood in silence as he rode by.

The stranger halted in front of the Bright Nugget saloon. Dismounting, he looked around as if assessing the town. When his gaze landed on her bookstore, Tabitha knew from his angle he couldn't see them watching through the window, but something made her take a small step back anyway. He was a good-looking man. Not young, but certainly not old. Not an ounce of city in his bones.

She watched as he moved around his animals, loosening the cinch of his saddle and then the packsaddle on his mule. *Is he just passing through?* she wondered. *Or has he come to stay?* One thought brought disappointment, and the other a warm flush of something she didn't recognize at all.

CHAPTER TWO

So this is the Bright Nugget, Hunter thought as he stood at his mule's side, his hand resting on the animal's prickly, warm hide. He took in the batten and board siding of the wide establishment. The place was in pretty good shape. Couldn't have been but a year or two since a new coat of paint had been applied. Above the batwing doors was a narrow balcony that ran the length of the building.

A place where the women advertise their wares.

Dragging his gaze away, he glanced up and down the wide main street of Logan Meadows, noting the variety of businesses at which he could procure just about anything he desired. Men's clothing, eats, general doodads, a sheriff (if one were needed to keep the peace), a hotel, a livery and forge, clean laundry, medical help—he thought of Malone's broken nose—and a bank. As he'd come into town he'd even seen a train depot and a few more streets crisscrossing the landscape.

Home sweet home.

Hunter patted his pocket, and the unpaid note that entitled him to half ownership in the Bright Nugget saloon. He still couldn't believe his luck, or lack of it, when Malone had said he was penniless and didn't have the cash to pay him the balance of the salary he'd promised. Instead, the sniveling businessman had signed over the last of his property in place of the thousand dollars he owed Hunter. Years ago, Quincy had lent Kendall Martin, a friend of his in Soda Springs, a grubstake to get started somewhere new. The agreement was to send payment each month with interest, until the note was paid off. Quincy had been so rich back then that when his friend stopped sending payments, he'd shrugged off the loss and forgotten about it—until now. If Hunter wanted to be paid for the last year of service he'd spent taking Malone's sister east, he'd have to get it from Martin.

Hunter turned back to the saloon. Hard to tell who'd gotten the better deal, Malone or Hunter. Still, he'd never owned anything before in his life. He'd always been free as a tumbleweed. Owning a business was an odd feeling, but one that was growing on him by the minute.

Stepping through the double doors, he spotted a man with a white apron tied around his middle, standing at the end of the bar, writing in a ledger book. Hunter guessed his age to be somewhere around fifty. *Kendall Martin?*

He glanced up and assessed Hunter. "Howdy." Setting down his pencil, the barkeep made his way to the other end of the glossy walnut counter and met him face-to-face on the opposite side just as Hunter lifted his boot to the bar's kick rail. "Name your poison."

"How's your whiskey? Not rotgut, is it?"

His smile disappeared. "No, sir, it's not."

"Fine. I'll take a shot."

"That all?"

Hunter nodded.

The bartender reached to the shelf behind him for a bottle and glass, poured, and then pushed the tumbler forward. "New in town?"

"Just rode in."

"I'm Kendall. Owner of this fine establishment."

Howdy, Partner.

"Hunter Wade," he replied, surveying the length of shelving behind the counter. The gold-plated mirror could use a good cleaning, but for the most part, the large rectangular room was just like a hundred other saloons he'd seen. In the shadowy rear portion of the area was a staircase that led to some rooms upstairs.

A woman in a knee-length blue satin dress watched from above. Black stockings encased her long legs. She smiled and raised her brows. Other than a single man standing at the middle of the bar, they were alone.

Kendall pointed to the woman and then to the man. "That's Philomena, and that's Dwight Hoskins."

Hunter nodded at Philomena and then at the man. Now was not the time to bring up business. He'd come back tomorrow morning, have a private conversation with Kendall.

He took a small taste of the whiskey. *Not bad. But could be better.* Intending on nursing the drink, he set the glass back onto the bar, switched feet on the boot rail, and thought about the legal deed in his pocket.

A young fella pushed through the saloon doors.

"Jake," Kendall called, his face brightening. "Good to see you. First drink's on me, being it's been a while since you've been in."

"Good of you, Kendall," the lanky cowboy replied, glancing at Hunter for several long curious moments. His gaze went from the long-fringed shirt to the gun strapped around his thigh. "Since I'm only having one, I'll pony up. Don't want anyone thinking I can't pay my own way."

"Suit yourself."

Hunter was used to being stared at. *Especially by women.* He'd grown up wearing the distinct and durable buckskin preferred by Thorp Wade, the man who'd raised him. A wagon-train master by trade, Thorp had guided a group of pioneers headed west some thirty-five years ago. Hunter and his aunt and uncle had been part of that group. As a five-year-old, and the ward of his relatives, Hunter didn't remember much about the trip, except for the day a band of Blackfoot Indians had attacked and killed his guardians, as well as others. The smoke; the hideous, high-pitched screams; and the flickering flames were scorched into his brain. He remembered the arrow that had pierced his leg all too well. The pain slicing its way through his small body. To this day, he could feel Thorp's large hand shoving him over an embankment, where he'd rolled down into a gully. The action probably saved his life.

Thinking of Thorp brought a small smile. He'd been a good man, a hard man. A man who'd taken on a wounded boy with nowhere else to go.

"What's the news with you and pretty little Daisy?" When Hunter surfaced from his thoughts, Kendall was speaking to the young fella called Jake. "I miss having that girl in here. She was one to catch any man's eye."

Jake slowly set down his glass, his smile gone. "Don't talk about Daisy. She's a good woman. I won't remind you again . . ."

The look that passed from the younger man to the older left no question that he was prepared to back up his request.

Kendall shrugged off the threat.

"Get off your high horse, Jake," the other patron called from down the bar. Dwight. The man must think the topic funny, as indicated by his smile. "Once a saloon gal, always a saloon gal. By the way, when's the wedding?"

Jake's face deepened in color, and Hunter could tell he was working hard not to let his temper get the best of him.

Hunter slugged down the last of his whiskey, then wiped his mouth. He'd get out of here before there was a brawl. "Thanks."

Kendall nodded. "If you're staying on, come back and see us."

We'll be seeing a lot of each other come tomorrow. For now, I'll make camp out in the meadow I spotted between the train depot and the town.

"I'll be back," he replied and smiled. May as well soften him up. "I like your place. Has a good feel." He glanced at Jake. "My grub's getting pretty low. I suppose your mercantile has what I need?"

The young fella cocked a thumb over his back. "Sure will. Maude or Beth'll be happy ta help." He stuck out his hand. "I'm Jake."

"Pleased to make your acquaintance, Jake." He glanced at Dwight. "And you too, Hoskins."

Hunter might not read especially well, but one thing he was good at was remembering names. Thorp had taught him as a lad to memorize an acquaintance's name to his face first thing, landscapes and trails traveled too—and the Indians they'd run across. For a wagon-train guide, a quick recall was an important quality, one that could save lives.

As he ambled to the batwing doors, he tipped his hat toward the balcony. Philomena nodded and smiled.

She reminded him a bit of Dichelle Bastianelli. Maybe if he invited Dichelle nicely, the lovely Italian songbird would leave Soda Springs and come work for him in Logan Meadows for a while. She always said she wasn't one to let the moss grow under her slippers. She wanted to be discovered. To do that, she had to get around. Ned would be none too pleased if he lost her. But Hunter couldn't worry about Ned. He had a business to think about, and grow. And truth be told, he'd miss Dichelle if he never saw her again. If he were ten years younger, just maybe . . .

I don't have much to offer a woman. Just worn-out boots from miles and miles of trail under my feet. When it comes to settling down, women want security, roots, family, social standing—money.

He stepped out into the sunlight. Proceeding down the boardwalk, he entered the mercantile. A display of cans with pictures of large colorful peaches on their labels brought moisture to his mouth. He'd get a few of those to hold him over until suppertime.

Edginess crept into his bones. He was used to a life spent outdoors, but this was the second building he'd entered today. Hunter breathed in, thinking of the camp he'd see to next. A little space would help. He proceeded down the aisle, just looking. Would he adjust to living in a room above a saloon? He'd been guiding wagon trains his entire life. Then the transcontinental railroad had been finished, and offers dwindled.

Since then he'd drifted around, taking work when he needed money. He never stayed in one place long enough to find out if he liked it or not.

From the other side of the store, an old woman raised her head from whatever she was doing behind a shelf. Her eyes brightened. "I'll be right with you, young man," she called. "Beth, break time's over. Come finish this while I wait on our customer."

"*Yeeees,* Maude. Be right there," a voice whined from the back room.

The woman came around the aisle corner wiping her hands on her apron. Her face was a mass of crinkles and lines. "That means *today,* Beth," Maude said over her shoulder. "The deep cleaning should have been done months ago. If the merchandise isn't enticing, who'll want to partake?"

She approached Hunter with a smile. "I may be old, but I'm not dead yet. She thinks I don't see these things."

He chuckled.

"Now, how can I help you? I've never seen you in Logan Meadows before, have I?" She stood very straight and sturdy for someone her age, but still she had to tip her head back to look into his face. "Did you arrive on the morning train?"

"No, ma'am." From anyone else the questions would have annoyed him. But not from her. "I rode in a few minutes ago. Cross country from Idaho Territory." *I may as well open up. Folks'll be curious about their new en-entrepren-eur,* he thought, stumbling over the difficult word he'd learned from an Ohioan he'd guided west, intent on opening a restaurant in California. The man's wife hadn't shared her husband's enthusiasm for the adventure, especially since Thorp had just forced several wagons, including her own, to lighten up. She'd been teary eyed for a week over leaving her piano behind for anyone to plunder.

"Your first time here?"

Before Hunter had a chance to respond, the mercantile door opened and a woman breezed in, a sense of purpose in her ramrod stature and uplifted face. She wasn't a girl—a venerability shone in her eyes despite her pretty features.

"Afternoon, Maude," she called out without really looking at anyone in particular. With single-mindedness, she marched over to the far side of the room and began scooping something from a wall bin into a small cloth bag that she carried in her hand. "Hope you don't mind me helping myself to some tea. I'm in a hurry. I had no idea I was out until I went to make a cup. Jessie's waiting on me at the bookshop and—"

She turned. When she saw him, her mouth snapped closed. At her interested perusal, his cheeks grew warm.

"Don't mind a-tall, honey. You help yourself to anything you'd like." Maude turned back to him. "What was it you said you was looking for? Did you ever say? I can't remember."

"A couple of those cans of peaches I saw when I entered the store."

Her face took on the expression of a pleased child. "Dandy! I also have some canned beans, if you'd like to try 'em. My customers rave right and left about how tasty they are. I like 'em as well. Would you like to try a can or two?"

"Sure, why not?" Until he worked out the saloon arrangements with Kendall, he might be camping for a while. He wasn't counting on it, but one never knew. Especially if a livelihood was at stake. Sliding his gaze to the left, he admired the woman's back as she waited at the counter to pay.

"Anything else?"

He shook his head. "No, ma'am."

"Fine then, I'll meet you up front. Did I mention that since you're a new customer, I'm taking five percent off your purchase? It's a promotion I'm trying. Does that make you happy? Make you want to return?"

"Absolutely, ma'am. Thank you very much. Every little bit helps."

Now behind the counter, the old woman stretched her neck toward the back room. "See, Beth! I told you so. He likes the idea and he's gonna come back." She looked around the woman waiting in front of him. "Soon? Will you come back soon?"

He nodded.

"He's coming back soon." Focusing her attention on the woman in line, she picked up her cloth bag and bounced it in her hand several times to gauge its weight. "That'll be ten cents, Tabitha. Did you want this on your account?"

"Please."

Taking her pencil, Maude jotted down the price in an open ledger next to a name.

When she was finished, she reached out and patted Tabitha's hand. "Have things picked up for you at the bookshop? I can't imagine there's much need for a business like yours in Logan Meadows, but who am I to say? I hope the venture doesn't turn out to be a boulder around your neck, so to speak. But don't worry, honey, God will provide."

A bookshop? Well, that suits her primness and properness just fine. Her straight back, too. He felt a smile coming on. *Never seemed to find the time to see to my schooling. Or, if I had the time, I didn't have the resources. Settling down in Logan Meadows may have just landed me both . . .*

The younger woman's stiff shoulders pulled back almost imperceptibly. "Thank you, Maude, I appreciate your concern. The Logans were just in this morning. In fact, Jessie's still there waiting on me for the tea. Business is fine. No need to think any different."

She's protesting too much. I'd predict her boat is sinking.

Tabitha gave a little dip of her head. "Thank you." She turned to leave.

"Excuse me," Hunter said, surprising himself. He had business to think about. He shouldn't let himself get sidetracked. But Tabitha turned, her vivid green eyes widening, and he threw caution to the wind. "Couldn't help but overhear that you're the proprietor of a bookstore. Would you happen to have a simple reader? Maybe a primer suitable for a child?"

Her eyes lit up like twin suns. "I do, sir! I actually have several to choose from."

An unfamiliar warmth swirled in Hunter's chest. "I'm in need of one."

"Then I'm the person to help," she enthusiastically replied. "Is it meant to be a gift?"

"Ah, well . . ." He didn't really want everyone in Logan Meadows to think him a dunce. He was going to have an uphill battle as it was, once he spoke with Kendall. Rubbing his hands together for a second, he nodded. "You might say that." *For myself.*

Her smile widened. "Perfect."

Looking at her, Hunter was inclined to agree.

CHAPTER THREE

Tabitha almost gasped with joy. A book sale! And to the handsome stranger she'd witnessed riding up the street. The transaction would be the first for her in a couple of days. Tabitha hadn't said Jessie was in to buy, but still she felt a bit guilty leading Maude to believe just that, even if her friend's comments had been a bit mean. Perhaps Jessie would fall in love with a title this morning, one she couldn't live without.

Now that she was within arm's reach of the windswept man—using Jessie's description—she could see he wasn't as young as she'd previously thought. She wouldn't be surprised if he'd passed his fortieth birthday—*several years ago.*

"I'm just down at the end of the block," she said. "Between Shady Creek and the sheriff's office. Storybook Lodge. It's not really a lodge, just a little bookshop. Stop by any time. I'm happy to help."

The man watched her intently, and if she didn't get out of the mercantile quickly, she just might say something stupid like: May I see if your buckskin shirt feels as soft as it looks? Or: Would you mind if I touched your cheek? I've never felt one covered in stubble.

Scandalous! What has happened to my thinking?

Perhaps her approaching twenty-ninth birthday was the cause of her sudden desires. Still, why she felt drawn to *him*, a man who looked as untamed as a wolf, was perplexing. "Are you just passing through?"

An amused expression crossed his eyes. *What in the blue blazes is wrong with my tongue?* Surely, someone this attractive had women falling at his feet.

"For the time being, I'm camping in the meadow between town and the train depot. Didn't think anyone would mind."

"That's the festival grounds," Beth Fairington said stiffly from behind the newcomer. "You'll have to get permission from the sheriff if you intend to camp out there."

Their conversation had snagged the curiosity of the town gossip. Tabitha had noticed Beth moving quietly forward, her ear turned in their direction. A spider stalking an unsuspecting fly came to mind.

Maude straightened. "Don't be so uncharitable, Beth! We're trying to make customers, not run 'em off. Albert won't have a problem a-tall with him staying out there. It's a free country, you know."

When his eyes met Tabitha's, the flush on his face deepened, and he returned her smile with a tentative one of his own. He must be used to people gawking at him or giving him censure for the way he looks. And yet, she'd hate to see him ride out of town so soon. He was interesting. Reminded her of the daguerreotypes she'd seen of Wild Bill Hickok, the gunfighter, or Grizzly Adams, the famous mountain man. He was a combination of the two—*only better looking*.

"Maude's right," Tabitha agreed. "There won't be an issue with you making camp in the meadow. The land is only used for special occasions, and we have none coming up at this time. Don't be put off by Miss Fairington"—she arched her brow at Beth—"and be warned. She's been known to fabricate stories and spread them around town to anyone who'll listen, which are few and far between in our good town, but still . . ."

Beth's nostrils flared, reminding Tabitha of an angry bull. "Say what you want," she stated without emotion. "Your words can't harm me."

"And neither can yours, me," Tabitha replied. "Even though you gave it a good try."

Maude held up her hand between them. "Girls."

As soon as Tabitha had arrived on the train with her many trunks and more than a handful of large pieces of furniture, Beth hadn't wasted one second whispering falsehoods that Frank Lloyd's spinster niece had fled to Logan Meadows to live out her disgraced, unmarried days far from the eyes of the town where she'd been rejected by every unmarried man therein. *Not so! If I'd wanted to, I could have had my pick of husbands. But I had dreams of owning my own bookstore someday, and that wasn't attainable in New York, where retail space is so costly. Beth is not but a year or two younger than me. If I'm a spinster, so is she. At least I'm not a spinster* and *a shrew!*

She'd learned of the clerk's slander from poor little Nate Preston, the sheriff's son. He'd come in red faced one day to look at the picture books displayed in the shop's front window. When she'd asked why he looked out of sorts, her small friend had hemmed and hawed, but she could tell something important was on his mind. Finally dragging out the snippet of chinwag, Tabitha had marched down to the mercantile to confront Beth. It felt good to put the gossip on notice. She'd not put up with one second of Miss Fairington's meddling, about her, or anyone else.

When an uncomfortable expression crossed the stranger's face, she regretted that her hasty words had pulled him into the fray.

"I'll keep that in mind when I come to make my purchases," he said.

"I'm Miss Canterbury, that's Maude Miller, and *she* is Miss Fairington." It went against everything Tabitha was to totally leave Beth out, even though she sometimes wished she could be more hard-hearted like the store clerk.

His large hand enveloped hers as they shook. "Pleased to meet you all. I'm Hunter Wade."

A jolt of awareness sparked from the contact with his palm and skittered all the way up her arm. *Silliness, to be sure.* She dug deep into her years of practice in proper conduct, poise, and grace. "My pleasure, Mr. Wade," she replied. "I'll look forward to our speaking again soon."

The rest of the day sailed by in a blur of errands, chores, and busy chatter. After Chase and Shane had collected Jessie, Brenna Hutton—who had married Logan Meadows's teacher the day of the horrible train wreck—stopped by just in time to help Tabitha move a small table upstairs. They'd placed it next to the door that opened onto a side balcony overlooking Shady Creek, which also had a view of the festival grounds.

The exact spot where Mr. Wade had said he would be camping.

Questions about him tumbled through Tabitha's mind. She sort of wished Beth had been her nosy self and asked a few personal questions. Then she wouldn't have this curiosity burning in her mind and making her waste hours in her day.

She needed to stop daydreaming about the new man in town and drum up interest in her shop! She couldn't just wait for customers to stumble in on their own, she had to go out and cultivate them. Plant the seed and water the ground. Bring them along like a new crop of wheat.

Reading was foreign to many in the Wyoming Territory, and yet their lives would be so much fuller, richer, if someone taught them a love for literature. *Cowboys, miners, and even drifters,* she thought with a smile.

Has God sent me here to do just that?

The door downstairs jingled, and she glanced at her bedside clock. Six o'clock. She'd come upstairs and neglected to turn the sign and lock the door.

"Tabitha?" A knocking on the door frame. "You upstairs? Your door is unlocked."

Hannah. She heard Thom, Hannah's husband, who was deputy sheriff, laughing in his deep voice at something his wife had said.

"Yes. I'll be down directly." Putting away her rambling thoughts, she picked up the hem of her skirt and hurried down the stairs. The couple stood arm in arm.

"I hope you don't mind I brought Thom along." Hannah glanced up at her handsome Irishman, her face full of smiles. "Susanna is finishing up at the restaurant, and Thom wanted to spend a little time with me before I headed for home. He's on the evening shift tonight and won't be home until later. We're taking a walk."

"Of course I don't mind. But it would be better if the two of you go along without me. It's a beautiful evening. Who knows how many more like this there'll be before the weather sets in. I'm so far behind in my work I shouldn't be taking time off anyway." In reality, she didn't want to be a third wheel. Sometimes witnessing their obvious romance incurred feelings of loneliness in the long evening hours. Best they go alone.

Hannah raised a brow, glancing around at her perfectly ordered shop. "Just try and tell me what you have to do in here, Tabitha. Not a thing is out of place. I insist you come along."

Even though she hadn't known Hannah long, the two had quickly grown close. Their family hailed from Ohio, but when Tabitha's grandparents died in an influenza epidemic, it had been up to Uncle Frank to support his two sisters. In his early twenties he'd taken a job as a teller in a bank. Marigold, Tabitha's mother, then nineteen, married a distinguished young man and moved to his family home in New York. A few years later, an opportunity arose for Uncle Frank to buy a bank in a small western town. Thrilled at the opportunity to make something of himself, he'd packed up his youngest sister, Roberta, and headed west. Soon after they arrived, Roberta met and married a young farmer, but he'd died when Hannah was only fifteen.

"Tabby, I'm not taking no for an answer," Hannah teased. "We planned this visit, and I've been looking forward to it all day."

Once Hannah set her mind to something, that was that. Tabitha sighed. "Fine then. Let me go fetch a wrap."

CHAPTER FOUR

With his knife gripped firmly in his left hand, Hunter sawed at the can of peaches with anticipation. He'd eaten one can earlier, and couldn't resist another. Prying the lid back, he licked the sugary liquid that spilled onto his fingers, then picked up his fork as he stretched back against a log.

All the comforts of home.

He stabbed a thick yellowy-pink slice of goodness floating at the top of the syrup. Forking the fruit in to his waiting taste buds, he wiped the drops that had landed on his chin with the back of his hand. His mouth exploded, and his eyes closed in ecstasy. Swallowing, he repeated the process, making fast work of the treat.

After he'd set up camp, he'd stabled his gelding and mule at the livery, knowing he'd draw less attention if they weren't staked out in the meadow. Win Preston, owner of the large barn and forge, was a friendly sort. They'd talked for a good forty minutes, the blacksmith filling him in on the train wreck the town had experienced a few months back. Later tonight, Hunter planned to go to the hotel and have a real meal of meat and potatoes.

"Hello in the camp?" a man's voice called. The slight Irish accent brought to mind a family he and Thorp had guided to Oregon. "Anyone here?" the voice called again.

Now what? He was minding his own business. He hoped that gossipy woman in the mercantile hadn't encouraged someone to run him off. He was tired. He wasn't going anywhere tonight. Still wearing his revolver, Hunter stood and stepped out into the clearing, surprised to see Tabitha, as well as another woman and a man.

The fella walked forward with purpose. "I'm Thom Donovan. Deputy sheriff of Logan Meadows." He gestured to the woman at his side. "My wife, Hannah Donovan. I heard that you've already met Miss Canterbury. We were out for a stroll, and I wanted to stop by and welcome you to town, Mr. Wade." He held out his hand.

Hunter grasped the deputy's hand, all the while sizing him up. "Thank you." He couldn't stop his gaze from meandering over to Tabitha.

She gave a small shrug. "Beth, in the mercantile, told Thom about you. I didn't know Thom and Hannah planned on walking out here until I'd already agreed to join them."

A mite defensive. "Glad you did, miss," he said on a half chuckle. After having Quincy's deed signed over to him, he'd been in a fine mood for days. Still was. He felt young again. Excited for this new chapter in his life.

She looked past him into his camp. "There's a hotel in town, and also an inn on the other side of Logan Meadows, in case you'd be more comfortable there."

"Camping is fine for the time being. That is, if I'm not breaking any laws."

"None," the deputy responded. "If you start trouble, now, that'll be a different story. You can count on seeing me or Albert then."

"That won't happen."

Thom's smile seemed friendly enough as he said, "Didn't think so after what Tabitha said about meeting you in the mercantile. We welcome newcomers. If you like Logan Meadows, you just might stay on."

Hunter nodded. "I just may do that, Deputy." He'd lived on the trail his whole life. Journeyed from Independence, Missouri, to various destinations in Oregon and California twenty-one times, a blanket on the ground his only bed. He was tired. The thought of settling somewhere was mighty appealing.

Mrs. Donovan sent him a smile. "I hope you'll stop in to our restaurant sometime soon. It's called the Silky Hen, located inside the hotel next to the lobby. Has the best food in town, if I do say so myself. Your first dessert is on the house."

"Much obliged, Mrs. Donovan. Actually, I was just about to amble in for a hot meal this evening. Plan to do that shortly."

The deputy's wife's face lit up. "That's wonderful. Be sure and mention to Susanna or Roberta—that's my mother—what I offered. Don't be shy. They'll know what you're talking about."

"I'm not shy, ma'am. I appreciate your offer and your recommendations."

"Also, I'd be remiss if I didn't tell you there are other restaurants in town as well," she added. "During your stay, if you tire of our food, I can recommend Nana's Place one street over."

"We should be going," Tabitha said, glancing back over her shoulder at the town. "Let Mr. Wade get back to what he was doing before we barged in. I'm sure he has things to do."

His chuckle slipped out before he could stop it. "Not much to do, Miss Canterbury, except to think about my next meal and how good my blanket is going to feel tonight. But I do appreciate your concern over my privacy."

Thom reached out and they shook once again. "I'm sure I'll see you around town."

Imagine so, when Kendall Martin finds out I'm his new partner.

As the three walked away, their conversation growing quiet, melancholy settled around Hunter's shoulders. He dug his fingers through his hair, remembering the camaraderie he'd enjoyed on each wagon train he'd led, filled with all sorts of different kinds of people. Down-home, helpful, hardworking, lazy, studious, gullible, and even deviant. He hadn't figured out what Tabitha was yet. *No doubt about it,* he thought as he watched them disappear from sight, *I look forward to learning more.*

CHAPTER FIVE

With a clean, moist cloth, Roberta Brown wiped down the table she'd just cleared, glancing up as a tall stranger walked through the restaurant door. He looked around at the few occupied tables, and then took a seat on the far wall where he'd have a good view of the door. She noticed his wide shoulders and interesting face. For a second, the gun on his hip put her off, but then his gaze met hers and he smiled. An unfamiliar pang made her breath catch. She left the rag on the table, went to the sideboard under the clock, and picked up a menu.

"Good evening," she said in her most polished voice as she arrived by his side. She handed him the paper.

"Evenin'," he replied, taking the menu, but his eyes didn't leave hers.

My, he's even more handsome up close! Heat crept into her cheeks, and she hoped they weren't turning red. "Would you like a cup of coffee?"

"Please."

Relieved at something to do, she turned for the kitchen. Pushing through the swinging door, she went directly to the stove, reached for a mug on the shelf above, and poured, noting a slight tremor in her hand.

"Roberta, is everything all right?" Daisy asked, concern in her voice. The petite seventeen-year-old was stirring a pot of stew, her face rosy pink from the heat of the stove. "Your hand is trembling."

"I'm perfectly fine," she replied, irritated at herself for letting a handsome face affect her so. Widows weren't supposed to have longings and desires. They were like horses whose race had been run and were now out to pasture. She thought of her late husband, Harvey, and how they'd met over a cup of coffee after church. He'd been tall and handsome, too, much like the man out in the dining room. Her older brother, Frank, had approved of the hardworking farmer and encouraged her to accept his hand. Their years working the land together hadn't been easy, but they had been years full of love, kindness, and respect. She'd known how lucky she was. Harvey was a gentle man who wouldn't hurt a flea. He didn't believe in carrying a gun on his hip, and never had. Not every woman was so fortunate. Janet, her girlfriend from back home, had written over the years with frightening stories of abuse at the hand of her husband. He'd hidden a hardened past from her until after the wedding. Soon, he'd gambled away every cent of their money and ended up in prison, leaving Janet without a penny to her name. Her life had been one of toil and hardships, making Roberta all the more grateful for the caring husband she'd had. And the wisdom of her brother, who'd watched out for her future.

Daisy, still frowning with worry, went to the door and peeked out into the dining room. "Oh!" she said, a smile replacing her frown.

"What?" Susanna asked from her position at the break table; she was cutting the last of the biscuits and placing them on a greased baking sheet.

Having already set the mug of coffee on the counter, Roberta pulled a small tray from underneath. She added a small pitcher of milk, even though she'd forgotten to ask the stranger if he'd like any. Someday, if the right man came along, maybe she'd consider a new marriage. That wasn't out of the question. "It's nothing!" She shouldn't sound so peevish, or the girls would surely think her behavior odd.

"What's nothing?" A masculine voice tinged with humor brought Roberta around. Jake, Daisy's beau, stood at the back door, his hat pushed back and a teasing gaze aimed at Daisy.

Daisy shook her head impishly. "Only a handsome stranger in the dining room who's caught Roberta's attention."

Jake stepped in and went to Daisy's side, kissing her cheek. "As long as he doesn't turn *your* head. There'd be trouble if that happened."

"You're a tease, Jake." She gave him a little push that didn't move him at all.

"Maybe so, but I can't help remembering how Dalton Babcock came to town and tried to steal Susanna away from Albert. That was a close call."

Susanna laughed merrily. "No one could steal me from Albert, Jake."

"That's not how it looked to us."

Susanna wiped her hands on her apron, finished with the sheet of biscuits. "Is that so? Well, it just so happens that Albert received a letter from Dalton last week. Seems now that his assignment in San Francisco is coming to an end, he's planning to return. Maybe even settle in Logan Meadows."

"Really?" Daisy's eyes widened. "All the single girls will be excited to hear that news. When?"

"I think almost immediately. He sounded happy that things had gone well, said he received a bonus for all he did to keep the bank's money safe. I'm glad."

Still standing close to Daisy, Jake asked, "How does Albert feel about that?"

Warmed by the lively banter, Roberta listened, feeling young and alive.

"Albert likes Dalton. Says it never hurts to have an experienced gun he can count on if need be. And he says he's going to start looking for a gal for Dalton right away."

Daisy laughed, then reached for a cloth-covered basket of golden-brown biscuits and added it to the large oval tray resting on a tray stand. "These two bowls of stew are ready to go out, Roberta."

"Let me deliver this coffee and I'll be back directly."

Roberta breezed out the door, the tray held up with practiced skill and an inexplicable excitement making her steps light.

CHAPTER SIX

What in the world am I doing! Tabitha flipped the page of the horticulture book laid open on her desk. *Sitting here with my window shade still rolled up as if it's the most natural thing in the world.* Normally, by this time of the evening the store would be buttoned up and she'd be upstairs, bathed, and snuggled deep in her bedroom chair, reading a novel. Few things she liked better in life—as a matter of fact, she couldn't think of one.

Except, maybe, waiting for Mr. Wade to walk by after having supper at the Silky Hen.

Her eyes wandered away from the sketch of a blooming larkspur to the flickering flame dancing in the lantern. She wasn't really reading, but thinking. Thinking of her life, and her situation since moving to Logan Meadows. Sometimes seeing her friends in their marriages made her wonder if she'd chosen wisely. To remain single, so she could accomplish her heart's desire of owning a bookstore. A bookstore couldn't laugh or talk or keep her warm in its arms.

Once she hit thirty, there would be no denying her spinsterhood, business owner or not. With each passing day, her odds of making a meaningful union, if she so chose to, diminished. The situation revolved around the word *meaningful.* In truth, she didn't have to remain single another day if she accepted one of the men here. Bachelors had made their interest known soon after she'd arrived. Kendall Martin, the owner of the Bright Nugget, who crossed her path almost daily, had told her straight out he'd even let her be a part of *his* business, if she cared to pair up. *How romantic.* She shook her head at the distasteful thought. The man, somewhere in his midfifties, and to her knowledge never married, was coarse and uneducated. He wasn't the worst in his cleanliness, but he certainly wasn't the best. When his eyes landed on hers in that oh-so-meaningful way, she had to stay the automatic shiver that threatened to take over her limbs. She'd happily remain an old maid for the rest of her years before yoking herself to him, *thank you very much.*

There was Winthrop Preston, or Win, as he liked to be called. The livery owner had become a good friend. And she liked him well enough. She was a few years older, but if she let him know she was interested, she felt sure the kindhearted fellow would ask for her hand immediately. He'd slipped into her church pew a few times, smiling shyly.

Her best fit was Dr. John Thorn. In his early thirties, they were a good match in age, but she'd had minimal interaction with him since moving here, even though their businesses were both located on Main Street. She'd not chase someone who hadn't shown any curiosity in her—there were limits to her boldness.

If she were *really* desperate, there was always Dwight Hoskins. In her first days here, he'd come by on several occasions, testing the waters, so to speak. He was handsome enough, but everyone had steered her away from Hannah's ex-brother-in-law with stories that had tinged her ear tops red. A country bumpkin was one thing; a shady, dishonest schemer, quite another.

There were also some ranchers farther out, and others from New Meringue, but not one of them moved her in any way at all beyond friendship or repulsion.

Shamefully, she banished the picture that popped into her head of Mr. Wade in his buckskin shirt. *There* was a man who could make a woman stand up and take notice. As appealing as he seemed now, he was a total stranger, she admitted to herself. One she knew nothing about. He could be an outlaw on the run. A bank robber. A totally unscrupulous man.

Stop pouting. Things aren't so bad the way they stand. She'd made a good name for herself in the community. She was respected. And a businesswoman. That had been her goal since she'd been a young girl. She'd get by. A bit on the lonely side, but that was better than in a bed of regret. The majority of men expected their mates to stay home. Do as they were told. They had power over their wives' every move. Her father's domineering ways were a very good reminder of reality when she began to imagine differently.

The thought of her parents always brought a healthy serving of guilt. She was their only daughter, only child. As much as she hated to admit the fact, she'd let them down. If only they could understand her dreams. As the years marched on, their unhappiness at her refusal to court any man turned into anger. She took a job in the library, working when other young women were looking for a husband. In her free time she read, whisked away to some foreign romantic place. On her twenty-seventh birthday, they'd been dumbfounded when she announced her intention to travel west. To a place where she could afford to realize her dream with the dowry that she wouldn't be sharing with a husband. Infuriated by her decision, her father, a rich man thanks to his speculative investments, had announced he'd put her money into a trust. One she couldn't touch until her thirty-third birthday. If she insisted on the crazy idea of opening a bookstore, something far below their family's standing, she'd do it on her own, without any help from them.

Someone knocked on her door. Tabitha glanced up. Recognizing Bao, wife of Tap Ling, owner of the town's laundry business, she hurried to the door and pulled it open.

"Bao, what are you doing? It's late. You should be home." *It's not safe for you after dark.*

Sometimes horrible stories reached Logan Meadows. Lawless men murdered migrants, with little or no repercussions. Tabitha's skin crawled at the thought. The shy woman, dressed in the same loose-fitting black pants and shirt that her husband wore daily, was unable to hide her growing stomach.

Bao gave a small polite bow. "Miss Canter*bury*, I see light. Run back for skirt so you not have to pick up."

"Thank you. But you didn't need to do that." Tabitha took the garment from Bao's hands, reddened from the harsh soapy water she used every day. "I don't want you to ever do it again. Where is your daughter, Lan?"

"Home with her father."

"Where *you* should be right now. I don't mind walking down to your shop at all. As a matter of fact, I'm coming in tomorrow anyway to pay my bill." On a tight budget, Tabitha usually washed her own clothes, but sometimes to help support Tap and Bao, she dropped off an item or two. It was a luxury she'd taken for granted back home. Maids, cooks—but no more. She was on her own. "You stay put from now on, all right?"

Two cowboys walked by in the direction of the saloon, giving her and Bao a wide berth. Tabitha hoped there wouldn't be a drunken brawl tonight, or guns shooting off to wake her in a panic.

Bao gave another small bow and hurried away.

Tabitha locked her door and returned to her desk, thinking how silly it was that she was still downstairs. When a shadow appeared in the corner of her eye, she thought it was the laundress returning. Seeing that it was Mr. Wade walking from the hotel, she buried her face in the pages of her book, all the while stealing secretive glances at his manly profile. Her heart thwacked against her ribs. She didn't want to be caught looking, and yet . . .

A soft tapping on her front window brought her head up.

Mr. Wade smiled.

Were her eyes too wide to be convincing? She hoped her astonishment didn't look contrived. After a brief moment, she smiled back, picked up the lantern beside the book, and made her way to the door. Unlocking it once again, she pulled the door open. "Why, Mr. Wade, what a surprise."

"Indeed," he replied. "Didn't expect to see you again tonight, Miss Canterbury."

Her face warmed. "How was your supper at the Silky Hen?"

The darkness of the night softened his features. He'd shaved, but wore the same clothes he'd arrived in. Now that the stubble was gone from his face, she had to work not to stare at his strong, manly chin or his chiseled lips. His eyes appeared to smile.

"As good as Mrs. Donovan promised it would be," he replied, rubbing his stomach. "I had chicken and dumplings with all the fixin's—as well as *two* slices of chokecherry pie. I can't remember a meal I've enjoyed more."

His words were casual, but his eyes seemed to be assessing every inch of her face. This one was bold. Perhaps it was because they were alone. She tried to stifle the unladylike gulp she felt coming at his scrutiny, but was unsuccessful.

"So you didn't forget to ask Susanna about the pie?"

He patted his stomach. "I'd never do that."

He looked back the way he'd come, at the Bright Nugget two doors down, his mouth pulling into a small frown. "Seems pretty quiet tonight in the saloon. Only four men when I looked in."

"That's because it's only Thursday. Tomorrow Kendall's business picks up, and it can get downright disorderly on Saturday and Sunday."

"Sunday, too?" Smiling now, a bit of wonder tinged his tone.

"Oh, yes. The Lord's day makes no difference to *those types*. Sometimes inebriated cowboys actually shoot off their pistols in the middle of the street! Then Sheriff Preston or Deputy Donovan has to arrest them and lock them up until they can sleep off their intoxication. I think the town should start fining anyone who participates in such irresponsible behavior. Lightening their pockets might make a difference."

He grunted. "Those types?"

"Men who enjoy wasting their hard-earned pay on drinking and gambling." She leaned a bit closer. "*And on women,*" she whispered.

"I see." He gazed off for a moment or two as if to ponder that fact, then glanced over her shoulder toward her desk. "Working late?"

"This isn't that late for me. I'm just attending to a few things I didn't want to put off until tomorrow." Well, that was true, to an extent. In reality, she liked to read into the wee hours of the night. Reading was work in a way. It helped her give honest recommendations.

"If you say so. I best get moving so you can finish up and get some rest. I don't mean to pester."

"Will you be stopping in soon for that reader you mentioned?"

His lips curved into a boyish smile. "I plan to do that tomorrow. What time do you open?"

She reached behind her for the small poster she had on the receiving table and held it out. "Ten to five. Monday through Saturday."

Mr. Wade touched a finger to the brim of his hat. "In that case, Miss Canterbury, I'll see you at ten."

"I'll look forward to it, Mr. Wade," she found herself responding a bit too brightly, then watched as he turned and started for the small bridge that crossed over Shady Creek.

What is wrong with me! I'm acting like a flirt. Besides, Mother and Father would never *approve of someone like him. He's the kind of man they loathe.*

Mr. Wade had long since crossed the creek and disappeared out of sight.

Tabitha closed the door with a soft click, turned the lock, and then pulled down the blind. Still holding the lantern, she leaned back against the door. *A handsome man tapping on* my *window. Imagine that.* She went upstairs, but before going to her armoire to change into her nightclothes, she took a moment at the balcony door, pushing aside the blue flowered curtain. Mr. Wade was out there somewhere in the chilly October air, planning to sleep on the ground. Winter was coming on, and frost would soon be on the pumpkins. She sighed.

Stop this nonsense! You have your lot, and it's this *store, in* this *town. You're as happy as you can be. Don't set yourself up for a heartache that may never heal.*

CHAPTER SEVEN

Feeling younger than she had in years, Roberta entered the home she shared with Hannah, Thom, and Markus, working the knotted ends of the scarf tied under her chin.

Hannah looked up from the sofa and smiled.

"Is Markus asleep?" It was well past nine o'clock.

"He is. But he said to blow you a kiss when you came in." Hannah kissed her palm, and blew the make-believe sentiment over to her mother. It was a ritual they had for whichever one of them came in last.

Roberta pretended to catch it. "He's such a sweet child. Thom home?"

"No, he has the late shift tonight. Water for tea is already hot," Hannah, already dressed in her nightclothes, said softly. "I'll have a cup ready for you after you change."

Sometimes Roberta couldn't believe her little girl was all grown up. Where had the years gone? Seven years she'd been a widow. Those first few months after Harvey's passing had been a struggle, filled with worry at how she'd carry on, shouldering the responsibility of providing for herself and her daughter. But she had. Hannah had married Caleb soon after, only to lose him, too, both becoming widows in the same year. Roberta had done her best, but at times had been criticized by others for the staunch positions she took.

"Bless you, Hannah. That sounds good." She ascended the staircase and went to change.

Feeling comfortable in her nightgown and wrapper, Roberta joined Hannah on the sofa, sinking into the soft cushions. "I'm glad to be home," she said, inhaling the aromatic steam of the peppermint tea. "Sometimes my life back on the farm seems like a dream. You as a baby, working the fields. That was a long time ago." She sighed. "The restaurant was a nonstop stream of hungry dinner customers almost from the time you left at six. We must have turned all the tables at least twice. I think you'll be very pleased with the revenue."

"I like the sound of that." Hannah blew on the hot liquid in her cup clenched between both hands. "Did everything go all right? Were there any problems?"

"Not at all. Having Daisy as a third person at closing makes all the difference. She's fast and efficient. That young girl has a heart of gold." She took a sip of her tea. "I know I wasn't happy with your decision to hire the ex–saloon girl last year, worrying that not everyone was as open-minded as you, Hannah. But I was wrong."

"She's a big help," Hannah agreed. "I've come to rely on her."

Roberta nodded. "She and Jake have been talking marriage for some time now. I wonder what's stopping them?"

Hannah rubbed a hand over her loose light-brown hair that reminded Roberta of a tall glass of sassafras. "I hate to contemplate this, but I think it's his lack of a last name."

"Did she say that?"

Hannah shook her head. "No, just a feeling I have. Not knowing his father seems to weigh heavily on Jake. Did Albert come in at closing time?"

"Doesn't he always when Susanna is on shift? He and that darling little Nate showed up a half hour before I turned the sign. It's nice he lends a hand with the mopping and such. Just emptying that water bucket is a chore. Being a newlywed does have its advantages."

Hannah gave her a look. "Thom always shows up to help and walk me home. And we've been married awhile. I don't think it's the time involved, but the person."

Roberta reached out and rubbed Hannah's arm. "Don't be so prickly. I didn't mean anything by that remark. Thom is the perfect husband, father, *and* son-in-law. It still shames me to remember what I thought of him all those years ago—and the shabby treatment he received at my hands." She shook her head and relaxed back onto the cushion. Lifting one leg, she rotated her foot in a circle, then repeated the exercise with the other leg, working out the kinks. "I was wrong about your Irish champion, and about a lot of other things. I've admitted that before, many times."

"I don't know what I would do if the two of you were still at each other's throats. Well, not him at yours, but you at—"

Her mother waved off the end of Hannah's sentence. "You don't have to remind me of my small-mindedness every chance you get, daughter. Isn't it enough that I've changed and freely admit to my flaws, if not to others, to you?"

"I'm sorry." Hannah softly laughed. "Forgive me for bringing that up."

"*Again*," Roberta said, smiling tolerantly. "And I'm sure this won't be the last."

"I'll work on that."

"Speaking of customers," Roberta said, thinking of the newcomer's intense eyes and wide shoulders, "we had someone quite interesting come in tonight." *He had me stammering like a schoolgirl. What would a romance with him be like?* "Wore a fringed buckskin shirt. Nate sure took a shine to him, asking all kinds of questions about Indians in the mountains, and Indians on the range, outlaws, bears, elk, and moose." She laughed. "Albert's son is not shy, to say the least. The man looks about as untamed as Win's buffalo. He couldn't answer fast enough before Nate was onto another subject. Albert finally had to tell his son to let the poor man eat in peace."

"You must mean Mr. Wade. Yes, we've met. He's quite pleasant, and I agree with you about him being interesting."

Roberta's gaze snapped up from her teacup. "Where did you meet? I was under the impression he'd just arrived."

"Beth told Thom about him. So when I got off my shift, we walked out to the meadow where he's camping. To say hello and welcome him to town. I think Thom also wanted to check him out, see what kind of man he seemed to be. Tabitha went along as well."

"Tabitha? Why?" The serenity Roberta had been feeling vanished, replaced by the usual apprehensions. "I feel totally responsible for my unmarried niece. I don't know what my sister was thinking to allow her to move west alone. I have enough worries of my own without having to concern myself over her daughter, as well as mine. Marigold may be older, but she doesn't have the sense of a scarecrow. She's placed me in a very difficult position. Sometimes I wonder how—"

"Mother!" Hannah laughed. "What're you talking about? Tabitha is her *own* woman. Not only did she travel here by herself, she managed to get an entire building built on time and under budget. She certainly doesn't need you to look out for her welfare." Hannah took a sip of her tea, her lashes blinking with agitation. "She'd be shocked if she knew you thought that. Uncle Frank doesn't feel like you, does he? Did Aunt Marigold specifically ask you to watch over her?"

Roberta counted to ten. The last thing she wanted tonight was an argument with Hannah.

"Mother?"

With a sharp click, she set her cup on the saucer none too gently, letting Hannah know she didn't appreciate being questioned.

"Of course Marigold didn't ask, she didn't have to. I'm sure once she learned Tabitha had set her mind to go, and wouldn't be stopped, she influenced her to pick Logan Meadows, knowing Frank and I were here to keep an eye out. And I have, quietly, in the background. I just meant that as a spinster she could easily be the target of any unscrupulous man." *Like Janet.* "Especially if they are charming and interesting." *Like Mr. Wade.*

Hannah snapped straight. "By *unscrupulous man*, I hope you're not referring to Mr. Wade! His long hair and leather clothes have nothing to do with what kind of a man he is. And what does he have to do with Tabitha anyway? I wholeheartedly pray cousin Tabitha *never, ever* hears you say that word."

"What word?"

"*Spinster!* That would be cruel. And as my mother, I know you're not that!"

"I didn't insinuate anything about Mr. Wade. I merely mentioned that I *worry* about *my* niece—as any aunt would."

Hannah's face clouded over.

"Do you think me so heartless to call her a spinster to her face?"

"I surely hope not."

"Well, thank you for that at least. Facts are facts," Roberta went on. "Tabitha will be twenty-nine years old next week. She's *unmarried.* That makes her a spinster. I'm not the one who makes the rules, Hannah, but you seem to think I do by that expression on your face." She sighed loudly and stood. "I guess I'll go to bed. I can't seem to say anything right."

The door opened and Thom stepped inside. His gaze went from Hannah to Roberta and back again. He slowly removed his hat and hung it on the hall tree, then unbuttoned his coat and did the same with that. "Problems?"

"Not at all, my brave, honorable son-in-law," Roberta said, feeling hurt.

"Mother was just getting up to refill our cups," Hannah said, her expression full of regret. "But I'd like her to sit back down. She's spent the evening at the Silky Hen and I'm sure she is worn out." Hannah stood and with a gentle touch to her arm, sat Roberta back down. "I'm sorry if I was harsh. I didn't mean to be," Hannah said, looking into her eyes. She picked up the tray and started for the kitchen. "There's plenty of hot water, Thom, if you'd like some."

"Indeed I would, Hannah." He came forward and eased down into the chair opposite Roberta.

If she wanted to keep the peace, Roberta would say nothing more about Tabitha. But her thoughts wandered back to Mr. Wade. Who was he, really? A drifter? That could mean anything. He did wear a gun, and was cut from a rough cloth, but sometimes opposites could attract. Especially if he was planning on making Logan Meadows his home. There was no harm in finding out.

CHAPTER EIGHT

After a visit to the bathhouse, where Hunter bathed, shaved again, and clipped his nails, and then a leisurely hour spent over a breakfast of fried eggs, bacon, and a basketful of hot, crumbly biscuits at Nana's Place, he set out for the bookshop. He wasn't completely illiterate, but needed to advance his learning so he could read the accounts book of the Bright Nugget, as well as other business dealings that may arise. As embarrassing as the admission of his ineptness would be to an accomplished woman like Miss Canterbury, he needed to make sure she knew the book was for him, and not a gift. Thorp had been a stickler for the truth. Misleading others was tantamount to lying to their face. Hunter had only to suffer once the long, disappointed stare from his adoptive father to know no truer words had ever been spoken. "A man's good word is his most vital possession, Hunter. Don't ever forget it."

Hunter might not have much, but he'd not trade his integrity for anything. Even if he were just a wagon-trail boss, saddle tramp, or hired gun.

Not so true anymore. You're the half owner of a saloon.

He arrived at Storybook Lodge as the door opened and Miss Canterbury stepped outside lugging a tall, blue-and-yellow sign. The board declared the place open for business. Once her surprise at seeing him faded, she smiled, bringing a gentle lightness to her eyes and a splash of color to her cheeks. He gently extracted the cumbersome object from her hands.

"Thank you, Mr. Wade. That thing is weighty."

"Good morning." Hunter glanced around the boardwalk, the sounds of the stream running beside the building making him raise his voice. "Where would you like this?"

She pointed, and then fluffed the folds of her brown skirt. "Right there, thank you so kindly. I wish I'd had the forethought to have my carpenter make that albatross half the size it is now. Every morning and evening, I begrudgingly think that very same thing." She laughed, glancing up the street and then back at him. "Although, I do suppose moving it around is good for the constitution."

"True enough. Once we reach our age, seems the more we move, the better. I know that's true for me."

Her eyes widened, and he hoped he hadn't offended her.

He patted his stomach, thinking he'd better watch himself, or living in town would turn him soft like most of the merchants he'd come across over the years. But it certainly wasn't true looking at Miss Canterbury. She had the willowy stature of a girl, even though she must be in her late twenties.

She stepped into her shop, waving for him to follow. He removed his hat and gazed around, warm air from a fire in her stove welcoming him.

She clasped her hands in front of her skirt. "You're an early bird."

Several freestanding shelves in the middle of the room held an array of books, as did more shelves built on the walls. "I've never been one to waste my working hours. Besides, it's not early. Half the day is almost over."

"At ten in the morning?"

"It is when I awaken at four. Rain or shine."

She gaped at him, and then laughed. "Four! I can't even imagine. But if that is the case, you're correct about the time. I have a habit of reading late into the evening. If a novel catches my interest, I won't be able to put it down for hours. Sometimes I'll read until three, which makes rising at seven a challenge. I guess I'm just falling asleep when you're getting up."

He pulled a volume from a shelf and turned it over in his hands. He didn't understand someone reading that much. "Spending that much time with a book seems a waste. I'd rather live my life than whittle it away in a story."

This time her lips flattened out to a firm line. She brushed at an invisible something on her sleeve. "What is it you do for a living, Mr. Wade?" she asked, her tone not quite that of the cheerful bird of a moment ago. He wondered if he'd said something to displease her. "What gets you up so early before the sunrise?"

He meandered over to the wall of books, wondering what he should say. He glanced at the spines. Kendall Martin was his next stop. He shouldn't mention anything about the Bright Nugget until all had been settled—especially since she didn't seem too fond of the saloon. Judging by her expression now, and her comment last night about what type of men enjoy wine, women, and song, it wasn't difficult to believe she was a bit uptight.

"For most my life, I've been a guide, bringing wagon trains over the Oregon Trail. Since the transcontinental railroad slowed demand considerably, I make my way doing a little of this and a little of that."

"A wagon master? How exciting!" She hurried to the opposite wall, beneath a sign overtop which he read to himself, *Lending Lib-b-ary*. She ran her fingers across the titles until she found what she was looking for and pulled out a book.

"This was published in late 1870 and features actual accounts of the early pioneers' migration on that exact route. I've read it four times myself and it's one of my favorites." She enfolded the book into her embrace, her eyes shining. "I'm sure you have some fascinating stories to tell."

Is fascinating the same as heartbreaking? He'd seen more death than any one man should. However, she made a good point. He'd also experienced more sunrises, seas of grazing buffalo, night skies so full of stars they didn't look real, unfettered exuberance when reaching a destination alive, and the like, than most men could claim. She was absolutely correct. "I guess I do."

"You must share a few before you leave Logan Meadows. There're several families who have had personal experiences with the western overland route. I'm sure they'd love to speak with you. Hear what you have to say."

I'm no public speaker. I'm not interested in sharing my past like a circus show.

She slipped the book back into its slot. "For now, how can I help you? Is it the reader you came in for?"

That and clearing up the misunderstanding about who it's for. He nodded.

"Wonderful, then follow me right over here." She took a small blue book off her back shelf and opened it several pages in.

There was a sketch of a black-and-white kitten that covered the whole page. *Cat. My cat. The cat. His cat. Her cat. Black cat. Wh-wh-white cat.*

He shook his head. "I'm beyond that. I can read all those words." *Almost.*

"The book is for you, Mr. Wade? Not a child?"

"That's right. I didn't want to say so in front of that gossipy woman you warned me about. Didn't want the news spread all over town"—*the town I'll soon be living in*—"that I'm somewhat illiterate. I grew up traveling back and forth on the trail. The man who raised me had no learning, but would solicit the help of any kind woman along the way who could instruct me for a time. I never had any formal teaching, but I'm pretty good with my sums. Adding and subtracting. After your warning about Miss Fairington, I thought it best I keep that small fact to myself. I don't feel good about deceiving you, but I stand by my reasons."

"I understand completely."

He shook his head, then glanced back at the picture of the cat, the book still resting open in her hands.

"I think that's very admirable of you," she said. "Desiring to further your education."

Even though she was a bit judgmental on drinking and gambling, and she whiled away too many hours reading that could be put to better use, he couldn't deny she was quite pretty. He wondered why a woman like herself hadn't married. "Would you have something a bit more advanced?"

"Of course!"

She pulled out another and opened it to the middle.

He gazed at the page. It had been years since he'd been tutored. This was going to be more difficult than he'd first thought.

"Mr. Wade?"

Embarrassed, he shook his head, then pointed to the page. "The only words I know here are, *the*, *but*, *look*, and *eat*." Disappointment pushed away his humiliation. *I really need to be able to go over the accounts. Reading is a necessity.* "I wonder if you might have some time to work with me? Just to get me started?"

She blinked, and her mouth opened a small amount as she thought over his statement. "You *would* progress much more quickly if I were close at hand to help with difficult words. Sounding out syllables takes time and practice, and can be discouraging."

Was she trying to convince herself?

"I've only been open a few months and I'm still working on finding ways to get townspeople interested in my wares. What I'm trying to say is, I have all the time in the world to help you." She pointed to a comfortable-looking chair by the window. "You could sit right there."

Footsteps on the boardwalk drew Hunter's glance to the window. Roberta Brown, the comely waitress from the restaurant, reached for the doorknob and entered. As she looked between him and Tabitha, her smile slowly disappeared.

"Aunt Roberta." Tabitha hurried to the door. She hugged the woman, and then stood back. "This is a nice surprise."

They're related. I've got a lot to learn about this town.

"It's—a surprise—to me—too, dear."

The jerky sentence was a contradiction to the lively conversations he'd had with her over supper last night. She'd seemed eager to talk, but he'd learned over the years that older widows didn't need much encouragement, which made him wary.

"Mr. Wade," she said, her tone much different from the last time they'd talked.

"Mrs. Brown."

"Did you come in to visit, Aunt Roberta, or are you looking for a novel to help pass the night?"

He understood long nights. Self-conscious, Hunter turned and strolled to the back of the room, tipping his head to better try to read the spines.

"I have a copy of *The Scarlet Letter* in the lending library that you might enjoy."

"No, ah . . ."

"If that's not to your tastes, what about *Uncle Tom's Cabin*? Or *The Legend of Sleepy Hollow*? Both are very good."

Hunter listened to Tabitha's quick footsteps as he kept his head down. "Here, this is what I was looking for. *The American Woman's Home*. It has ideas on healthful cookery, home decorations, gardening, illnesses, and much, much more. It's a wealth of information! I've only had a quick look, but I think you'd like it very much."

He could hear the woman's sputters without even looking.

"No, no, Tabitha. I came in to invite you to Sunday supper. I was afraid if I let it go, I'd forget, and the weekend is almost here."

"How thoughtful of you," Tabitha replied. "I'd love to come. What can I bring?"

He looked over his shoulder to see Roberta mouthing something to Tabitha, a none-too-pleasant frown on her face. Her eyes darted to him and then back to Tabitha. *She's talking about me.*

The woman blinked and straightened. "Just yourself. Hannah and I have everything covered. Say, six o'clock?"

"Thank you," Tabitha replied. "I'll be there."

He waited for Roberta to turn and leave, but she didn't. Instead she said, "Just out of curiosity, what are the two of you talking about?"

He caught Tabitha's glance toward him. She snatched up several more books and covered the beginner volume in her arms. "Mr. Wade is looking for something to read. He hasn't yet made a decision. I'm assisting him."

Roberta tipped her head to one side, as if weighing that answer. Her eyes narrowed when she glanced down at his .45 Colt and then up into his eyes. "In that case, I'll let the two of you get back to work. I'll see you on Sunday, dear." With perfectly ladylike posture, she turned and left the store, disappearing out of sight after passing the window.

Hunter watched her leave, feeling something wasn't right. "I appreciate you keeping my secret," he said tersely. "By the time men reach my age, most can read, write, and do sums quite well. I'm a bit sensitive about my lack of education."

Tabitha smiled. "Sounds like all you need is some practice."

He stepped toward the door, securing the hat dangling in his fingertips back onto his head. "I don't think your aunt likes me very much." He didn't appreciate the disapproval he'd sensed from Roberta. She'd been friendly enough before. The reversal didn't sit well, and he felt the need of some cool air on his face.

"Why would you say that? Of course she does." Tabitha lifted the books she still held. "Aren't you going to make a decision?"

"I'll come back later if I find some time. I have some pressing business I need to attend to before any more of my day gets away."

At his hard tone, she searched his face, but her smile never faltered. "Whatever suits you, Mr. Wade. You know where to find me."

What suited him was for others to stop judging him by the way he looked. Roberta Brown, in particular. He'd had his fill of overly righteous women. He could spot 'em a mile away. As his thoughts turned from aunt to niece, he wondered if the apple fell far from the tree.

Mr. Wade glanced over his shoulder at her once before following in Aunt Roberta's footsteps. Tabitha fingered the book in her hands, acknowledging to herself that she'd enjoyed the encounter with Mr. Wade more than she'd like to admit. Straightening her spine, she set the primer back on the shelf and gave the book a little pat.

So, she wasn't as immune to the opposite sex, at least not this particular man, as she liked to think. She went to the door and looked out on the town. A tickle in her stomach, feeling very much like butterflies, made her lips tilt up. Was this what it felt like to have a crush? She'd never had one, but she rather liked the feeling.

She hoped Aunt Roberta hadn't frightened him away. He'd acted put off by her. Reading was the love of her life; she was sure once Mr. Wade, with his love of travel, got a taste for it, he'd see the value in stories that could transport a person anywhere.

With a sigh, her thoughts turned back to business and she moved to her desk. She stared down at the poster she'd been working on before opening the shop this morning and running into Mr. Wade.

Come One, Come All, to a Public Reading!
Great Expectations by Charles Dickens
Every Tuesday evening two chapters will be read aloud.
This exciting novel follows the coming-of-age
experiences of an
orphan named Pip. Good entertainment for the whole family.
Storybook Lodge, Six O'clock
Refreshments Will be Served

Tabitha wrinkled her brow. *Well, it's a start.*

If this didn't get customers into her shop, and readers interested in the books she had to offer, she'd have to try something else. Perhaps she'd have a sale in conjunction as well. She rubbed her chin. No, she couldn't afford to discount any of her inventory just yet. She'd wait. See how the event went. Back home in the city library, authors often came to read their works. She never missed one. She wasn't Charles Dickens, but an oration would be something different for Logan Meadows.

Tabitha glanced around the interior of her shop. How many people would Storybook Lodge hold? If she moved the center bookshelves to the side, several more rows of seats could be added, which all depended on what she'd use for seating. Who would attend? Hannah, Thom, and Aunt Roberta would be here, and Uncle Frank. Most likely Jessie and Chase. Susanna and Albert. Brenna, Greg, and their brood. If Nell wasn't too busy on the ranch, maybe she would drag Charlie out, and even Maddie and Julia, the nice young woman who'd broken her arm when the train crashed a few months back.

What about Mr. Wade? Would he come as well?

A spark of excitement skittered around in Tabitha's heart. Maybe he would. Even if a quarter of her friends came to the first reading, that would be a great start. And she'd be content. A list of other acquaintances filtered through her head. Mrs. Hollyhock, Maude Miller. Dr. Thorn seemed the type who might enjoy a night out, as did Reverend

Wilbrand. Win would come just to be supportive of her—and if these readings really started to catch on in the months to come, maybe some of the folks would venture over from New Meringue.

Just imagine how many books she could sell then. She hadn't thought ahead to have extra copies of *Great Expectations* available for purchase, in case some customers showed an interest. She'd put in an order to have in two to three weeks.

Tabitha leaned back in her chair. Rome wasn't built in a day. Or a month. Or even a year! She couldn't get discouraged. She had to have faith.

She went to the shelf for her feather duster. She had things to do besides speculate on possibilities that may never happen. And that went as well for Mr. Wade. She still didn't know his past, but she did know a little more about him than she had yesterday. And if he actually did come in for reading lessons, she'd get to know him even better.

CHAPTER NINE

Let me see that!" Kendall Martin roared, grabbing for the document as Hunter pulled the note out of the angry bartender's reach. "It's a fake! I don't owe you nothin'. You're not gettin' the Bright Nugget! I built this place on my own. Now get out of this office before I throw you out on your backside."

Hunter had known this wouldn't be easy before he'd stepped through the batwing doors. No man wanted another staking claim to his livelihood. He understood that, but he had to think of himself as well. He'd done the job for Quincy Malone, and the once-rich land baron owed him a bundle. Kendall Martin had owed Malone, and hadn't paid up. If he had, he wouldn't be in this predicament. This was the only property Malone had left to give. It was so insignificant, he had completely forgotten about the saloon until Hunter had made him search the safe hidden away in his closet, from top to bottom.

"You may have stopped paying, but you still owed Malone. And Malone owed me. It's as simple as that. Signing this over was Malone's way of paying off his debt to me. I can't say it any plainer. We're partners. Equal in every way. Get used to it!"

The two had been standing face-to-face in the small liquor storeroom Kendall called an office for the past twenty minutes, yelling at each other. A droplet of sweat trickled down Hunter's temple, but he stayed the impulse to brush it away. Martin might mistake any quick movement for him going for his gun.

Martin's face relaxed. "We'll take it to the sheriff. See what Preston has to say. He's not going to let some stranger waltz in and take over."

"Good idea. Let's go." Hunter knew the signed document was legal and binding. There wasn't a thing Martin could do to change the inevitable.

Martin threw open the door and stormed out. Philomena watched with wide worried eyes as Hunter followed the bartender out the front door.

Sheriff Preston's head jerked up when the bartender angrily threw open his office door, banging it against the wall with a loud crack. Hunter had met the sheriff the night before in the restaurant. "What's this?" Preston barked. A large dog by the woodstove pounced to his feet and growled.

"What in God's name is wrong with you, Kendall?" The sheriff's gaze followed Hunter as he went to one side of the sheriff's desk, and Martin the other.

Martin jabbed a finger in Hunter's direction. "He's trying to hoodwink me. Says he has documentation stating he's now half owner of the Bright Nugget! He's a liar and a fool if he thinks I'm going to turn my life over to him just like that! It's a forgery, and—"

"Just settle down, Kendall, until I have all the facts," Preston said, glancing over at Hunter and then back at the red-faced bartender. He gestured to the chairs in front of his desk, but the two remained standing, so he stood as well. "What claim do you have on the Bright Nugget?" he asked. "Explain everything to me the same as you did to Kendall. Don't leave anything out."

Hunter nodded. "I did a large job for a businessman in Soda Springs by the name of Quincy Malone. A contract that took more than a year to complete. When I returned for the pay that was owed me, I learned Malone had mortgaged himself to the devil and had lost everything. Had no way of paying. But on closer inspection, he found this one, forgotten note that Kendall Martin had taken out with him years ago. Malone had provided Martin a substantial grubstake to get started. Martin made payments for a few years, but somewhere along the line, stopped. Since Malone was building his empire, the note went forgotten. He signed it over to me in payment."

"Did you have a loan with Malone?" Albert asked Kendall.

Kendall's nod was barely perceptible.

"Do you have the money to pay off your debt to Mr. Wade?"

Kendall shook his head.

Hunter withdrew the paper from his pocket.

"May I see that?"

Should he trust the sheriff? Without the signed note, he had no claim on the saloon. Hunter glanced at Martin. "If you don't give it to him."

The sheriff gave Martin a no-nonsense stare. "Behave yourself, Kendall."

Sheriff Preston unfolded the legal paper and scanned it over. He checked the date several times. "So, if I send a telegram to Soda Springs to check out your story, the sheriff will have knowledge about this?"

"You bet he will. I was sure to cover my back, anticipating just that."

"It's a setup," Kendall complained. "Maybe his men killed everybody and took over the town, just waiting for you to contact them."

"Over the Bright Nugget?" Sheriff Preston's tone spoke volumes. The Bright Nugget wasn't worth that much trouble to anyone.

"You can be sure I'll be sending some telegrams of my own," Kendall mumbled. "I used to live there. Nobody's gonna barge in on me."

The sheriff refolded the document and handed it to Hunter.

"I'd like to move in to one of the upstairs rooms," Hunter said.

"What! That ain't possible. I live in one and Philomena the other."

"I saw four doors at the top of the stairs."

"One is rented out to Wilson's Feed and Seed for extra space. The other one has been torn up for years. Needs two new walls, and the mice have eaten out a couple holes in the ceiling, which need to be patched. It don't even have a bed."

"You sure aren't getting the most out of your saloon, Martin. You'll be glad I showed up to help. I'll bet I can double your profit in three months."

"Why you . . ." Martin lunged across Preston's desk, going for Hunter's throat.

Sheriff Preston threw his arm around Kendall's neck and wrestled him away, the large bartender grappling at anything within his reach, knocking items to the floor. Preston pushed Kendall up against the wall, the sheriff's face red with anger.

"*Don't* make me lock you up, Kendall! I will if you don't stop this foolishness." The sheriff stooped over and picked up an ink bottle, frowning at the black puddle on the wood. "Mr. Wade is minding the law. You should follow suit. Let me check out his story before you try to kill him."

"Thank you, Sheriff," Hunter said, ignoring the hate-filled scowl coming his way. "I guess I can throw my bedroll in the back of the saloon until I figure out where I can live, for a time anyway. Or better yet, stay in the meadow. Doesn't bother me to camp."

Preston stared at him so long he feared the tide might be turning against him.

"You won't have to do that. There's an empty apartment directly above here. I moved out when my son, Nate, came to live with me. The place has a bed, and some other useful things."

"Sheriff!"

"Be quiet, Kendall."

Hunter couldn't believe his good luck. "Thank you. Next door to the Bright Nugget will be handy."

"*And* next to the bookshop," Kendall spat. "Miss Canterbury don't like all the noise the rowdy cowboys make on Saturday night. You'll find that out soon enough. Now you'll have to contend with her yourself."

That didn't sound so bad. An image of Tabitha almost made him smile, but he didn't want to rile Kendall any more than he already had.

"Come on," Sheriff Preston said. The sheriff grabbed his hat as he strode over to the door. "I'll show you the apartment before I go to the telegraph office."

Kendall's face twisted. "Isn't that putting the plow before the ox?"

Preston shrugged and walked out.

That evening Hunter stood behind the bar, essentially watching Kendall and copying whatever he did. How difficult could it be to pour whiskey and talk to men? Whenever a patron put coins on the bar top in payment, they went directly into Kendall's pockets behind the apron tied around his belly. When those began to bulge, he discreetly emptied them into a box below the bar, attached to the shelf with a chain. Alongside that was a loaded shotgun, as well as two .45 Colts. Out of habit, Hunter still wore his Peacekeeper on his thigh, thinking someday he might feel comfortable enough to go without, but that was doubtful.

The saloon was filling up. The length of the bar was standing room only, and the tables more than half full. Sheriff Preston had stuck his head in at ten o'clock, taking stock, he'd said. The friendly feel of the early-evening customers had morphed into a more serious nature. Farley, the pleasant, middle-aged piano player, pounded out songs on the piano keys, and when Philomena found herself free from delivering a tray full of whiskeys, some cowboy would swoop her into his arms and dance her around the outside of the tables, shuffling through the shavings.

"You told that joke five minutes ago!" an angry drifter-type yelled over the piano music to the bleary-eyed man at his side, the two directly in front of where Hunter stood behind the bar. "I'm tired of your repeating everything you say a hundred times over. Shut your trap! You're givin' me a headache."

The man he was addressing belched loudly then pulled a steel blade from somewhere below. Hunter lunged forward and grasped his arm, bending the fella's wrist back until he yelped. The weapon clattered to the bar surface. Men looked over.

"There'll be none of that tonight," Hunter said sternly, looking them all in the eyes. "Keep it nice, or get out."

"I didn't mean nothin'," the knife holder sneered. He took up the gut sticker and slid it back into his belt. "I was just gonna give my friend a haircut. That's all. Hey, Kendall," he hollered over to the bartender, who was pouring two shot glasses of whiskey. "This new fella's a darn sight stronger than you!" He circled his wrist several times, to the snickers of others. "A darn sight!"

Shouting broke out deep in the room. Hunter glanced at Kendall, but he just shrugged and tossed back one of the drinks he'd just poured. He wiped his mouth with the back of his hand and sent Hunter a hate-filled stare. It was easy to see his partner had yet to soften. The fella Kendall had just refilled smirked, making Hunter think that perhaps he was the topic of their conversation. For one instant, he recalled the quiet bookshop, and Tabitha agreeing to tutor him. Only two doors down, but a world apart. He wondered if she was upstairs reading right now.

Crash!

A bottle flew past Hunter's head and landed in a rack stacked with clean glasses, the tumblers exploding into shards. A table in the middle of the room was upended, and one man dived for the other's throat. Hunter dropped the damp rag and dashed around the bar, hoping to stop the fight before too much more of his new property was ruined. If he'd been worried that becoming a business owner would make him soft, he realized that wouldn't be a problem. He pushed through the throng of men that had surrounded the combatants, ducking one misguided fist, but taking another to his gut. Tending a saloon after midnight was much like wrestling a bear. Which of the two was more unpredictable was yet to be decided.

CHAPTER TEN

Midmorning Saturday, Violet Hollyhock ignored the ache throbbing in her spine as she lifted the large fruit jar of fall leaves, arranged just so. She positioned the container, accented by a few cattails collected from the banks of Shady Creek, on one side of the church's altar. The room was quiet. The only illumination streamed through the six rectangular windows, three to each side, that ran the length of the simple nave.

She rotated the jar, careful not to spill water on the snowy-white altar cloth she'd just laid down. After a long scrutiny through discerning eyes, she turned the adornment back to its original position.

"It's simple, Lord, but the best I can do this time of year. Hope ya like it."

When the door opened, she turned. Reverend Wilbrand, wearing brown trousers and a light coat, stepped inside and stopped. "Violet? What a nice surprise. I didn't expect to find you here this early."

"Just dressing the church for tomorrow's service."

The reverend came forward. Although he was in his midforties, the preacher's face always reminded her of a mischievous boy's. He was tall and trim. Had come to Logan Meadows some ten or twelve years back, passing through on his way to Washington. When he'd discovered their preacher had taken sick and died, he stayed on.

"Don't you usually do this in the afternoon?"

"Ya know me pretty well, don't ya, you young whippersnapper?" Sentiment swirled in her breast. Would anyone miss her after she'd passed?

He cocked his head and chuckled. "Yes. I think I do." His astute gaze took in her face. He came closer. "Is something wrong, Violet? Are you feeling well?"

She straightened her spine, despite the bolt of lightning it caused, putting on a good front for the reverend. "I'm as fit as a fiddle, as you can see." She pointed to the broom, dusting rags, and jar of lemon oil she'd left next to the wall after she'd given the pews a good polishing, and the floor a thorough sweeping. "I jist wanted ta get done a mite early. No sin against that, last time I checked—though things may have changed?" She narrowed her eyes at him. No youngster was going to boss her around, even if he was the preacher. "I have some bakin' ta do later on." *And I'm movin' slower than a turtle this week. When Pansy crowed this morning, I had ta force my ol' bones from the warm covers. Right then and there I knew iffin I didn't start early, I might not get finished on time.*

He put his hand on her shoulder. "You need to let the other ladies help you. I know a handful have offered more than once. Susanna, Hannah, Brenna, Tabitha, just to name a few, but you always turn them down. It's not a crime to grow older, Violet. Or to ask for some help."

"I don't do it for them, I do it for the Lord!" She gazed at the ceiling, imagining a multitude of angels looking down at her from puffy white clouds. "He and I have a standing date. I'm not givin' that up for nothin'."

The patient look on the reverend's face almost made her scowl, but that wouldn't be right in the house of worship.

"I'm not asking you to give it up, Violet. All I'm saying is let the others help. Have you ever thought that you might be robbing them of their chance to do something for God? Maybe they'd like to have a standing date, too."

"Let 'em do something else. This job will be open soon enough."

She hadn't meant to sound so crotchety. It was just that she wanted to live her days out until the end *her* way. If she stopped doing, and being, and saying, what kind of life would that be? Not one to contemplate in her way of thinking.

Reverend Wilbrand took a deep breath, and slowly turned a circle. "Everything looks very nice. Like always. Thank you for all you do."

That was better. She nodded. "My pleasure, Reverend. Now, I best put these things away, and get on to my other errands. Time's a-wastin'."

With her basket of eggs over her arm, Violet took the little dirt path that led down the hill from the church to Main Street. Halfway there she noticed Bao Ling come out the back door of the laundry. The poor woman, large and past her sixth month, lumbered toward the clothesline with a basket of linens in her arms.

Violet hurried over. "Give me that! Ya gonna hurt the peanut."

Bao resisted, but Violet wrested the clothes away. She might be old, and in pain, but she was still stronger than most women she knew.

Bao blinked several times. "Mrs. Holly*hock*," she breathed out on a sigh. "Let me have back."

Violet marched to the taut rope strung between two medium-sized oaks and set the load on the ground, pushing back the groan in her throat. "After I hang these, I'm gonna have a word with that man a' yours. He can't be expectin' you ta do the things ya did afore you was with child." She took a sheet from the basket and snapped it out. She stuck a few clothespins in her mouth, then went down the line fastening on the sheet. Bao hurried to get the other end.

When she went for another sheet, Bao stopped her with a hand to her forearm. She looked into her face. "Please, no do that."

"But ya need help, honey. Think of the little one."

Bao's face clouded over and she glanced away. Violet was sure it was to hide her tears.

"We get by."

Maybe now they got by. But in another month, all the hours over the boiling pots would take their toll. Violet had seen it before. She didn't want to see this sweet woman lose her baby.

"Ya gots ta hire some help." Surely they could. They were the only laundry business in town, and were always washing. "Just for a few months. Until the babe is born."

She shook her head, sending her long braid swishing back and forth. "Can't afford."

Lan, her young daughter, stepped out the back door. When she saw Violet, she stopped and slowly stepped back in. That was strange for the friendly child. Turning, Violet fetched a nearby chair and set it by the basket.

"Sit yerself down. Jist for a minute while I string these up. Your face is redder than any beet from my garden." When the shy woman tried to resist, Violet narrowed her eyes. Bao sat.

"That's better." An expert after many years of hanging her own laundry, Violet was finished in ten minutes. "What other heavy work ya got planned fer the day?"

"That's all."

Violet lifted a brow.

Bao smiled. "I promise."

"That better be the truth." Once the wet garments were dry, they would be much easier to remove from the line. "I'll be by tomorrow ta handle your sheets."

"No. Sunday. You have service."

"And you have work. I seen ya. You and Mr. Ling work seven days a week. I can't say as I understand that, but I won't harp." When Bao began to object once more, Violet pointed a finger in her face. "God put you protector over that little one. You have ta think of him or her first."

Bao dropped her eyes. "Thank you," she whispered.

Violet patted her arm. "I'll be on my way now, but look for me around this time tomorrow. I'll be here."

CHAPTER ELEVEN

Whisk broom in hand, Hunter brushed the shards of glass strewn over the Bright Nugget's bar onto a tray, wondering how much it would cost to replace the broken glassware. A pretty penny, he was sure. Sheriff Preston had warned him that the saloon could get rowdy, but Hunter had thought the lawman had been exaggerating, since Logan Meadows wasn't the largest of places. Boy, had he been wrong. His first night working the bar had been an eye-opener.

A door opened upstairs. Hunter didn't even look up. Kendall was still giving him the cold shoulder. He guessed he'd feel much the same if someone horned in claiming half of his territory.

Footsteps clomped down the stairs.

From the corner of his eye, Hunter saw Kendall pull his suspenders up over his shoulders as he passed Hunter without saying a word. The man continued behind the bar where he poured himself a short drink and tossed it back.

Hunter set the tray down. "Feel better?"

Kendall glanced his way with bloodshot eyes and rumpled hair. "I'm not talking to the likes of you."

"That's gonna make things a mite hard, Kendall. Just get over it. I said I was sorry." He'd eat a little crow to hasten the bonding process.

"You never said you were sorry! Not once."

"Guess you're right. Well, I'm saying it now."

Kendall's gaze dropped to Hunter's hip and the gun he'd strapped back on this morning after only a few hours of sleep. Kendall placed both palms on the bar top and watched the people walking past their front door. The paunchy bartender didn't look like he felt very well.

One thing Hunter couldn't abide was a hangover. Thorp Wade, a teetotaler for as long as Hunter had known him, was a smart man. When Hunter had been old enough to be curious about the whiskey jugs being passed around the campfires at night, Thorp hadn't forbid him. He actually provided Hunter with a small bottle of his own. After vomiting his guts into the prairie grass and a few bouts with a head that felt like a buffalo herd had used it for a river crossing, Hunter wised up. From that time on, he only allowed himself one drink. The rule had served him well over the years. He'd seen many a good man fumble when it counted the most, and be killed.

His apology hadn't garnered a response. "Kendall, what do you say we bury the hatchet? I can handle this cleanup if you want to go to the bathhouse and then relax for a few hours." *A bath might help our business.* "I don't mind at all."

Kendall scowled and began wiping down the other end of the sticky bar. "What? So you can go through the books?"

"You got something to hide?"

The man Hunter recognized as Dwight Hoskins pushed through the batwing doors. Another man followed. "We're not open yet," Hunter said, thinking of all the housekeeping ahead.

Kendall shot him a glare. "We're always open to paying customers. Especially Dwight."

"New rule. We open at one. That's only two hours away and will barely give me time to clean up this mess and repair the broken tables and chairs from last night. We'll need them if tonight is anything like yesterday. I noticed more in the back alley, too. Things around here can use some repair." *You've been shirking your chores for some time, Kendall.* "If the men want coffee, we can do that."

Hunter was surprised that Kendall didn't offer more resistance. He had no problem if others wanted to throw their money away. He'd gladly take it. But the sooner they got to drinking, the sooner more fights would break out. This place needed some down time. With both him and Kendall now, maybe they could make some headway on the chores, since Kendall didn't seem to have the desire.

Dwight and his friend exchanged a glance, then went to the bar.

Clyde, a regular who, according to Philomena, spent every day in the saloon, came in and ambled to a table in the back. He plunked down without saying a word, content to doze right there until a decent hour to begin drinking.

Since Kendall was moving slower than molasses, Hunter went to the stove for the pot of coffee he'd brewed not long ago. Returning, he brought up two mugs from under the bar and placed them before Dwight and his friend.

"Here you go, fellas," he said all friendly-like, filling each mug to the brim with steaming black liquid. "It's on the house."

Hunter hadn't yet had time to figure out Dwight Hoskins. The man had a shiftiness to him that kept Hunter on edge. Almost like the ruthless flimflam men he'd seen plenty of who didn't bat an eye when stealing from a muddled old man. The other individual was a different matter. Hunter had seen his share moving back and forth between states and territories on the hunt. Predators. An aura surrounded them like the stink of a rotting carcass. This man was a killer. Hunter wondered what business he had in Logan Meadows.

A shout of warning from outside brought Hunter around. He set the coffeepot down and sprinted out from behind the bar. Grasping the tops of the batwing doors, he glanced left and then right.

Nothing.

Only one feeble old woman crossing the street with a basket over her arm. Her lips moved rapidly as if she were holding a heated conversation with herself.

Another shout.

From the direction of the livery, a buffalo charged down the middle of Main Street headed directly for the unsuspecting woman. *That's Max! No, it's Clementine, the wilder of the two.*

Hunter blasted out the doors and sprinted as fast as he could.

I'm not going to make it. She's too far away.

The pounding of the enormous hooves shook the ground. As he drew alongside, he saw the animal's eyes rolled toward the top of her skull in fear. She'd mow down the scrawny woman and not even notice.

He shouted and waved his arms.

The woman glanced up. Her eyes grew round and she clutched her basket to her calico-clad chest.

His only chance was to dive. Hunter gathered his muscles and pushed off his feet, ignoring the pain that sliced through his weak knee. He reached out, not wanting to hurt the old woman, but his blow would be better than the animal's hooves enforced with a thousand pounds of meat.

Clementine's hot breath scorched down his back.

CHAPTER TWELVE

Tabitha swallowed a scream, both hands pressed against the glass. Everything had happened so fast. At a loud crash, she'd bolted from her desk to the bookstore window. A second later, Clementine streaked by faster than Tabitha thought possible for such a large animal, heading directly for Violet.

She grasped her skirt and ran out the door.

Outside the saloon, Mr. Wade took two running steps and dived from the boardwalk just as the buffalo was about to run Violet down.

The two tumbled in a cloud of dust as the beast thundered past.

It took an eternity to get to their side. Entwined in each other's arms, they lay still as the prairie grass at sunup, a mixture of dirt and egg yolk covering them both. Surely, Mr. Wade wasn't dead, but Tabitha worried about Violet. She crouched down and touched Mr. Wade's shoulder.

He opened his eyes. "Did I make it in time?" He tipped his head down to inspect Mrs. Hollyhock cradled in his arms.

"I'm not sure," Tabitha replied, keeping her gaze on Mrs. Hollyhock. "You both took a bad fall."

"Is this heaven?" Violet patted around Mr. Wade's chest, her eyes closed. "Sure feels like heaven ta me."

Tabitha squelched a thankful smile that the old woman was still alive and had retained her sense of humor. "Let's get you up." She helped Violet climb to her feet.

Mr. Harrell had run from his haberdashery to see what the commotion was all about. Kendall had arrived, as well as Dwight and another man she didn't know.

Tabitha's gaze traveled down to the large, shiny gun strapped to Mr. Wade's thigh. This was the first time she'd seen him since the news had gotten around town about his dubious history in Soda Springs. Kendall had told Dwight, who'd in turn told her aunt, who in turn had told her, that Mr. Wade was a gunfighter. A killer. Kendall's friend in Soda Springs had replied to Kendall's telegram the same day. When Tabitha had heard the words, she'd found them difficult to believe. *Is a gunfighter determined to better his education?* She didn't think so, but she couldn't be sure. Since he hadn't returned to the shop after the encounter with Aunt Roberta, she hoped they hadn't, in some way, discouraged him. She'd felt a friction between them. Still, concerning the information Kendall had discovered, she wouldn't turn a blind eye.

Dwight shifted his weight.

Mr. Wade flicked several eggshells from his shirt and pants. "I didn't think I was going to make it. That critter is fast."

"Well, ya did," Violet said, her voice filled with emotion. "Ya done robbed me of my heavenly reward." She glanced up at him with a wobbly smile and her eyes softened. "Even though I don't get to go see my mama and pappy today, I'm still grateful to ya. Yer faster on yer feet than the grim reaper himself." She gave him a long look up and down and nodded her approval despite the egg and dirt. "You must be that handsome new fella come ta run the tavern."

Kendall harrumphed.

Win galloped up on a horse, a rope in hand. He slid to a halt. Short leather blacksmith chinks covered his thighs, singed in places from work at his forge. He wasn't wearing a hat. The panic on his face was impossible to miss. "Everyone all right?" he shouted.

"They're both fine, except for needing a bath," Kendall replied.

"'Cept fer my basket of broken eggs I was taking to the mercantile." Mrs. Hollyhock's eyes narrowed on the livery owner.

Mr. Wade bent, retrieved the wicker carrier, and handed it to her. Yellow yolks and white shells spotted the blue-and-white-checked cloth inside.

"You know I'll make good on those, Violet," Win said, a hurt expression darkening his eyes. "Pay for your dress as well, if it's ruined." His horse danced nervously. "Something spooked Clementine when I went in to fill the water barrel. There was a noise and then Clementine crashed right through the slightly ajar gate with her impressive set of horns."

Violet straightened. "They ain't so impressive ta me."

"No, I guess not." Win shook his head. "She's never acted crazy like that before. Cantankerous, yes, but . . ." He straightened in the saddle. "I better go find her. Which way did she go?"

They all pointed down the street.

Win nodded and galloped off in a shower of dust.

The onlookers meandered away now that the excitement had passed and Violet was going to live. The usually stubborn woman actually let Tabitha and Mr. Wade help her over to the mercantile side of the street.

"I'd like ta thank ya. What's yer name? Mr. Way?"

"It's Wade," he corrected. "And there's no need for thanks, ma'am."

Violet pulled back, affronted. "What? Yer gonna deny me the chance to thank ya, ta bless ya? After what you gone and done? That's a disgrace!" Color suffused Violet's blanched face. "Why not? Don't ya think you're good enough for a simple thank you?" She reached out with a claw-like hand and took ahold of the fringe of his leather shirt. "How many others have ya turned away, Mr. Wade? You're a good actor, I'll bet, but I can see the uncertainty in your eyes."

Stunned, Tabitha watched Mr. Wade drop his gaze to the boardwalk. Was that true?

"Well, Mr. Wade, ya gonna let me bless ya?"

He nodded.

A smile blossomed on Violet's face. "Thankee." She reached across and took the hand that dangled at his side. "You saved my life, young man, and I'm indebted to ya. You risked yer own neck to help a crotchety old woman ya didn't even know. In my way of thinkin', that makes you the best kind of man. I thank ya, and bless ya, and hereby proclaim myself yer granny."

A lump of emotion squeezed Tabitha's throat. She wished she weren't here to witness such a private moment. Chancing a glance at Mr. Wade's face, she saw sentiment and pain lurking deep in his eyes. Was that regret over men he had killed?

He swallowed once. "Thank you, ma'am, but I'm old enough—"

"Hush!"

"It's just that I've never known a grandmother before, ma'am, and I can hardly remember my own ma and pa. Your sentiment has moved me deeply."

Mrs. Hollyhock straightened. Now that she'd gotten her way with Mr. Wade, she seemed back to normal, except for the spots that marred her skirt and brown calico blouse, or the long gray strands of hair that had escaped her bun and straggled in front of her face. "Dandy. That makes two of us. I expect ta see my grandson at my place each week for supper—every Thursday night. I live at the Red Rooster. You know where that is?"

He nodded. "Yes, ma'am. I do."

Tabitha took a small step back and they both looked at her. "Violet, would you like to go down to my shop and sit in my soft chair? You're looking a little peaked."

"No, missy. I have lots ta do today." She looked down at the basket in her hands. "I need ta let Hannah and Maude know I won't have any eggs fer 'em today. That might present a problem. Best take care of that right now."

Mr. Wade kept ahold of her elbow. "I'll escort you there."

"As will I," Tabitha added. "Just give me one moment to run down and lock my door." As strongly as she'd felt drawn to Mr. Wade in their encounter in the bookstore, perhaps he was one of those types that could snap on a dime. Listening to Aunt Roberta, she'd believe anything was possible. Tabitha would feel better about Violet's safety if she went along to keep an eye on things.

CHAPTER THIRTEEN

Scrunched in with Mr. Wade and Tabitha at a small table in front of the window, Violet enjoyed the two young people's company and conversation. It was a far cry from speaking with Beth Fairington, the woman who lived at Violet's boardinghouse. Depending on which way that girl's wind was blowing each day, one could never know if she'd ignore you, or bite your head off. Violet had to walk softly until she knew which side of the bed she'd crawled out on. That made company with these two all the sweeter.

Lifting her teacup with both hands, she took a sip. Funny how Tabitha colored up each time Mr. Wade addressed her. Her strong spirit was a good match for his insecurities. Violet might just have met her new grandson, but that didn't mean she couldn't see through several layers of his character. One had to look past what was on top. Just like peeling an onion . . .

"What do you make of Clementine getting loose?" Tabitha asked.

"Critters have a way of gettin' out," Violet answered. The warm tea had settled her nerves considerably. She relaxed in the chair as she watched through the window. The Wells Fargo stage pulled to a halt in front of the hotel. "I'm sure some of the townsfolk will put up a squawk, worried it might happen again."

Mr. Wade just listened, looking uncomfortable with the little china cup held in his large hands. He'd wanted to skedaddle once they'd arrived, but she'd kept him on, knowing Tabitha had taken a shine to him—not that the girl likely even realized it yet.

She hid a smile. Tabitha reminded her of herself when she was that age, feisty and headstrong. By then, Violet had been married ten years. This gal believed she was old, spent, when in reality, she was just a babe, with her whole life in front of her, and now here was a man interested in opening her eyes. As hard as Violet tried, she couldn't keep her teacup from trembling as she raised it to her lips, recalling the short, but heady years she'd had with Bruce. Oh, how she missed that man. Her heart swelled, feeling again sixteen and bursting with hopes and dreams that would fill an ocean.

Outside, two men climbed out of the stagecoach and ambled away. Ralph, the driver, stepped to the conveyance's door and put out his hand, helping a woman to the ground.

Violet gasped. Her teacup clattered to the table. Tabitha and Mr. Wade both leaned back, their eyes wide, and began blotting at the puddle on the tablecloth.

"I'm sorry ta leave ya with this mess, but I need ta go."

Both youngsters responded with a *why*.

"Never you mind. I have someone I need ta talk to."

Violet stood and hurried away, her energy back, and ready for a fight. Within seconds she was next to the stage. "What in blazes are ya doin' in Logan Meadows?" she barked out.

The medium-sized woman she'd recognize from anywhere turned. Her hand went to her mouth in shock. "So, you're still alive. Doesn't surprise me, though. You're too wicked to die. God doesn't want you."

Violet, still in disbelief, stared at Jake's mother. Marlene had been a saloon girl in Valley Springs where Violet had owned a mercantile. Marlene's once-thick black hair had thinned, and her rouge stood out on her powdered face. Time had not been kind. Her blue eyes, usually clouded with drink, were clear.

"Your hollow words don't scare me," Violet mumbled.

The woman's lips pursed. "By now I thought you'd be long gone. A lump in some lonely graveyard."

In no mood for games, Violet grasped Marlene's arm. She came close so no one else would hear. "What do you want?"

"I only want to speak with my son. See how he is."

"I don't believe you. You've never had a kind thought for Jake. You only had a use for him when you needed something. Was hungry or wanted him to find you a bottle. I won't let you near him. He doesn't want you in his life. When he was jist a tyke, I was the one to bathe him, feed him, and make sure he had somewhere to sleep. He grew up like a wild wolf pup. You never loved him then, and ya don't love him now. Jist get back on that stage and keep going!"

Unfortunately, Ralph, the stage driver, was watching the exchange with a troubled brow. The last thing Violet wanted was for everyone to find out Jake's no-good mother had shown up in Logan Meadows. With as much strength as she had, she dragged Marlene sideways into the alley between the hotel and the mercantile, where they'd have a little privacy.

Marlene jerked her arm free. "Stop it, you witch! That hurt." She rubbed her arm when Violet's hand fell away.

"You be quiet, or I'll put a spell on ya."

The woman had always believed the herbal remedies Violet made from plants she gathered were magic potions, instead of healing medications. Disliking her from the bottom of her core, Violet never took the energy to correct the floozy. Perhaps she just might be able to use the misconception to her advantage.

"I'll put a spell on ya right now if ya don't leave!" She curled her fingers and pointed them at Jake's ma. "Jake's built hisself a good life with the Logans. He don't need ya and he don't want ya. You will only make him miserable." She'd dare not say anything about Daisy, and Jake's intention to marry the girl, in case Marlene was here to make trouble.

Marlene stumbled back, holding out a hand as if she could ward off any spell Violet might conjure. When she gulped in fright, Violet wanted to laugh.

"Violet, stop! Please wait until you hear what I have to say. Jake will want to speak with me. I have good news."

Nothing this woman could do or say would ever change Violet's opinion of her. She didn't have a decent mother's bone anywhere. Violet remembered little Jake, knocking on the mercantile door after dark, grimy and dirty, asking if she had anything he could do to earn a piece of bread. Her heart ached, and then hardened. Seeing Marlene now brought back all those hard times.

"Spit it out afore this spell slips from my fingertips. They's hard ta control when it comes ta people I don't like." With her other hand, Violet struggled to pull the outstretched hand back to her chest.

Marlene's eyes grew wider.

"J-Jake's pa sent me a l-letter." She patted her reticule without taking her eyes off Violet. "It's in here."

Flummoxed, Violet just stared. All these years she'd known! Memories of a tiny Jake crying noiselessly into his pillow almost robbed her of breath. Marlene had claimed she didn't know who Jake's father was. Held true to the story for years. And now this! *How dare she!* Violet felt like clawing her black-lined eyes from her skull. Her lies had all but destroyed that poor child.

"You're a liar!"

"I'm not lying about this."

"You're an evil, evil woman, Marlene. I wouldn't want ta be standin' in your shoes when ya go ta meet yer maker. Now, what's this about Jake's pa?"

Color had returned to her face. "I'll tell Jake."

Violet stretched out her arm again. "You'll tell me, or I'll turn ya into a salamander. Then throw ya in front of the stage coach. The team will crush ya into a gooey mess and no one will ever even know you were here." Violet searched her brain for some curse-sounding words. "Eye of newt," she whispered in a gravelly voice, "tail of pollywog—"

Marlene threw her body back against the brick side of the mercantile, her hands covering her face. "Wait!" she choked out. "Please! He's dying. Jake's pa is on his deathbed and wants to see Jake before he dies."

Violet knew how much Jake longed for roots of some kind. To have a last name. But would meeting his pa only make things worse? She didn't want to cause him more harm.

"Mrs. Hollyhock, is everything all right?"

She turned to see Mr. Wade and Tabitha watching. When they started her way, she held them off. "Jist fine. Just reminiscing with my long-lost friend who came in on the stage. Sorry for running out on ya like that."

The two exchanged a glance.

"There's a satchel over here," Mr. Wade said. "Do you want me to bring it to you?"

Violet pushed her lips into a convincing smile. "It'll be jist fine there for a few more minutes. But, thankee." She waggled her fingers at them. "You two can go about yer day."

Again, Mr. Wade and Tabitha glanced at each other. They waved and started off.

She had to come to a decision. Jake was a man now. Perhaps his pa would give him something of value besides his name. Maybe even some love.

"All right. I'll let ya speak with Jake. But I'll arrange it. Where ya gonna stay?"

Marlene shrugged. "I don't know. I used everything I had just to get here. I hoped Jake would take me in."

What nerve. Marlene had rarely let Jake stay with her in her room. He was either at the mercantile with Violet, or in the storeroom in the saloon—hearing and seeing who knew what. That poor boy had lived a lifetime already.

"He lives in a bunkhouse out at the Broken Horn with the Logans, where he works. Ya ain't going ta stay there."

Marlene had her over a barrel. Violet had rooms to let, but Marlene had no money to pay. She'd mooch off anyone who would let her. Violet wouldn't stand for that. "Ya can stay with me," she said distastefully. "I have an empty room. But yer gonna work for yer keep. There won't be any freeloading here."

"Doing what? I don't know much except salooning."

"Yer gonna learn ta do *laundry*. Anyone with two hands can do that."

Marlene scrunched her fingers together. "Laundry? That'll ruin my skin."

"Yer skin's ruined already, ya old biddy, so stop yer yammering."

"I'm tired of you throwing insults at me, Violet! I've never done laundry and I don't aim to start. Surely the saloon could use another girl."

I'll never let her shame Jake that way!

"You'll learn, and you'll keep yer mouth shut about who you are and about your past. You'll smile and be nice. At least until ya talk with Jake and he either believes ya, or boots ya out of town. If ya do that, I'll house ya and feed ya fer as long as yer here." *That way I can keep my eye on you! And little Bao will have some help as her time approaches. Maybe, jist maybe, this might work out for everyone concerned.*

Marlene straightened and put both hands on her hips. When she opened her mouth to protest, Violet squinted, curling her fingers. "I guess ya like the idea of slimy green skin . . ."

Marlene snapped her mouth closed.

"So, from here on out, yer my dear friend from Valley Springs." She pointed across Main Street to the narrow row building that sat between the telegraph office and Cottonwood Lane, which led to the

Red Rooster Inn. If Marlene had to stay in town, the arrangements couldn't be better. "There's the laundry house."

"Tap Ling's Laundry," Marlene gasped, her heavily made-up eyes blinking in quick succession. "You mean to put me to work! Real work?"

"That I do, my sweet dearie. And yer gonna start right now." Violet took in her tightly corseted middle and almost smiled. "Let's pick up yer satchel and head over."

CHAPTER FOURTEEN

Hefting the posthole digger chest high, Jake was about to slam the tool into the earth when the sound of approaching hoof beats stilled his motion. He turned and searched the horizon, as did Gabe and Tyler Weston.

Chase? What's he doing out here? He always picks up supplies on Monday morning. He'd left early with the buckboard to pick up several additional rolls of fencing wire.

A nervous energy edged its way over Jake's shoulders. He reached for his canteen, and the other two men followed suit.

"Wonder what he wants," Tyler said, leaning a shoulder on a nearby tree trunk while they waited for their boss to arrive.

The twenty-four-year-old, from somewhere over in the Dakotas, had become a friend. Other than Gabe, he was Jake's closest comrade in the bunkhouse. The fella had hired on several months ago and had yet to open up about his past—which was a fairly common occurrence. Saddle tramping was a solitary business. One didn't have to spill his guts to get hired, which was attractive to the drifting sort.

That was fine with Jake. He rarely divulged his past, since it brought back hurtful memories. He'd gotten over a lot of it in the last few years. Chase had helped, as had the rest of the family. The past was the past, and there wasn't a thing he could do to change it. Most importantly, Daisy didn't seem to mind that he didn't have a surname, or that his mother had worked in a saloon. She herself had left a similar type of existence. She was his sun on a rainy day.

"Don't know." Gabe swiped at water that had splashed on his chin, then glanced up at the sky. "Must be important that the news couldn't wait until quitting time."

Chase reined to a stop and stepped off his mount in one fluid movement. "Men," Chase said, sparking suspicion in Jake with his formality.

Chase strode to the fence they were stringing, and leaned close to the top wire. Closing one eye, he inspected their day's work. He pulled back and nodded. "Good and straight. How long till you're finished?"

Another strange question. He knew they were waiting on the wire to finish up. "As soon as we get what you went to town for, the rest shouldn't take long. You did get the wire, didn't you?"

A look of embarrassment crossed Chase's eyes.

Jake glanced at the buckboard Gabe had driven out, where one roll remained. "We'll make this last acre with what we got left. But if you didn't pick up the supplies, we're dead in the water."

"I got the fencing." He looked off over the prairie.

What in the devil was going on? His, Gabe's, and Tyler's orders had been to string the fence as far as they could go, and then they'd have more wire tonight for the rest of the week. What was the cause for this impromptu, unneeded meeting out in the middle of nowhere? Chase had to have something else on his mind. When he plopped his hand on Jake's shoulder, he was sure of it.

"Gabe, Tyler, go ahead and head back. Take the rest of the day off. You've been putting in long hours. Go fishing or something."

"What about the roof on the bunkhouse?" Gabe asked, his brows drawn down in question. "Did ya pick up the shingles needed for that? If yes, I'll get to reroofing."

Gabe, always industrious, could work the rest of them to shame.

Chase sprouted his first smile since he'd arrived. "If you're so inclined, Gabe, then you'll find everything you need in back of my buckboard parked in the barn. Be careful on the roof. I don't want you sticking your foot through the places that are paper thin. I believe that bunkhouse is fifty-some-odd years old."

Gabe nodded. After one confused glance toward Chase, he went to the wagon and climbed onto the bench.

Tyler fetched his horse and mounted. "See you back at the ranch," he said in his low, gravelly voice.

Jake and Chase watched in silence as the two moved away.

"So, what's up?" Jake asked, not sure he was ready for the answer. It had been years since he'd seen such a mixture of anguish and uncertainty on Chase's face. Not since the morning Jessie's daughter, Sarah, had been abducted by the scoundrel that had followed them to Logan Meadows from Valley Springs—some five years ago. "Spit it out, Chase, because I can tell whatever you have to say is bad. Is Daisy all right? She hasn't gotten hurt, has she?"

Chase shook his head. "No, no, nothing like that. Everyone is fine. Saw Daisy this morning in the Silky Hen and she looked as pretty as ever. Said to tell you hello."

Jake rolled his tight shoulders. His boss meandered back to the fence and tested the post. Jake's gut was a mess of twisted knots.

Chase turned and stared. "Your mother's in town. She's staying at the Red Rooster Inn with Mrs. Hollyhock. She wants to speak with you."

Jake's breath burst from his lungs.

My mother?

In Logan Meadows?

He turned to hide the animosity that ripped through his chest. *What's she want? Money? A place to live?*

The tangy taste of bile rose in his throat. No. He didn't want to hear anything she had to say. Mrs. Hollyhock was the closest thing to a mother or grandmother that he'd ever had. She hated his ma. Why would she house her at all?

"Jake?"

"I hear ya, Chase. That was a mouthful you dumped on me. I don't know why that woman would come here—*now*—after not hearing a word from her since I left. It's not because she wants to see me." Jake searched Chase's face. "You know why, don't you? I can see it in your eyes."

Chase nodded.

"Well?"

"She has news of your pa. Has a letter for you."

Revulsion for the woman who'd birthed him soured his mouth. *She's known all along who my father is?* "What do you mean? A letter from years ago?"

"A new correspondence. You should be happy, Jake. You've wondered about this for years. You'll finally know who your pa is and have a family history, some roots. It's what you've been longin' for."

"Family?" Jake scoffed, glancing back at Chase. "I'd hardly call *him* that. I can't imagine why, after all this time, he wants to see me. You and Jessie are my family. Gabe and the children, too." *But you'll have a name. Something real to give Daisy. If for no other reason, you should be glad about that.*

Chase gripped his shoulder. "'Course we are. And that will never change. But, he's dyin', Jake. The doctor thinks he may only have a few weeks to live. You've wondered about him for a long time, and now's your chance to get some answers. Jake?" Chase's heated tone was not lost on him.

"Yeah, I'm delighted. Glad he waited until he was out of time to look me up."

Chase let go of his shoulder and gazed into the sky. "Maybe this is how fate planned it, Jake. You're your own man now, not some boy looking for a handout. You can meet him on your own terms. You're a *good* man, too. Never doubt that. You've made a home and name for yourself here in Logan Meadows. You've got a small piece of land and a bride to boot. The mares you got from Nell and Charlie all have nice foals by their sides and are bred back to our stud. Your band of horses is growing. You don't *need* him now, and that's a good thing. That should give you some peace of mind. Some pride. Jessie would say this was God's way of leveling the field. That fella may be surprised at the man who walks into the room."

Jake's heart swelled. What would have become of him without this man standing here? Jake didn't like to contemplate. Once he'd been given the opportunity to move away from the squalor that he called home in Valley Springs, he'd never looked back. Perhaps he'd have gone bad, been on the wrong side of the law. Robbed a bank, or worse. Maybe he'd even have been strung up from some hanging tree for rustling or killing.

"When?" he asked, the thought of seeing *her* distasteful in his mind. "When does she want to talk?"

"Violet's making her work off her board by doing laundry for Tap Ling. She'll be off around four today. Violet said if you wanted to come out to the Red Rooster tonight for supper, that would be a good time. Violet's told no one but me about who Marlene really is, or why she's here."

Jake took a stumbling step back at the mention of his mother's name. He hadn't heard it spoken in years.

Hey, Marlene, don't you look purty tonight. Come on over and give me some sugar.

"The Lings don't know her history, but of course, Beth Fairington does, being she's from Valley Springs as well. I'd prepare yourself that others are going to hear the story once the ol' gossip starts nattering. Violet had her promise to keep quiet, but you know as well as I do that the temptation will be too great."

Jake nodded, not caring who else found out. He'd never tried to hide his history. A part of him wondered what his mother looked like now. The woman who'd been dead to him had just been resurrected.

"I'll go," he said, looking Chase in the eyes. "Tonight."

CHAPTER FIFTEEN

At a round table by the back door of the Bright Nugget, Hunter plopped into a chair next to Kendall, who was counting the money they'd taken in last night.

The bartender turned to him, a look of annoyance in his eyes.

"Just taking a short break." *To watch you count the earnings.* He'd offered to do it—amid repairing the damaged tables and chairs, as well as patching the ceiling and walls of the dilapidated room upstairs—but this was one job Kendall wasn't turning over. Today was the first time Kendall had brought out the ledger, and Hunter pulled the volume close. The columns were a mess. Black smudges marred the pages where Kendall had made mistakes and started over. One half of a column was completely crossed out. How Kendall kept anything straight was a mystery.

"Give me that." Kendall snatched the accounting book back to his side of the table.

Hunter shrugged and picked up a deck of cards left over from last night. He shuffled and dealt out a hand of solitaire. Made four moves, counted through the deck. Once, twice, three times, moving cards to the top four places.

Kendall organized the money in piles, counted it three or four times, and then, with head bent over the ledger, entered his sums. He pressed the pencil so hard Hunter expected the lead to snap.

Finished, Kendall pushed back from the cigarette-burned tabletop, a good-sized grin splitting his face. "Not bad. Not bad at all. I'd say we'll end even with what I did last October." He ran his finger down a crumpled sheet of paper, one corner at the top burned away. He jotted down the amount, two hundred ninety dollars, next to the date. "Fall's when business starts to dwindle. Weather gets nasty. Men stay home by their own stoves instead of venturing out."

"Just even? Shouldn't we be making more? I thought the idea was to grow business every month."

The obvious hung over them like a dark cloud. The profits would be split between the two owners now that he had arrived.

"Can't always grow, Wade. Sometimes nights are slower than others. Wives get cranky and keep their men at home. Salooning is give and take." He rubbed his belly and glanced to the woodstove where a pot of beans was heating, and then back at him. "You've got a lot to learn."

The older man's biting tone rankled, but Hunter shrugged it off. Kendall was getting tired of his many questions, and had said so on numerous occasions. He once again counted out his three cards, and then stilled. "Maybe, but I've been thinking."

Kendall scowled. With both hands, he scooped the coins and paper money into the cash bag to take down to the bank. They'd do *that* together. "You're always thinking about something. What is it now?"

"I know a pretty little singer in Soda Springs. Sounds like an angel."

Kendall swiveled and looked him in the eye. "Go on."

"Since the room upstairs will soon be repaired and livable, why don't I send her a telegram? Maybe she'll come to Logan Meadows."

"We got Philomena."

"Miss Dichelle's not a working girl, she's a performer. She draws a large crowd at Ned's every Friday and Saturday night. Just like clockwork. She's looking to be discovered. She may be the goose that lays *our* golden eggs."

A look of skepticism crossed Kendall's face. "Women round here won't like that. You know, their men going off to ogle another woman flaunting her wares, even if they can't touch."

Hunter felt his eyes go wide. "When have the rules of a saloon been dictated by the female element of a town?"

Kendall rubbed the black stubble on his chin, knocking off a few dried crumbs in the process. "You haven't gone up against the likes of Mrs. Logan, Mrs. Donovan, Mrs. Hutton. Or the sheriff's new wife, Mrs. Preston. They can be a handful, to say the least. If I keep a low profile, they pretty much leave me alone."

Suddenly, Kendall's eyes grew as wide as a barn door.

Hunter couldn't stop his curiosity. "What?"

"Or *Miss* Canterbury. She's the worst of 'em all. Ever since she built that dollhouse out of a fairytale two doors down, my life has been a living hell. She won't like more men crowding in, taking up hitching rail space, creating more manure that'll bring more flies. She's talked to the town council three times." His hand dropped to the table like a stone. "I've even tried sweet-talking her. Nothin' seems to work. Once that spinster gets a bone in her craw, there's no yanking it out."

At the mention of Miss Canterbury—Miss Hoity-Toity as Hunter started thinking of her in light of Kendall's comments—he couldn't stop a grin of his own. He'd not call her a spinster—not just yet. She was a shrewd but pretty businesswoman. One that wasn't frightened to speak her mind. One with a very good head on her perfectly straight shoulders. "That might be so," Hunter said, all the while thinking out his plan. "But Dichelle Bastianelli would be worth the fight."

Kendall cocked his head. "What kind of a name is Bastianelli?"

"Italian, my dear man. And she's as pretty as she sounds."

Kendall's eyes narrowed suspiciously. "She *your* girl? That won't sit well with the men. There's only so much you can keep under wraps. And a relationship ain't one of 'em."

"Nope, she's young enough to be my daughter. I may be coarse and a bit uneducated, but I'm no lecher. I'd be a liar, though, if I said I don't appreciate her attention. We're good friends is all. I like her singing and she likes my stories. If I ask nicely, she just might come. If that happens, you leave Miss Hoity-Toity to me."

Jake stood at the hitching rail of the Red Rooster Inn a good five minutes, stalling. Going inside was a double-edged sword. Once he opened the door to *that woman*, he'd not be able to close it again. But, he was curious and excited to find out about his pa.

Taking the steps two at a time, he rapped on the thick wood.

Violet opened the door, causing a rush of emotion. *This* was the person who'd raised him. Made him hot chocolate on Christmas day, washed behind his ears, scolded him for cussing. She'd stood him in the corner when needed, or switched his behind when he got out of hand. Her care and love were the only constant in his life.

"Mrs. Hollyhock," he said, feeling shy. He took his hat from his head and smiled.

She searched his eyes, keeping the door closed enough to keep their meeting private from snooping glances.

"Jake, boy," she said for only his ears, her gravelly voice a soothing medicine to his heart.

As was his habit, he leaned down so she could kiss his cheek.

"I know this won't be easy on ya, but I feel ya just might benefit. Iffin I didn't think so, I'd've sent her packin' just as soon as she stepped off that stage."

"Thanks for puttin' her up." He hated that his ma would inconvenience Mrs. Hollyhock. His mother was a thorn in his old friend's side that just wouldn't go away. Even after all these years. It wasn't only a few times that he'd found Violet smoldering over something his ma had said or done. And now, here she was again . . .

"Come in outta the chilly air." She took his arm and pulled him inside. "May as well find out what this is all about. Things that don't kill ya will make ya stronger."

Just inside the door, he shrugged out of his coat, hanging it and his hat alongside a few others on the rack on the wall by the door.

Feeling someone's gaze, he turned. Standing in the alcove between the living room and kitchen was the woman he remembered. She was older. Thicker. More lines marked her face. But the eyes were the same. Blue as a field of bluebonnets, but missing the hot resentfulness. He'd been an inconvenience to her all those years. And perhaps, he still was.

"Jake," she uttered, blinking several times in quick succession. Her face, void of the rouge he remembered so vividly, changed to a deep ruddy pink. "Look at you! You're a man!"

He squelched the shiver her smoke-tainted voice produced. He pushed away the memories of her drunken rages, and quick hands eager to slap.

Not wanting to call her *Marlene* or *mother*, he just nodded. He stepped toward her as stiff as a dummy set out to ward off the crows.

"You look good. You've grown tall." She reached out for a moment, but let her hand fall back to her side. "Thank you for giving me this opportunity to see you. I realize you could have said no."

What did she expect him to say? Even if he had any words, they'd not be able to get past the boulder wedged in his windpipe.

At his silence, she turned and looked at the table set behind her. "Violet's made all your favorites. Let's eat before the meal gets cold, and then I'll have answers for all your questions. Does that sound good?"

Shocked that she'd asked, instead of demanded, he felt himself nod. It wasn't going to matter what was on his plate. He doubted he'd be able to eat even a bite.

The meal passed with barely a spoken word. When they were finished, Violet insisted they go into the living room and sit by the fire while she cleaned up. She'd sent Beth to stay over at Maude's house tonight so they wouldn't be interrupted. Jake felt five again, as he fiddled with a piece of string in his fingers, waiting for her to make the first move.

"As you know, I got a letter from your father. He's dying. He wants to see you if you're willing."

He looked up into her eyes. "You said you didn't know who my pa was."

The sounds of Mrs. Hollyhock banging around in the kitchen kept their conversation private. Any other time, Jake would have insisted on helping, but tonight he'd let her drag him into the living room, the wiry old woman adamant on doing the dishes herself. After they'd cleared the table, his mother had gone into her room, returning with the envelope she held in her hands. He'd not beg.

"I knew. I knew very well."

"Why didn't you tell me? At least when I'd grown older?"

"I had my reasons, Jake, ones I'll not share with you. You can hate me if you want. I'm sure you already do." She held the letter out to him.

His name was right here in this letter. How many years had he pondered on who he was? He swallowed and took the missive. "I'll just step outside."

Marlene nodded. "I'd do the same. I'll be here when you have questions."

Jake retrieved his jacket, and picked up a lantern set on the small table by the door. He stepped outside and put the lantern on the wide porch rail. Drawing the note from the envelope, he opened the paper, thankful that Gabe had insisted on teaching him to read.

> *Marlene, I hope you will indulge a dying fool. I'd like to meet the boy you claim is mine. If you still know where he is, ask him to come quickly. I have a longing to see if*

what you said is true before I die. I hope it is. You know where to send him.

—James Costner

Jake stared at the signature. So many emotions swirled inside he couldn't make out one from the other.

Costner. His name was Costner. Jake Costner, son of James Costner.

The door creaked open.

He looked around.

"You all right, Jake boy?" Mrs. Hollyhock asked, her face looking fifty years older than when he'd arrived. "Yer ma said you was out here."

He held up the letter. "My pa's name is James Costner."

She gave a wink. "Imagine that," she said in a whispery-soft voice, one he remembered from the times she'd tenderly tucked him in.

Exactly. *Imagine that.* The backs of his eyes pricked painfully, so he dropped his gaze to the flickering flame of the lantern.

Costner.

His mother knew where to go to meet his father. When his heart tried to soften toward the woman waiting inside, he purposely brought to mind how his fingers and toes had felt in the shivering cold every time she'd forgotten to fetch him into the saloon to the small area she'd arranged for him under the staircase. She'd not be let off the hook just because she offered up something that she should have done years ago. Not with how many times he'd begged her for the information. No one deserved absolution so quickly.

"You going ta see yer pa?"

He nodded, folded the missive, and put it back where it belonged. "Just as soon as I get a few things arranged. I can't do anything until I speak with Daisy."

CHAPTER SIXTEEN

Tabitha was a flurry of nerves. She'd spent all day yesterday preparing Storybook Lodge for tonight's event, baking, and making sure the dress she intended to wear was perfectly ironed. She'd read and reread aloud chapters one and two of *Great Expectations*, going so far as to practice how she held the volume in her hands, how Pip would sound, at what part of the story she'd pause or add inflection, who she'd look at, and whose gaze she might avoid.

Mr. Wade? Will he be interested in a public reading?

Surely not. The wagon-train guide turned saloon owner had been the talk of the town since last week. Half the townsfolk backed Kendall, thinking the newcomer was stealing a man's property right out from under his nose, while the other half understood that he was collecting on a debt owed him, but still gave him a wide berth because of his gun. The rumors of his background had some people scared. He'd yet to return for the book he'd said he was interested in acquiring, which disappointed her more than she wanted to admit.

Stop thinking about him.

She needed to forget about Mr. Wade altogether and concentrate on a performance that would bring everyone to their feet. This was her big chance. She had to make the night entertaining enough for the partakers to return next week for chapters three and four. And the week after that as well. *And maybe even buy a book! Or two, or three . . .*

Susanna Preston stepped into the shop with a tray of cookies in her hands. Her friend's shiny black hair was pulled back in a messy bun as if she'd fashioned it in haste. A clean, pressed apron was folded over one arm. She must be on her way to the restaurant.

"Bless you!" Tabitha cried, rushing forward. "These will help immensely. I wish I knew how many people to expect. I certainly don't want to run out of goodies and set the old men to grumbling on my very first night." She lifted the tray to her nose. "These smell delicious. Pumpkin?"

Susanna smiled and nodded. "Yes, Nate helped me bake them. That child is such a delight. I can't imagine my life without him."

"Or Albert?"

"Or Albert." A shy twinkle danced around in Susanna's eyes. "*Especially* Albert. I've married the most thoughtful man. He spends hours a day thinking of ways to make me happy. I had no idea married life would be like this."

Still a newlywed of only a couple of months, Susanna was living on cloud nine. Anyone with two eyes in their head could see her match with the sheriff was one of true love. Albert had been rambling around town with a smile on his face ever since they'd tied the knot. Heard tell he even went softer on the petty offenders now, which Tabitha found difficult to believe. He was a lawman through and through and wouldn't let outside influence cloud his judgment.

"I'm sure you keep him just as happy, Susanna. The three of you make a darling family." Tabitha walked the cookies over to a shelf she'd cleared to hold the treats for tonight; she set them next to a cake Brenna had dropped by and a pie made by Hannah. Along with the three dozen walnut cookies she'd baked at five o'clock this morning, she felt sure she had plenty of refreshments to serve at intermission. "Thank you so much for making these. I can now rest easy."

"You shouldn't be nervous. We're all your friends." With her hands now free, Susanna picked up a cookbook, turned it over, and looked at the back. "By the way, Mr. Wade came in for supper again last night." She glanced up at Tabitha and smiled. "I'd guess he's about the same age as your aunt, wouldn't you? I like him. I think he's interesting."

Tabitha straightened. Mr. Wade and Aunt Roberta? That thought had never entered her mind. "I suppose he is," she answered, not wanting her friend to know she found him not only interesting, but fascinating. "I still can't believe he's half owner of the Bright Nugget and has taken Albert's old apartment. Living next door, he walks by my front window at least several times a day." *But hasn't stopped in.* "You've heard the rumors about his past."

"And that's exactly what they are."

She shrugged. "I feel kind of duped that he came into town under a different pretense than he let on. He never said anything about the Bright Nugget."

Susanna gently closed the cookbook and set it back on the shelf. "Oh? What did he tell you when he arrived?"

Tabitha thought on that for a moment, realizing that he really hadn't said much of anything. She'd filled in the blanks on her own. "Well, I got the distinct impression that he was just passing through. Here to buy a few supplies and then would be gone." She felt a bit silly for having brought up the subject in the first place. "Actually, I asked him just that, and he said he was camping in the meadow, which was a totally ambiguous answer if I do say so myself."

"I wouldn't say that at all. I said I was camping, and I was."

Both Tabitha and Susanna swung around at the deep voice of the man standing in the open doorway. His hat was tipped back and perspiration ringed the armpits of his cotton shirt.

"I'm not totally sure what *ambiguous* means, but I can tell you I wasn't trying to mislead anyone! Not on purpose. Not by a long shot."

"Mr. Wade!" Tabitha cried, her voice choked with embarrassment. "How long have you been listening to our conversation?"

"Long enough to know you think I intended to make a fool of you, of everyone here in Logan Meadows, which isn't the truth at all."

He stood tall, mussed, and devilishly handsome.

"I had to speak with Kendall before I said anything," he said. "And then the sheriff. I'm sure you can understand that."

As he proceeded into the shop, he removed his hat, exposing the sweaty hair underneath. Susanna glanced Tabitha's way, a spark of merriment in her eyes. "I need to get to the restaurant. Nice to run into you, Mr. Wade. If I don't see you before tonight, Tabby, break a leg."

Tabitha glared teasingly at her friend's abandonment. "I just may." She laughed, deciding not to take herself so seriously. "Thank you again for helping out with the baking."

Susanna left. They were alone. Mr. Wade's large frame took up much of the space in her small shop. Her every little move felt like a conscious effort. Perhaps his wanting a book he could practice his reading with had all been a yarn.

Three breaths, five blinks, and one swallow later he said, "I'm working upstairs at the saloon. One of the rooms was in shambles. I should be finished later today."

That was the reason for the cotton work shirt, his disheveled appearance, and his back and forth in front of her window. The feed store stocked building supplies.

"I'm on my way to the Feed and Seed for more nails right now." He lifted a muscular shoulder, which brought a fluttery feeling to her lungs. He glanced around at the open space she'd created in the center of the room with Albert's and Thom's help. There were two rows of borrowed chairs, then three rows of long boards set atop overturned buckets. It would have to do for the time being.

"Looks good. Tonight's your big night. You excited?"

He didn't owe her any explanations about who he was and what his business was in Logan Meadows. He was free to do as he wished. She smiled. "More nervous than excited, I guess. Wish I hadn't taken this on at all." She liked the way his thoughtful eyes made her feel. *Young. Desired.*

"I'm sure you'll knock 'em dead, Miss Canterbury." He fingered his hat. "I best get back to work." His gaze strayed over to the baked goods and lingered.

"Mr. Wade," she all but blurted as he turned to leave. He slowly looked back. "Would you like a couple of cookies? Several batches are fresh from the oven."

His eyes widened. "Will you run short?"

"Not at all." *I hope.* Tabitha selected her largest walnut and one of Susanna's pumpkin and placed them in his palm. "After our conversation last week I went through my books and found one I think will be of interest to you. It's not a beginner, and yet, it's not all that difficult either." Tabitha hurried to her desk for the novel she'd put there to have handy on the off chance he stopped in. She returned to his side and held it out. He was just swallowing the first cookie.

"The Ad-vaaan . . ."

Tender warmth seeped into her heart as she watched him struggle. One small crumb clung to the corner of his lips until he brushed it away, and his earnest gaze dropped to the floor beside her.

"Adventures."

He nodded. "The Adventures of Tom Sawyaer," he read jerkily.

"Sawyer. The 'aw' creates a 'so' sound."

In a swish of green, Daisy Smith breezed past the bookstore window.

"Can you excuse me one moment, Mr. Wade?"

"Of course," he said with a gracious smile.

Tabitha rushed to the door. "Daisy? Oh, Daisy! Do you have a moment to spare?"

Daisy stopped and turned. The shade of her modest emerald dress brought out the beauty of her green eyes. Only seventeen, the girl's youth and beauty always amazed Tabitha. It was difficult to believe she'd ever worked in a saloon. At twelve, she'd run away from her abusive father, and somehow, three years later, ended up here in Logan Meadows working at the saloon. Tabitha didn't like to speculate on how that was accomplished, being young girls were a rare commodity, especially unprotected ones that were as pretty as her friend.

Daisy hurried back to where Tabitha stood in her doorway, and then they both stepped inside.

"The book you ordered for Jake's Christmas present came in last week. Let me get it for you." She hurried to her desk and picked up the new volume of *The Last of the Mohicans*. Returning, she set it in Daisy's hands. "I just love this story. I've read it at least ten times." She sighed, thinking about the long-haired, heroic Natty Bumppo, who could set her blood humming through her veins. She glimpsed at Hunter and caught him watching her exchange with Daisy. She smiled, thinking he, in a way, reminded her of Natty. "Would you like me to wrap it for you?"

Daisy's smile faded. "Actually, I'll have to wait until payday. I don't have the funds just yet."

"Well, I was thinking about that. You know I'm having my book reading tonight and have just finished baking several batches of cookies. I know you love to cook, and in truth I'd much rather do something else with my time. What if we traded your labor and fixings for five batches of cookies, for the next five readings?"

Daisy gasped. "That's not enough in exchange. I need to pay you something."

"It is. By then the weather will turn and I'll have to stop until spring. I'd say that's a fair trade."

A smile replaced Daisy's hesitation. "Only if you're sure."

"I am. Will I see you tonight?"

She shrugged.

Tabitha reached out and touched her arm. "I hope I do." Because of her past, Daisy kept to herself. If she wasn't in the restaurant, she was at home. Tabitha wasn't sure if she worried about running into an old customer, or if she was truly frightened of men, afraid they might take advantage of her. She wished she could help the girl more. "You best get on your way."

Daisy hugged the book to her chest. "Thank you, Tabitha. Jake's going to love this. Might take him a year to finish, but that won't stop him."

Daisy departed and Tabitha went back to Mr. Wade, who was staring down at the open page. "Thank you for waiting."

He groaned. "I don't think this book is easy enough."

"That's what sounding out is for. You'll do fine. Try it and see. Since you're actually a new part of the community, I picked something from the lending library. If you find it too difficult, or not to your liking, bring it back. Or better yet, come in when you have some time and read a few pages in my reading chair." She gestured to the soft chair on the side of the front window. "I can help. Just like we did with the title. That way, you won't get discouraged and be tempted to quit. Being able to read well will open up your world to people and places you won't expect. Trust me. You'll be amazed."

His clean-shaven cheeks blossomed pink, and she realized she may have been a bit heavy-handed in her sell. He'd just finished the second cookie in two bites. She dared not give him any more.

He took the book. "Thank you. I'll do that. Don't know when, though. My next project is to add another hitching post out front in that ten-foot gap."

"Another hitching rail? But the street is already a mess from overcrowding on the weekend! I can't imagine more horses out there. And the flies they will create with their . . ." She tried to tamp down her rising displeasure. "I've spoken with the town council on the matter. It wouldn't be bad if Kendall would get out there and clean the street on

Sunday morning, before the horse manure had a chance to bake in the sun, but he's not willing to do that. Every time I open my windows, the reminder floats in. Really, Mr. Wade, think of the other businesses around you. The Bright Nugget isn't the only one on Main Street."

His charming smile only angered her more.

"I *am* thinking of you, Miss Canterbury. During the day, when the saloon is slow, all your bookstore shoppers can tether down at our new hitching rail. Won't that be convenient?"

She looked at him in shock, feeling as though she was only just now seeing his true colors. He knew very well she didn't have any customers during the day—or the night. He was playing with her. Making her the fool. And here she'd gone and lent him one of her books!

He reached out to touch her arm, but she stepped back. Dropping his hat on his head, he said, "I'll consider what you said about the manure. Maybe we can work something out there." He touched the brim and turned. "Good day, Miss Canterbury."

In stunned silence, she watched him walk away. He was just as bad as Kendall. Or worse. And to think she'd been worried that she and her aunt had doused his desire to improve his reading. Ha! Turning on her heel, she headed for the stairs. It wasn't a good day. Not any longer.

CHAPTER SEVENTEEN

From the front door of the Bright Nugget, Hunter watched as the town poured out to support Miss Hoity-Toity. By the stunned look on her face earlier, he knew that she was annoyed with him. Well, that was just too bad. He was annoyed with her as well. Who ever heard of shoveling manure from the street? He didn't know where she was from, but *this* was Wyoming! He sucked in a deep breath to chase away his aggravation. Still, he hoped that she'd sell a few books for all the trouble she'd gone through to get people into her store. He had to admit, it was a good idea. The bar was near empty, but that wasn't unusual for a Tuesday night. Not every night could be Friday or Saturday.

Buckskin Jack, one of the regulars he'd paid to play the piano tonight for an hour or two, pounded away at the keys as if he were churning butter. Hunter supposed the gap-toothed man was trying to give a good show for the half dollar Hunter had promised, but his enthusiasm was wearing a bit thin. Their normal musician, Farley, had taken ill a few days ago with a bad stomach. Hunter was anxious for his return.

"Guess her public reading wasn't such a dumb idea after all."

Hunter turned to find Kendall watching the street over his shoulder, a bar glass and towel moving in his hands. "At first I thought the notion kinda harebrained," Kendall went on. "A scheme of sorts. Now, not so much."

"Harebrained?" Hunter said dubiously. "Miss Canterbury seems to have a pretty knowledgeable head on her shoulders."

"I see whatcha mean."

Four spur-wearing cowboys rode up and stopped in front of the bookstore.

"I can't figure where she's gonna put 'em all," Kendall complained. "Who woulda thought cowboys would enjoy listening to a book being read to them like they was babies. Wouldn't they rather drink whiskey? And play cards? I don't get it."

Hunter turned and gaped at Kendall. Didn't the man know anything? Miss Canterbury was a darn fine-looking woman. She wore her age well, a saying Thorp was partial to about women on the wagon trains. And she was single, probably the most important reason of all. But, even better, Hunter liked the things she came up with. Too bad *she* wasn't his partner. Surely, the saloon would be standing room only if she got ahold of the reins.

"You serious, Kendall? They're not coming to listen to the story, they're coming to *watch* the show. She's single, if you've forgotten. Nothing better for drawing men than an unmarried woman."

Kendall shrugged. "You're right. I guess I'm just trying to make myself feel better about her good fortune and our lack of it."

"That's not very neighborly."

"You need to send for that girl. That Italian singer."

To their left, Frank Lloyd stepped out of the bank and locked the door, testing the doorknob to be sure it was firm. Wasn't hard to guess where he was headed. He stopped in the doorway when he reached the saloon.

"Boys," he said friendly-like. "You coming to the reading?"

"Can't," Kendall replied. "Work to do."

The banker's brows arched as his gaze swept around the nearly empty room. "Why don't you close her up for the night? Not often you have a civilized chance such as this."

Lloyd had to shout because Buckskin Jack, having seen activity at the door, began a jaunty rendition of "Sweet Betsy from Pike," intending, Hunter was sure, to draw whoever it was they were talking with into the saloon. Hunter's ears rung so loudly from all the sour notes the half-sober fella hit, he wondered if he shouldn't cut his losses and pay the man to stop playing, now that he knew just how awful he really was.

"I'm doing inventory later," Kendall said without missing a beat.

Frank smiled and shrugged. "Suit yourself."

When the banker left, Hunter turned and headed for the back door. "I'm going up to my place and get my book. I'll be right back."

They weren't going to have a rush of drinkers tonight, no way, no how. Philomena didn't even glance up as he passed the table she used when business was slow. Her head bent over some knitting project and a cup of coffee at her side.

Ducking out of the saloon, Hunter hadn't gone more than five steps toward the back of the sheriff's office when he heard a woman's halfhearted cry for help.

He stopped.

Listened.

It was difficult to discern where the sound had come from over the thunderous piano music trailing him out the back door. Not hearing anything more, he continued until he reached the stairway to his apartment. He stopped again and listened carefully. Fifty feet beyond, far enough out from the Storybook Lodge not to make a stink, soft light glowed from the insides of Tabitha's outhouse.

The silly building had garnered a laugh from him his first day in town. About twice the size of a regular privy, hers was a tiny replica of the bookstore with all the frippery and finery of the larger building. When no one was looking, he'd taken a fast peek inside. Along with the obvious necessities, there was a miniature pump that flowed into a bucket. A pipe at the bottom of the container disappeared into a round hole that had been drilled through the lower portion of the wall, and the waterline was stretched out to a small kitchen garden, something he was surprised to find in town. If that hadn't been enough, the place had a latched roof so anyone inclined who wanted fresh air could raise up one side of the roof. Pretty ingenious, he grudgingly admitted. The small building was the fanciest outhouse he'd ever seen, and a darned good idea.

"Help me," a voice called faintly. "Help me, please." It was Tabitha, a controlled panic coloring her tone.

Hunter rushed over. "Miss Canterbury? What's wrong? Are you sick?"

"Oh!" came the unsteady reply.

Several seconds crept by.

Laughter from the folks congregated in the bookstore reached them.

"Mr. Wade, thank heavens you heard me! Be careful out there. There's a skunk rooting around my back door. I tried several times to escape, but it's as if he knows I'm frightened, and that I don't have time to waste. Every time I open the door, he stands his ground and threateningly shakes his tail."

Her voice wobbled. Was Miss Hoity-Toity about to cry?

"I-I'd hate to get sprayed when I've invited all those people to my store."

"I see your point." Turning, he examined her back porch. The darkness made seeing much of anything near impossible. "I can't see much from this distance. You wait here, and I'll take a gander. Maybe it's gone."

"Please don't shoot it, Mr. Wade!"

He squelched a smile. "No? Why not?"

"It's not the poor animal's fault. He must have smelled my trash. After baking this morning, I didn't make the time to properly take it to the dump this afternoon, as I should have. There were eggshells and greasy papers from butter. I'd hate to see a creature come to a bad end because of my stupidity."

He looked down at his gun. "No, I won't kill it, if it's even still here. I better get moving. It's almost six o'clock and you have a packed house."

"Packed?"

"Absolutely packed."

"Yes, yes, please do. I appreciate your help tremendously."

There she goes again, using those long words. "You'd do the same for me."

Hunter walked the path to her shop with a sharp eye, the faint aroma of the stink kitty apparent on the chilly air. He stopped every few feet to scan the darkness. Most likely the critter was gone; if not, it could have burrowed down into the dirt of her foundation. He didn't want to get sprayed either. He'd experienced that once when he was a boy, suffering the consequence—and Thorp's laughter—for weeks.

He took the three steps to her back door, and still didn't see what she'd been frightened by. Nope, the skunk was gone.

He returned to the outhouse. "All's clear," he said, thinking how embarrassed she would be when she actually came out. "The animal has either hightailed it away, or is in hiding, and we won't find him tonight."

She didn't answer.

"Miss Canterbury? You still there?"

"I am, Mr. Wade." The reply was soft, hesitant. "I'll never be able to thank you enough. Would you mind terribly leaving now before I come out? I can't seem to bear the thought of facing you tonight. Not after such an embarrassing situation."

"Totally understandable." Sometimes she sounded just like a little girl. "Good night," he said, his previous annoyance feeling trite. "Knock 'em dead."

CHAPTER EIGHTEEN

Tabitha placed the bookmark between the pages, and gently closed the volume. Books were like people and should be treated with respect, handled carefully, and loved until their timely death.

A thunderous applause erupted. She glanced up, gratitude for this night weighing light in her heart. They'd loved it! At least so far. Thank heavens Mr. Wade had come to her rescue. For all his rude behavior before, his sensitivity to her embarrassing situation made her wonder. Maybe he wasn't the tough saloon owner he pretended to be. After Mr. Wade had cleared her way, she'd skirted inside while gathering her wits, said her hellos, and began. By then, everyone was seated. Perhaps they believed her delay was a dramatic part of the performance.

"Bravo, bravo," the crowd cried.

There must be fifty people here. Tabitha couldn't believe it.

Aunt Roberta, along with most of her girlfriends, and a sprinkle of the older people of the town, took up the first two rows, as well as the benches. Their husbands and the single men stood around the sides, and lined the back wall entirely. Jessie, and her family, were absent, which surprised Tabitha a little. As did Mrs. Hollyhock's absence. She hoped her dear old friend wasn't feeling poorly tonight. She'd promised to come when they were having tea on Saturday. Uncle Frank's face beamed with pride, bringing her another rush of emotion.

She swallowed back a knot of joy. How she'd longed to see that same look on her father's face once or twice, or even her mother's. *If only they could see my success tonight.*

"Thank you so much, ladies and gentlemen," she said, placing the novel on the side of her desk as she stood. "Thank you for coming out for the first of many nights of entertainment at Storybook Lodge. As you can see in the back, Susanna and Hannah are at the refreshment table, ready to assist you." *And to hand the treats out judiciously so we don't run out.* "I'll be available for anyone who might have any questions about this book, or others. Please feel free to browse." She pointed to the left corner. "And be sure to take a look at our Lending Library. There are twenty-three titles for your reading pleasure. We'll be resuming at ten minutes past seven, which gives you fifteen minutes to stretch your legs."

As people stood, talking and making their way to the goodie table, Tabitha returned their smiles, all the while sneaking glances at the plate-glass window. *Mr. Wade is not coming! Nor should I wish him to. Especially after tonight. It'll be all too embarrassing the first time we have an encounter.*

Nell Axelrose held Maddie's hand as they got in line for refreshments while Charlie, her husband, spoke with some of the men Tabitha didn't know, who must be from one of the ranches. Roberta had a firm hold on Markus, and Nate stood quietly at Albert's side. When Nate glanced her way, she smiled, but the boy quickly dropped his gaze to the floor, his winsome smile nowhere to be seen. She wondered why. Hadn't he liked the story at all?

Two cowboys along the wall, hats in hands, smiled at her. *More men I don't know. I expected to see more women tonight.* The way the one on the left's eyebrow raised in invitation, she didn't think he was here to further his literary awareness. Her face pricked with heat, even more than it had been already. She nodded and politely turned away.

"Miss Canterbury, may I have a moment of your time?" Mr. Hutton, the schoolteacher, approached. Brenna, his wife, stood at his side nibbling on a walnut cookie, her eyes bright with the pleasure of the night, Tabitha supposed.

"Yes, of course."

"You read beautifully. I couldn't help wondering if you might come to the school every so often and read for the children. You have a way of making the story come to life. I felt as if I were there."

Such praise coming from the schoolteacher! "I'm sure you can do the same, or better, Mr. Hutton."

"I think not. Besides, it's good for the children to see that others besides myself have a love for books and the written word. They already know I do. Your presence will give weight to what I've been trying to drill into their heads. Good readers find other aspects of their life easier."

"I believe that's true, as well," she agreed, thinking of her conversation with Mr. Wade about the many places a good story could take him. Surely he'd come around to her way of thinking on the hitching rail, see her concerns, and soften. He was new to Logan Meadows. He'd been so good with Violet, and then again with her tonight. It was only a matter of better communication between them.

"I'd be so appreciative if you'd agree. May I schedule you?"

"I'd be pleased to help in any way that I can. And actually, it sounds like fun. You just give me a day and time and I'll be there."

Mr. Hutton glanced at Brenna, a warm smile on his face, and then looked back at her. "Perfect. I'll look at my schedule, and then let you know."

"What would you like me to read?"

"Anything age appropriate that you'd like. Surprise me."

Over Mr. Hutton's shoulder, Mr. Wade appeared outside the glass of the front door. His gaze started on the far side of the room and tracked slowly around it, causing her a small flutter of warmth. *Is he looking for me?* When his search ended and their eyes met, a jolt of awareness made her inhale. He'd washed, shaved, and his hair was properly combed. The soft buckskin shirt that had grabbed her attention in the mercantile brought a smile to her lips. She was glad he'd come. Embarrassment or not, her heart filled with anticipation. He opened the door and stepped into the shop, made cozy by all the warm bodies. A hush descended for only a moment, and then the chatter picked back up.

Because of her proximity, she had to greet him right away or else look rude. She hoped her face didn't give her away. "Mr. Wade." She remembered the outhouse, and how his gentle voice had sent tingles up her back.

His eyes crinkled at the corners when he smiled. "Miss Canterbury. Did I miss the reading?" He glanced around. "Is it over?"

He means to stay? Listen? "Not at all. This is intermission." She glimpsed the goodie table and found Susanna watching them. "If you hurry, there are still a few treats left." *Maybe he came for another round of cookies.*

He glanced at the others still circling the refreshments three deep and then back at her.

Mr. Hutton and Brenna had wandered off and were gazing at a book in the history section. *Oh, to sell a big book like that.*

"I'm relieved to hear I didn't miss the whole thing. Business is slow as molasses over in the saloon. I offered to let Kendall attend while I watched the bar, but he said he might get claustrophobic being squished in here with all these people." He chuckled as he again glanced around. "He insisted that I come, and represent. Show the people of Logan Meadows that the owners of the Bright Nugget are forward thinkers." His muscular shoulder lifted and he ran a hand down his leather shirt. "I hope you don't mind. This was the best I could do."

"Mind?" For some strange reason she felt exceedingly happy. *Be careful. Words have power.* "Not at all. I'm delighted you came. The cadence you'll hear from me will help you with your own reading."

His look was skeptical. "Even after I told you about the hitching rail?"

It's not built yet. "We'll discuss that later."

He chuckled. "I'm not the most popular person in Logan Meadows, these days. I suppose I can understand why. Either people like me or hate me. Seems there's no in-between."

"Surely, you're exaggerating, Mr. Wade. Everyone likes you. And as soon as they get to know your charming self, the situation will even itself out."

When people began taking their seats, Tabitha glanced at the tiny watch she had pinned to her bodice.

"Oh, it's almost time to recommence."

His eyes widened and he shuffled uncomfortably.

"Begin again. I don't mind your staying. The way I see it, I owe you a great deal. If you hadn't stumbled across me outside"—she avoided the word *outhouse*—"I might still be trapped. And no one would be the wiser. Thank you again for that."

Aunt Roberta, dressed to the hilt, navigated the crowd toward them. It touched Tabitha deeply that Roberta thought so highly of her to dress the part. But the frown on her face . . .

"It's twelve past seven," her aunt said, her expression none too pleased as she glanced between her and Mr. Wade. Only moments ago, before he'd arrived, Roberta had been singing Tabitha's praises, and telling her what a wonderful job she'd done. Now she looked as if she'd just stepped in a fresh pile of horse droppings with her best shoes. "Time to resume," she said curtly. "Some of your guests have a long ride home. Tomorrow is a workday, as well as school. I wouldn't want to keep them later than necessary."

"No. I don't want to do that. Punctuality is important."

"I'll just find a place to stand," Mr. Wade said. He nodded politely and walked away.

Maude, from her seat in the second row, held up a book to show Tabitha she'd found something to buy. Uncle Frank did the same in the back of the room. Tabitha smiled and nodded back, excited that her plan seemed to be working.

Hunter found a small spot in the back and was able to slide one shoulder in to lean against the wall. Most of the people seemed friendly, but a few still sent scowls in his direction. *Kendall's friends, I'm sure.* He recognized Maude Miller, the clerk from the mercantile—but he didn't see the younger busybody.

An hour passed in the blink of an eye. He found he enjoyed listening to Tabitha's voice. He'd decided her brown hair reminded him of roasted hazelnuts. The way it was fashioned, it seemed as if the thick mass might tumble off her head at any moment. He watched, mesmerized, waiting for the event to happen. The soft light from the lantern on her desk made her green eyes appear mysterious and filled with unspoken questions.

Surprised at how many things he liked about Tabitha, he wondered if she'd ever been kissed. *Really kissed.* The image that thought conjured up made him smile. She'd be all shocked and businesslike, but soft and vulnerable, too. Why hadn't some lucky man snapped her up the minute she arrived in town? She delivered a line, then paused for theatrics, her mouth formed into a perfect little rose.

You can like her, and be friends, his conscience whispered, *but don't go getting romantic thoughts. You've never been much good at that. You have a knack for messing things up. Logan Meadows is your hometown now. You'll be living here for a good long time. Having to face a relationship gone bad day after day would be uncomfortable . . .*

Winthrop, the livery owner, nodded to him from the other side of the room. Hunter hardly recognized the man in his clean clothes and jacket. So many other men here tonight, too. He'd like to have them in the saloon.

Tabitha leaned forward, her eyes opened wide. Her voice, a good imitation of a male speaking broken English, breathed the story into life right before their eyes. Hunter had come in late, but had put together that a young lad named Pip was in all sorts of trouble.

"Mrs. Joe has been out a dozen times, looking for you, Pip," she read, glancing up from the book from time to time. "And she's out now, making it a baker's dozen."

"Is she?"

"Yes, Pip," said Joe; "and what's worse, she got Tickler with her."

"At this dismal intelligence, I twisted the only button on my waistcoat round and round, and looked in great depression at the fire. Tickler was a wax-ended piece of cane, worn smooth by collision with my tickled frame."

Tabitha read with earnest, and Hunter couldn't hold back his admiration. The children in the crowd leaned forward in anticipation, almost shivering in fear of the whipping Pip was about to receive, the room so quiet he could have heard a snowflake melt. Adding another point to her list of good qualities, Hunter leaned back and enjoyed the story.

CHAPTER NINETEEN

"Jake, what's wrong? Has something happened?" The happiness Daisy had felt when she'd opened the door to her small living quarters behind the hotel evaporated the moment she saw her love's eyes. He was troubled, and hurting.

"We need to talk, Daisy. Do you have a few minutes? I know it's late, but this is important."

She didn't dare invite him inside at eight o'clock at night. With her reputation, that would surely start the gossipers to talking. As a reformed saloon girl, she had to be doubly careful about the things she did, or said. She'd been in love with Jake since she was fifteen years old. Back then, he'd been her stalwart support. Helped her out of her old life, finding her employment at the Silky Hen and moving her to this tiny place. Trading Tabitha baking for the book she'd ordered had strengthened her today. There were all kinds of opportunities, if one just looked for them in the right places. She had to remember that. But the unreadable—and disconcerting—expression on Jake's face worried her. What was wrong?

Leaning inside, she lifted her shawl from the back of the battered old Queen Anne chair that belonged to the landlord, then stepped out and closed the door. They walked around to the front of the hotel and sat on the bench outside the establishment's glass front doors, in the respectable amount of light. It was their usual meeting place, where townsfolk could see they were keeping their relationship chaste until they married.

She took his warm hand into her own, finding comfort in his strength, the roughness of his palm, the way his thumb moved over her fingers in a never-ending promise. He'd been her champion for over two years. Her only thought from sunup to sundown. She couldn't wait until they were man and wife. Just as soon as he saved a little more money and felt ready to take on the responsibilities of starting a family, he'd promised that was exactly what they would do.

"What's happened?" she asked. "I can see a storm brewing in your eyes, Jake. Don't try to hide it from me."

His face clouded over. "Yeah, something's happened," he said low, leaning toward her. "Something I never thought would. I don't know completely how I feel about it yet myself."

"Well, *tell* me, *please*. This waiting is killing me."

He sat a little straighter. "Jake Costner."

"What?"

A small smile played around the corners of his lips. With his free hand, he patted his chest. "I have a name, Daisy. I'm Jake Costner."

She sucked in a deep breath. "What?" she said again, completely at a loss. "How?"

Three riders approached the hotel, so Daisy waited to continue until they rode past. The moment gave her time to gather the feelings thundering around her chest. Change was in the air. How would it affect them? "Jake, I'm so happy for you. How on earth did this information find you?" Her happiness for him mixed with trepidation. Would this discovery alter his feelings? With a complete identity, once the missing wound where his father was healed, would he still want someone as damaged as her?

"My mother is here in Logan Meadows."

"Your mother?" This was so unreal.

"Yes. I spoke with her tonight. She gave me a letter from the man she claims is my father." With his free hand, he pulled a dented envelope from his pocket and set it on his lap. "He's dying. Want's to meet me."

"Dying from what?" *Lack of heart?*

"The letter doesn't say."

Unable to look him in his eyes for fear he'd see her distress, she kept her gaze trained on his hand held firmly in her own. What did this mean? Jake was leaving? There wasn't an inkling of doubt in her mind that he would respond, go when summonsed away from Logan Meadows. After he learned what he'd been seeking, would he ever come back? After all was said and done? Or would he stay on? Did this mean he didn't want to marry her anymore?

"Daisy, darlin', what're you thinkin'? Why're you so quiet?"

With a gentle finger, he lifted her chin and found her gaze.

She gave a halfhearted shrug. "Hearing this is just such a shock. I don't know what to think." *You're leaving me, Jake, that's what I know. That's why my heart is breaking and sorrow has its hand tight around my throat. I love you. I don't want you to go.*

"I know. I felt the same. And still do."

"Where's your ma now?"

"She's staying at the Red Rooster with Violet."

"Violet? I'm surprised. Mrs. Hollyhock is a Christian woman, but sometimes she even has limits. I'm astonished, is all."

"She's making the effort for me. But, I feel the same as you."

Well, it's plain to see he's going. I won't stop him. And if I love him like I do, I'll make it easy to go . . .

"When will you leave?"

He let go a whoosh of air, and a full-blown smile stretched across his handsome face. "I'm happy to hear you say that, Daisy. I didn't know how you would respond. I'd never do anything to hurt you, or us, but this is something I have to do. For the both of us."

"Of course, I want you to go find your pa. Any woman worth her salt would. I love you, Jake, and I only want what makes you happy. If traveling away from Logan Meadows for a time will do that, then I say you better go. What does Chase say about losing you for a while?"

"He's fine with it. Says I need to go meet my father before he passes away. That's why I need to hurry."

Oh, how she wished she could give him a kiss.

Nothing was certain any longer. The queen of spades had dealt her a vicious blow, as she always did, wanting to muddle up any good luck that came Daisy's way. Well, she wouldn't fret just yet.

This wasn't the end, she reminded herself as he gazed lovingly into her eyes. It was the beginning of their future. *Together.* She desperately wanted to trust her thoughts, but something inside kept twisting her heart. She'd believe it when he walked back into her life.

CHAPTER TWENTY

When the reading concluded, Hunter was one of the first out on the boardwalk. He sucked in a deep breath of air, appreciating the openness and the sight of the stars in the sky. His roots were in the wide-open spaces, the prairie, the mountains, the long-forgotten ghost towns.

Great Expectations had been engaging. He'd like to get a copy of the book and read it himself, but only after he finished *Tom Sawyer*. He'd worked for some time today on that project, getting to the end of chapter one. Standing back, he nodded as people exited, chatting excitedly about the event, then proceeded on their way home. Through the window, he could see Tabitha taking money from a few hands in payment. She'd made some sales. Good. He wondered how Kendall had fared in the saloon. Frank Lloyd came out of the bookstore, smiled, and continued on his way home.

Charlie Axelrose, his wife, and their little girl exited next. Yesterday, Hunter had taken his stock out to their horse ranch to board, being their place was within walking distance. Since he wasn't using his mule or his horse at this time, keeping them out there was more affordable than at the livery in town, though Win hadn't been happy to lose his business. The young woman who cared for the Axelroses' blind daughter stood close to their side. He'd heard she'd lost her only aunt the day of the train accident and broken her own arm. With no other relations, she'd stayed on in town.

Tabitha breezed out into the evening air with a shawl draped over her shoulders, riding high from her accomplishment. There was just enough lamplight to see her pink cheeks and bright smile. Her arms moved around in animation as she thanked her guests and bid them good night. Feeling awkward without his usual hat, he stood alone a few feet away from the Axelrose group. He stuffed his hands into his pockets, in no rush to leave.

"There you are, Julia," Tabitha said, taking one of Julia's hands after darting a quick inquisitive look at him. "I've been trying to catch your eye all night. I wanted to see how you've been. I haven't seen you in town for a few days."

"I've been busy watching this little gal." She set one hand on Maddie's shoulders. "And I'm perfecting my cross-stitch."

Nell smiled at Julia and then winked at Tabitha. "You haven't mentioned a thing about riding, Julia. I seem to remember several long outings you and Gabe have taken."

The shy girl ducked her head. "Yes, that's true. In his spare time, Gabe's decided to teach me to ride."

"I see," Tabitha responded with a tone full of meaning. She reached out and stroked the blind child's hair. "Hi, Maddie. Did you like the story?"

"A lot," Maddie responded. "But not that mean man with the chain on his leg. He scares me. He wanted to eat poor Pip's cheeks!"

The group chuckled.

"I know. Isn't that horrible? He scares me, too," Tabitha replied, again glancing his way.

Hunter kept a stoic face but wanted to chuckle.

"You being scared means I'm doing my job, Maddie. I hope you come back next week."

✿

Is Mr. Wade waiting on me? Tabitha kept up her chatter with Nell's family, and all the while Mr. Wade's tall, imposing presence continued to distract her thoughts. When she'd first seen him standing outside on the boardwalk, she'd thought he was just hanging around to speak with friends, but now, most everyone was gone. When the Axelrose family left, they would be the only ones left on the quiet street.

"We'd better get moving before Maddie falls asleep on her feet," Charlie said, lifting his little girl into his arms. The group started off.

"Have a nice walk under the stars." Surreptitiously, Tabitha glanced down both directions of the street. *We're alone.*

She peeked over at Mr. Wade, who was already looking at her. He closed the distance between them.

"Can I help you with something, Mr. Wade?" She sounded so silly. So formal.

"Yes, as a matter of fact, I was waiting for you. I want to tell you that I read a whole chapter of the book. I had to skip some words, but I got enough to know what's happening."

He gave a boyish shrug, as if reporting to a teacher whom he wanted to impress.

She clapped her hands together. "That's wonderful! Good for you. You'll be reading well in no time."

"I don't know about that, but I would like you to order a copy for me to buy. I'd feel better purchasing instead of borrowing. 'Be not a lender or borrower,' Thorp liked to say."

Does he feel sorry for me? I sold five whole books tonight, doing much better than I ever expected. I would have been happy with one. "Thorp?"

"The man who raised me."

"That's not necessary. I don't expect you to buy the book. You should finish reading it first, to see if it keeps your interest."

"My interest is captured, I can assure you."

At his warm, tingle-inducing tone, she jerked her gaze away from his, feeling her face heat. She fastened her eyes on the lantern hanging by her front door. *Are we talking about the same thing?* His ability to make her feel eighteen years old was uncanny, *darn him*. Unable to stop herself from glancing back, she caught his smile. His warm gaze roamed slowly over her face. When it landed on her lips, she felt as if she were sinking into a patch of quicksand.

Surely, he knew how deadly his gaze could be. Especially on a spinster. He wasn't a boy—far from it. He must have seduced his fair share of women in his life, and by his casual manner, enjoyed doing it.

He glanced up at the stars. "Look at the blanket of stars the Lord has laid out for our enjoyment."

She followed his gaze. "Beautiful. The stars were never so bright in New York. Here, they amaze me."

He chuckled.

"What?"

"Had you pegged as a city girl."

She returned his smile. "Well, you're correct. I'm on my way out for a little night air before I turn in. I'm much too keyed up to go to sleep just yet." She rearranged the shawl more securely around her shoulders.

"By yourself?"

"I don't go far—just up one side of Main Street and return on the other. I always stay within the lamplight. Most nights, I go out much earlier, but tonight the reading has put that off by a few hours. Sometimes I cross the street and say good night to Max and Clementine." *Be quiet! He'll know how desperately lonely you are. Have a little pride.*

His brows raised a smidgeon. "Mind if I go along—for your safety. I wouldn't want to wake up to hear a wolf had stolen you away." He stepped closer, offering his arm. "And besides, I've been so busy with the saloon, I've let some of the things I cotton to most go by the wayside. Like walking to the light of the stars. Time I corrected that."

What am I doing? Aunt Roberta would have a heart attack if she saw us. Stop this foolishness before it's too late!

"Just let me get my key and lock the door."

CHAPTER TWENTY-ONE

A few moments later, Tabitha found herself strolling down the desolate street at a loss for words. They'd already passed the empty sheriff's office with the one lantern burning in the rear by the stove, and the quiet saloon. Now they were in front of the bank's large front window. "Have you been inside?" she asked, gesturing to the bank, pleased to finally have something to say. She felt like a schoolgirl walking with her first suitor. Well, she'd walked out with a boy in the eighth grade, but beyond that, no one.

He tipped his head toward the building as they passed it by. "I opened an account."

"Of course."

"Pretty darned fancy, if I do say so myself. Reminds me of the banks and businesses I've seen around St. Louis, Chicago, and even farther east. I didn't expect something so nice in Logan Meadows."

"I've forgotten about all of your travels, Mr. Wade. Are you sure you'll be able to settle down here? Grow some roots?"

His steps slowed, and he stopped, the dark mercantile and the overhang making her feel invisible to the rest of the world.

"Will you *please* call me Hunter? Seems strange to keep hearing you call me Mr. Wade. Every time you do, I think of Thorp. We've known each other for a few days now and see each other often. I just think it would be nicer."

"Maybe nicer. But, I'm not sure it would be proper."

He mulled that for a few moments.

Could she? Should she? Loneliness squeezed her insides. She didn't want to feel something for this man. He owned the saloon. The one she'd taken a stand against. Surely, a relationship couldn't go anywhere.

"Well, at least think about it, *Miss Canterbury*. Just thought that might make things a lot simpler between the two of us."

Simpler? Actually, more complicated . . . and risky. He didn't agree with her philosophy on reading, although he was learning how, and he'd voiced his opinion on her wasting time that could be spent better elsewhere. And he wanted to bring more business to the saloon, when she'd like the place to close at midnight. A future with Mr. Wade was asking for trouble.

At the end of the street, they ran into Daisy speaking in hushed tones with Jake on the bench in front of the El Dorado. Feeling conspicuous on Mr. Wade's arm, she smiled and nodded at the couple, but kept moving. A few guests inside the parlor of the hotel sat with newspapers in front of the lamp, but didn't even look up.

She and Mr. Wade—*Hunter*, she tested the name in her mind—crossed the road and started back toward her shop on the opposite side of the street. A light still shined from the back of the laundry house where the Lings did their washing. *How late will they work?* Bao, in her seventh month, needed to slow down. That woman was a true workhorse. Tabitha worried about her.

"Have you met Tap and Bao Ling?" she asked. "Owners of the laundry house."

He let out a small chuckle. "I have, and their little girl. Cute little thing. In a town the size of Logan Meadows, meeting everyone doesn't take long. Especially if both your businesses reside on the main street. I've known a few Chinese in my travels, most coming west to find their fortunes. Hard workers. Most are unassuming and fair. They aren't looking for any handouts."

She nodded in agreement. "You're absolutely right about that. It's shameful how they're treated. And now this law that allows anyone who's come into the country after 1880 to be sent back. I think it's reprehensible." When he gazed down into her eyes, clearly confused, she added, "Morally wrong. Unkind. Families ripped apart perhaps never to see each other again."

His lips flattened as they moved down the boardwalk. "I haven't heard about that, but I agree with you. Doesn't seem right."

She nodded, amazed at how much she and Hunter had in common. Yes, they were at odds over the saloon, but they could agree on other things. If someone would have asked her two days ago, she would have laughed at the thought. Her and a buckskin-wearing trail boss? "I read about the law last year, before coming west. Speaking of the saloon," she went on, liking the ebb and flow of this discussion, "how's Kendall treating you now? Has he accepted the inevitable? Come around to the fact that he has a partner in the Bright Nugget? I'm sure he likes all the repairs you've done. The place must be looking quite nice inside. I couldn't help but notice all the boards you've carried past my front window from the Feed and Seed."

Even in the darkness, she could see his smile. They proceeded from one lantern to the next, stepping down into the dirt each time they had to cross an alley, and then back up onto the boards where the walkway picked up again.

"I repaired four tables and more chairs than I'd like to remember," he said, chuckling and shaking his head. "Kendall had a stack piling up out back. I guess he'd rather buy new than restore the broken ones. Some were unsalvageable, but a good portion came through. The upstairs room is once again livable. I wouldn't say yet that Kendall has warmed to me. I keep one eye on him most of the time. He still won't let me count the till at closing time, but he's gettin' there." He gazed at her, a good-hearted smile shining in his eyes. "I'm an honest man, if nothing else."

He took a deep breath and looked around. She wondered if she'd imagined the feel of his palm briefly brushing the top of her hand. She didn't dare look to see if she were correct.

"This is more what I'm used to," he said, gesturing to the quiet street. "No walls, the night air. Even rain on my face if the weather turns. Sometimes when I'm sleeping in the apartment the air feels tight. I think about taking my blanket out to the festival grounds. That's what I'm used to," he said. "Not streets, businesses." He glanced around. "Not all this. Or a bed with sheets. That darn thing feels so soft I think sometimes the mattress is going to swallow me up. It's like a big cloud. Or a swamp pit."

Tabitha couldn't stop herself and laughed. That only seemed to encourage him.

He shook his head. "You think that's funny? I don't know how everyone else does it—live inside all their lives. They don't know what they're missing. Thorp always said the same. He'd take a blanket on the ground to a fancy hotel any day of the week. Guess I'm the same."

Hunter was the most interesting person she'd ever met. But to sleep on the ground? Not only would it be as hard as a board, the thought of what might crawl over her during the night, when she was asleep and unprotected, was enough to make her hair stand on end.

With his next step, Hunter faltered, and almost dragged her to the boardwalk when his knee buckled and he grappled to stay upright.

"Hunter!" she yelped, pulling on his arm. "What happened? Are you all right?"

He straightened up and ran his hand through his disheveled hair. "Just the leg I took an arrow in when I was a kid. It goes out sometimes on uneven ground." He looked at her closely. "Are you all right? Did I hurt you?"

"I'm fine." She wondered if he was okay. He went down quickly, and she'd heard a loud rap when his knee hit the boards. His brows were still tented in worry over her. "Really, Hunter, I'm not hurt in any way. Just surprised."

He put out his arm, his lips twitching up.

"What?"

"You called me Hunter. It slipped out before you knew what you were saying."

"So I did." She placed her hand back through his arm and they resumed their promenade. "And you may call me Tabitha." She was playing with fire. Setting herself up for heartache. Not only were they adversaries, but Hunter might come to find living in a town not to his liking. Anything could change. From what he said, the wilderness was deeply ingrained.

"How and when did you take an arrow?"

"On my first wagon train west. I was a small boy, traveling with the aunt and uncle who took me in after my parents died. Indians attacked. Killed my relatives. Thorp pushed me into a ravine, but not before I took the arrow. Luckily, there was a doctor along."

They walked on. A far-off coyote broke the silence.

"What happened to Thorp? Is he still alive?"

"Sixteen years after he took me in, and many trips back and forth across the country, Thorp fell off his horse, dead from some kind of seizure. From then on I was wagon master." They paused, and Hunter gazed once again into the dark sky filled with stars. "May he rest in peace."

What a life! What a heartbreaking life for someone so young to experience. A nomad. No family. Tended by a grizzled old man who offered him food and shelter. Well, she wasn't sure Thorp was grizzled, but that's how the mountain men from the books she'd read appeared. Moved by all that Hunter had shared, she wondered about the rest of his life. If he'd ever been in love, perhaps married. A thousand questions filtered through her mind.

Feeling daring, she hugged his arm. "And you never married?"

His head tilted. "Getting rather personal, aren't you, Tabitha?"

She shrugged. "You've told me everything else. Just wondering is all."

"I had a sweetheart once," he said in his slow, easy voice. "I was twenty. Brought her and her family west to Oregon with a wagon train some fifty-five families strong. Along the way, Mable and I fell in love. Her parents, not too keen about their sixteen-year-old daughter marrying up with someone like me, talked her into postponing the wedding until Thorp's and my next trip out. By then, she'd be seventeen, plenty old enough to be a wife." He shook his head, and a whimsical smile pulled at his lips. "She promised to wait, which would constitute a twelve- to fifteen-month delay, if you counted our riding time back to Missouri, and then making sure all the settlers were prepared for the grueling journey. As fate would have it, bad weather delayed us another four months, and hostiles three more. That can happen. One thing that's sure on a wagon train is that nothin' is sure." He looked meaningfully into her eyes. "By the time I made it back, Mable Firth was Mable Hasselburg. She'd up and married the young preacher in her town, much to her parents' relief. And she was already in the family way. That was my one and only brush with the institution. Decided I liked myself better on my own."

She squeezed his arm. He'd lived through so much. "Memories."

He made an agreeing sound in his throat. "I haven't talked about that with anyone ever before. Feels like yesterday, and I'm twenty years old again. How about you, Tabitha?"

He made her name sound like a caress.

"I can't imagine why a good catch like yourself isn't hitched by now."

Reaching Dr. Thorn's office, they stopped when the door opened. As if a person were the last thing he'd expected to see, the doctor pulled up short when they were about to collide. His eyes widened when he saw her hand in the crook of Hunter's arm.

"Good evening, Miss Canterbury. Mr. Wade," he said, looking first at her and then at him. "I enjoyed your reading tonight, Miss Canterbury. You read very well."

"Thank you so much. My head is going to be a mile wide by tomorrow with so much praise from my friends."

Hunter pulled her hand closer. "Don't be modest . . ."

At the long pause at the end of Hunter's sentence, she feared he'd go and call her Tabitha in front of Dr. Thorn. This was a dangerous game she was playing.

". . . Miss Canterbury," he finally finished with a devilish twinkle in his eyes. "You deserve all the praise coming your way. I've never been that spellbound watching someone read."

She gave him a look that said to be careful. She didn't want to give anyone the impression they were stepping out. "Have you ever listened to an oration before?"

He cocked a brow. "Well, no."

"Didn't think so."

"I won't take up more of your time," Dr. Thorn said. He buttoned up his jacket against a light breeze that had kicked up, and started off. "Enjoy your walk."

"So?" Hunter said when the doctor was good and gone.

"What?" She'd hoped he'd forgotten he'd asked about her past.

"You were saying why you aren't married."

"That's right, I was. Well, my case is a bit different. I'm sure you won't understand at all—as my parents don't."

"You're stalling."

"You're right. I've never been engaged, and never had a beau. But I've always had a dream of owning my own bookstore. I could picture the building, the interior of the shop, and the books in my mind from the time I was six years old." She shrugged, finding the saying strange even to her ears.

His gaze was filled with questions. "Do you cotton to the fairer sex?"

"No!"

"Just sounded like a question that needed asking."

"But I do cotton to having a life to call my own. And being in control of such a life, as much as a person can be. I believe anyone can achieve whatever they set their mind to—as long as it's a burning desire. All-consuming. Much to my parents' dismay, I've been strong-willed since childhood. If I married, my shop would belong to my husband, as would I." She shrugged. "That's not my idea of a life . . ."

She let her words trail away. He didn't need to know about her parents' betrayal with old Mr. Brackstead, how when they'd learned she *really was* going west, they tried to hoist her off on a wealthy old man. Some things were better left unsaid.

"I see."

His warm breath, still scented from the cookies he'd eaten, slid gently across her cheek, causing her imagination to run wild. What would his kiss be like? Or the feel of his arms? Stories about romance were some of her favorites.

She slipped a quick look at him as they passed the haberdashery. Was he an honorable man, or was he looking for a fling? Why had he asked to come along? And why was he flirting? Their attraction was irrefutable. *You're turning twenty-nine on Thursday, Tabitha, take a fling if he's offering. His affections may not be true love, or forever, but isn't a few days in heaven better than never knowing?*

She heaved a sigh, rounding up her wayward thoughts. She knew she wouldn't. Her honor meant a lot to her. As it should. It was part of who she was. If God wanted them together, it would have to be in the proper way.

"Something wrong?" he asked, his eyebrows tented with concern.

He must have noticed her quietness and felt her sigh. "No. Just enjoying the night. You're quiet as well. What's on your mind?"

"Things."

"Like?"

"The Bright Nugget. There's still a lot of fixing to do before the saloon will produce up to its full potential. Right now, Kendall only has one working girl."

Her feet ground to a halt. His words were an imaginary slap across her face. "Working girl? You mean Philomena?"

He chuckled. "Who else? I haven't seen any other women in the saloon since I've arrived."

"You mean to bring in more, more—"

He held up a hand. "Tabitha, a lady like yourself doesn't need to say the word. We're both old enough to know about the birds and the bees—and what transpires when the lights go out. Saloons and soiled doves go hand in hand. You can't have one without the other."

"I've always hated that moniker! I picture a little white dove with sad eyes . . ."

His amused expression turned hard. "What do you want me to call them? Scarlet ladies, fallen angles, nymphs du prairie? They're all one and the same."

Heat prickled her face over the indelicate topic. The lack of saloons and taverns was one thing she loved about Logan Meadows. The fact that there was one only, when most towns had three or four—*or ten*—made her new hometown cozy and nice. Less drunks, less shootings, less trouble. She didn't want to see things change. "What if we don't want you to bring in more *working* girls? We like Logan Meadows the way it is now."

He gave her arm a tug with his elbow, trying to bring her closer, but she held her ground.

"No one seems to mind what happens inside a saloon. That's for men to do and to decide."

"That's because you're a man!"

"True enough."

"The women mind! They mind *very* much!"

His eyes widened. "Don't get riled. Nothin's been decided. It's just an option I've been tossing around."

Disregarding the intimate feel that only minutes before had clouded her usual good judgment and had her considering an inappropriate affair, she felt compelled to speak for all her female friends. "You'd best review long and hard, *Mr. Wade*. If not, you just might find yourself on the wrong side of all the women in this town. That's a place you might not like to be."

With agitation rippling inside, they started again toward the store. She stilled the impulse to yank her hand from the crook of his arm and march away. She'd gone against her own best reasoning to walk out in the first place. She knew better. How dare he bring more saloon women here, which in turn would draw more of the wrong sort of men?

When they were drawing close to the bridge, with Storybook Lodge just across the street, a buggy appeared down the road, approaching from the direction where Uncle Frank lived, and Aunt Roberta, too. It was still too far away to know for sure, but one of the occupants looked like her aunt. The conveyance sped forward, turned, and crossed the bridge, stopping in front of her shop.

Tabitha jerked her hand free and widened the distance between her and Hunter. Cool air sharpened her mind, opened her eyes to what this looked like. She didn't dare chance a look at Hunter to gauge his reaction, but she could feel his gaze on her face.

On one side of the buggy seat was Aunt Roberta, with Thom at the reins.

It was evident from the scowl on her aunt's face that she'd seen them—and had drawn the worst possible conclusion.

CHAPTER TWENTY-TWO

Tabitha yanked her hand from Hunter's arm and stepped away as if he were a coiled rattlesnake ready to strike. She was toying with him! And like a stupid fool, he'd fallen for it. She knew her place, and it wasn't walking in the moonlight with the likes of him. Was he a plaything, the forbidden fruit? Now close to the buggy, Hunter pushed back his anger and buried his injured pride.

"Aunt Roberta, what brings you back into town this evening?" Tabitha's normal calm, intelligent tone held a tremor of uncertainty.

"Once I got home, I discovered I'd accidentally left my reticule at the bookstore."

Her chilly tone made Tabitha blink. "Couldn't it have waited until the morning? It would be safe with me."

Thom pushed up his hat, and he heaved a healthy sigh, his eyes heavy with fatigue.

"That's what I told her, but she wouldn't listen. Especially when she wanted me to fetch the buggy and horse from the livery first, instead of just walking back the short distance. I offered to come myself, but she wouldn't think of it."

"I wanted to keep you company," Roberta said. The smile she gave Thom was strained.

"For all of three minutes?" The deputy began to climb out, but Hunter waved him off. He quickly approached Roberta's side of the cart. "Stay put, Thom, I'll help Mrs. Brown down. I can run in and get your reticule for you. That way you can be on your way more quickly."

Her eyes widened. "No thank you, Mr. Wade. I'd like to retrieve it myself. The back of the brooch I was wearing snapped off, so I tucked it away in my reticule, which I put in the desk drawer. It was a gift from my late husband, and is very important to me. I'm sure you can understand I'd be nervous about losing something of such sentimentality."

Roberta put her hand into his, and let him help her to the ground.

Tabitha already had the door unlocked, and had gone inside to light a lamp. Her aunt marched through the opening like a battalion sergeant, and Hunter followed behind. She went straight to Tabitha's desk, opened the drawer, and pulled out a small woman's handbag.

She turned. "Here it is." Her gaze tracked back and forth between him and Tabitha.

He could feel her discomfort from five feet away.

"I'm sorry you had to come back for it, Aunt Roberta," Tabitha said in a hollow-sounding voice.

Roberta lifted her chin. "I'm only down the street."

Her aunt made no attempt to move. It hit him that she was waiting for him to be the first to leave. What did she think? That he was going to climb the stairs and compromise her niece here in her own home on Main Street? Anger tightened his gut. "I'll be going now, Miss Canterbury. Thank you for the walk."

Tabitha glanced his way.

"I hope I didn't intrude on you too much."

Her eyes, a few minutes ago alight with—what, he didn't know—were now anxious and worried. "It was my pleasure, Mr. Wade. Thank you for coming to my reading tonight. I appreciate the support."

He went to tip his hat but realized he wasn't wearing one. Turning, he stepped out into the blissfully cool air once more, understanding this was where he belonged.

CHAPTER TWENTY-THREE

Roberta charged through the door of Hannah's house totally unconcerned with the noise her clomping boots made on the hardwood floor. *What is Tabitha doing? Throwing away all that she's worked so hard for?* She yanked the scarf from around her neck and tossed it onto a chair. That was when she saw Hannah watching her from the supper table, bookwork strewn across the top.

"What on earth?" Hannah gasped. "Can you please be a little quieter? Your grandson sometimes has a difficult time staying asleep."

Markus! "I'm sorry. I totally forgot." Roberta let out a moan and began pacing the floor. "I *knew* this would happen. Tabitha in her naïveté is ripe for the pickings. She's fallen for that gunslinging buffalo hunter who's all too charming for his own good!" *Like I almost did.*

"Buffalo hunter! Charming?" Hannah closed the ledger and stood, watching her mother walk the length of the room. "Who? Mr. Wade? You're jumping to all sorts of conclusions. Besides, he was a wagon-train guide, Mother, not a buffalo hunter."

"Same thing!"

"No, not at all. And why on earth are you upset? He was a perfect gentleman tonight at the reading. Now that he's a partner in the Bright Nugget, he's also a business owner, just like me. You should stop judging him so unfairly."

"Surely you've heard what Kendall said. He's a gunslinger and has killed indiscriminately. Doesn't that worry you?"

Hannah followed her mother's steps over to the small writing desk against the far wall. "That's nothing but hearsay. If he were a murderer, he'd be locked up or already hung. You know as well as I do, Kendall has an ax to grind. I'd not believe what you heard unless it came from Albert or Thom, and it didn't. As long as Mr. Wade doesn't kill anyone here, he deserves a chance. There are two sides to every story, in case you've forgotten."

Roberta pulled out the chair and plopped down, her hands shaking as she opened the drawer and took out a sheet of paper.

"Mother, what did Mr. Wade do that has you so upset?"

Roberta didn't answer, just began writing as fast as she could.

"Mother?"

"He and Tabitha were taking a moonlight stroll. She had ahold of his arm, and they looked rather lovey-dovey to me. Marigold has a right to know what is transpiring with her daughter. I'm doing what I should have done the moment he rode into town and turned Tabitha's head. I'm sending word to her mother!"

CHAPTER TWENTY-FOUR

Hunter descended the steps of his apartment early the next morning, anticipating a cup of hot brew at the sheriff's office. He knew either Albert or Thom was already below because the savory scent of coffee seeping through his floorboards had driven him from his covers where he'd lain awake the whole night.

Rounding the corner into the alley between his place and the bookstore, he paused. Irritation stabbed him. He glanced up to the second story, feeling his lips flatten into a frown. With a hand to his whiskered jaw, he contemplated the object of his frustration, most likely still in bed sleeping away the morning. Her rejection last night stung. His pride had been dealt a serious blow.

As a young, unattainable wagon master, he'd been adored by most of the women moving west. They were grateful for his help to their men, and had let him know with their smiles, secretive glances, and even a soft, womanly hand to his biceps now and then.

When he was fourteen, and old enough to begin noticing the unsaid innuendos, Thorp had given him a strict lecture about his responsibilities. What his position of authority would be as he grew older. The women would be attracted to the man, *any man*, they felt held their life in his hands. He was not to abuse that power. Hunter was to be polite and considerate without encouraging flirtations. And never to partake of what they offered, no matter how they insisted their husbands didn't understand them.

Oh, he remembered those lessons well. But now, he found himself single at forty. And if he were truthful, feeling more alone than any man ought to. He longed for something more meaningful than the Bright Nugget saloon. If loneliness was a slow killer, he had one foot in the grave.

Was Miss Hoity-Toity still asleep? By her own words, her habit was to read far into the night. Had she done that last night, unable to get her thoughts off him? He remembered her expression when he'd come to her reading and she'd seen him through the window. Her eyes had softened, and her lips had pulled up in a secretive little smile.

He might be a plaything to her, but she liked him well enough. She'd just not admit that fact to anyone else, least of all herself.

Damn her! He hadn't come to Logan Meadows to pine away over some past-her-prime businesswoman. *Especially one who doesn't want me.* His best course of action would be to kiss her as soon as he had the chance. Get her out of his head so he could move on. Once he did that, there was sure to be a slap, condemnation, and a demand for him to stay away.

That would be paramount for them both.

The sooner the better!

Albert Preston looked up from his desk when Hunter stepped into the sheriff's office. His son, Nate, was perched on his knees on a chair beside him, leaning over his father's desk. With pencil in hand, he was writing something on a piece of paper.

"Mornin', Wade," Albert said, a friendly smile on his face. He had a stack of official-looking papers in front of him. "Come down for your usual cup of coffee?"

"You mind?"

"'Course not. That's why I asked." He glanced at his son, who was watching Hunter with wary eyes.

Hunter forced the smile he wasn't feeling. "Mornin', Nate," he said, wondering why his small friend was now regarding him as if he'd grown sharp teeth.

More often than not, Nate was here working on some kind of schoolwork before class. Seemed Preston was awfully thankful for the son he hadn't known he had until a handful of months ago. In the slow hours of the saloon, Kendall had filled Hunter in on the sheriff's situation, as well as that of just about everyone else here in Logan Meadows. The man was a wealth of information. If there was something Hunter needed to know, he went straight to Kendall.

Albert cleared his throat. "Son, you have something you'd like to say to Mr. Wade?"

Nate set his pencil down, his mouth pulling into a frown.

"You forget to do your homework, Nate?" he asked, wondering if the boy knew how fortunate he was to have a pa watching over him to make sure he completed his studies.

Nate came forward a step. "No, sir, Mr. Wade. Just writin' my spellin' words one more time. If I get 'em all right today, my pa's takin' me froggin' after school."

At the child's scared tone, Hunter was mystified. Shouldn't he be happy and excited about froggin'?

"Nate?" Albert prodded. "Go on. It's best just to spit it out."

His small chest expanded. "I'm sorry for scaring Clementine."

Confused, Hunter cut his gaze over to Albert.

Albert raised his brows.

"Clementine?" *Ah, the reason for the buffalo charge.* He hunkered down and looked Nate in the eyes.

Nate nodded. "I was in the loft when Uncle Win went into the buffalo pen to water Clementine and Max. I was shooting at things with my slingshot, and, well, I wasn't trying to hit nothin' really . . . Still, I shot Clementine in the butt."

Hunter held back his chuckle.

"That's why she stampeded out and almost run over Mrs. Hollyhock," he mumbled, his eyes cast at the floor. "—and you, too. I'm real sorry for that."

"No harm—"

Albert, seated behind Nate, narrowed his eyes and shook his head. The boy's father didn't want Hunter to go too easy.

". . . was done—*this time*. Yet, the situation could have been much worse, being Mrs. Hollyhock is so advanced in age. I accept your apology, and thank you for being so truthful."

"I think Nate should do something to make up for his carelessness, Mr. Wade. So the next time he's tempted to shoot his slingshot, he'll be a bit more careful what's in front of his aim. What do you think?"

Hunter took his time mulling over a punishment that wasn't too difficult for Nate, but would still be one he'd remember. "Well," he finally said when Nate had swallowed for the third time. He didn't want to traumatize him too much either—parenting wasn't easy. "The saloon's no place for a boy, but I'm sure Miss Canterbury could use a hand in her bookshop. Maybe sweep up her boardwalk, take out her trash, or dust her bookshelves?"

Nate jerked his face to Hunter's, his eyes glowing with eagerness. *Ah, he likes Miss Hoity-Toity.*

"I'm sure she'll have some ideas of her own to keep you busy." He sent the boy a meaningful glance. "Does that sound fair?"

Nate nodded.

"And of course, you're also going to apologize to Mrs. Hollyhock, right?"

Another nod.

"Good." He reached out and ruffled Nate's hair. "Glad to hear that. Now, you best get back to your spelling words. You don't want to miss a chance to go froggin'. Come by the bookshop this Saturday. I'll let Miss Canterbury know to expect you, and why." He stood. "Now, for that coffee."

Seemingly relieved of the guilt he'd been carrying around since last Saturday, Nate heaved a healthy sigh, then went back to his paper. He resumed his work, the pencil looking large in the boy's small hand.

At the stove, Hunter noticed an empty cup warming on the iron cooktop, but not directly on top of the heat. He glanced up at Albert in question.

"Yep, it's for you. Go on, it's clean."

With a chuckle, Hunter wrapped the thick potholder around the hot handle of the coffeepot and filled the mug to the brim. He took a swig, being careful not to burn his mouth. The coffee, stronger than most, plunged down to his empty belly, feeling warm and heartening. He ambled toward Albert while noting the quietness of the street outside.

Albert took a drink from his own cup. "You don't have to open the saloon for hours. I usually don't see Kendall until late morning."

"Old habits die hard," he answered, looking at the faces on several wanted posters tacked to the board just inside the door. His apartment walls were closing in on him more than ever. "I thought I'd take a ride this morning." *Right after I send that telegram to Dichelle.* "See some of the country. Haven't gotten much of a chance since I arrived. Everything that needed fixin' in the saloon is pretty much fixed." He turned to Albert and gestured to the papers before him on the desk. "Business?"

The lines between Albert's eyes pulled together in thought. "Seems contentions have grown worse in Rock Springs. White workers don't like the Chinese getting all the jobs at the local mine. The immigrants work cheaper, and the owners keep hiring them first. They've had some dustups. One Chinese man was beaten, and another turned up missing. I don't like it. It's a powder-keg situation."

Nate looked up from his spelling words. "What's a powder-keg situation, Pa?"

"It means something's ready to blow."

"Like when you blasted through the train car with dynamite?"

Albert chuckled. "Sort of. But when I say it now, I mean with people. Men. When a group of fellas are stewing for a fight, and nothin' is gonna stop 'em." He reached out and placed his hand on Nate's shoulder. "Disagreements should be settled with words and laws. Not violence. Taking into consideration everybody's needs, not just those of a few."

Nate regarded his pa earnestly, rolling the pencil back and forth in his mouth. He bit marks into the yellow coloring, and then looked at them.

Albert motioned to his spelling words. "Keep at it, son. It's almost time for you to skedaddle to class."

The door opened and Thom came in, his dog, Ivan, bringing up the rear. "Morning," he said. After hanging his hat on the hat rack, he went straight to the coffeepot and filled a mug.

Hunter supposed the apologetic look was because of last night. Surely the deputy saw how Tabitha had jerked her hand from his arm.

"Morning," Albert and Hunter replied.

"You're here early as well, Thom," Albert said. "I wasn't expecting you for a few hours. You and Hunter know something I don't?"

Thom gave a quizzical look, clearly not understanding what Albert meant. "Not a thing," Thom finally said. "The kitchen was just a bit crowded with Hannah, Markus, and Roberta clamoring around. Makes thinking a bit difficult, if you catch my drift. Thought I'd get a peaceful cup of coffee down here before the day began."

Hunter pictured a room filled with loved ones, still warm after a long night's sleep. Angry with himself, he pushed away the thought. He had a good thing going with the saloon. That was soon to get better if they could arrange some unique entertainment.

And the sooner he'd banished that little bookworm from his mind, the sooner he could get back to business. That chore would be taken care of straightaway, the first spare moment he had. Today!

CHAPTER TWENTY-FIVE

Packed and ready to meet the twelve o'clock train, Jake entered the laundry house, his stomach twisted in a tense knot. The moist air, smelling of scorched cotton, clung to his face and hands, weighted his lungs.

The entry was empty. Stepping to the open dividing door between the reception area and the work place, he looked into the long, narrow building. With only the two small windows near the rear, and one along the alley, the place was dim, adding to the suffocating feel.

Mr. Ling worked at a large ironing board, his face dripping in sweat.

Marlene was bent over a washtub, vigorously scrubbing some article of clothing on a washboard. She extracted the garment, inspected the collar, and placed it in the large tub beside her.

Mr. Ling looked up. He set his iron on the stove and hurried over. "Mr. Jake," he said courteously. "You speak with mother?"

Jake turned his hat in his fingers. "Yes, Mr. Ling. Can she spare a minute?"

He nodded, and then proceeded to guide him through tables with stacked laundry, clean, folded and ready for pickup. Piles of dirty garments lined the wall.

Marlene looked up. Her eyes widened.

"Please, you go out back," Mr. Ling said, pushing open the back door to a rush of fresh air. "Speak in private."

"Thanks." Jake's tight throat was almost painful. He should be angry, resentful when he looked at the woman, but all he felt was sadness.

She dried her hands on a small towel.

Jake couldn't help noticing when she straightened her skirt, that her hands were red and painful looking from the hours spent in the soapy water. She swiped at several strands of straggly hair falling into her eyes, and then dried her face with the towel.

The air outside felt downright chilly in comparison with where he'd just emerged.

"Jake," she said after several moments passed in strained, uncomfortable silence. "You're going then? To meet your pa?"

He nodded. "Today. In a few minutes." He gazed off to the small church on the hill. Reverend Wilbrand appeared on the porch and closed the open door. "Thanks for delivering his letter. You didn't have to."

She fiddled with the towel still clenched in her hands, her gaze trained on him. "You mean, you're surprised that I did."

He nodded again, noting the whiteness of her eyes. Seemed he couldn't ever remember her sober. "It's not an easy trip from Valley Springs."

The sound of laughter caught her attention, and for one instant her eyes lowered to the ground at his feet and her lips wobbled.

"Why didn't you tell me sooner? I must've asked you over a hundred times." He wouldn't bring up all the instances when he'd been small and she'd thrown him outside unmindful of the weather. Once he grew tall and strong, she'd not handled him anymore. That almost seemed worse than the spankings and arm-twisting.

"I just didn't. That's all."

"You don't know why, or you won't say?"

Her shoulders slumped, and for a minute, from the longing in her eyes, he thought she was actually going to do as he'd asked, and tell him why she'd kept such an important fact secret. One that could have changed the course of his life.

She must have realized from the hopeful look on his face that he thought she was going to comply. Her mouth pulled down into the expression he remembered all too well.

"I just said no, boy. That's all you're getting from me today. Now, get going. Go meet your pa. See what he wants."

Her going out of her way to travel to Logan Meadows was a mystery, unless she thought his pa was going to give him something of value. Did she want a piece of the action? Most likely yes. She'd made the costly trip for herself, and not to see him. Or help him.

And that was fine with Jake.

The door to the shanty that sat in the back of the laundry house opened and a very expecting Mrs. Ling came out, her small daughter in tow. She pulled up when she saw them only a few feet away.

Jake nodded. "Mrs. Ling," he said politely, then smiled at Lan.

"Mr. Jake."

Her soft reply floated over him, reminding him there were good people in the world. Ones who weren't just out for what they could get.

"You best get going, boy," Marlene said, her voice curt. "You don't want to miss your train."

Thinking that was the smartest thing to do, Jake strode away, across the land, headed to the train station where Daisy waited to say goodbye. He steered clear of Main Street, not wanting to speak with anyone else. He'd said his goodbyes this morning to Chase, Jessie, and Gabe, as well as Sarah and Shane, insisting they needn't come to the depot.

Jake Costner was off to meet his new destiny.

A bundle of nerves, Daisy paced back and forth on the wooden decking of the Logan Meadows train station, the wrapped copy of *The Last of the Mohicans* clutched in her arms. The cool breeze pulled the corner of her cape and she grasped at the ribbons of her bonnet to be sure it was securely tied. It was a bit out of season, but she'd worn it anyway for Jake. He'd given it to her last Christmas, after she'd exclaimed in June over a display in the window of the haberdashery, which had begun carrying a few items for women.

Hoot, hoot, hoooooooooooot.

She whirled.

A quarter mile away, the Union Pacific rounded the bend. The tall smokestack puffed black and gray plumes into the air, leaving a long trail of soot billowing in its wake.

Joker, Jake's horse tied at the hitching rail, danced nervously in place, then pulled on his reins. Where was Jake? He should be here by now. If Jake was late, he'd instructed Daisy to have the conductor load his horse into the stock car. His bag, hardly large enough to hold more than a change of clothes, sat nearby. Had something happened? Would he miss his train?

Maybe he's changed his mind, she thought, then tamped down the selfish hope.

Mr. Hatfield hurried out the depot door, over to the tall water tower, and, hand over hand, began climbing toward the platform where he'd regulate the influx of water to fill the steam engine's tank.

Still forty yards away, brake pads met metal wheels, and great clouds of steam whooshed out from below, followed by an ear-splitting screech. Gradually slowing, the huge silver-and-black train approached. In an onslaught of noise, it pulled up to the depot platform, and rolled to a stop.

"Darlin'."

With all the noise the Union Pacific was making, she hadn't heard Jake's approach. Turning, she fell into his waiting arms, the book between them. "I thought you weren't going to make it, Jake," she whispered, her lips brushing his ear. His warm cheek on hers, heady. She longed to stay that way for all time.

"Shhh, no need to talk. I can hear the tears in your voice. Everything's going to be all right. I'll be back. Nothin' could ever stop me."

Hot prickles burned the back of Daisy's eyes. She'd promised herself she wouldn't cry. She wanted Jake to remember her with a smile on her face. So he'd want to come back, no matter what great things he discovered about his father.

"I know, Jake. I don't think you understand how much I'll miss you while you're away. Nothing will feel the same."

He cupped her face between his hands, so close now she could see the honey flecks in his expressive brown eyes. "Time will fly by, sweetheart. The Silky Hen will keep you busy." He looked down at the package. "What's this?"

"A surprise to make your trip go faster." *And something to remind you of me.*

His brows pulled down. "But I don't have anything for you."

"I don't want anything, Jake." *Just your return.* She placed the package into his hands and watched expectantly as he unwrapped the book. A swell of love lifted her chest when he read the title and smiled.

"Sweetheart, I love it. Thank you. I'll start it on the train." His earnest gaze held hers. "Don't know how I got so lucky to win a girl like you."

Enjoying his praise, she felt herself blush. "How long will you be gone?" It was the question she'd been wanting to ask since he'd told her the news.

"No way of knowin'. The letter said my pa was dying. I'll send a telegram if I can. Promise you'll wait for me, Daisy. That you won't do something foolish if it takes me a while. Like run off with another man."

She pulled back. "Jake! You know I love you."

He chuckled. "I do. Now, I have somethin' serious I want to ask."

Daisy held her breath.

"You've known for a long time what's been on my mind. My cabin on Shady Creek has been put to rights with Chase and Gabe's help, and is ready to be lived in. My herd of horses is growing and—"

"Jake!"

"What I'm trying to say is, I love you, Daisy. Will you marry me the minute I get back? Make me the happiest man in the world?"

Unable to stop herself, she went up on tiptoe and kissed Jake's lips. She'd worried this day would never come. "Yes, yes! You know I will."

"I'm sorry it's taken me so long. I never had a name to give you, honey. Now I do. Daisy Costner. I don't know what I'll find in the next few weeks, but I know what I'll be coming home to."

She laid her palm against his cheek. "I love you, Jake. I can't wait to be your wife."

The train whistle blew again, and he stepped away. "Good. I was praying you'd say that. Now, I have to get my horse loaded. There's not much time before we pull out. Remember, Chase and Jessie have promised to look after you. Gabe, too. If you need anything, anything at all, go to them." He pulled her into his arms one last time, and she felt his love, and longing. "You have nothing to fear."

With a new purpose, Jake strode away toward his horse, the animal still pawing at the hitching rail. Daisy worried her bottom lip. How she wished he didn't have to make this trip. She wouldn't sleep well until her beloved was back in Logan Meadows, safe and sound.

CHAPTER TWENTY-SIX

With *The Adventures of Tom Sawyer* tucked under his arm, and a mission firm in his mind, Hunter opened the door of the Storybook Lodge and stepped inside to the heady aroma of cinnamon sticks cooking on the woodstove. Tabitha, the picture of proficiency, stood at the back shelf, speaking with a heavyset woman he'd never seen before, a volume in the customer's hands, her head tipped thoughtfully to one side. A small blue traveling case sat at her feet.

Must have arrived on today's train.

Miss Hoity-Toity glanced up. Her eyes widened. She looked mighty pretty in her formfitting yellow dress with a white ribbon tied around her small waist.

"Good day, Mr. Wade," she said in a light, airy voice. "I'll be with you in one moment."

He gave his most congenial smile. *I'll not be able to take care of business just yet. Not until we're alone.* "No rush at all, Miss Canterbury. I'm just here for"—he dropped his voice—"a reading lesson." Back to normal voice, he went on. "Don't rush. I have all the time in the world." Which was true—unfortunately. The near-vacant saloon was easy for Kendall to handle on his own. He wondered if Dichelle would even take the time to answer his telegram. They needed her desperately, but he didn't hold out much hope she'd actually come. She had a good gig going where she was. Why upset the apple cart?

He ambled over to the chair by the front window and sat, listening to the quiet conversation in the back. He smiled at the sales pitch Tabitha was laying on the woman. No one would know from her relaxed charm how desperate she was to make some sales.

"Wonderful," he heard her say. "I'll write this up. Your purchase will make the rest of your travel time fly by in the blink of an eye."

As they came forward, he opened his book and flipped the pages to chapter two.

Albert appeared on the other side of the glass and stopped when he spotted Hunter. With a quizzical grin, the sheriff tapped on the glass and waggled his fingers. When their gazes met, the sheriff's eyebrows rose in humor and Hunter shrugged. Albert shook his head and moved on.

"There you are, Mrs. Petrowich. I hope you enjoy the rest of your trip. Thank you so much for stopping in today." Tabitha handed the book to the portly woman, who exited the shop with a smile on her face.

"Now, how can I help you, Mr. Wade?" Tabitha asked, walking in his direction.

If only you knew. You're going to help me banish your hoity-toity face, your hoity-toity voice, and your hoity-toity ways from my brain once and for all. He stood as she approached.

She smiled. "Actually, I'm a bit surprised to see you. After our disagreement last night over the—"

"Soiled dov—"

"Don't say it! I haven't given up. Can't you see how buying a woman for pleasure isn't right? A woman isn't an object that can be bought and sold. She's flesh and blood, with feelings, hopes, and dreams. It's demeaning. And wrong. My friend Daisy used to be a saloon girl, but has worked hard to change her life."

Hoity-toityness at its best! "Just settle down. You're giving me a headache. Your friend didn't have to go into that profession if she didn't want to."

"So typical of a man to say. You think a beautiful young woman—or *any* woman for that matter—wants to be pawed, and *everything else*, by some smelly ol' man she doesn't know! Daisy was young, running from an abusive home with nowhere else to turn. When she got hungry enough, some man looking to make a profit offered to give her shelter and food for something in return. Think about it. To me, that's tantamount to blackmail!"

Irritation mounted at her use of inch-long words.

"The survival instinct is strong, Mr. Wade, especially in women. When there isn't any other way to subsist, women do what they must. It's our obligation as a society to try to help when we can."

Hearing enough, he held up his hand, reining in his own agitation. "I don't know what you're going on about. Saloons, and *women of the night*, have been around forever!" Darned if she didn't make him angry. *I can't let her derail me from the reason I'm here. This conversation proves it all the more. I best get to it.* "I didn't think up the profession, *Miss Canterbury*. I came in for another reason, not to have my head bit off."

She actually blushed.

"You're very right. There's a time and place for everything. I shouldn't have attacked you as I did. I'm just very passionate about the subject." She glanced at the chair behind him. "Please sit back down and get comfortable."

He stood looking at her, thinking it best if he came back later. Now he was mad. No telling how his mission would turn out.

She raised her brows. "Sit, *please*."

He did. Looked at the page. "Can you help with this word?" He pointed to the first long word that he saw. "Can't figure it out. Soon as I do, I'll take myself out of your company."

She circled behind the chair and leaned over his shoulder. Her clean lavender scent, mixed with the cinnamon in the air, fogged his mind.

"Which word, Mr. Wade?" she asked stiffly.

There would be no first-name basis anymore, he was sure. "Right there."

"Oh, yes. Fra-fra . . ." She sounded out the first part for him. When he didn't respond, she turned her head to look into his face, only a few inches from hers.

My Lord! Can eyes be that green? He swallowed.

"Any ideas?"

Her breath caressed his cheek.

"Read the last four words."

He forced his gaze back to the sentence his finger still marked. "B-Blos*soms* filled the a-air," he read haltingly.

"Does that give you a hint on what the difficult word might be? Blossoms in the air?"

"Nope."

Her lashes fluttered at his ignorance, and her cheeks blossomed as well. *This is quite entertaining.*

"Begin the sentence again, please, and read it through."

"Sure thing, Miss Canterbury." He forced his smile away. "The lo*cust* t-trees were in bloom . . . and . . . and the fra-fra—"

He shook his head. "I can't get it."

"Finish the sentence."

". . . the *something* of the blos*soms* filled the air."

He looked over at her, distracted again by the proximity of her face and other womanly parts so close to his shoulder.

She took a deep breath, enhancing her other womanly parts, bringing them all the nearer.

She leaned closer, tracing the sentence with her finger. "The locust trees were in bloom and the *blank* of the blossoms filled the air," she read, then gazed at him expectantly. "Fra? Fra?"

Maybe this wasn't the smartest way to banish her . . .

"What could the word possibly be?"

He bit the inside of his cheek to keep from laughing. He might have found a way to pay her back after all. "I know!" he barked.

Her smile bloomed.

"Frustration! The locust trees were in bloom and the frustration of the blossoms filled the air." He paused for a good long moment. "That's awfully strange," he added, keeping the laughter from his voice. "I don't know what that means. This reading is more difficult than I'd wagered on."

A small, agonized sound slipped from her throat.

Brenna Hutton, the seamstress, opened the door, making the tiny bells above ring out. Relief passed over Tabitha's face.

"Keep at this, Mr. Wade," Tabitha said to him softly. "Read forward, and I'll be back to help in a moment."

After watching her speed away, Hunter dropped his gaze to the word, thinking Miss Canterbury's *fragrance* had filled his heart. No! That wasn't true. She was just a challenge because she was holding back. She thought him below her. That's what was troubling him, not her pretty smile, expressive green eyes, or her well-put-together womanly parts. It was most certainly not her quick mind. He had to stick with his plan if he ever wanted to be free of her.

CHAPTER TWENTY-SEVEN

Thank the Lord for small favors—and for sending Brenna into her shop when she needed her most. Tabitha hurried forward, ushering her friend over to her desk, to put space between herself and Hunter. His inability to sound out the frustrating word wasn't what had her almost shaking. It was the nearness of his attractive mouth, his gold-flecked blue eyes that were playing havoc with her insides. He was pure man, and spoke to every womanly cell in her body. After he'd made his intentions about the saloon known last night, she shouldn't let him get to her in this way. It was madness!

"Tabitha, is everything all right?" Brenna asked, setting the rented copy of *Moby-Dick* on her desk. She glanced over to where Hunter sat quietly reading, and then reached out and took Tabitha by one shoulder. "Your face is extremely red."

Tabitha quieted her tapping toe. "I'm fine."

"I'm not so sure." Brenna placed the back of her hand on Tabitha's forehead. "You're not coming down with something, are you?"

Agitated, Tabitha marched over to the door and opened it a couple of inches, letting in a cool breeze, then returned to her desk. "It's just warm in here. I've already had one customer today, and now Mr. Wade is taking advantage of the quiet of my shop for a little spare reading."

Brenna's brows scrunched together.

"I offered the place to him. We were just talking. Everything is fine."

"I'm not so sure," Brenna whispered behind her hand. "He's not making a pest of himself, is he?"

"Not at all."

Brenna would find it more believable if the wagon-train master were here for help with his reading, not just relaxing in her shop, but Tabitha was bound to keep his handicap a secret. His large form did look rather silly in her flowered chintz chair next to the tiny Queen Anne side table.

"If you say so." Brenna glanced at the returned book. "I'm dropping this off. It was so exciting! I could smell the ocean and feel the salty spray on my face." She gave a small laugh. "I even got seasick a time or two. The book is one of Gregory's favorites and he's read it many times. I did feel quite bad for all the sailors in the end, though." She extracted a quarter from her pocket and placed it on top of the book.

"That's too much. You know the rental fee is one-fifth of that."

"I've kept it much longer than I should have. Now don't argue. I insist."

Her friends were worried about her. She didn't want them to be.

"Please."

"Thank you," Tabitha said with as much ease as she could muster. She didn't like to be on the receiving end of charity, but to be gracious, and because she could use the money, she accepted.

"Gregory also wanted me to ask you about your schedule. He's very keen on getting you into the class to read."

Seriously? She'd thought he was just being nice. "I guess any day that he'd like. I can close up for an hour. No one will miss me."

Mr. Wade cleared his throat.

When she glanced over, his head was buried in his book. Was that a coincidence?

Brenna smiled. "I'll tell him that and let him choose. I believe he's thinking sometime next week. Is that too soon?"

"That will be perfectly fine. You just let me know."

"Wonderful. I guess I better get back to my mending, because this is the evening I bake for the Silky Hen. My life feels fuller than full, and I'm loving every second of it."

Brenna stepped forward and gave her a hug. A moment later, she breezed out the door.

Tabitha took her time adding the quarter to her money sack, which she kept in the back of the desk drawer. Once a week, she walked her earnings down to the bank to deposit into her savings. She wasn't making much headway on her loan to Uncle Frank. Still, she wasn't going to worry—yet. She'd not let anxiety ruin her days. She needed to give the shop some time to prove itself, as she did all she could to keep her clientele growing. Add events like the Tuesday-night readings, and help people become better readers, as she was doing with Mr. Wade—she'd turn more people into readers and perhaps might eventually start charging for her tutoring. Even though her days here in Wyoming were uncertain, the time was much more productive than when she'd lived at home. And much more pleasant.

She glanced at Mr. Wade. Things here were proving to be quite exciting compared to living under her parents' restrictive thumbs. She could never go back. She'd never want to.

Noiselessly she closed the desk drawer, then ventured back to Hunter. She hoped he'd figured out the word. And that he'd forged ahead.

"Well, how's it going? Did you figure it out?"

His look was quizzical. "It's not frustration? I thought it was, so I read ahead, but got stuck on the first word of the next sentence, so I've just been waiting until you were finished."

"All this time?"

He nodded, closed the book, and set it on the table. "I don't mind." With palms to the armrests, he pushed himself to his feet. "I need to stretch my legs a little. I'm not used to sitting around with my nose in a book for any length of time. Not like some people I know."

She bristled.

He ambled through the room looking at things. He seemed different today. She followed a few steps behind, curious.

"Where was—" He turned. Pulled up when he found her so close. "You're very light on your feet."

All of a sudden, everything grew so quiet she could hear her own heartbeat. Even the street outside seemed deserted. When he took a step forward, she held her ground. If she wasn't mistaken, he meant to kiss her. With a determined tilt to his brows, he wrapped her in his arms and lowered his lips to hers.

Her world tumbled forward as she gripped the front of his butter-soft shirt. After all her wondering about what his lips would feel like, here they were, warm and firm on her own. His annoyance with her came through, though. His grip was strong, and she could hardly breathe. Her mind said she should pull away, but her heart screamed this might be her only chance. His head slanted and he pulled her closer, sending a rush of warmth through her body.

A moment later, he pulled away, their ragged breathing the only sound in the shop.

The amusement she'd expected to see in his eyes, on his lips, wasn't there.

His eyes narrowed. He took a tiny step forward, backing her up to a bookshelf, and then took her face between his large palms, his lips again only inches from her own.

With the most perplexing expression, he silently searched her eyes so long she thought she might faint. Or die of want of another kiss just like the one before.

He closed the distance, but this time the kiss was different. Where the other was aggravated, this one cherished her. With a mind of its own, her hand stole up his chest and gently caressed his cheek.

She'd felt horrible last night, pulling her hand from his arm as if she'd be caught doing something dirty. The action had haunted her sleep, and robbed her of any rest at all. She'd been sure her betrayal of his trust had cost his friendship. That she'd seen the last of him. But today, he'd surprised her, venturing into her shop.

And now this. What was she supposed to think? Her heart felt like a sparrow with a broken wing. She had no idea how to proceed, or even if she should. Should she wait to hear what he'd say first?

He pulled back just far enough to gaze into her eyes. "Your *fragrance* is mighty nice."

It took a moment for her to realize he'd been teasing her when he couldn't get the word in the story. He'd known the difficult word all along . . .

"Tabitha!"

Aunt Roberta! Not again!

Ripping away from the warmth of Hunter's chest, Tabitha pulled back, and without thinking of the consequence, in a reaction born of the disdain she felt coming from her aunt, reared back and slapped him across the face.

He blinked, looked at her for several long moments, and then . . . *smiled*?

"You've gone too far this time, Tabitha!" Roberta cried, turning back to the door. In a quick move, she ripped down the shade, which did little good at all because the large window at the front of the shop was still uncovered. "What if someone else were to walk in on you behaving like a floozy? And with someone like him!" She pointed a finger at Hunter. "He's a wagon-train guide no-account at best and a killer at worst! Please—use your good sense. What would your mother think? Or your father? They'd be scandalized is what. A saloon owner!

Once he's gotten what he wants, he'll leave you in the dust." She slowly shook her head. "I-I'm totally speechless, to say the least . . ."

Hunter's anger was easy to feel. "It was just a little kiss," he said slowly.

"A little kiss? I think not!" She drilled him with a hot stare.

"Aunt Roberta, let me explain . . ."

"I don't know what's gotten into you lately, niece of mine! Last night's impropriety is what I came to speak with you about. Walking out and making a public show. I just thank the stars I came in today. Before something much more shameful could happen." Her gaze cut to Tabitha's second-story bedroom. "What on earth has been going on between the two of you? Don't you know I'm responsible for you? What befalls you lies on my shoulders."

"Since you've thrown out a mouthful, I'd say you're anything but speechless, Mrs. Brown," Hunter said on a growl of irritation. He stepped away from Tabitha, toward his hat on the table. Four perfect finger marks were outlined on his cheek. "But just so you know," he said to her aunt as he looked at Tabitha, "Miss Canterbury had nothing to do with what you witnessed. She was an innocent bystander."

He pulled on his hat and then tapped the rim in salute. He strode out the door, leaving his book on the table.

CHAPTER TWENTY-EIGHT

Leaving the mercantile with the supplies she needed to bake a cake for Tabitha's surprise birthday party tomorrow evening, Violet halted on the edge of the boardwalk. She glanced both ways. She'd learned her lesson last Saturday, when she'd been daydreaming. Because of Mr. Wade, she hadn't been severely hurt when Clementine charged down Main Street in a slingshot-induced frenzy. Repositioning the basket on her arm, she realized that the next time, she might not be as lucky. Little Nate Preston, with a shaky voice and downcast eyes, had confessed his transgressions, and she'd put him to work cleaning her henhouse. That lad warmed her heart. Reminded her of her boy, Tommy, when he'd been that age. A familiar burn pushed at her heart. "Hurry home, Tommy, if ya want ta see yer ol' ma again," she muttered to herself. "My time's about run out . . ."

Across the street, Dr. Thorn exited his office beside Ling's laundry house. When he saw her about to step off the porch, he hurried to her side and took ahold of her free arm. "How're you feeling today, Violet?" he asked, walking slowly beside her.

She felt his evaluating gaze. The thirty-something whippersnapper was always thinking she was on her last leg. Most likely he'd be glad when she did pass, considering she was his main competition in Logan Meadows.

"Jist fine. And you?" Turning her head, she gave an exaggerated gander at his person, slowly looking him up and down.

His face blossomed pink.

"You look a might paltry fer someone yer age." Successfully crossing the street, then stepping up onto the boardwalk, she cocked her brow. "You been gettin' enough iron in your feed? I suggest ya boil a couple of rusty nails in a cup of water. Add a splash of vinegar and drink it morning and night."

At his mollifying smile she lifted a shoulder.

"Thanks, I'll keep that in mind. I was just asking because of your fall the other day." His tone was a bit self-justifying. "You having any dizzy spells?"

"I'm fit as a fiddle in the fiddle player's hands. I don't know why you keep askin'. I'd tell ya if somethin' was wrong."

"I didn't mean to upset you."

Mr. Harrell came out of his clothing store and waved him over.

The doctor smiled, seeming relieved to hurry away. "See you later, Violet."

"That you will," she muttered under her breath. "For a good *long* time, too."

Big words, but I can't deny, no matter how much I'd like ta, that Ol' Violet Hollyhock is slowin' down. She swallowed, and gazed down the street. *I love this place. These people. Best keep moving if I don't want to stop for good.*

Reaching out, she grasped the doorknob of the laundry house and struggled with the door, concerned about keeping the items in her basket from jiggling around too much.

Warm mist enveloped her. Not waiting to be helped, she went directly into the back work area in search of Marlene. She spotted Jake's ma bent over a washtub in the back of the room, and Bao working the water pump into a hefty bucket. The small, sweet-natured woman brought a smile to her lips, even though Violet still worried over the long hours she worked.

"There ya be, missy. How's the tadpole?" She pointed at the large protrusion under Bao's apron.

Bao hadn't heard her approach, and looked up in surprise.

"Mrs. Holly*hock*!" She placed her hand on her growing belly.

Marlene straightened, dragged her sleeve over her wet brow, and stood there.

"Well?" Violet looked expectantly at Bao.

"I feel well. And strong."

"I better not catch you overdoin', ya hear?"

Bao nodded. "I not work too hard. I take easy." Mr. Ling, busy at the iron, looked over, smiled, and kept working.

Violet glanced around in search of their child. "Where's Lan?"

"Napping," Bao said. "Soon wake up."

Things looked as if they were working out well with Marlene's help. Hopefully, Bao was getting a little more rest because of her. "Why don't you jist go lie down fer a few minutes yerself. The work will wait."

Longing passed over Bao's weary face. She rolled her shoulder, then glanced at Tap. He nodded.

"Five minutes, is all," Bao said. "I won't be longer."

"You stay as long as you like. That's what Marlene is here fer. You need ta depend on her."

Bao smiled her thanks and went out the back door.

Violet turned her attention to Marlene. "I brought ya somethin'." She carefully set her basket on the floor and went through her items. She pulled out a cloth napkin with both hands, careful not to drop anything out. She handed it over to Jake's mother.

Marlene's brows drew down. Her face, void of any rouge, powder, or lipstick, looked younger. "What's this?"

"Open it and see."

Cautiously, she unwrapped the gift. "A piece of pie?"

Feeling almost silly, Violet nodded. "Maude's doing. Baked it for the customers in the mercantile. When she offered me a slice, I thought you might like some since you're working harder than yer used ta."

"That's why you came by?" She looked down into her hands and then back into Violet's face.

"That and ta tell ya that Jake's gone. Off to find his name. I pray to God some good comes outta this."

"I know. He came to say goodbye."

He did? To say goodbye? I hardly think so. He musta had other reasons. "What're yer plans now?" Violet asked. "Since ya done what ya came fer? Go back ta the rock you crawled out from under?"

Marlene shook her head. "Don't have the money. I'll need to save some before I can leave."

"How ya gonna do that? You ain't working for pay. All yer time here pays your room and board."

"Don't know yet, but I'll figure something out. Don't lose any sleep over my plight."

"You can be sure I'm not. I jist wanted ya gone before Jake returns. You've brought him enough grief in his life." *She's sticking around ta see if he comes back with anything of value. Wants ta get her claws into some money.* "You best eat yer pie and get back ta work. Try and get most of this done before Bao comes back."

"Yes, ma'am!"

Violet narrowed her eyes. "Don't ya be sassin' me." Straightening her finger, she pointed, and the woman cringed back in fear. "Or I may change my mind about not turnin' ya into a lizard, toad, or slimy creek salamander . . ."

"I didn't mean to rile you. I'll think on how I can save money for the stage."

Satisfied, Violet picked up her basket and headed toward the front of the laundry house, intent on seeing her newly adopted grandson before she made the walk back to the Red Rooster. That brought a smile to her lips. She liked Mr. Wade. He needed her, more than she needed him. She could tell by the loneliness lingering behind his blue eyes.

CHAPTER TWENTY-NINE

In a mood just about as foul as they came, Hunter dipped the mop back in the bucket of water and swished it around. Seemed any chore that took more energy than lifting a rag, Kendall gave to him. He was only going along with him now to build a little goodwill. Eventually, he'd insist they split everything, chores and money. Since he'd arrived, every cent had gone into the bank, and he'd worked harder than he had in years.

Actually, this was a good way to work out his frustrations after the way he'd gone and muddled things with Tabitha. He flopped the mop's wet cotton tendrils into the wringer, then leaned forcefully forward, pushing his muscles to the limit.

"You're gonna bust that thing," Kendall said from behind the bar. "Then we'll need ta buy a new one."

He shot Kendall a look of warning, and went back to his mopping. His plan to banish Miss Hoity-Toity from his mind once and for all had done the opposite. Since the moment he'd walked out her door and back into the saloon, she was the only thing he could think about. Her downy-soft lips, the way her womanly curves fit perfectly in his arms, the passion with which she'd kissed him back.

Damnation! He'd let her under his skin. *I'm forty years old. I know better!*

"Be careful. You're sloshing dirty water everywhere. Making the floor worse."

"I don't know why we stripped out the shavings just to mop the floor. They cover the mess."

"We gotta change 'em out from time to time, and mop the floor. If we don't, this place would stink to high heaven."

"It already stinks to high heaven. This isn't making anything better."

Hunter looked around in time to see Kendall make a face. The original owner was getting angry.

"I'll say it again. It's strong in here," Hunter said. "I'm not lying." The wide-open prairie, with its sweet-smelling air, came to mind.

"And *that's* why we swept the old shavings into the alley and we're mopping the floor. After which, the new shavings from the mill will be good for another six months. The sweet scent of woodchips covers up the sweat, muck, and spit. Understand?"

"You make it sound so enticing."

"Don't get smart. You can leave anytime you want."

"Yoooo hoooo?" a scratchy old voice called from the front door. "Mind iffin I come in?"

Hunter turned to see Mrs. Hollyhock in a blue calico dress. Seemed she was waiting on an invitation to enter. He sloshed the mop back into the bucket and wiped his hands on the towel he had tucked in the waistband of his trousers. "You sure you don't mind coming into the saloon, Mrs. Hollyhock? We can talk out front, if you'd like."

"I'm too old to bother about things like that, Hunter boy. There're things in life worse than saloons, ya know."

Yes. He knew about that. Things like desire, confusion, and the dull ache in his heart.

"If I mean ta visit you any time I please, I'll need ta do it in your place of business."

"Fine then. We don't mind, if you don't." He put out his elbow, and escorted her inside.

She looked around wide-eyed, and then smiled at Philomena, coming down the stairs in her low-cut, pink dress. Violet wrinkled her nose at the murky water sloshed around by his bucket.

"Don't mind the mess, we're doing a bit of spring-cleaning."

"In October?"

"Late spring-cleaning."

"Hello, Violet," Kendall said. "Never thought I'd see you in here. Can I get you something? On the house, of course."

She rolled her eyes. "What would I want from the bar, Kendall?"

"I don't know, that's why I asked."

"I've come ta see my *grandson.*"

"Grandson?" Kendall hurried around the bar just as Hunter pulled out a chair at the table closest to the door. "I think that fall in the street knocked some of your brains loose. You're not making sense."

Hunter felt a smile coming on. "I'm her adopted grandson, Kendall. And she's come for a visit. I think that's mighty nice."

Kendall slapped a large palm to his tall, shiny forehead. "Well, why didn't you say so sooner. You scared me there for a moment."

She took the chair he offered. "Thankee kindly." She looked around. "On second thought, would ya happen ta have any tea behind that long counter? I see a woodstove in the back of the room—feel its warmth. Wouldn't take but a few minutes to brew up a few cups."

Hunter cut a questioning gaze to Kendall, who shook his head.

"We don't," Hunter replied. "But Kendall can run down to the mercantile and get some. I don't know why we didn't think of that sooner. Kendall!" he barked when the bartender just stood there.

"Oh, right. I'll be right back."

Kendall banged out the door with all the grace of a bull in a ballet.

Philomena hung around the far end of the bar. Hunter caught her curious look every now and then. A pang of something stirred in his chest as he remembered what Miss Hoity-Toity had said about women being bought and sold. Them not wanting to do what they did. He'd never really given the quandary much thought, being the women he'd run across seemed to have enthusiasm for their profession. Was that all an act?

Violet cleared her throat.

He pulled out the chair beside her and sat, wondering what they should talk about. It wasn't like when he'd rescued her from the buffalo. That day was filled with excitement. It was hard to get a word in edgewise. There was plenty of inspiration, as well as egg to rub off. And Tabitha had been there to help the conversation along whenever it petered out.

"Philomena, have you met Mrs. Hollyhock?" he called. "Come on over and say hello."

The saloon girl's head jerked up. She moved it back and forth.

"We'd like you to. Mrs. Hollyhock won't bite."

Mrs. Hollyhock waved her hand. "Come on down and say hello, sweetie. I've met ya before. Don't ya remember? Several times on the street, and once when ya was takin' a walk out behind my inn. I asked ya if you'd like some lemonade, and you told me no, but thanked me all the same."

Philomena came forward, doing her best not to sashay in front of their guest. She suddenly looked shy and young. He wondered how long she'd been working here, and felt a prick of shame that he'd never taken the time to find out. Her perfume wafted around.

Mrs. Hollyhock patted the chair beside her. "Have a seat right next ta me. I always thought you had a pretty smile."

As Philomena did Violet's bidding, Farley came through the doors and stopped dead in his tracks.

Mrs. Hollyhock waved the piano player over. "Don't be shy, Farley, come have a seat, too. We're just getting ready to have some tea."

Farley stood in stunned silence, his gaze tracking between Hunter, Philomena, and old Mrs. Hollyhock.

Kendall came through the door, a bag in his hand. "Maude said to boil some water, stir in the tea, then let the brew sit for a few minutes. I'll have to wash some cups if everyone is going to partake."

Hunter nodded to Kendall. "You best get busy."

Farley spun on his heel. "I came to collect my earnin's, but I can come back."

"You're feeling better, I see, Farley," Hunter said. "Will you be able to play this weekend? I don't think I can stand another day with Buckskin Jack at the keys."

"I'll be here." Farley darted out the door.

"I wonder where he's off to like a bat outta hell," Mrs. Hollyhock muttered. She looked at Philomena. "Aren't ya cold, honey? I'm sure my grandson won't mind iffin you cover up some when there ain't no men to impress." She looked around at the empty bar. "Isn't that right, Hunter? No one in here now for the little missy to entertain. The fall air is gettin' chilly. We wouldn't want her comin' down with nothin'."

Hunter sat straighter. *My adopted grandmother might present a problem.*

Kendall showed up with a tray of rattling coffee cups filled with hot water barely colored at all, drawing Violet's attention away from the question she'd just asked. He'd really rather not address the Philomena situation at the moment, or where it might lead.

"Here we are," Kendall said. He set the tray on the tabletop, and passed out the cups.

Violet jerked her head up and narrowed her eyes. "Ain't ya havin' any?" Jittery hands reached out to touch the cup in front of her.

"No, ma'am. Tea makes me sick. Never could abide the stuff."

Her face softened. "Well, thankee then, for makin' this. It'll strengthen my soul." She blew on the hot liquid, and Hunter found Kendall's gaze over her gray head. *Thanks*, he mouthed, reaching for his own cup. Kendall nodded and started for the bar.

Philomena was no help at all. The tea party progressed in starts and stops and the saloon girl never said a word. Just smiled at anything anyone said, happy to drink her tea and listen.

"Yer probably wonderin' why I came ta see ya, Hunter," Violet said after drinking her last sip and setting the cup down with a clunk. "I'd like ya to come out to my place for supper. Tomorrow evening. Just like I mentioned."

Thursday night? He didn't have any plans, but after struggling for conversation today, another evening with Violet felt a little daunting.

Her hopeful gaze caught his.

"Sure. Kendall's been running the bar without me for years. You make up a list of things that need fixing or doing while I'm there. I'm happy to help any way I can."

"Now, I'll let ya all get back to your saloonin'." She stood, and Hunter followed suit. She pulled him down and kissed his cheek. "Four o'clock. Don't be late."

Hunter escorted Violet out, the action raising a few eyebrows from townsfolk on the street. "Do you need me to walk you home?"

She adjusted the basket once more on her arm. "I walk this all the time. Gives me time ta have a little chat with my creator. I don't want him not ta recognize me when I show up on his doorstep, iffin you catch my drift."

Hunter smiled and nodded. She was pretty wise, in this way of thinking. He could use a little walk time himself. He hadn't given the state of his soul any consideration for a long time. He glanced over to Storybook Lodge, wondering about Tabitha. What was she doing? Her aunt most likely had chastised her up one side and down the other. And with good reason. He didn't have anything to offer such a woman. Nothing at all.

"Penny for yer thoughts."

He'd forgotten Violet was there.

"Just thinking how happy your visit made me."

She winked. "My pleasure, grandson, my pleasure."

CHAPTER THIRTY

With cumbersome movements, Bao maneuvered around the warm brick workroom as gracefully as the water buffalo she remembered from China. All she lacked were the long, curved horns. She brushed away the sweat from her forehead, remembering the cool forests and rice paddies of her homeland, where she'd played as a little girl, no older than Lan. Thinking of her daughter, pride warmed Bao's heart. She was so smart. Learning her letters and numbers. She would do fine in this new world. She wouldn't be a laundress imprisoned by a business or town where she didn't feel safe venturing out. This was America. The land of opportunity.

Setting a stack of folded linen on the table by the wall, she stopped to stretch her aching side.

"You feeling all right, Mrs. Ling?" the woman who went only by the name Marlene asked. "You've put in a long day. Why don't you quit? Now that I've gotten the hang of how all this works, I'm getting faster."

"Will in moment, thank you." She returned her smile. "Need to make lye. Almost out." Marlene didn't know that in truth, she was trying to keep busy. Tap had gone to the mercantile to get a few eggs and a bottle of milk, and until he was back safely in the four walls that held their world, she was a bundle of nerves.

"Do you need help gathering the ashes from the fire pit? I don't mind doing that. Gets me outside for a while."

"No, thank you. I do." It was more important the woman finish the ironing that Tap had begun. Thursday, several accounts came in to pick up their laundry. Tomorrow would be here soon.

Eager to be finished, Bao went through the back door, over to the fire pit where they warmed large kettles of water. Moving slowly so as not to hurt her baby, she lifted several shovelfuls of wispy ash from the rim of the fire—being careful not to pick up any dirt—into a bucket. Carrying that to the wooden ash hopper, she added her load to the small amount of water left at the bottom of the barrel, leftover from the last batch. When that was done, she added more water. Later, she'd pull the cork, and let the lye drain into the bucket below. Tomorrow, with the new lye, they'd be able to make soap.

That complete, Bao took a moment to enjoy the cool evening air. She gazed across the way and up the hill to the school that sat on the same knoll as the small, white Christian church. Would they accept Lan next year in their school? Some of her friends said yes, but Bao had her doubts. She'd begun to prepare her daughter, who didn't understand. Bao didn't want a fight on their hands. Or for anyone to be hurt if things turned violent. When her daughter's eyes filled with tears, she wished there was something she could do to change people's hearts.

"Why?" Lan would ask. "Why do they hate us?"

"I do not know." Although she did, and very well. "Someday when Lan is woman, she change way people think? Yes?"

That would bring a smile back to her daughter's face.

"Yes, Mama, I will. I will do that for you."

In her stillness, a rustling sound between her building and the telegraph office caught Bao's ears. Lan was not permitted outside the shop or the shanty without either of her parents. What was she thinking?

As swiftly as she could, Bao moved that way, expecting to see her child. Instead she pulled up short at the figure of a man trying to peer into the window of the laundry house. She jerked back, turned to run . . .

"Wait!"

The voice was familiar. She was far enough away she'd be able to dart inside if he tried to grab her. She turned. She recalled the face. A cowboy who'd come into the laundry house with Gabe Garrison and Jake. Their friend? Was his name Tyler?

"I'm sorry if I gave ya a fright, Mrs. Ling. I was just passing by on my way to the saloon and, well . . ."

You look in my window?

"Ma'am?"

"That all right," she forced from her lips. She gave a small bow and hurried away.

Tabitha opened her eyes and looked at the ceiling in her bedroom.

My birthday.

Twenty-nine years old.

Spinster.

The hated word pained her like a prickly pear on baby's skin. *How had this happened? My life has whizzed right past, each year faster than the last.*

She took a deep breath, and then let the air out slowly. If she were home, her mother would whisk her off to Lady Em's Tea House where they'd eat miniature cream-cheese sandwiches flavored with dill, and finish with a plate filled with slices of pecan pie, the portions tiny enough for a doll's hands. A cozy fire would be burning in the corner. Bright fabrics, pictures of queens, and small British flags everywhere. Women would chat the day away in breathless conversations about gowns, handsome men, and good matches. In the evening, when her father returned home from work, he'd reminisce about the huge parties his parents had thrown over the years for his popular sisters, attended by an abundance of friends, male and female, always ending the story asking why Tabitha never wanted a party of her own.

Her heart ached. Every year was the same.

She wasn't like other girls. She'd rather spend the day in the library, with a favorite book, where she could sail away to distant shores, go into battle, or ride an elephant through a thick jungle laden with dangers around every corner. She wasn't, and didn't want to be, that person her mother and father wanted. She marched to a different drum.

Well, at least no one here in Logan Meadows knew that today was her birthday. Aunt Roberta, as mad as she'd been yesterday, hadn't mentioned it. *Thank God.* Her face heated, recalling the angry exchange. Hunter's bridled irritation. The slap.

Rolling onto her side, she saw the volume of *Tom Sawyer* on her nightstand. Last night, for some strange reason, she'd brought the book up to her bedroom. She'd read bits and pieces of the story she knew so well. The fact that Hunter had left the book behind when he'd stomped out of her shop was still a prick to her heart. She'd not only slapped him, but stole away his newly awakened desire to read.

She sighed. She couldn't change the past. She reached for her watch.

Six o'clock. Several hours before time to open.

Slipping out of bed, she threaded her arms into her wrapper against the early morning chill, and pulled tight the sash. Before anything else, she'd build a fire downstairs. Feeling melancholy, she pushed aside the curtain and looked down at the cheerful creek below.

A buckboard driven by Win rattled across the bridge. Sheriff Preston and Nate were approaching from the other direction on their way to the office. Tabitha could imagine Susanna, cozy and warm in her little yellow home, kissing her new husband and stepson goodbye before sending them off for the day.

Life. And love. She felt left out.

Win pulled the wagon to a stop to speak with his brother and nephew. Albert laughed at something Win said. Slapped his thigh. Nate tried to climb up onto the wagon, but his pa pulled him back.

In her sad state of mind, the homespun scene was almost too much to watch.

She spotted Hunter on his way back from the festival grounds or the train station.

She dropped the curtain and stepped back. Hurt and confusion made her breath catch. Had she really said all those things to him? Their words had been heated, but then he'd gone and kissed her, and she'd slapped him.

Unable to stop herself, she peeked out to watch his progress. He was so tall. So handsome. Her heart thwacked against her ribs as she remembered their conversation during their walk under the stars—before he'd brought up the girls. A smile curled her lips when she thought about how he'd thrown himself into danger to save Mrs. Hollyhock. Not just any man would do that. Not only that, but he'd kept her secret about being trapped in the outhouse. He'd been her friend. What if she hadn't slapped him? Would he have continued kissing her? Courted her? She didn't know, and now she wouldn't ever find out.

Hunter must have called out a greeting, because Albert turned. When he was close enough, Albert clamped his hand on Hunter's shoulder and gave a little shake, large smiles all around. Nate skipped over to the side of the bridge and looked over at the water.

A sob gushed from Tabitha's throat. She let the curtain drop and backed away. She'd been happy here once, hadn't she? She'd loved the process of building. Then slowly stocking her shelves. Life had been good. Livable.

Then Hunter came to town.

With his arrival, Tabitha realized she'd just been subsisting. Living in the shadows of everyone else's happiness. Was it so wrong to want her own? With the back of her hand she stifled the jerking sounds of her sorrow, then sat on her unmade bed, tears trailing down her face unchecked.

The sounds of the men on her boardwalk reached her ears. Nate's silly giggles brought a shaky smile. Look at what Susanna and Albert had just gone through to find their contentment. It hadn't been easy. A lot of give and take had been involved. Was there a chance for her and Hunter? Even if she weren't twenty-nine years old and facing spinsterhood, she realized she'd still be attracted to Hunter. But was attraction enough? They were complete opposites. He owned a saloon, encouraged men to drink and partake in the sins of the flesh. She read about and admired Josephine Butler, Florence Nightingale, and Elizabeth Wolstenholme, women who had made a mark trying to improve the plight of the prostitute.

What am I doing? One kiss does not a marriage proposal make. I'm putting the novel before the hours, months, and maybe years it takes to create such a project. Most likely, Hunter grabs a kiss wherever and whenever he can. Why do I think I'm anything special to him? I just slapped him silly in front of my aunt . . .

Tabitha closed her eyes.

She took a deep breath and wiped the tears from her face. She'd allowed herself this self-pity, but now she was through. Today was her birthday. She'd wrap up her sorrow in a neat little box and stash it under her bed.

She'd make this day special, and no one would be the wiser.

CHAPTER THIRTY-ONE

In the happiest mood she could muster, Tabitha moved around the shop with her feather duster, admiring her books as she cleaned. Even though it was silly, this morning she'd dressed in one of her finest frocks, despite the fact nobody but her would know why. The garment was made of a silk-cotton mixed fabric and had a beautiful green-and-pink paisley print. She'd brought the gown from home, and had yet to wear it here in Logan Meadows. She felt a little silly being so gussied up on a regular Thursday, but that wasn't going to stop her. After she was satisfied with her clothing, she'd carefully woven her hair into a French braid down her back and tied it with a matching ribbon. Her mother would be pleased.

That had been hours ago. Now, she lifted a decorative vase from the shelf and whisked off invisible dust. This wasn't so bad. So what if she was twenty-nine? One day older than twenty-eight didn't feel a bit different.

A chorus of laughter sounded outside. It must be three, and the schoolchildren were on their way home. She stepped outside, rolling her shoulders against the brisk north wind. Winter would be here soon. She was ready. She was ready for any change life brought her way.

A buggy came across the bridge at a good clip driven by Jessie, most likely on her way to pick Sarah up from school. Excited to see her, Tabitha waved, hoping Jessie would stop and chat for a moment, as was her habit, but her friend just waved back with a bright smile and kept on going.

Disappointment lodged in Tabitha's tummy. Her shop had been unusually quiet—more so than ever. Not one friend had stopped by to talk. Not Win to speak about the weather, not Dwight to try and flirt, and not Uncle Frank just to say hello. And certainly not Hunter for any reason at all. It wasn't unusual for Hannah to pop in for a quick cup of tea, or Susanna to bring her a cookie on her way home from her morning shift at the Silky Hen.

She'd seen Nell and Charlie ride by in their ranching clothes, but those two were always so busy she didn't expect them to take a minute out of their day to look at books. And Aunt Roberta? She'd probably never see her again.

When Beth Fairington had walked by her window, a scarf wrapped around her head and covering her ears, she'd almost been tempted to invite her in. She struggled so long with the decision, by the time she decided to do it, Beth was gone.

Well, so what if no one had stopped in. Recounting her disappointment had pointed out to her just how many good friends she had here in Logan Meadows. Keeping her face trained away from the saloon, she turned and went back inside, feeling the best she had all day. She put a smile on her face and gazed into the small mirror in the back of the room. Celebrating a birthday by oneself was rather fun. She had a secret. As the morning had dragged on, she'd even baked a batch of fig cookies and eaten all but five. Perhaps, later, just before closing, she'd walk down to the mercantile and see if Mother and Father had sent a post.

Tabitha ambled over to the back shelf where the plate of cookies, or what remained of them, was covered with a clean cloth. She picked up one edge. Her tummy felt a little queasy from the handfuls she'd already consumed. *You mean stuffed yourself with, don't you? It'll be days until your appetite returns.*

Her gaze tracked to the side of the dish where the volume of *Tom Sawyer* sat, just waiting to trip her up and make her feel sad. So silly of her to carry it around all day as if it were a kitten or puppy.

Maybe she should take it down to the saloon. That would get the book out of her sight. She'd just knock on the batwing doors, and hand it over without saying a word. He'd know why. She didn't want to stand in the way of his progress. Or hers of getting over his kiss. Since this morning, she hadn't had any more glimpses of him, to her utter disappointment.

"Hello, how're you?" a female voice called.

Excited, Tabitha twirled and hurried to the door, but stopped with her foot halfway out.

The voice had been Mrs. Harrell calling to Dr. Thorn across the street. They stood beside the road having a lively conversation. Tabitha backed away.

Hunter arrived at the Red Rooster Inn several minutes before four o'clock. This was his first time here, so he took a moment to admire the ruggedly built lodge-type building that looked considerably old. The place appeared well kept, and he wondered how someone as old as Violet accomplished such a feat. Climbing the steps, he knocked on the door.

While he waited, he turned and looked past the dirt road, to the distant hills. *Pretty. Peaceful.* This is where the town must have begun. Since Violet didn't answer, Hunter descended the stairs and walked around back where part of a shed could be seen from the front. Maybe she was doing some chores.

He saw her just returning from a chicken yard. When she saw him, her eyes lit with pleasure.

"There ya are. Welcome ta my humble home."

He laughed, and strode forward. When he got to her side, she pulled him down to kiss his cheek, making a tendril of warmth spiral through his chest.

"It's hardly humble, Mrs. Hollyhock. I'd say it's quite the place. How do you keep it up so well?"

She winked and threaded her hand through his arm for the short walk to the back porch. "By the efforts of many wonderful people in my life. I'm blessed, ta say the least. Gabe Garrison comes by once a week ta make sure I have plenty of firewood. And, even though I don't need it, a buggy load of women come by every other Wednesday ta clean. The rest I keep up, albeit a bit more slowly than I used ta."

He took the back steps carefully, making sure she was steady on her feet.

She opened the door and they went into the kitchen.

The kitchen was orderly. A large cake was set off to the side, next to a stack of porcelain dishes. His brows drew down. Was she expecting more company than just him? Something good smelling was simmering on the stove.

He proceeded a few steps farther, where he could see the large front room. Although it was clean, the furniture was pushed back in a strange-looking way.

He glanced at her in question.

"All in good time. First I wanna know what you think of the inside? I owned a store once, but this place has captured my heart. It's a good place ta live—and die."

Not knowing how else to respond, he scoffed. "Who's dying? Certainly not you."

The rumble of wagon wheels sounded out front.

Hunter followed her to the door, feeling more than a little cautious. Something was in the making and he wished he knew what it was. Her tiny boots barely clomped as she hurried out.

"Thom, there ya be. I was beginnin' ta think you'd taken a wrong turn."

Thom Donovan? Deputy Sheriff?

"Whoa there, now," Thom called to his team. He waved, and then stomped down on the brake. "I had to take the long way around. Didn't want Tabitha to catch a glimpse of what I'm carrying."

Heat shot to Hunter's face. *Tabitha!*

"And then halfway here, there was a downed tree in the road too large for me to move without tools, so I had to backtrack a little and take a route through a meadow. Had to go slow so I wouldn't break an axle. But, I'm here now." He was already at the back of the wagon, lowering the tailgate.

With a multitude of questions filling his mind, Hunter descended the steps and arrived by Thom's side. Several benches, a crate of dishes, and several wrapped presents were stacked inside. "What's all this about?"

Thom shot him a quizzical glance. "Hannah's throwing Tabitha a surprise birthday party. And we better get moving. Guests should be showing up anytime, and the guest of honor at five thirty."

"Get that stuff in here, Thom!" Violet called, waving her arm. "We need ta move the wagon. So Tabby don't get suspicious when she arrives. Don't want to let the cat outta the bag afore she steps inside."

Dismay, and a tiny button of anger, popped up in his belly. The very *last* person he wanted to see tonight was Tabitha. And especially on her birthday. But he couldn't let on. That would hurt Violet. She'd shanghaied him. And he'd been had. What happened to a nice, quiet supper with his adopted granny? A home-cooked meal and soft-cushioned chairs?

Thom reached for the closest pinewood bench and drew it out.

Hunter did the same with the next one. Carrying the cumbersome seat, he mounted the steps and went inside, careful not to bang any walls or break any knickknacks.

"Where would you like this?" Now the furniture arrangement made complete sense.

She gazed up at him through the spectacles on the end of her nose, her eyes sparkling. "Right here, Hunter boy."

Finished with the bench, he turned to her. "Why didn't you say something about the party? I don't feel like I fit in. I'm new." That wasn't the real reason, but what else could he say?

"For them reasons, I feared ya wouldn't come. I saw how the two of ya looked at each other when we was having tea in the Silky Hen. They weren't normal friendly looks, I can assure you that. She likes ya. And you like her."

"Mrs. Hollyhock—"

"Call me Violet."

Thom came back in with the crate of dishes. There was nothing Hunter could do now. He just hoped Miss Hoity-Toity didn't get the wrong impression. Embarrassment for what was to come, and a bit of anger, too, warred with other feelings.

"Fine." He turned and went out for another load. Tonight would be full of surprises for Tabitha—and possibly him as well.

CHAPTER THIRTY-TWO

It was ten minutes past five when Tabitha realized the time. Rising from her comfortable chair by the window, she went outside for her sign and lugged it inside. She locked the door and turned the door sign to CLOSED.

Not one visitor. Not one customer.

No matter how hard she tried to keep a stiff upper lip, she found her spirits flagging. She hadn't even taken the time to put up her BACK IN TEN MINUTES sign to go to the mercantile to check the mail. When four o'clock had rolled around, she'd finally opened *Tom Sawyer*, and started on page one.

She heaved a sigh, and ran her hands down the front of the dress that had brought her so much joy this morning, feeling anything but. The street looked quiet. She started when a buggy driven by Aunt Roberta crossed the bridge.

What now? I hope she's not here for round two. Maybe if she doesn't see me, she'll keep going.

Tabitha took one healthy step back from the glass, trying not to look conspicuous. The kiss, as well as her aunt's dressing down, popped into her mind. As much as she tried to feel a little shame over her and Hunter's actions, she couldn't. The kiss had felt right. The slap was another story entirely. A deep humiliation pushed in her chest. Once in his arms, she'd encouraged him, she knew she had. And then, in her finest glory, she'd stepped back and given him her best. How she wished she could do that moment over.

Aunt Roberta pulled back on the reins and rolled to a stop in front of Storybook Lodge. When she smiled and gave a friendly little wave, heat rushed to Tabitha's face, as well as guilt for her uncharitable feelings.

Tabitha unlocked the door and stepped outside, being careful not to look toward the Bright Nugget. She couldn't help but wonder if Hunter was standing just outside the batwing doors, as was his habit. "Aunt Roberta, it's nice of you to stop by."

Her aunt fidgeted in her seat. "I was wondering if I could ask a little favor."

The woman appeared nervous. Aunt Roberta was never nervous. Just the people around her.

"Of course. Anything."

"Violet has something she'd like to speak to me about."

"Violet?"

She nodded. "Hannah and Thom are visiting Susanna and Albert, and Win is occupied shoeing a horse or something, or else I'd ask one of them. You know how I don't like to drive by myself."

"Yes. Because you had a buggy accident when you were a girl."

A small frown formed between her aunt's brows. "That's exactly correct. Would you have a moment to come along? So I don't get nervous."

"Right now?"

"Well, yes. That's what I was hoping. I promise not to keep you long."

Tabitha glanced back at her shop, her heart still beating quickly. She didn't want to go anywhere in her fancy dress. She'd feel silly.

"Just there and back."

"Do I have time to change out of . . ."

"Oh, no. You look lovely. I don't think I've seen that gown on you before. It's beautiful with your green eyes." She patted the seat next to her. "Why don't you grab your shawl and come along."

"All right. I'll run upstairs for my things and lock up. I'll be right back."

The Red Rooster Inn was packed to overflowing. Soon after Hunter had arrived, buggies and wagons came trailing down the road, unloaded, and a few of the fellas drove the empty conveyances farther down the road and out of sight.

Hunter detested tight, confined spaces and was having a hard time not bolting out the back door. Men and women alike were squished together in the back of the kitchen area so when Miss Hoity-Toity came in, they could jump out and yell surprise. It was warm, he noted when he dashed away a drop of sweat from his brow.

The inner intuition that had served him well over the years, and kept him alive on the trail, told him now that Tabitha was not going to be delighted that everyone had made such a big fuss about her turning another year older. For a woman, the subject was touchy; one, if given the choice, he stayed away from with a ten-foot pole.

Violet waved her arms. "Shush! Here they come, right on time."

Albert glanced at him and winked. Was probably remembering him sitting in Tabitha's reading chair.

From the front of the throng, Dr. Thorn turned, his wide smile directed at Hunter. "You want to come up here, Hunter, where she'll see you first thing?"

Hell no! "I'm fine back here, thanks." Earlier, as the women were setting up the food line, the doctor had sought him out. He'd made a point about mentioning seeing him and Tabitha out for a stroll the night of the reading.

Knock. Knock.

Everyone held their collective breaths.

Mrs. Hollyhock went forward.

"Howdy, dears," Mrs. Hollyhock could be heard saying. There was a murmur, and sound, and then the heavy door closed. Footsteps sounded, then they all jumped out.

"Surprise!"

Tabitha fell back a step, her eyes wide in horror, her hand at her throat. She blinked several times, and her hand covered her mouth. Hannah crowded in. As did Susanna Preston, Maude Miller, Brenna Hutton, the rancher Nell Axelrose, Violet, Roberta, and a few more he hadn't yet met. Charlie's blind daughter, Maddie, hung back, and the young woman with the auburn hair that watched over her stood behind her with her hands on her shoulders. Everyone was laughing, smiling, and talking. From where he stood in the kitchen, Hunter couldn't make out all the individual words, but the emotions that stormed past Tabitha's eyes were a sight to see. As her astonishment ebbed, a bright red stain slowly climbed her neck until her whole face was covered.

"She's beautiful, don't you think?"

Hunter had thought he was alone. He turned to find Frank Lloyd assessing him.

"And she's intelligent, too," the banker went on. "A man could look long and hard before he found a woman as deep as Tabitha. She has a lot of layers to her, and I'm not talking about that fancy dress she's wearing."

Tabitha's uncle was waiting on a reply. Only, he didn't know what to say. Any direction he took would be the wrong one.

"Guess you're right. I don't know her that well," he mumbled out the side of his mouth, turning back to watch what was happening before Lloyd could react. Hunter didn't appreciate the pressure the men had been dishing in his direction.

Maybe he should make a quick getaway out the back door. He turned his head slightly, but Frank was still there, blocking his way.

"Hunter, come up here," Albert called, waving him forward. "Don't be shy. We know you'd like to wish Tabitha a happy birthday."

CHAPTER THIRTY-THREE

Hunter? Here! No, *dear God*, this couldn't be happening. Tabitha wanted to find a mousehole and slowly creep away. Trying not to be too conspicuous, she glanced around the room until she finally saw him in the far reaches of the kitchen.

Tall.

Wild.

Deadly.

He leaned against the drainboard, his arms crossed over his chest and her uncle Frank at his shoulder. When she met his gaze, his wide shoulders pulled back imperceptibly, and a teasing smirk marked his face. Surely, he'd been roped into this and had no way of escaping either.

Her already warm face blazed with shame. All she could think about was the kiss, and then the slap, followed by his confusing smile as he'd walked out her door.

"Come on, Wade, get the lead out," Albert called to him again. A few of the others laughed, but she caught Aunt Roberta's startled face as she stared into the kitchen. It was obvious she hadn't known that Hunter had been invited.

Feeling overdressed by a mile, Tabitha smoothed her skirt with one hand, while putting on the best smile she could muster. Mother always said, when you found yourself in an embarrassing situation, just throw back your shoulders and smile—and the rest would take care of itself.

No one seemed to notice her discomfort except the tall man making his way to her through the sea of bodies.

"Happy birthday, Cinderella," he said, the timbre of his voice bringing a warm flush. His gaze reached deeply into hers. Her breath caught. "That's some ball gown you have there. Surprised?"

Good. His sarcastic teasing made it easier to shelve her guilt over slapping him. Perhaps he deserved the palm of her hand on his cheek after all.

"Surprised? Yes. Very." She blinked as she gazed around. "I can't believe all these people came out for me. It's wonderful. It's glorious. I'm overwhelmed, to say the very least. Look—"

His brow rose. "Still a chatty chipmunk I see. Don't overplay your hand."

Mrs. Hollyhock appeared at their side, a huge grin splitting her wrinkled face. "Well, now, sweetie, happy birthday. We have a nice potluck of dishes ta choose from. All your friends pitched in. Looks as if everyone spent their whole day cookin' away." She looked around until she found Chase Logan. "Chase," she called over the crowd. "You mind slicing the meat? I'm sure everyone's mighty hungry. Takes lots of energy ta plan a surprise party—and keep it secret."

Everyone laughed and nodded.

"I wanted to come by today so badly," Susanna said, squeezing in front of Hunter. "But I didn't want to give anything away. I'd hate myself if I were the one to let something slip."

That's why no one came in. They were afraid of ruining the surprise.

"Me too," Brenna added. "I found myself on my way to your shop before I knew what I was doing, and had to turn around. I was all the way on the bridge. Did you see me? I thought you might have stepped out the door."

Tabitha shook her head and laughed, totally ignoring Hunter standing behind Susanna. "No, I didn't." *But I could have for all the forlorn gazing I did.* How silly she'd been feeling sorry for herself. The plethora of friends crammed into the Red Rooster Inn was heartening.

"Come on, Tabby, you gotta go first. Chase is about done cutting the meat." Mrs. Hollyhock took ahold of her arm and pulled her away.

In the kitchen, Mrs. Hollyhock stuck a plate into her hands and walked her to the far end. "Ya start here and just make yer way down the line. Don't be shy. No eatin' like a bird."

Tabitha went down the row of delectable creations taking a little of each, all the while wishing she hadn't eaten so many cookies. She wondered if Hunter still followed behind. She didn't dare look. First, she forked a slice of the roast beef, and then took one scoop of mashed potatoes. There was a green-bean dish, some creamed corn, pumpkin squash, and a basket filled with biscuits.

Something that looked suspiciously like blackened frog legs was last. Since there weren't nearly enough for everyone, she felt compelled to leave the delicacy for the others.

With her knife, she took a scoop of butter. And another of jam, recognizing Brenna's jars. She eyed the three cakes that sat apart from the supper food in the middle of Violet's table. Those would be for later. Everything looked so good.

When she was finished filling her plate, Violet personally walked her into the front room where the benches lined the walls. She'd been here many times over during her year since moving to Logan Meadows and never tired of looking at the beautiful quilts that decorated the log walls. All made by Mrs. Hollyhock.

"Now, sit ri'chere," Violet said, setting her in the most significant chair next to the fireplace. "I'll be right back."

For the moment, Tabitha was alone. She looked down at her supper. Quite different from the cream-cheese dill-flavored finger sandwiches. Mother and Father would be surprised at her popularity. That brought a bubble of sadness. Why did she always feel she had to defend herself? Like she had something to prove.

When she glanced up from her plate, she sucked in a surprised breath. Violet led Hunter her way. He hadn't been shy. Food heaped his plate. Although he smiled, she could tell he was not pleased.

Without any objections, he sat next to her. Violet patted his shoulder, and scurried away.

"Hunter," she whispered. "I'm sorry. I don't know what's gotten into everyone." Heat prickled her cheeks and she hoped he wouldn't notice.

"Why are you sorry? You didn't do anything, did you?" he whispered back, his lips shrouded by his raised hand. "As a matter of fact, you didn't even know about the party."

"Did you?"

"Hell no. Do you think I would have intruded? Violet got me out here with a promise of a nice home-cooked meal." He looked down at his plate. "I guess she didn't fib."

Tabitha felt a smile coming on. Her dress was so wide the skirt splashed out and actually went so far as to touch Hunter's leg. She wondered if he noticed. If she weren't so mortified, she'd enjoy sitting next to him. She couldn't help but recall when she'd been helping him with the difficult word. *That was a setup*, she reminded herself. He'd been baiting her. But why? Why had he done that?

She looked up and saw Aunt Roberta watching. That made her remember when she'd all but ripped her hand from his arm. Had he come into her shop to pay her back for that? It was possible.

"Well, I'm sorry you got roped into coming. And don't tell me I don't have to be sorry. I am. Seems it's been one thing after the other when it comes to you and me."

The front door opened, and Beth Fairington stepped inside, removing her bonnet with slow hands as she glanced around the room at the commotion. Her gaze caught Tabitha's. She gave a halfhearted smile.

"Happy birthday," she said. Her gaze strayed over to Hunter and then returned to Tabitha.

Poor Beth. Tabitha felt sorry for her even though she knew the woman worked hard to keep up her prickly reputation.

"Thank you," Tabitha replied. "Food's just been served. Why don't you go get a plate?"

Beth's gaze darted into the kitchen where the line had shrunk, and others were making their way into the front room to find a spot to sit and eat. She peeled off her coat and, not finding a space on the hooks by the door, made a face. "I'll have to go put this in my room first, I guess."

"Yes, do that. Then please come back and join us."

"I thought you said that was the town gossip?" Hunter said quietly. "For me to keep my eye on her."

"I did, but I shouldn't have. I think people will act the way we expect them to. When she walked by my window today, I actually smiled at her but she ignored me. She must be very lonely. Even though she's lived here much longer than I have, I think I could count the people she's friendly with on one hand. That sort of makes me feel bad."

And she felt bad about her conflicting feelings for Hunter. Was there any point in keeping his friendship? With their ideas so different? She wasn't going to change, and by their clashes, it didn't sound like he would either. But what would she do if he did? If he'd heard her reasoning, and didn't bring more women into Logan Meadows? Her heart leaped at the possibility.

CHAPTER THIRTY-FOUR

From her spot on the hard bench, Roberta all but fumed. Why had Violet put Mr. Wade up in front with Tabitha? What was he doing here, anyway? Now all of Logan Meadows would think they were courting. Taking a bite of mashed potatoes that tasted like sawdust in her worried state, she chewed and swallowed, her mind a million miles away. If only there were some other more respectable men here in Logan Meadows. Someone who didn't make his living pouring whiskey and gambling, or have a reputation with a gun. A different suitor with whom Roberta could distract Tabitha's attention. Seemed all of a sudden, the girl had a mind to get married, and with her foolish behavior she might end up like Roberta's friend Janet—poor, penniless, or worse.

Violet shuffled up, a plate in her hands. "Is this spot taken?" she asked, sitting down next to her before Roberta could respond. The innkeeper wiggled a few times, making herself comfortable.

Perhaps Violet was so old, she didn't realize what harm she was doing to Tabitha's reputation. As much as she hated to do it, Roberta understood she'd have to enlighten Violet, or else her matchmaking actions might continue.

"Violet," she whispered, the room semiquiet with all the guests enjoying their meals. Hannah sat to Roberta's right, and Thom next to her, so she needed to keep her voice down. The Logans were across the room with the Huttons next to them. Maude, Nell, Julia, Frank, as well as others stood holding their plates. The children had found comfortable spots around on the floor, and any place there was an opening.

"Yes, Roberta?"

The old woman didn't look up, just kept preparing her plate before she dug in.

"Why on earth are you encouraging this relationship between my niece and Mr. Wade? They're totally unsuited. Nothing good can come of it. Tabitha will end up with a broken heart. He hasn't a thing to his name except half a saloon. He's been known to use those guns he always wears. You heard what Kendall said after he got word from Soda Springs. Mr. Wade will take advantage of her, and she'll be jilted. Once the gunslinger is through, no respectable man will look her way. Tabitha is too naive to know how these things go. I ask you to please stop meddling."

"Oh, fiddle-faddle," Violet whispered back. "First, that man is no more a killer than I am. You can bet yer sweet tootie on that." She broke open her biscuit and lathered on a healthy dollop of butter. "Second, you don't know a thing about the heart. If you did, you'd be able ta see those two are meant for each other—jist like potatoes and gravy, butter and bread, griddlecakes and maple syrup." She took a bite, chewed with great movement of her jowls, and swallowed.

"They are *not* meant for each other! She's so far above him, it's not funny. She's beautiful, refined, educated, and owns her own business."

"And comes from yer family—that's what's really up yer craw, Roberta. Go on and admit it. You don't want him because he ain't good enough. Jist like you didn't want Thom because he was Irish. You should be ashamed of yourself."

Roberta hoped her face wasn't as red as it felt. "I *forbid* you to encourage them any more than you already have. He's an old man, for goodness' sake!"

Hannah glanced over at their animated whispers, her brow crinkled. "Mother, is something wrong?"

She patted Hannah's knee. "No, dear. Just enjoying the evening." She stabbed a slice of beef with her fork, smiling into her daughter's face. Hannah would be fit to be tied if she discovered Roberta was still concerned about Tabitha's love life. "The food is marvelous. Everyone did such a good job." She put the forkful inside her mouth and chewed.

Hannah smiled and turned away. When Roberta turned back to Violet, the woman met her with a squinty-eyed stare. She'd been waiting.

"Mr. Wade is *yer* age, Roberta, iffin I'm recallin' correctly. And she's just about ten years younger. I'd say their union would be perfect. Unless you're saying someone yer age can't love no longer." Her brows arched, creating a forehead filled with wrinkles.

Roberta took a deep breath and counted to ten. She shouldn't have started this conversation at the party. To make her point, Violet might go and do something stupid. "Of course forty isn't too old to fall in love." *When put like that it does feel a little different.* "I'm just saying they come from two completely different backgrounds. They aren't suited."

Glancing forward, the picture of the two smiling into each other's eyes had Violet clucking. "Yeah, I see yer right," Violet whispered back, then had the gall to cackle like a hen after a handful of scratch. "Not suited a-tall."

"Everyone, Tabitha is going to open her gifts now," Hannah called. "Come in and watch." Dinner was finished and the dishes had been cleared away.

At that point, Hunter stood, and ambled for the kitchen. He couldn't sit next to the guest of honor a moment longer. As much as he smiled and nodded at the conversation sent his way, his nerves were stretched to the limit. Pretending he wasn't attracted to Tabitha wasn't easy. All the men kept nodding, and sending him raised eyebrows. He felt like a fool, and worse. Why couldn't people just mind their own darned business?

Grasping the pump handle, he worked it a few times over a sink filled with stacks of dishes and glassware. He filled a glass and downed the whole thing at once.

"I'll take one of those."

He turned to find Albert and Thom behind him. Without a reply, he repeated the process twice and handed each man a glass.

"Getting a little too hot in there for ya?" Thom asked.

What was that supposed to mean? "Just need to wash down my supper. I hope that's not a crime." They were being nice. He didn't need to make enemies.

"I'm agreeing with ya, Wade," Albert said. "I've never taken to being in the spotlight either. She's a lovely girl."

Don't dig your hole deeper tonight. Ignore them, and move on to something else. Problem was, he couldn't think of anything else to say. Neither man seemed to notice his discomfort.

"By the way," Albert went on, addressing him. "Sheriff in New Meringue sent me a telegram to say there's a bounty hunter hanging around the territory."

"Is bounty hunting against the law?" He still felt put out by Albert's teasing.

"No. But a lot of the men I've met think they're above the law. Just want to keep an eye out. Have you seen anyone suspicious in the bar? Or fishing for information? I like to keep abreast of newcomers and what they want."

Hunter let go of his anxious breath. Here was a conversation he could sink his teeth into. "As a matter of fact, I have. Nothing outright, just a feeling I had. In my travels, I've met all kinds, and this fella had a bad feel about him. Came into the saloon with that Hoskins fellow from New Meringue."

"When was that?" Albert asked, his smile gone.

"Couple days after I arrived. They talked quietly and had some coffee. I didn't like the way he was looking around, though. I made a point of taking a good look, in case I ran into him again."

Albert exchanged a glance with Thom.

Hunter shrugged. "In my former business, forgetting someone's face could get a man killed. I remember everyone I meet. The practice has always served me well."

Albert clapped him on his shoulder. "Well done, Wade. Let us know if he comes back in the saloon, or you see him somewhere else. Some bounty hunters are nothing more than killers. I don't like to think of one hanging around the area. And yet, if he's here, he must be looking for someone. I don't like not knowing."

A burst of laughter came from the front room. Tabitha was still surrounded by women.

"I think she's looking for you, Hunter," Thom said, jabbing him friendly-like in the ribs with his elbow. "Maybe you should get out there, help her celebrate her *twenty-ninth* birthday."

When the deputy stressed her age, Hunter couldn't remain silent a moment longer. If his mouth caused her a problem, so be it. "I don't know what the two of you are going on about, as well as the rest of Logan Meadows. Miss Canterbury and I are just friends. Nothing more." *Miss Hoity-Toity made sure I knew where I stood with her. And the slap still stings.*

Thom pulled back. "No? You sure about that?"

"I just said it, didn't I? All I'm concerned about is bringing more business into the Bright Nugget. I have some ideas in the works."

Both men looked interested.

"But you'll just have to wait with the rest of the town to find out what they are."

CHAPTER THIRTY-FIVE

After a wild Friday night in the saloon, Hunter ambled around the littered room of the Bright Nugget picking up glasses and empty bottles. Stopping before a table full of glassware, a bottle lying on its side, and an overflowing ashtray, he frowned. None too gently, he stacked them on the tray until there wasn't room for one more item, and started for the maple bar.

A flamboyant snore rattled from the back of the room.

Clyde!

He hadn't seen the drunk last night in the late hour and dimness of the room. The town sot was slumped over a tabletop, one arm stretched past his ear, and the other dangling by his side, his fingers almost touching the shavings. How he stayed atop the surface in that position was a mystery. His mouth, wide as a barn door, quivered as several snorts shot past his lips.

Hunter set the tray on the bar top, and then made his way toward the well-oiled man.

"Hey, wake up," he said, giving the man's shoulder a good shake. "It's morning, time to go home." *Past time to go home. Hours past time to go home.*

Cranky from the little sleep he'd gotten, Hunter mentally counted to ten. Because of his habit of waking just past four, he'd only slept a total of one hour. His eyes burned. Feeling a need to be outside, he'd gone for a long walk. The crisp, cold air had cleared out his head and lungs from all the smoke.

"Clyde, wake up! You can't stay here!"

For several moments, Hunter contemplated slinging him over his back and dumping him in the chair Kendall kept in the back alley for just that purpose. The frosty air would wake him fast enough. In the short time Hunter had been in Logan Meadows, Kendall had done it three times to the fella.

"Whass . . . ? Whass matter?" Clyde slurred, lifting his head for three whole seconds before letting it fall back to the table with a clunk. A groan slipped past the man's lips.

Darn drunk. Why did men have to get wasted? It didn't make any sense. The memory of Hunter's one and only hangover made moisture spring into his mouth. Feeling a mustard seed of compassion for the man, he strode to the woodstove and poured a cup of thick, black brew, then returned. "Here, drink some of this."

Clyde rolled his head back and forth. "Hunter, thass you, man? Why're ya screaming in my ear? Feels like ya got yer boot on my skull."

"I'm *not* screaming in your ear—just drink the coffee. You can't stay all morning."

"But I like it here . . ."

Thank heavens for the new shavings. The placed smelled a good sight better than it had when he'd first come to town. Leaving Clyde with his untouched cup of coffee, Hunter went behind the bar. One by one, he loaded the dirty glasses into a bucket of water.

With heavy lids, he ran a hand over his stubbled chin. After Miss Hoity-Toity's birthday party, the woman had kept a low profile, staying in her shop or somewhere else out of his sight. He'd not seen her out in the evening in front of her shop like he sometimes used to.

Kendall clomped down the stairs, pulling his suspenders up over his shoulders. At the bottom of the staircase, he rubbed his eyes and yawned. "What time is it?"

"Nine fifteen," Hunter replied after glancing at the clock behind the bar. Why the man couldn't just look for himself was beyond Hunter. "Time to rise and shine."

"If you say so. Anything on the stove for breakfast?"

Hunter had made coffee, but eating the day-old beans in the pot left from last night didn't sit well with his stomach. He planned on heading to the Silky Hen in a few minutes. "Just the beans from last night and a fresh pot of coffee."

Kendall grumbled something about ungratefulness, and ambled to the back of the room.

"Where's Philomena? Seen her yet this morning?"

Hunter shook his head. "Nope. Not a peep."

That was another thing that had begun to bother him. Before he'd come to know the woman, he hadn't had any trouble thinking about how she made her living. But now, after nine days in town, he was beginning to feel a bit protective over their one employee. As the days passed, he'd come to know the kind of joke that would make her laugh, or how her eyes lit up with curiosity, and something deeper that he didn't want to think about, while she stood at the door, watching the town from her protected spot. It made him feel sad. She had a pretty smile. Did she have hopes and dreams, like Tabitha said?

A light rapping sounded at the door. *Who knocks at a saloon?*

Hunter strode over and pulled open the inner door to the batwings hoping it wasn't Violet.

"Morning, Mr. Wade."

Hunter dropped his gaze. Nate Preston stood in the doorway. Glancing toward the sheriff's office, he spotted Albert watching from his office, a cup of coffee in his hand. He smiled all friendly-like and nodded toward his son.

"Mornin', Nate. What brings you out so early?" The boy had a freshly scrubbed face and his clothes were clean. His small boots were as shiny as a new penny.

"It's Saturday!"

Was it? Yes, that was true enough, but Hunter didn't know what that had to do with him. "And?"

"You told me to come to the bookshop on Saturday morning. To do chores for Miss Canterbury. You know, because I made Clementine mad, and almost killed ya?"

Hunter held back a chuckle.

"Did you forget? Pa thought it was a good idea if I checked in with you first to see if you had anything spa-spa-*cific* ya wanted me to do."

Clementine! The bookshop. *Miss Hoity-Toity.* How had he forgotten? "You're right," he said. "Saturday didn't waste any time getting here." *And now I'm going to have to search out Miss Hoity-Toity again. Oh, joy.* "It's darn good of you to remember."

The child just looked up at him expectantly. He wasn't going to be able to get out of this one.

"Are ya comin' along?"

Hunter reached back and untied the apron around his middle. "Sure I am. I wouldn't miss this for the world." He tossed the semiwhite apron onto the closest chair and reached for his hat. "I'm with you all the way."

CHAPTER THIRTY-SIX

At the sound of the whistling teakettle, Tabitha rose from her desk and hurried to the floral drapes that sectioned off her small kitchen area from the rest of the store, and swished between the split curtains. In a few minutes, she'd need to pull up the shades, turn the door sign, and lug out the billboard onto the boardwalk.

Hopefully today she'd have a customer or two. It all depended on whether the Union Pacific had a train scheduled to stop. And if said train brought with it anyone interested in books. One could only hope . . .

She'd not get discouraged. Rome wasn't built in a day, she reminded herself. She needed to be patient—as well as cheerful. By nature, she was a happy person. Even if she were lonely, going into debt, and had mixed feelings about Hunter, she'd keep a stiff upper lip. Her birthday party had made her realize just how blessed she was to have so many friends.

Yesterday she'd had three whole customers. One who wanted their own copy of *Great Expectations*, one who wanted a dime novel, and the last bought a large picture book for his wife's Christmas present. That purchase had been the most expensive, and she'd made a whole two dollars profit.

Tabitha drew the whistling teakettle to the side. She stirred the bubbling pot of mush, finding it not yet thick. Going to her eclectic teacup collection, she chose her favorite, a blue-and-white bone china teacup from England. She dropped in some loose tea she'd purchased the day Hunter had ridden into town, and set the cup aside.

Footsteps sounded outside, drawing her attention, but that was nothing new. People walked by all the time. When hushed voices stayed outside her front door, her curiosity grew. She glanced at her clock. Ten minutes until ten. Hoping whoever it was might be a customer, she crossed the room and pulled open the door.

Shock registered. Hunter stood there looking gruff and unshaven. Next to him was small Nate Preston, a wide smile splitting his face. "G-Good Saturday morning," she stammered, excited and wary at the same time. "May I help you?" The sight of Hunter's bloodshot eyes made her stomach clench. She'd never seen him so unkempt. A dark shadow of a beard darkened his square jaw. A dangerous spark glimmered in his eyes.

"Nate, in his quest to make up for spooking Clementine, has volunteered his services. Being a saloon isn't a fit place for a boy, I suggested he see what you needed doing. I had intended to tell you a few days ago, Wednesday to be exact, and forgot. Today's the day Albert has let him off."

He winked for her to play along.

"How did you spook Clementine?" she asked, glancing down at Nate. "I'd think that would be difficult to do."

"I shot her in the butt with my slingshot. Not on purpose," he hurried to say. "I was in the hayloft, and she just sorta got in my line of fire. Then she stampeded through the gate Uncle Win had partially opened."

The scene played over in Tabitha's mind. "I see."

"I already worked for Mrs. Hollyhock," he said. "Cleaning out her chicken coop." He wrinkled his nose and waved a hand in front of his face.

"Oh. Well, I won't have anything like that for you to do today. Nothing stinky, but I do have some things you could help with." She eyed Hunter who waited quietly through the conversation. "Mr. Wade, are you sure you don't have something Nate can do for you? In your apartment or caring for your animals?"

"Nope. My animals are out at the Axelrose ranch, and my place is so small it's easy to keep up with the chores. You're the perfect person for him to help."

"Oh, why's that?"

A muscle clenched in his jaw. And he looked grumpy.

"Being unmarried, you don't have a man to do for you. Thought you would appreciate some support."

All right. She'd deserved that, she supposed. After their arguments, and then the slap. And him being thrown into the party against his will. She was resilient, and could easily handle whatever he dished out—especially since his revenge was well merited.

"In that case . . ." Tabitha held the door wide and waved them both in. Did Hunter intend to stay and supervise? A flutter of excitement took her by surprise at the same moment a gust of wind sent a cold blast of air whistling into the shop and up her skirt. Her burst of laughter brought a wariness to Hunter's eyes. "Hurry in, before all my warm air escapes." She rubbed her hands up and down the sleeves of her dark-green dress, giddiness making her feel all of sixteen. "I have a kettle on for tea, if either of you'd like a cup."

Hunter and Nate both looked at each other and then back at her. They nodded.

"Wonderful. I knew there must be a reason I heated so much water." She placed a hand on Nate's shoulder. "First Nate, would you please roll up all my window blinds, since it's time to open? When that's finished, turn the sign on my door." She pointed behind him. "After that, please take my billboard out to the boardwalk and place it between my door and the creek. That way all my customers will know we're open. But be careful, it's heavy."

During her direction to Nate, Hunter had leaned a hip against her desk, an amused smile pulling his lips. Maybe he wasn't in such a bad mood after all. His gaze meandered the length of her in a slightly suggestive way, causing fire to rush to her face. At the realization of what he must be thinking to have such a devilish look in his eyes, the air charged with an unusual energy she'd never experienced before. She tried to pull her gaze away, but was powerless to do so. She liked it! *Him!* Her racing heart and carnal thoughts. What his silent expression was promising.

Amid his lack of decorum, she jerked her gaze away. She whisked behind her kitchen curtain and pressed her palms to her heart, willing herself to calm down. *I'm twenty-nine years old. A man with a sensual smile should not be able to send me scampering for cover.* When she reached for two additional cups and saucers, they rattled in her hands. "Mr. Wade, have you eaten your breakfast?" she called. "I know you get up early, but I have a pot of mush back here you're welcome to. You too, Nate."

She glanced at the small pot. She could quickly add more. Opening the door to the oven's fire compartment, she stirred the coals to life and added two more logs. "Mr. Wade," she called louder this time.

"That wouldn't feed a fly."

She straightened, surprised to find him in her kitchen sanctuary. She spun so quickly she lost her balance.

Hunter reached out and steadied her, his hand on hers producing a sizzle of tingles.

"Oh! I didn't hear you enter."

His fingers remained on hers.

"You were working the fire." He gazed around, slowly took his hand away. "You wouldn't happen to have any eggs and bacon around here, would you?"

Although he'd initially asked about the food, his gaze strayed to her lips.

He came a step closer.

She took a step back.

"A-Actually, no, but I can run down to the mercantile for the eggs and the butcher for some bacon. They'll both be open by now."

"I can go."

He stood so tall; it made her room shrink around them. "No, Mr. Wade, I want to do this for you." *To make up for the slap.* "I can be back in ten minutes. Can you keep an eye on the place until I return? No one will come in."

He nodded, his eyes hooded. She wished she knew what he was thinking.

"I'm done, Miss Canterbury," Nate said from the other side of the curtains. It was then Tabitha realized how improper it was for her to be alone in here with Hunter. She grasped one panel, tied it back with its sash, and then did the same with the other.

"My, you're a fast worker," she hastened to say, feeling fluttery and distracted. Carrying the empty teacups intended for Hunter and Nate, Tabitha hurried out and went to her desk. Setting the cups down, she reached for her feather duster and handed it to the boy. "Here you go, Mr. Preston. I'm running out for a few minutes. While I'm gone, I'd like you to go about dusting the bookshelves. Some books, the ones on the walls, you may need to take out and get behind. Can you do that for me?"

He nodded.

"Be careful. Treat them like good friends." Feeling totally conspicuous with Hunter watching her, she raced upstairs for her shawl. Descending, she wrapped the wool garment around her shoulders and tied the ends. "I'll be back shortly."

She couldn't stop a smile at Nate's large eyes. He looked as if he'd been left in charge of a candy store. She knew the place was in capable hands. At that thought, she snuck a peek at Hunter's large hands, his arms crossed in a nonchalant way over his wide chest. Yes, those were good hands if she'd ever seen any . . .

CHAPTER THIRTY-SEVEN

Tabitha hadn't been gone three minutes when the door opened and two women entered the bookstore. They stopped and looked around. Hunter groaned inwardly. *Why now?* One moment before their entry, his mind had been reliving the seconds in Tabitha's small corner kitchen when he'd actually been contemplating kissing her again. Really! He must need his brain examined!

She was like a sickness to him. He'd never run across a woman who'd so fully captured his attention.

The thought brought a swift punch of anger. She'd looked beautiful, soft, and innocent. His heart had thumped forcefully against his ribs and the sensibilities of his mind had fuzzed. She'd drawn him like a field of catnip did a tom.

The prettier of the two new arrivals smiled when she noticed Nate on his knees, dusting the bottom row of novels on the far side of the room. Looking like sisters, the older jerked back in surprise when she spotted Hunter lounging by the kitchen drape, watching. He supposed he did look rather disreputable.

"Good morning, ladies," he said in a polite voice. He ran a hand over the stubble on his face, surely the reason they were eyeing him dubiously. Or perhaps it was his red, gritty eyes, or his rumpled clothes still reeking of smoke. "May I help you find something?"

They turned to each other for a moment, then back to him. "Are you the proprietor?" the older slowly asked. "We'd heard this place was run by a woman—who was now holding public readings."

The wariness in her voice almost made him laugh. "That's true. Miss Canterbury had to step out, but only for a moment. She will return shortly."

Nate, still on his knees, had turned and was watching the women standing in the doorway.

"We came over from New Meringue to visit a sick friend and wanted to see the new shop. Thought we might find something to brighten her mood. Would you have something inexpensive like that?"

Something to brighten a sick woman's mood? Do they write books like that? If yes, I wouldn't know what. Still, Tabitha needs this sale. Surely I can come up with something to their liking.

"Well," he began glancing about. They wouldn't want a book from the renting section if they intended their purchase to be a gift. The large picture books would be much too expensive for a friendly memento. Panic began to register.

Hunter walked quickly to the place where he'd seen a few people looking at dime novels. "Over here are some Western stories, outlaws, and lynchings."

The older brushed off that suggestion as if she were swatting a pesky fly. "I was thinking more along the lines of poetry." When she turned to him, Hunter stopped the wild search of his gaze. "Sir, where would I find the verse and rhyme section?"

"Look at these, Dorothy!" the younger woman called to her companion. She'd wandered over to Tabitha's desk and was holding a bright-pink flowered teacup. One Tabitha had brought out of her kitchen before she'd left. The woman lifted the saucer and turned it over. "It's from England. Lucy would love this. You know she collects teacups."

Dorothy rushed over.

Nate stood, the feather duster forgotten in his hands.

"Oh, yes," Hunter said. "Miss Canterbury just got those in. The one you're holding is from, er, England, just like you said."

"But, Mr. Wade," Nate spoke up. "Those are—"

"Hush, Nate," Hunter said. "I'll be with you in a minute. These two ladies are looking for a gift, and I think they have a keen eye. I'd imagine there're only a few of those mugs, uh . . . cups, *teacups* in the territories. I believe they're quite rare."

The woman fairly shook with excitement. "Do you know how much she's asking? I don't see a price."

How would I know! He'd never bought a china cup before. He wanted to make a sale for Tabitha, but he wanted to be sure he asked enough. He'd seen a whole set in the mercantile; if only he'd looked to see the price, that might give him an idea.

"Sir? Do you know?"

Nate hurried to Hunter's side. "But—"

"Not now, Nate. You're interrupting." He pointed to the far wall. "Those books need dusting."

Dorothy's eyebrow peaked in a silent reprimand. "The boy is only trying to help."

"The teacup is two dollars."

Both women's eyes widened. "That's quite a lot."

Not appreciating Dorothy's admonishment about Nate, he crossed his arms over his chest to let her stew—set now on making this deal. "Miss Canterbury did mention she was having a sale next week. I'm sure she wouldn't mind me passing along a small discount since you've come all the way from New Meringue. That special gift to delight your friend will only cost you a dollar fifty. Seventy-five cents each." He gauged their reactions. "That's as low as I can go. Think about it. Every time Lucy takes a sip, she'll thank you all the more."

"I can afford that, Dorothy. What do you think?"

"That's still a lot of money, Etta. I don't know." Her lips pulled to the side as she gazed at the cup in Etta's hands. She reached out, took it, tested the feel. All the while Hunter hoped she'd say yes.

"All right. Let's do it. I just won't tell Edgar." She laughed and Etta joined in.

"Good choice!" Hunter took the cup and began wrapping it as he'd seen Tabitha do for the woman from the train. Finished with the cup, he wrapped the saucer. Dorothy and Etta beamed with happiness. They took the money from their reticules and placed it into his palms.

"Please tell Miss Canterbury we're sorry we missed her, but we'll be back again another time. And depending on our husbands being able to drive us over, we might even be able to make her reading this week. We've heard nothing but good things about this cute little store. I'm happy to see she's expanding her goods from just books."

"Good day, ladies," he said, walking them to the door. "I'll relay your words to her just as soon as she returns. Thank you for stopping in."

He stepped out behind them and waved when they turned back to give him one last look from the bridge, Tabitha's pink teacup well on its way to its new home. Would Miss Hoity-Toity be angry? Maybe that was a treasured item. Swiveling, he glanced toward the mercantile. Well, he only had one second before he'd find out.

CHAPTER THIRTY-EIGHT

Customers! Leaving Storybook Lodge with a paper-wrapped package. Hunter waving goodbye. Tabitha hurried forward, her purchases clutched in her hands. As she drew closer, Hunter waved at her, a look of unease crossing his face.

"Hunter . . . Mr. Wade," she corrected quickly. "Was that what I think it was? Did you make a sale while I was out?"

He blinked and rubbed a hand over his face. "Yes. But right now, I'm famished. Would you mind putting on the breakfast before we get into all that?"

Hurrying inside, she pressed her free hand to her racing heart. Mr. Seton, kind man that he was, had taken forever at the butcher's, cutting each slice of bacon with the speed of a sloth. Then at the mercantile, Maude shared a story about the do-gooder bringing the laundry off her line, all folded neatly, and set by her back door. She was filled with questions about who the Good Samaritan might, and might not, be. Tabitha had to practically sneak out when she turned her back. But that couldn't be helped. Hunter and Nate were waiting on breakfast.

"Yes, of course, I'll put on the bacon right now. It takes the longest." She gazed off longingly in the direction of the two women, wondering which book they had chosen. It was exciting to see people she didn't know patronizing her business.

In the kitchen, Tabitha set her purchases on the counter and reached for a heavy iron skillet, setting it on the stovetop. She smiled at the forlorn-looking pot of mush. In reality, she hadn't wanted that either. Thoughts of bacon made her mouth water. She put two strips each for herself and Nate into the warming skillet, and a generous five for Hunter. He looked hungry. She didn't want him leaving in want.

"How you doing out there, Nate?" she called out. "Still busy?"

"Yes'm," he called back.

"Good boy. I'll have breakfast whipped up in a jiffy. You hungry?"

"Yes'm."

She smiled. This was fun. She wondered what Hunter was doing. She didn't dare look out in case he was looking in at her. Did she have time to make a batch of biscuits as well? Bacon, eggs, and biscuits sounded like a real man's breakfast. She'd do it. Discreetly, as not to draw attention to herself, she untied the bows holding back her drapes and let them swing shut. She wanted the biscuits to be a surprise.

Scooping two generous cups of flour into her bowl, she quickly added water, a pinch of salt, a teaspoon of baking powder, a spoonful of lard, and stuck her hands in, mixing as fast as she could. With that done, she spooned heaping portions of the gooey dough onto her cookie sheet, and slipped them into the already hot oven. A gushy warm feeling took ahold of her heart. Hunter had his rough edges, but they were getting smoother the longer they knew each other, yes, they certainly were.

Reaching for the eggs, she carefully broke eight into a bowl, then added a splash of milk, and a pinch of salt and pepper. She whisked the mixture well, then poured it into the melted butter of the skillet heating on the stove. He could be maddening, for sure, but he had a way of making her think all sorts of fanciful things, like maybe marriage wasn't so far out of her wheelhouse after all.

Deciding to be formal, and use the tea infuser, she filled the device and went to her desk where she'd left the two teacups. Only the white with the gold rim was there. She glanced around. Had Nate moved the other?

Hunter ambled over.

"Almost ready. I'm just—"

"Looking for something?"

"Yes." She laughed. "It's strange. I'm sure I brought out two teacups, and now there's only one. Do you happen to know what happened to the other? It was a pink-and-white floral."

Nate appeared at Hunter's side and gazed up into his face. A few moments passed with nothing but the sound of the sizzling bacon for distraction.

"Either of you?"

"Yes'm."

The look of distress in Nate's eyes all but answered her question. Moved by his sad look, she squatted to his level. "Don't worry, Nate. I'm not mad that you broke my teacup." *It's just the only thing I have left of my grandmother. But it's only a cup. And you're a child. Your feelings are much more important.*

"No, ma'am, I didn't—"

A frown furrowed Hunter's brow. "What Nate's trying to say is he didn't break your cup."

Completely confused now, Tabitha stood and took another quick look around. "No? It's not broken? What happened to it then? Where'd it go?"

Nate pointed to the street. "Out the door with them two ladies."

What? "I'm sorry. I don't understand."

"I sold the cup to Dorothy and Etta. The two women you noticed leaving when you arrived. They were looking for a get-well gift for somebody here in Logan Meadows named Lucy, and it was the only thing I could think of. Actually, Etta discovered it on your desk and just assumed it was for sale. I went along because I thought you could use the business."

He sold my gramma's heirloom teacup? To strangers?

The whole situation was so strange she burst into laughter. Soon Hunter was laughing and so was Nate. On impulse, she touched his arm, and let her hand linger, gazing into his eyes.

"How in the world did you come up with a price? I'm trying my best to figure this out and every time I see you giving a sales pitch on a cup, my mind breaks into giggles. You have to admit, it's pretty funny."

"So, you're not mad?" Nate asked. "I tried to stop him, but he wouldn't listen."

Hunter shrugged guiltily. "I got a dollar fifty. I hope that's enough."

That was a lot for a single cup and saucer. More than she'd have made in profit on most of her popular books. "You did well."

Hunter stuck his nose in the air.

The bacon! And biscuits!

One cup short, but with a happy heart, Tabitha dashed into the kitchen enjoying this day immensely. She wasn't going to mess that up by getting angry over a teacup. Nothing could spoil her mood today.

CHAPTER THIRTY-NINE

A rush of attraction jerked Hunter straighter when Tabitha came through her kitchen drapes, a heaping plate of vittles in each hand. Her flushed face looked more beautiful than ever before, proud of the breakfast she'd prepared. She seemed almost joyous today, and he wondered the reason. The feel of those soft lips were never far from his mind.

Their gazes met, held. His face warmed as a line he was becoming quite familiar with began just above the collar of her dress, and crept up her face. Desire and longing rose up within him. *Miss Hoity-Toity,* he reminded himself, *isn't interested in more than friendship*—or at least that was what he'd thought. Now he wasn't so sure. He took the plate she offered with a smile. He best keep this business. He was here to make sure Nate fulfilled his obligation, nothing more. The boy had been a good little worker so far, keeping to himself and completing each job efficiently.

"Please, sit here, Mr. Wade," she said, pulling out the chair at her desk. She quickly cleared away her pen and paper and a few other things to make room for his plate, leaving down a pad of paper he could use as a mat.

She must take her food upstairs, because there wasn't room for a table between her bookshelves. She must be used to eating alone. "Thank you kindly."

"Nate, you come over here on this stool. Can you balance your plate in your lap?"

"Yes'm. This sure looks good. Thanks." He took the plate as soon as he'd climbed up. The way he was gazing at his bacon almost made Hunter laugh.

"You're welcome. After you eat, you can help me clean up the kitchen and then you're free to go. I can't thank you enough for all the help."

"You sure?" Nate asked. "I like working here. It's better than the livery where I have to clean stalls."

This time Hunter couldn't stop a bark of laughter, which drew a smile from Tabitha and Nate. As a boy, Hunter had cared for the animals. He'd been stepped on, bitten, and even kicked a few times. Although he'd never had to clean stalls, he could commiserate with Nate.

Hunter finished one strip of crispy, almost-black bacon and reached for one of the two fluffy, generously-given golden-brown biscuits. "This is mighty good, Miss Canterbury," he said. "I was heading to the Silky Hen before Nate stopped by to remind me what day it was. I'm glad I got to taste your cooking. For some reason, I never pictured you as a cook." He shrugged, scooping in a mouthful of eggs. "You know, because of all the books and all. Just thought . . ."

Albert stepped into the shop with a curious smile on his face. He approached Nate and stole a strip of bacon off his plate. Chewing, he said, "I thought you were here to work, son." He winked at Hunter and Tabitha. "You've been gone a good hour. What have you accomplished?"

Nate's spine snapped as stiff as a rod. "First, Pa, I came in and put up all Miss Canterbury's shades. Then I turned her sign and put out the other big one on the boardwalk." He swiveled and pointed out the window, as if waiting for his pa to say something.

"That's all fine and good, but couldn't have taken you more than five minutes."

When Nate held up a hand, signaling he wasn't yet finished with his explanation, Hunter almost choked on his laughter.

"I dusted this whole shop, Pa! All the books. Look how many there are. Then, when Miss Canterbury went out, me and Mr. Wade sold one of her teacups."

"Teacups? Did I hear that correctly?"

"I'm afraid so, Albert," Tabitha said, amusement still clearly in her eyes. "Two ladies came in and when Hunter—*and Nate*—couldn't find a book the women wanted to buy, Hunter sold them a teacup right off my desk."

"I hope it was clean," Albert chortled, and then slapped his leg. "That's a good one. I'll have to remember that next time I can't mollify one of my outlaws. If they don't want to be locked up, I'll invite 'em out to supper. Sounds like a good plan."

"One of the women took a fancy to it," Hunter explained. "What was I supposed to do then? Tell her no? She got the impression Miss Canterbury was branching out into other items besides books, and was excited she might be starting a gift shop. I just played along. I didn't think she'd mind too much," he finished, looking directly at Tabitha. She hadn't really said one way or the other. "They were speaking about attending your reading next week as well."

"That's wonderful! And I've never considered branching out into other areas. But I guess I could if I wanted."

The Union Pacific gave a toot on its horn.

Hunter looked toward the window. "Here comes the train. I wonder if anybody will be getting off?"

"That's anyone's guess," Albert replied, ruffling Nate's hair. The boy hardly seemed to notice as he shoveled in his scrambled eggs.

Tabitha was only picking at the food on her plate. "I have a good view of the depot from my second floor," she said. "I can see people coming and going. When I'm not busy, and hear the whistle, I go up and take a look."

Nate's face brightened. "Can I?"

Albert shook his head. "Miss Canterbury doesn't want you upstairs, Nate. That's private. You stay put."

Tabitha waved away his statement. "I don't mind, Albert. It might be fun. It's all right with me if it's all right with you. Let him go up and see."

Albert took the plate from Nate's lap and the boy hopped down. He was up the stairs in a blink of an eye.

A happy smile stretched all the way across Tabitha's face. "Keep going through the room to the far window."

"The train's just sittin' there on the tracks. Not much happenin'. Wait. Looks like Mr. Hatfield is starting this way with his buckboard."

Albert nodded. "For a fee, he'll transport anyone who'll pay the quarter mile to town. Sometimes ladies have too much to carry," he said to Hunter.

"There's a lady sitting next to him."

That got everybody's attention.

Albert moved to the window.

Tabby went to the door, her attention on the bridge, and Hunter flanked her shoulder just as curious as to who might be arriving.

"She's got a parasol over her head," Nate called. "It's white and lacy."

Could it be? He'd not gotten any return telegrams from Dichelle, but then she always was one for surprises.

"Lots of trunks in the wagon, too. Whooeee, they're piled high. The wagon's almost to this side of the festival grounds."

Albert stepped outside and they all filed out behind.

Hunter blinked in astonishment, wondering if he was seeing things.

CHAPTER FORTY

"Hunter!"

Tabitha, who the moment before had been warm and fuzzy from the sensation of Hunter standing so close to her back, jerked her gaze away from the gorgeous young beauty sitting next to Mr. Hatfield to stare openmouthed at Hunter. He'd gone and done it. Sent away for more . . .

Nate bolted out the door, and skidded to a halt beside her. "Jumpin' Jehoshaphat," he exclaimed loudly. "Who's that!"

"Whoa there, Blacky," the depot master called to his mule, who plodded along, his head down and eyes shrouded by blinkers.

Just then, the Union Pacific tooted its horn and began chugging away, the sound a death knell to Tabitha. Its important cargo sat in the wagon before her, looking like she should be on a fashion runway in New York. Hunter knew this girl? This *young, beautiful* girl? Had sent for her? She'd thought they were making headway. That he was coming to see her reasoning. Their discussion had only been a handful of days ago. He'd said things hadn't been decided. He'd lied. Tabitha swallowed down her hurt, but the emotion clawed its way back up her throat as anger.

"Ciao, amore!" the beauty called from the wagon, all but standing with excitement, before the buckboard had stopped completely. "I

packed my things the moment I received your telegram and boarded the first train I could." She glanced up the street, a wide smile displaying her perfect white teeth, all the while twirling her parasol above her head. Her tiny waist was no larger than Tabitha's two hands touching finger to finger. Oh, that was an exaggeration of course, but if Tabitha didn't make a joke, she just might burst into tears—or kill Hunter. Neither option viable at the moment.

Hunter hurried to the wagon's side, took ahold of that impossibly small waist, and whisked her down with no effort at all. "Dichelle! You should have let me know of your arrival so I could meet your train." He took her arm and brought her over to the boardwalk, having the decency to look embarrassed.

"Everyone, I'd like to introduce an old friend of mine, Miss Dichelle Bastianelli. Dichelle, this is Miss Canterbury, the proprietor of this bookstore, that's Sheriff Albert Preston, and his son, Nate."

Old friend? Ha! The girl couldn't be more than eighteen years old. Tabitha found herself nodding and smiling, although she felt completely betrayed. What had all those sultry looks been about this morning? And the lingering touch of his fingers? She was such a fool! Just like Aunt Roberta said.

"Pleased to make your acquaintance, Miss Bastianelli," Albert said first, sounding out her last name slowly. He doffed his hat. "What kind of an accent do I hear?"

She gave a small smile. "Italian."

Trying to look normal, Tabitha felt her chin dip, and was acutely aware of her eyelids blinking. She must look a fool. "Welcome to Logan Meadows, Miss Bastianelli." There. She'd gotten the words out. From the corner of her eye, she noticed Kendall rushing over from the saloon.

Albert nudged Nate.

"Hello, m-ma'am," he sputtered.

"Oh," she exclaimed. "*Bel ragazzo*—he is so darling." Her kid leather–gloved hand fluttered to her breast, and then she fanned it in front of her face. *"Penso di essere innamorata!"*

Tabitha had to look away. Nate's adoration was enough to make her cry. She wasn't sure what she'd said, but was almost certain it had something to do with love—and hypnotizing the male species. Her accent wrapped around the men like warm chocolate.

Kendall arrived with a red, excited face. "Is this her, Hunter?"

"Uh huh." Hunter kept his gaze away from Tabitha.

An approving whistle emanated from the bartender. "You weren't kiddin', were ya?" He was about to go on, but Hunter clapped a large hand on his partner's shoulder.

"Meet Miss Bastianelli, Kendall. Dichelle, this is my partner in the Bright Nugget, Kendall Martin."

"She's the goose that'll lay us the golden eggs," Kendall chortled. "Just like you said."

"Oh?" Miss Bastianelli lifted a softly penciled eyebrow at Hunter. "Is that right?"

Hunter shot Kendall a dirty look and the man clamped his mouth shut.

"Maybe. A few anyway. Best not to get ahead of ourselves, though. She's come to help us revive the Bright Nugget. You can't fault a man for wanting to do that."

Mr. Hatfield loudly cleared his throat. "If we're all finished, I'd like to get her trunks delivered and get back to the depot."

"Of course. You can leave her things here and Kendall and I will take them to the saloon."

Miss Bastianelli put out a questioning hand. "What is this, Hunter? You expect me to room in the saloon?"

Tabitha wanted to laugh when the smile fell off Hunter's face. "Well, yes. I've spent all week fixing a room just for you. Right next to Philomena's."

"And mine," Kendall added.

"Oh, *no, no*, that will not do. You must book me a room in the hotel. Your finest." She looked over her shoulder and down the street. "Is there one nearby?"

"Right down the street," Mr. Hatfield pointed to the El Dorado. They'll have a room for you, Miss Bastianelli. If you'd like, I'll take your things there straightaway."

The woman looked to Hunter.

"Go on, Mr. Hatfield. Take her things to the El Dorado. I'll walk her down after she sees the Bright Nugget."

A crowd of onlookers had gathered on the other side of the street. Tabitha took a small step back, thinking how much she was going to enjoy slipping into her shop and closing the door. If she could sneak away unnoticed, she'd do it this very second. As it was, Mr. Hatfield had climbed back onto his buckboard and shook the reins over Blacky's back. The wagon lurched forward, and then rolled away.

"Let's go, Nate," Albert said. He took a step and then stopped. "That is if you're all finished with him, Miss Canterbury."

Thank heavens! Something sane to speak about. "Yes I am, Albert. He did a fine job." She looked down at the boy. "Thank you, Nate. I appreciate all your hard work."

"Isn't he supposed to help you clean up your kitchen?" Hunter asked, his gaze trying to catch hers. His warm voice tried to stir her heart, but she wouldn't let it. "By now, those skillets will be tough to scour. Let him help you."

She lifted her eyes to his, praying her hurt wouldn't show. "That's not necessary, Mr. Wade. Nate's done enough for the day, and paid his debt to you."

With a firm nod, Hunter's gaze left hers, and he laid his hand on the small of Miss Bastianelli's perfectly straight back. "Ready?"

"*Sì*. I wish to have a nice, hot meal with you, Hunter." She smiled warmly into his face. "Catch up on old times."

The bittersweet memory of the morning that had brought Tabitha so much joy only a few minutes ago made her sick. At this moment she thought she might never feel happy again. Taking a tiny step back, she watched as Albert and Nate started for the sheriff's office. Mr. Hatfield was already alongside the El Dorado, and he was letting down the wagon's tailgate. None of that mattered, though, not like the sight of Hunter and Kendall holding the saloon door open for Miss Bastianelli. Would he glance back? See if she were still standing where he'd left her?

Don't wait to find out. Be gone if he does.

Listening to her inner voice, Tabitha squared her shoulders and stepped inside Storybook Lodge, resigned to the fact that she was a businesswoman. A *happy* businesswoman. The scent of bacon still lingered in the air. Going to the kitchen, she grasped her pump handle, working it until water gushed into the sink.

Hunter Wade had hurt her for the last time. He was what her aunt had proclaimed. A saloon owner with no scruples at best, and a killer at worst. No, she corrected herself, a *lying* saloon owner with no scruples at best. She'd not forget that anytime soon.

CHAPTER FORTY-ONE

With shaky hands, Mrs. Hollyhock pulled the amber embroidery floss through the white linen in her needlepoint loop, then fingered the basket-weave stitch. Dissatisfied with her work, she silently harrumphed. Getting old wasn't easy. Beside her, the fire popped, and the front door to the Red Rooster opened.

Marlene stepped inside. The woman, who'd been at the laundry house since early morning, gave her an uninterested look, then continued on into the kitchen.

Violet set her work aside and pushed herself out of the chair. Going to the kitchen, she halted to see what Marlene was doing.

"Yer home early." She glanced at the clock on the wall. "Ain't even noon yet."

"The Lings told me to take a break for an hour, get something to eat."

All Marlene had on her plate were two slices of bread and a glob of butter. "That's not much. Let me scramble ya a couple of eggs." She noticed Marlene's reddened hands. Not used to washing every day in the soap, they'd taken a beating and looked like they hurt more than she was letting on.

Before Marlene had a chance to answer about the eggs, Violet shuffled down her hall and came back with a jar of cream she'd made from beeswax, almond milk, and honey. She set the half-full jar beside Marlene's plate. "Go on and rub some on."

Marlene looked up at Violet from where she sat, slowly chewing. "What's all this about? You don't have to pretend you care."

"I ain't pretending nothin'! Just do as I say." She shuffled to the back door and went onto the porch for her basket of eggs. She took up three and went inside, shivering from the chilly fall air.

Taking out a mixing bowl, Violet carefully cracked all three eggs and whipped them. Pulling out a skillet, she scooped in a large spoonful of butter and then stoked the stove. It wasn't but a moment before the melting butter had spread across the pan. She poured in the eggs and salted and peppered. "These'll be done in a minute more."

"I never said I wanted any."

"I say you do. So shush up."

Marlene harrumphed.

A knock on the door preceded the sound of it opening. Violet turned from her cooking to see who had arrived.

"Violet?" Jessie called. "You home? I see a nice cozy fire burning."

"Come in, darlin' girl! I was jist thinkin' about you." She hurried to the door and enveloped Jessie in a hug. "What brings ya by?"

"I wanted to say hello. I've been feeling pretty low since Jake left and—" Seeing Jake's mother, she snapped her mouth closed. Who could forget the awful way the woman had treated him in Valley Springs when he was just a boy? Her drunken rages and foul mouth.

"Hello, Marlene," Jessie said, dipping her head.

Jake's mother seemed to pull back in her chair as if she'd like to disappear. "Mrs. Logan," she replied softly.

"I'm interrupting. I'll come back another time."

Violet caught Jessie's arm as her friend tried to retreat. "Oh, pooh, yer doin' nothin' of the sort. Hungry? I'm scramblin'. No trouble a-tall to add a couple more."

"Oh, no, I've eaten. I can't stay but a minute." She crossed her arms over her chest. "Gabe and Sarah are watching Shane for me so I can run a few errands. Do you need anything at the mercantile?" Her gaze kept straying to Marlene sitting at the table with her plate of bread.

Violet went to the stove, scraped the cooked eggs onto another plate, took it to the woman, and set it alongside the other dish.

"Nothin', dearie. I'm just sittin' by the fire workin' on some Christmas presents. But there is something I've made up fer you." She waved Jessie past Marlene, who was very good at ignoring everything that went on around her, to the back of the kitchen. She opened a cupboard and took out her lacquered wooden box of herbal remedies. Opening the lid, she reached for a small sack made of red cloth tied up with a string, and handed it to Jessie.

Jessie's brows drew down. "What's this?" she asked softly.

"Jist make yerself a nice cup of brew each night. It don't have ta be strong, just get into a habit that it's the last thing you take before crawlin' under the covers with that man of yours."

Jessie's eyes went wide. "Mrs. Hollyhock! What're you talking about?"

"You know very well what I'm talkin' about. You've been a wife fer a while now. Don't tell me ya don't know about the birds and the bees, cause Shane would prove ya wrong."

With one hand on her hip, Jessie glanced behind, and lowered her voice even more before whispering, "I'm not sick. What is this? What's it for?"

Violet searched her friend's face, hoping Jessie wouldn't be angry for her butting in. "Jist a mixture of yarrow, parsley, red clover, and dandelion."

Jessie's eyes narrowed. "I'm not drinking anything until I know what it's for."

"I'm thinkin' Shane's gettin' pretty old now. Almost four." She glanced down at Jessie's trim midsection and wiggled her eyebrows. "This'll speed things up."

Jessie's lips wobbled.

"See, I knowed ya been thinkin' about it, too." She picked up Jessie's hand and held it between her own. "That's why I'm still here. You ain't got nothin' ta worry over. Jist do as I say and all will be well."

CHAPTER FORTY-TWO

Three hours after Dichelle's arrival, Hunter exited the saloon and headed to the Feed and Seed for more lumber. Dichelle had nearly swooned when she'd seen there wasn't a performance stage anywhere in the Bright Nugget. She'd insisted there was no way she could perform in a room full of men standing by the piano. Someone of her stature must be lifted above, where pawing hands couldn't touch. Kendall wasn't happy about the mounting costs of the songbird, between a hotel room and a small stage at the end of the bar accessible by way of the staircase. Hunter hoped his idea to bring Dichelle here wouldn't prove to be a bad one.

Charging several two-by-fours to the saloon's account, Hunter carried the boards on his shoulder past Storybook Lodge, keeping his gaze trained straight ahead. Tabitha's hurt expression haunted him. He'd felt something warm brewing last Saturday when they'd sat with Mrs. Hollyhock in the Silky Hen. They'd weathered two arguments, a kiss, a face slap, and then this morning, something more had changed. He'd seen it in her eyes, too. And then Dichelle had arrived. Seriously! It boiled his blood when he recalled Tabitha's accusatory look. Did she really think so little of him? Could she actually believe he'd be involved with a woman young enough to be his daughter?

Almost past the sheriff's office, Albert and Susanna stepped out. He stopped and wiped his moist brow.

"More carpentry work, Wade?" Albert asked. "Thought you were finished with the upstairs room."

If he could believe his eyes, Susanna Preston was not happy to see him. The half-friendly smile on her lips didn't reach her eyes. Surely, Nate and Albert had filled her in on Logan Meadows's newest arrival. "I finished that room several days ago. And if I do say so myself, it turned out pretty nice." *But not nice enough for Dichelle.* "This is for a small performance stage."

Albert whistled. "A performance stage, you say? You sure are making some big changes. Between your Italian and Miss Canterbury doing a reading each week, I feel like we're living in a metropolis. Keep up the good work."

"Metropolis?"

"A large city," Susanna explained, a tone of censure to her voice. That was all right, the women would adjust. For business's sake, he hoped they would. The clerk at the El Dorado had been only too happy to check Dichelle in for an extended period of time. But fifty cents a day would add up fast.

Albert and Susanna were about to move on when Hunter remembered something. "Albert, I saw that fella I told you about that had been in the saloon with Dwight a while back. The one you asked me to keep an eye out for."

Albert stopped, his face going serious. "When?"

"Last night. I stepped out of the saloon for some fresh air and to stretch my legs. He was standing in front of the telegraph office. When he saw me, he left at once as if he were up to no good."

"Dwight with him?"

Hunter shook his head.

"Who, Albert?" Susanna asked.

"A stranger. Heard tell he may be a bounty hunter. I don't like bounty hunters in *my* town. Most of 'em are ruthless. Shoot first and ask questions later. I won't have that here in Logan Meadows."

Hunter couldn't help but notice how the color drained from Mrs. Preston's face. Her gaze darted across the street and all the way down to Ling's Laundry. It was almost as if she knew something they didn't.

"Mrs. Preston?" Hunter asked. "Is something bothering you?"

Albert turned to his wife in question. He wasn't in on it. Now Hunter's curiosity was really piqued.

"Susanna?" Albert asked. "Is there something you aren't telling me?"

Her gaze went back and forth between him and Albert.

"Yes. I was sworn to secrecy, but in light of this news, I feel compelled to speak."

Albert's eyebrow peaked. "Go on."

She paused, letting her gaze rest on Hunter.

"I best get back to my work." Hunter hefted the boards onto his shoulder, being careful not to hit anyone.

"Stay," Albert said. "You were good enough to keep an eye out, and then to let me know what you'd seen. I trust you." He looked at his wife.

"I trust you as well," Susanna said. "But if this has nothing to do with what the two of you think, you must promise to keep it to yourself. Never to speak of it. The fewer people who know of this law, the better."

Albert looked puzzled. "Law?"

"Bao told me about it a few months ago, right after the train crash at Three Pines Turn. Any Chinese coming into the country after 1880, by law can be deported. Tap Ling came here a couple years before he sent for Bao and Lan. And now Bao is going to have another baby. She's frightened that, because of the animosity growing in Rock Springs, someone will find out about her. Could someone be paying the bounty hunter to find Chinese to deport?"

"Susanna, I'd appreciate if you left the sheriffin' to me, darlin'. I had no idea the Lings were worried. I need to be aware, to be able to keep people safe."

"I heard about that from Miss Canterbury. More people know about it than just the Lings. That's something to keep in mind."

"I can't believe how cruel men can be," Susanna said.

Albert clenched a fist. "Money talks. Someone you might never suspect might be tempted. You'd be surprised."

Kendall stepped out of the Bright Nugget, a broom in hand, and began sweeping the front boardwalk. When he saw Hunter, he called, "You gonna stand there all day, Wade? That performance stage ain't going to build itself. Only have a few hours before the Saturday crowd rides in."

"Kendall's right. I need to get to work." With no more distractions, his thoughts drifted back to Tabitha, and he wondered if perhaps Miss Hoity-Toity was watching them out her window. She was one aggravating woman, all right. One he'd let get under his skin. Best not to think about her at all, now that Dichelle had arrived. He had enough on his plate as it was.

CHAPTER FORTY-THREE

With the conclusion of Sunday service, Tabitha gathered her reticule off the pew and followed Aunt Roberta, as well as Hannah and Thom, out into the sunshine. Circles formed, men in one group and woman nearby, as residents living farther out of town were hungry for interactions with their neighbors. The circles fairly buzzed with chatter. Reverend Wilbrand's sermon on the evils of alcohol indulgence seemed apropos for all the attention the Bright Nugget had gotten over the past few days.

Hunter hadn't shown up. She told herself she was glad, but she was having a difficult time convincing her heart. Even after how he'd hidden the fact that he'd already made the decision about bringing more saloon girls into town when they had their heated discussion, but led her to believe otherwise.

The congregation had been shocked when Miss Bastianelli had come in quietly, a few moments after the service had started, and sat in the last pew by the door, then exited a few minutes before its conclusion. She was already down the hill and out of sight by the time the worshippers had emptied the church and began their social hour.

"I'm surprised she had the nerve to enter a house of worship," Maude said, her plentiful wrinkles coming alive with her surprise. "First time I known of a soiled dove coming to church or staying in a hotel."

Tabitha felt compelled to respond, having put up such a case to Hunter about Daisy and Philomena. "She's a child of God, too, Maude. She has nowhere else to worship. If Reverend Wilbrand doesn't mind, neither should we."

"If you say so," the mercantile owner mumbled, raising her brows.

"I agree with Tabitha," Jessie added. "Who am I to judge others? My beginning was somewhat colored."

Hannah nodded, gazing around the group. "I feel the same."

"You're all being very charitable," Roberta said, brushing a hand down the front of her skirt. "But don't forget, the element of Logan Meadows is changing. One person at a time. That's how it begins. Next week someone will open another saloon, and then a gambling hall the next. Shall we keep an open mind to that too? Then the train will arrive with a carload of fallen women to fill the rooms and help keep your men happy." Roberta flicked a quick look at Tabitha, and then went on. "What if Chase and Thom decided they needed a little time out this weekend? Will you kiss their cheeks and send them off to the saloon now?"

Dichelle walked quickly, keeping her eyes trained forward and her hands securely inside her fox-fur muff. Sitting in the last pew of the small country church had reminded her of home, her parents, and the life she'd left behind five years ago. As she descended the slight incline, she passed the quiet school, then headed straight for the saloon where she'd heard the sounds of construction going on earlier this morning on her way to the service. She wouldn't think of home today. This was a new town. A new chance. Perhaps here someone of importance would hear her sing, and offer her a way to get to New York, and the stages of the plays she dreamed of acting in.

Arriving at the boardwalk between a doctor's office and a small bakery, she crossed the deserted road. Seemed everyone was at the church. Without a hint of shyness, she opened the saloon door and stepped inside. Scents of coffee, wood shavings, and smoke enveloped her. She spotted Hunter working on the newly constructed stage.

"*Ciao*," she called out cheerfully. Back in Soda Springs she'd heard the stories around town of how Hunter had become part owner of the Bright Nugget. She hadn't thought anything could make the trail boss settle down. For as long as they'd been friends, he'd regaled her with stories of the wide-open spaces he loved so much. The dim interior she gazed at now was a far cry from that.

Hunter rolled back from his hands and knees and stood, brushing off the shavings that clung to his legs and hands. "Morning, Dichelle. How's the room at the El Dorado? Does it suit you?"

A small jab of guilt pricked her mind. She'd felt bad about insisting on that—a nice large room in the best hotel, especially making the request of Hunter, but it couldn't be helped. If she began staying in boardinghouses and saloons, her reputation as a performer would be tarnished. She had to act the part. With her head high, she continued over to her old friend.

"The accommodations are very nice, thank you." She glanced around, never fully comfortable standing in a saloon. "I can't stay long. I just wanted to see the progress you've made." She put her hand on one of the new posts and tested its strength. Unable to move it even the smallest amount, she smiled at the tall man watching at her side. "It's very strong, *amico mio*."

A niggle of loneliness pulled at her. Later, to dispel her melancholy and pass the long hours in her hotel room, she'd unpack her painting easel, canvas, and paints from her trunks and begin a new project. Something Western that depicted this town. That always lifted her spirits.

The back door opened. The man who'd been introduced to her as Kendall Martin came through carrying a garbage can. When he saw her, his face lit with pleasure. "Why, Miss Bastianelli, what brings you by the Bright Nugget this fine Sunday morning?" His red eyes and slow step attested to the late night he'd had.

"I wanted to see Hunter's progress on the performance stage," she said, nodding at the eight-foot-square landing. They wouldn't be booking in any large acts. "When will it be finished?"

"It's almost finished now," Hunter said, assessing his work.

"When will I first perform?"

The two men looked at each other.

A devious smile pulled the older bartender's lips. "I say we unveil our secret weapon on Tuesday evening! During the spinster's reading. That's coming up, you know."

Hunter scowled. "I thought you liked Miss Canterbury."

That brought Kendall up short. "Whaddaya mean?" he stammered. "'Course I like her! When she's not being bossy."

"I've never seen her bossing you about the saloon."

Kendall hurried away and rounded the end of the bar, coming up along the backside. "You ain't been to any town meetings."

Hunter took a deep, calming breath. "Kendall, we're not competing with Tabitha. Period. Not now, not ever. She can have her Tuesday nights, and we'll plan on having our first big show nine o'clock Saturday night. Make a big splash when the bar is full." Hunter paused and stroked his chin.

"What if none of the women let their men out? We'll only get the bachelors."

"I had a few censoring glances from the women in church," Dichelle said. "Kendall may be right."

Hunter just stood there tapping his boot on the floor. "On second thought, why don't we have a preopening show, the day before, on Friday afternoon?"

"Friday afternoon?"

"Yes. Mrs. Preston seemed none too pleased with me yesterday. I don't want to set every female in Logan Meadows against us from the start. We'll have a women-only show."

"The women!" Kendall barked, his face squished up like a prune. "They wouldn't be caught dead in here."

"I'm not so sure. If they're curious about Dichelle now, wait until they find out she's really a famous singer. They'll want to see her clothing and culture. If the women partake—even just a few—how can they forbid their men from coming? At least it's a start. We're into Dichelle for quite a few dollars." He gave her an apologetic smile. "With the women happy, I'll bet we'll sell a lot more tickets and pour more whiskey for the men." Grinning, he plopped his hands on his hips in satisfaction and looked around. "We'll call it Ladies' Day Out." He looked to the door and then back at Dichelle with a big smile. "Miss Canterbury isn't the only one who can start a new trend in town. We'll need to get a few posters up. And a few in New Meringue and Rock Springs as well."

"We're going to charge for the show?"

"Of course we're going to charge for such fine entertainment as Miss Bastianelli! But only the men. A dollar a ticket."

Hunter's devilishly handsome smile made Dichelle laugh. He was such fun to be around. She'd had a crush on him since they'd met three years ago. She'd missed him when he took the job to go east. He insisted they were only friends, and treated her like a daughter. That still didn't keep her from wishing.

"The women's show will be complimentary, and we'll pour coffee and tea."

Kendall made another face. "And serve petits fours?" He held up his fingers as if putting a small something into his mouth.

"Cookies," Hunter countered. "It'll work, you'll see."

"Don't seem fair that we let the women in for free. The men are paying a whole dollar."

"We want them to come, don't we? If we charge, we'll only get a couple. What's a few pots of coffee to us when the bar is normally quiet? Trust me. This will work."

A sly smile began on Kendall's face as his gaze meandered up to the ceiling. "I think you're on to something, Partner," he said, scratching his whiskered cheek.

"Of course I am, *Partner.*" Hunter laughed, and then winked at Dichelle. "I'm glad you're finally starting to realize that."

"This is all good and fine," she said. "Do you have a competent piano player? One that will practice with me at least a couple of days."

"Of course," Hunter said. "Leave that all up to me."

If the piano player was anything like the saloon, Dichelle had her doubts. Perhaps it had been a mistake to make Ned mad by leaving Soda Springs. The midsized town wasn't so bad, after all. At least the crowd she'd been attracting filled the room. Here in Logan Meadows, she didn't know what to expect. As much as she wanted to trust Hunter, she knew he was working on hope and prayers. But hope and prayers wouldn't get her to New York.

CHAPTER FORTY-FOUR

"Tabitha, have you seen this?" Susanna pushed through the bookstore door late Monday afternoon, her face alight with excitement. She held up a paper. "The owners of the Bright Nugget are inviting *the women* of Logan Meadows to a showing of Miss Bastianelli—"

Without waiting for Susanna to finish, Tabitha slipped the announcement from her friend's fingers, her insides quaking. "You mean Mr. Wade and Mr. Martin," she said just for something to say as she scanned the notice. Hunter would steal her audience away from her Tuesday evening reading with his fancy Italian saloon girl! Her heart felt like a scorched desert as she tried to find the date on the quivering, hand-printed paper. For the last two days, she'd missed speaking with him. They hadn't traded a single barb since that young woman had arrived to Logan Meadows. As angry at herself as it made her to admit the fact, her emotions were taking a toll. She should have been smarter, guarded her heart.

"Tabitha? What's wrong?"

"Nothing. I was just so sure the woman's show would be tomorrow evening, the night of my reading." She pointed to the date on the bottom of the flyer. "It's Friday, at three in the afternoon. And then Saturday night for the open show. I'm just surprised is all."

"Mr. Wade wouldn't do that to you." Susanna's brows drew down and her reprimanding tone matched her expression. "He seems like a nice fellow. We'd all thought you both were moving toward—you know—getting sweet."

"Well, you're all wrong. He was tricked into coming to my birthday party. When I think of that night, I couldn't be more humiliated if I tried."

"You're mistaken. I spoke with him several times. You're being silly."

Her friend didn't understand. Tabitha would change the subject. She pointed to the paper. "I didn't know she was a professional singer as well as a—well, you know—did you?"

"No. She must be really talented to say the least—as well as beautiful."

That went without saying. "Where did you get this?" Tabitha asked.

"Mr. Wade brought it by the Silky Hen this morning and asked if he could tack it up on the news board by the door. Almost everyone that's come in today read it. This was my first opportunity to bring it by."

Kendall must have written the posters. Or, perhaps, Miss Bastianelli herself. . I should do a few of my own to place around town.

"What do you think?" Susanna asked.

"Think? About what?"

"The show!"

"In the saloon, Susanna? I wouldn't dream of attending such an event. I already have enough troubles with Aunt Roberta as it is. Besides, if we went, we'd be encouraging the men in their salacious activities. Don't you think?"

"That was my initial thought, but . . ." Susanna's eyes brightened. "Roberta isn't your mother. You shouldn't give her so much power over you." Her friend's mouth scrunched to one side in contemplation. "I can't decide how offensive it would actually be. How many chances like this will we get? To hear a professional singer, especially one who's

Italian. I'm sure she sings as beautifully as a bird. Albert said she arrived with a wagonload of trunks. Think of the dresses and gowns she must have. To tell you the truth, I'm intrigued."

Jealousy clawed up Tabitha's spine.

Susanna shrugged. "If we all went together in a group, it might be fun." She stabbed the paper. "Says right here no men will be allowed in the saloon during the women's show. The Bright Nugget is just a building. It's what we do inside that would or wouldn't be scandalous. Don't you agree?"

Tabitha could easily see where this was going. "Have you talked to Albert yet? I can't imagine he'd let you go."

Her brow arched. "Let me go?"

"Yes! Let you go. He is your husband, remember?"

Susanna pulled up as tall as she could get. "No, I haven't spoken with him yet. I came straight here."

"I see. Would you like me to tag along to temper his outrage when you ask?" Already not herself over the invisible pitchfork of jealousy poking her backside, she struggled to push back her irritation.

Brenna burst through the front door, her face bright with excitement. She held a paper in her hand. "Have you seen—"

"Yes," Tabitha and Susanna said in unison.

Brenna tipped her head. "I can't imagine Gregory would be in favor of me attending an event in the Bright Nugget. What do you think?" She looked back and forth between them. "Susanna, what did Albert say?"

The excitement in Brenna's voice was unmistakable. Her eyes shone with mischievousness. Susanna wasn't the only one who wanted to go.

"I haven't spoken with him yet."

"He's in his office. I saw him on my way here. Will he allow it? If he says yes first, I think that may influence Gregory. Everyone is talking about Miss Bastianelli, and I'm curious myself. As far as I know, besides church service on Sunday, she's stayed holed up in her room."

Tabitha glanced between her excited friends, a niggle of unease growing inside. Seemed Hunter Wade was a shrewder businessman than she'd given him credit for. He was looking for more than just the men in his saloon. He wanted everyone—even if it caused strife between the couples.

Albert smiled when Susanna stepped through the office door. She usually stopped by on her way home from the restaurant, and today was no different. He anticipated kissing her soft lips and spending a few minutes alone with his new bride. Nate was a gift from above, but private moments with Susanna weren't bad either.

"Susanna, did you stop in for a kiss?" He stood to greet her, but pulled up the moment Brenna and Tabitha followed her through the door. The three looked between themselves before Susanna handed him a sheet of paper.

"What's this?"

"Look and see," Susanna responded sweetly.

Heat rose to Albert's face. Did his wife actually want to go to a saloon show? Did the other women? Impossible!

"What do you think?" Susanna asked, expectantly looking into his face. "Would one show hurt?"

"I'd think a saloon show in the Bright Nugget would be the last place you'd ever want to go. You know what goes on inside a tavern. Actually, I'm flabbergasted you're even asking."

"She's a professional singer, Albert," Brenna said, standing beside Susanna, her voice low but steady.

Albert considered Brenna, then Susanna, all the while rubbing his chin in deep thought. Tabitha stood a step behind, her gaze unwavering. This could easily get out of hand if he put his foot down. He had to walk lightly. It was three against one. “I’ll admit, I don’t know much about the woman. What did Gregory say?”

“I haven’t spoken with him yet.”

“Are you planning to go on Saturday night?” Susanna asked, gazing expectantly into his face.

He dropped his attention back to the paper in his hands. The women-only show was at three o’clock on Friday afternoon with another showing the next evening at nine. It didn’t specifically say for the men, but that’s what everyone would think. “I’m the sheriff. I have to go and make sure no one gets too rowdy. You know, to keep the peace.”

Characteristically, one of Susanna’s eyebrows slowly arched.

Brenna crossed her arms.

Tabitha stared, unblinking.

“It’s my *job* to go, ladies. Not something I *want*, or *like*, to do.”

If he put up a fuss, Susanna was sure to dig in her heels. After the few months they’d been married, he knew her well enough to know what her reaction would be. He glanced between the faces, realizing they had safety in numbers. He wouldn’t mind a little backup himself before he made a stand. What if he said no, but the other men said yes. He didn’t favor his wife going by any means, but he also didn’t want to be in the doghouse for months either. They were practically still on their honeymoon.

Thom came through the office door. When he saw the three women, a wide smile drew across his face. He swept his hat from his head and gave a low bow. “Ladies. This is a nice surprise.”

Albert almost groaned. Thom didn’t know what was about to hit him.

Susanna tipped her head thoughtfully. “Afternoon, Thom,” she said in a pleasant tone. “I guess you’ve heard about the singer that arrived in Logan Meadows on Saturday . . .”

“Hasn’t everyone?” Thom’s gaze trailed over to Albert, but he didn’t leave it there long enough for Albert to warn him. Thom’s usual good instincts were overwhelmed by all the femininity in the office.

"I guess then you'll be going to her show Saturday night?" Susanna went on, leading him easily down the path of no return.

"Of course. I wouldn't miss it. An opportunity like this doesn't present itself every day. I hear Hunter has even built a stage. I'm looking forward to it."

When he caught Albert's frown, he blinked several times and snapped closed his mouth.

Brenna's toe began to tap a fast rhythm on the wooden floor. "Yes, why wouldn't you, Deputy?"

Thom's smile was now nowhere to be seen. "I mean, I'm sure Albert will agree, there should be someone there to be sure the men stay nice and polite." He shrugged. Turning, he marched over to the stove and poured himself a cup of coffee, running from the exchange like a frightened dog.

Albert put his hand on Susanna's shoulder. "Today's only Monday. We have time to figure this out." *And I have time to speak with the other men.* It was obvious Thom didn't know a thing yet about the women's show. Hannah, being the forward thinker that she was, was sure to want to go—and would lead the way into the Bright Nugget with her head held high. He still couldn't believe it. What was the world coming to? The saloon was the men's sacred ground, so to speak. A place a fella could go and not worry about offending anyone's sensibilities. And Jessie? What about her? Would she want to go? Nell, Maude, Julia, Violet . . . the list was endless. What Wade was up to with this, he couldn't fathom. But he was sure going to find out.

CHAPTER FORTY-FIVE

With so much going on making sure Dichelle was settled and happy, Tabitha's Tuesday evening reading caught Hunter off guard. The sound of laughter drew him from a sink full of dirty glassware to the saloon's batwing doors. With a towel in his hands, he watched as townsfolk gathered, turning out in droves to support their local bookstore owner. Good. He was glad. She'd most likely sell some books and turn a profit. Would the residents do the same for him and Kendall on Saturday night?

He hadn't seen or searched out Miss Hoity-Toity since Dichelle had arrived. The devastation in her eyes had rocked him to his socks. That was not a feeling he wanted to relive—not today or ever.

Still, at the sound of merriment coming from the quaint bookstore, Hunter was tempted to meander over, as he'd done last week, and join the festivities. The memory of his gaze first meeting Tabitha's through the windowpane brought a pang of awareness. Then inside, the sugary scented air had warmed him inside and out. He'd felt included, accepted by everyone, even in his buckskin shirt. So different than being in the saloon. Her awareness of him had been heady, and he'd reveled in the feeling. At least until the end of their walk when she'd jerked her hand from his arm, embarrassed at being caught consorting with someone like him.

He'd not go over tonight. She didn't want to see him. His presence might even upset her so much she might not be able to perform. She'd kept away, and hadn't been on her nightly walks. He recalled the unseen stink kitty, and the tremor in her voice when she'd asked him not to kill the varmint. With a melancholy smile, he turned and headed back into the room.

"What're you smiling at?" Kendall asked, pouring a whiskey for Dwight. Several other men stood at the bar talking. Buckskin Jack sat at a table alone, nursing the only whiskey Hunter was allowing, and two ranch hands played a game of poker that had gone on all day. He hoped they didn't end up killing each other. Twice he'd had to break up their aggressive conduct with the threat of kicking them out.

I'd rather be at Storybook Lodge. "Nothin' in particular," Hunter replied. "Just thinkin' business is a little better than it was last Tuesday night. At least Farley's at the piano, and not Buckskin Jack."

Buckskin, catching his name, looked up.

"You know what your problem is, Wade?" Kendall said loud enough for everyone to hear. "You *think* too much. Business will never be the same one night to the next. Things were a hell of a lot simpler before you showed up."

Truer words were probably never spoken. Hunter ignored Kendall's gibe and ambled to the back of the room where the back door beckoned. He wished he hadn't been so hasty to give Miss Hoity-Toity back her book. Getting lost in *Tom Sawyer* felt better than hanging out here with a bunch of men intent on getting drunk. He wished he could get the feel of her hand on his arm off his mind. Or how soft her lips had been during the kiss that was supposed to wipe her out of his head. And yes, even her know-it-all smile had a way of lightening his day. Damn!

He folded his arms across his chest and leaned back against the wall, feeling antsy to get outside.

"When we gonna see that new gal—*the singer*?" one of the card players called, after throwing down his cards in a snit of anger. "Does she do more than sing?"

Hunter bristled at the slur to Dichelle. The cowboy winner collected his money from the center of the table with an outstretched arm, threw back what was left in his glass, then laughed in glee.

"Saturday night, nine o'clock. Told you that before, *Terry*," Hunter bit out.

"I'm looking forward to the show," Dwight said. "Nothing much ever goes on in New Meringue. That place is as dead as a doornail. Don't know why I ever moved over there in the first place."

"I do," Buckskin slurred. "You was shamefaced after Sheriff Albert fired yer backside."

Dwight scowled.

"Let's not forget, you almost hanged Jake for rustling cattle he'd never seen," Kendall said. "That might've played a part in your decision."

Dwight tossed back his whiskey, then slammed his glass onto the bar. "Can't a man drink in peace?"

Buckskin hiccuped, then wiped his arm across his lips. "Yer the one who brought it up, Dwight . . . I was just makin' conversation."

"Well, don't!" Dwight pulled out a coin and flipped it onto the bar top. "Where's Philomena, anyway? Haven't seen her all day."

"Has the night off," Hunter said, walking forward. It had been years since he'd gotten into a fight—*a real fight*—but tonight the temptation to punch someone in the face was growing increasingly attractive. "No need for her to twiddle her thumbs when we can handle things around here."

Dwight turned, looking Hunter up and down. His chin jutted out and his eyes narrowed to snake slits. "Isn't it her *job* to entertain customers?"

Poker Winner snickered.

Hunter's already-ruffled annoyance grew. "Sometimes it's her job, and sometimes it's not. Tonight, it's *not*."

"Wade!" Kendall barked in a warning tone. "You're supposed to stop fights, not start any of your own."

"I'm not fighting Dwight," he said, sizing Dwight up and finding him lacking. He may have been younger, but Hunter could have taken him down in seconds. "I don't like him asking about our saloon girl when she's clearly not here. He should show a little respect."

Dwight's mouth dropped open. "For Philomena?" He let go a laugh, and the other men in the room, minus Kendall, joined in.

Before he knew what he was about to do, Hunter had Dwight by the shirtfront and yanked him up close to his face. "Yes, Hoskins, for Philomena. That's exactly what I said."

Hunter thrust Dwight away. Dwight slammed his back against the bar, grunting in pain.

With a laughable display of anger, Hoskins straightened the front of his shirt, avoiding Hunter's hard gaze. "I won't be back anytime soon, Kendall. I can promise you that."

"Good," Hunter retorted. "Go drink in your own saloon! The one in New Meringue. You're here so much, I doubt that's even true."

As fast as Kendall could move, he hurried around the long bar to meet Hoskins just as he was about to exit. "He didn't mean it, Dwight. He's just riled tonight."

Hoskins jammed on his hat, tromped through the door, and was gone.

Kendall's furious expression didn't faze Hunter. "We're supposed to be making customers, not throwing 'em out!"

Kendall was right. He'd let his anger and frustration get the best of him. He pushed his hand through his disheveled hair, feeling prickly and out of sorts. Maybe it was time he made peace with Tabitha, talked with her to see what she was thinking. Even if they got into an argument, that was better than this deafening silence he felt coming from her shop.

CHAPTER FORTY-SIX

Feeling ever so optimistic, Tabitha, dressed in a soft pink dress, finished her afternoon bookkeeping and put the money she'd earned from last night's reading securely in the little cloth bag she used to transport it to the bank, anxious to see Uncle Frank. The smile she felt in her heart spilled onto her lips. Last night had been standing room only, and she'd sold eight books. The best she'd ever done in a single day, grossing a whole forty-four dollars. Only eight dollars of that was profit, but if she multiplied that amount by thirty days, sometime in the near future her monthly income would be enough to pay the mortgage. One could dream . . .

A few minutes before people had begun to arrive, she'd decided to have a raffle. Ten cents a try. Everyone had participated, and many bought three or four chances to win a copy of *Alice's Adventures in Wonderland*, a secondhand book in good condition. The winner from New Meringue had been delighted.

Gathering her shawl, reticule with the money safely inside, and her key, Tabitha put up her Back in Ten Minutes sign and locked the door. Only when she turned toward the Bright Nugget did her bubble of happiness burst.

Hunter. She hadn't allowed herself to think of him since yesterday morning. Every time her mind tried to stray his way, she roughly pulled it back to safer ground. *How was he*, she wondered, hearing the sound of merriment coming from inside the saloon as she passed. She didn't turn her head and look into the room. Perhaps Miss Bastianelli was there. A rush of bitterness squeezed her insides.

Reaching the bank, she huffed out her discontent and pulled open the door to Uncle Frank's foyer. The oak siding gave the place a manly feel, but the chandelier offset the room with an elegant touch. With a quick glance in the mirror, Tabitha was just about to make herself comfortable in a chair when she heard her uncle laugh. A moment later, he appeared in the hall with Hunter directly behind.

What are the chances?

Had she imagined it, or had Hunter's eyes just brightened?

"Tabitha," Uncle Frank called happily. "I've been expecting you. Last night was a resounding success. I've had a smile on my face all day. Tell me, did you sell many books? I saw you taking money for two."

Ignoring her warming cheeks, she nodded. "Eight." She jingled her reticule. "I'm here to make a deposit." She couldn't stop her gaze from straying over to Hunter, whose warm smile was all too disarming.

"Congratulations, Miss Canterbury," he said. "I wish my business was doing as well."

She could tell by his twitching lips he was kidding. The saloon did well enough on the weekends to make up for the slower days during the week. She felt bold with her uncle at her shoulder. "Thank you, Mr. Wade. I missed you last night. After your presence at the first reading, I assumed you were also a lover of books."

"Not since I lost my tutor. I guess that sort of burst my sails."

She pulled up. Her gaze cut to Uncle Frank. Was he catching any of this?

Her uncle had pulled out his watch, and clicked open the lid. "If you mean to make a deposit, we should do that now. I have an appointment coming in in a few minutes."

Disappointment dropped like a stone in Tabitha's tummy. She'd had so little time with Hunter, these few moments felt like gold. "Yes, of course. Should we go into your office?"

"Certainly." He extended a hand toward Hunter. "Good to see you. I think what you have planned is very forward thinking. Let me know if I can help."

That was mysterious.

She smiled at Hunter and said, "Good day, Mr. Wade."

He nodded, still holding his hat in his hands, and she proceeded down the hall with her uncle.

Hunter felt like following Tabitha back into Frank's office. It seemed like years since they'd had a verbal sparring, and he missed her arched eyebrow and censoring smile.

Disconcerted over his feelings, his hat clutched in his fingers, he ambled over to the wall and studied a painting of a stag and a herd of does in a snow-covered meadow. The lighting in the picture was subdued and gave the painting an overall dreamlike feel. He imagined Logan Meadows would look much the same after the first good snowfall. Glancing behind the counter to a calendar on the wall, he stared at it blankly, minutes passing until the door down the hall opened.

"Thank you, Uncle. I'll see you soon."

Tabitha pulled up when she saw him still standing in the foyer. Her gaze darted to the door, and then back at him. "Mr. Wade . . . you're still here." Her tone held a mountain of caution, and he guessed he couldn't blame her.

He swallowed. "I'm waiting on you. Thought to ask after how you were. I haven't seen you around town like I used to."

"I've been busy in the store." She smiled, touched the side of her hair. Her disinterested expression said she hadn't noticed the separation at all. "You know, thinking up ways to entice people inside. Take a look at what I've got. Maybe buy a book or two."

There! The arched eyebrow. He felt better. Less neglected.

"You've been busy as well, I'm sure," she went on speaking softly. Very ladylike. "I've heard your hammer working long hours throughout the mornings and evenings, building your new performance stage for *Miss Bastianelli.*"

Leave it to Miss Hoity-Toity to get directly to the point. He nodded her along, sure it was best if she voiced all her grievances now. Bringing Dichelle here may not have been in his best interest. Her beauty, even for the most gorgeous young woman, would be a difficult pill to swallow. He'd noticed Tabitha's reaction to some of his innocent comments pertaining to their ages—a fact of life they couldn't deny. He was forty and she had just turned twenty-nine. No spring chickens anymore, but hardly old. She thought wrongly if she believed she didn't measure up to Dichelle. Tabitha was beautiful, but her mind made her so much more attractive to Hunter. Sometimes all he could think about were her jibs and jabs.

"The new stage in the Bright Nugget and the women's show is about all that anyone talks about these days," she said. "I'm sure you have to stop the pounding in the afternoons when customers come in. Am I right?"

"Yeah, you're correct. I do what I can early on and put the hammer away about two o'clock. Are you planning on coming to the women's show Friday?"

"I've yet to decide."

"Well, I hope you do."

Hunter motioned to the two chairs set out by the window. "Would you like to have a seat? So we can talk?"

Her brow scrunched. "In the bank?"

"Why not? For now, it's private and quiet." He walked over to the nearest chair, but waited for her to comply.

"Uncle Frank . . ."

"He's busy in his office. I'm sure he won't mind if we pass a little time in his lobby."

A rosy blush crept into her cheeks. "All right, but I don't have much time. I left my sign in the window and I don't want to keep anyone waiting."

Relieved that she agreed, he waited until she was seated before sitting himself. Quiet wrapped around them. He was at a crossroads. He knew, because each time he woke up or right before he fell asleep, Tabitha was on his mind. Each hour of the rest of the day was filled with thoughts of her and their time in the bookstore or their walk under the stars. Since Saturday, the arrival of Dichelle, and the hurt he'd seen in Tabitha's eyes, he'd been irritable with everyone. It was no way to live.

"I was wondering if I could come back to the bookstore for my reading lessons?"

She sat back, assessing him with her soft green gaze. Hunter knew he never wanted to be on the wrong end of her affections again. What would it take to win her over? It was her aunt. If he could just get past Roberta Brown, change her opinion of him, Tabitha would crumble like a cake too soon out of the pan.

"Would you have some time for me? Maybe later today?"

She looked up at him with a small smile. "I don't have any plans for this afternoon if you'd like to come by. I'm glad you haven't given up altogether on your desire to read better."

That's not the only thing I desire, he thought, smiling back. He reached out and she placed her hand in his, transporting him back to their starry stroll on the boardwalk.

The door to the bank opened and Dichelle, dressed in a soft cream-colored dress, stepped through the door, the shade emphasizing her dark beauty. She smiled brightly when she saw them and hurried over.

Tabitha pulled her hand away.

"*Ciao*, Hunter. Miss Canterbury. I am happy to . . ." Her voice trailed off and she took a tiny step back. "Actually, I just remembered something I forgot to do! Forgive me." She quickly turned before he could say a word and pushed back through the door, frigid air rushing inside in her wake.

"I think we should forget about the reading lesson, Mr. Wade. I don't think you have time, with your new girl in town. I'm sure she'd like some of your attention."

"That's uncalled for! Dichelle is working for the saloon. Nothing more."

"When we had our discussion about you bringing in more working girls to Logan Meadows, you specifically said nothing had been decided. And then four days later, your secret weapon arrived. Where I come from, that's called a lie."

Anger rolled in his gut. Darn her hoity-toityness to hell and back. She was the most aggravating women he'd ever met. He'd not clear up the misunderstanding. He'd let her stew. She deserved it.

Tabitha stood and shook out her dress. "It's been nice speaking with you. Now, I really must get back."

He stood, then went to the door and opened it for Tabitha. "Good afternoon," he said to her retreating back as he fastened on his hat. Frustrated, he shook his head. That woman was more trouble than she was worth.

CHAPTER FORTY-SEVEN

One hour later, as Tabitha was taking the tea infuser out of her teacup, she noticed movement outside her window. Miss Bastianelli stood out by the bridge behind a painting easel, the paintbrush in her hand making little swishing movements across her canvas. She'd donned a beautiful navy wool hat and coat, both trimmed in some sort of white fur.

She's an artist as well!

It made sense. Gifted people usually had more than one talent.

Feeling the coolness of the shop, Tabitha added several logs to her woodstove and draped her shawl over her shoulders, all the while sipping the hot cup of orange tea and trying not to look at the beautiful young woman outside, painting the stream and bridge. Tabitha straightened one shelf, moved around a display, then went to fetch her broom. Returning, she leaned the tool against the wall and picked up her cup, watching Miss Bastianelli. The girl looked up at the sky at the tiny snowflakes that had begun to fall.

A little snow this time of year wasn't unheard of.

Tabitha took another sip. The warmth of her cup felt good in her hands.

Miss Bastianelli shivered visibly, then glanced down the street.

It must be lonely in a new town where all the women were envious of your beauty. Not one person had stopped to talk. Was she cold? Moved by compassion, Tabitha went for her coat, slipped it on, and hurried out to find the woman packing up her things. The Italian singer appeared a little leery as Tabitha approached.

"You must come inside and warm up, Miss Bastianelli. Have a cup of tea with me." She pointed to her shop, but the woman didn't look convinced. "I get lonely sometimes," Tabitha added.

At her words, a smile appeared on Miss Bastianelli's face. "*Sì,* I understand. A cup of tea and conversation sounds delightful. The temperature has dropped even since setting up my paints. But only if you will call me Dichelle."

Tabitha smiled and nodded. She lifted Dichelle's bag while the saloon girl took her painting off the easel, then lifted that as well. "I'm glad your shop is close," she said, hurrying across the bridge and into the bookstore. "Oh, that warmth feels good."

"It does," Tabitha agreed. "I've added more wood to the stove so it won't be long and it'll be warmer still. The water is hot, so this will only take a moment." They both slipped out of their coats, hanging them on pegs by the door.

In silence, Tabitha fixed a second cup and refreshed her own. Carrying them into the main room, she found Dichelle looking down a row of books. Tabitha handed her the beverage and smiled, taking a sip of her own.

Dichelle took a sip. "Oh, it's good. *Grazie.*"

Feeling a little contrite about judging her so harshly before, Tabitha went over to the painting leaning by the door. The stream, the bridge, and her shop in the background. She sucked in a breath. "It's lovely. You're very talented." Shady Creek and the bridge were finished, or so Tabitha thought, but her shop was just in the beginning of development. Watercolor blues washed over the canvas, mixed with browns and tan.

"Oh, I am just learning. But it helps to pass the time when I'm away."

"Away? Where are you from?"

The young woman's smile faded. "Over the last mountain."

"I see." *She doesn't want me prying. I can't blame her. I don't like Aunt Roberta's snooping into my life either.* Tabitha took a sip and gazed out the window.

Dichelle gazed at the snowflakes that had grown in size. "An early snow, *sì*?"

Across the street, and several doors down, Mr. Harrell pulled his display table of sale items inside the haberdashery. Sheriff Preston ducked inside after him.

"It is, from what I've heard. I'm new to town myself. I arrived in Logan Meadows last November."

Dichelle turned to her with vivid blue eyes. "Did you know Hunter from before?"

Well, they knew so little about each other, the woman was most likely searching for something to speak about. She didn't blame her. "No. We met when he came to town. Why do you ask?"

She lifted a shoulder, a small smile pulling her lips.

Curiosity filled her. "Dichelle?"

The singer turned back to the window, the empty street outside looking more and more like a Christmas scene.

"The way he looks at you when you're not watching. He was protective of your reading night on Tuesday and wouldn't let Mr. Martin schedule my performance then, so it would compete." She turned and gazed into Tabitha's face, a knowing smile on her lips. "Little things like that. I don't know . . . I just thought the two of you must be *very* good friends . . ."

A warm goodness seeped into Tabitha's heart. Hunter had looked out for her?

"You like him. At least a little."

Tabitha didn't know how to respond. Her feelings were all mixed up. She motioned to the chintz chair by the window. "Shall we sit? I have some throws we can put on our laps."

Dichelle's eyes twinkled. "Yes, let's. I have some things I'd like to share."

Tabitha retrieved her desk chair and set it on the other side of the small table as Dichelle made herself comfortable, already unfolding a small knitted blanket. Tabitha hurried upstairs for the small blanket she kept on her bedroom chair.

Returning, Tabitha got comfortable and picked up her cup.

"First, I'd like to clear up a common mistake that I run into when I come to a new town. I am not a lady of the night, saloon girl, prostitute. Because I sing in taverns and bars sometimes, I'm mistaken for such. I'm a professional singer and actress. I aim to perform in New York someday."

Tabitha blinked, realizing her mistake. She'd assumed, and Hunter hadn't corrected. He hadn't lied to her at all. Shame filled her chest.

"At one time, I had hoped Hunter would develop feelings for me," Dichelle went on proudly. "I tried hard to get his attention. I wasn't worried about the age difference. As well as being devilishly handsome, he was kind, and looked out for me when other men had other ideas. I think the world of him. And for a while, I was in love with him. We are now just friends."

Tabitha lifted her teacup to her lips, trying not to let it shake. Dichelle's admission cut her to the quick. Why the woman would be so candid with her, Tabitha didn't know.

"You two seem like very different people," Tabitha began, not quite sure what she wanted to ask. "He's cut from a different cloth than you, rougher. A wagon-train master. You're refined, and cultured." Shocked at herself, she realized that she sounded as small-minded as Aunt Roberta.

There was no judgment in Dichelle's eyes. "Is that what you think of him?"

Tabitha's moment of truth. It felt good to finally acknowledge her feelings. "No. But it's the opinion of my aunt, who lives here in Logan Meadows. She's very vocally set her will against us."

Dichelle nodded as if she understood completely. "Has Hunter shared with you the time he delivered a baby?"

Tabitha's hands jerked, rattling her cup and saucer. She shook her head.

"He's a good man, no matter the cloth from which he's been cut. The wagon train he and Thorp Wade were guiding was almost to Oregon when they reached a chasm that had opened up in the trail. Each wagon had to be unloaded, then lowered down a small cliff, and then reloaded. It was an ordeal that lasted several days. Hunter was sent on ahead with the wagons that had already been lowered, to a meadow where they would camp and wait for the others. A woman went into labor while her husband and the rest of the men toiled back at the cliff. She was frightened. Hunter was young himself, maybe twenty. Before they could send a runner back for her man, she delivered into Hunter's hands. He never flinched from what he needed to do."

Dichelle's solemn gaze met Tabitha's over the rim of her cup.

"Another time, he stayed behind to help a new widow plow and plant her fields after they'd learned her husband had been killed by a cougar and she was all alone. Hunter has a big heart. He's loyal to a fault. If you look beneath his rough exterior, Hunter is pure gold. A rare find. If you have feelings for him, I'd not let him slip away. In my mind, there isn't a woman alive good enough for him."

As if she realized her comment was a judgment on Tabitha herself, Dichelle moved her gaze outside. She laughed and pointed to Markus and Nate, who twirled in the deserted street with outstretched arms, their heads tipped back as they caught snowflakes on their tongues. Neither boy wore a coat or hat.

"Oh, my," Tabitha said, barely seeing them for all the sentiments about Hunter warming her heart. How he'd reached out to her today in the bank, and her chilly response. "I wonder if Hannah and Susanna know."

Dichelle winked. "Boys will be boys, *sì*?"

"Yes, you're absolutely correct."

Finished with her tea, Miss Bastianelli stood. "I should be going." She went to her coat and put it on. "Thank you so much for your kindness," she said, slipping the hat over her head and pulling it down over her ears. "You've touched me deeply. If you'd like to hear more about Hunter's chivalry, let me know. I have many, many more stories I could share. But, I'd rather you hear them from him."

Before opening the door, Dichelle leaned forward and pressed a quick kiss to each of Tabitha's cheeks. *"Arrivederci."*

Tabitha gently fastened the door tight as she watched the young woman walk away with her things. She was wise for someone so young, and Tabitha would do well to heed her words.

CHAPTER FORTY-EIGHT

Hunter surveyed the gussied up Bright Nugget, feeling a rush of satisfaction for a job well done. He and Kendall had cleaned the place to its utmost. Thank goodness they'd so recently swapped out the floor shavings, because now the place smelled better than most businesses on Main Street. They'd hung large blankets across both front windows so men couldn't look in, as well as over the staircase so the ladies couldn't see the doors of the upstairs rooms. No use making them uncomfortable. They'd done the same with the balcony that overlooked the downstairs, and rehearsed their explanation as wanting to give Dichelle a private place to make her entrance. All the whiskey bottles had been placed in the storeroom, spittoons removed, pumpkins and old cornhusks added for decorations.

They were ready.

He glanced at the clock. Fifteen minutes until they'd open the doors and start seating. A small group of women waited on the boardwalk outside, their chatter and laughter audible. Tabitha was not among them. He tried not to let her absence bother him. Since she'd left him standing in the bank, the kiss that was meant to free him from her spell had intensified in his memory. It was all he could think about.

In a few swift strides, he crossed the room and went to the stove in the back to make sure at least two of the seven borrowed coffeepots were brewing.

Philomena looked up at his approach. She'd dressed in a high-necked white blouse he'd never seen before, and a demure black skirt. There wasn't an inch of skin exposed that wasn't supposed to be.

He smiled. "You look nice. Are those your clothes?"

She returned his smile, appearing a little self-conscious. "I borrowed them from Daisy."

He didn't know much about Daisy, but he was glad Philomena had a friend to turn to. "Everything set?"

"They are on my end," she replied. Two trays of mugs were set on a table she'd pulled close to the stove, as well as several platters of cookies. "We owe Maude for the baking, when you get a chance."

"I'll settle up tomorrow. Wait until most of the women are seated before you ask any if they'd care for a beverage." He chuckled. "I doubt any will belly up to the bar. Kendall will be back here helping you."

She nodded. "Stop worrying, Hunter. I know how to pour a coffeepot and carry a tray."

She was right. He needed to relax.

Kendall banged through the back door almost mowing Hunter over, the large trash barrel that belonged behind the bar in his arms. His hair hung down in his sweaty face.

"You need to clean up, Kendall!" Hunter said, trying to hide the disgust he felt. "Get up to your room and change, wash your face, and comb your hair."

"I'm going. I'm going."

"I hope so. We don't want to scare the ladies the minute they walk through the door. Make it fast. As soon as Farley arrives and starts the music, I'll open the doors. Let Dichelle know the show will begin in about thirty minutes."

Hunter glanced at the door. "Where is Farley, anyway?"

"Here!" The small man hurried through the back door, a bow tie Hunter had never seen before fastened around his neck. The fellow's hair was uncharacteristically combed, slicked back, to be exact, and he wore Sunday go-to-meeting clothes.

"You look presentable, Farley. Thank you for taking the time to clean up. Now get over to the piano and start tickling the keys. Not too loud, mind you. The ladies will be chatting, and we want them to be able to hear each other."

Farley saluted and hurried to the piano.

Excitement hummed in the air. Would Albert allow his wife to attend? Thom too? Chase, Charlie, or Gregory? The men had been very closemouthed about the whole affair after he'd assured them there would be no alcohol served. Just coffee and tea.

When Farley began a soft rendition of some song he didn't recognize, Hunter took a deep breath and sauntered to the door. This reminded him of the evenings they had on the trail, when the wagon master, either him or Thorp, would gather everyone around the campfire and review the past few days and talk about the days to come, what obstacles they might incur, the weather, Indians. He was not frightened to speak to a crowd. His only nerves were caused by wondering if Tabitha would actually show up.

He opened the door. In the few minutes since he'd last checked, the crowd of excited-faced ladies had grown.

"Good day," he said loudly, the crisp air snapping at his face. The snow from Wednesday afternoon was gone. He stepped out and fastened the swinging doors in the open position. "Welcome to the first ladies' day at the Bright Nugget! We have a very nice show in store for you."

He saw Maude and Beth standing in the crowd. As well as Violet, Mrs. Harrell, Nell Axelrose—Seth Cotton's sister—standing with a woman he didn't recognize. He did recognize the two women from New Meringue who'd bought Tabitha's teacup. They gave a bright smile when they caught his eye, their faces rosy from the cold. In the very back, he spotted Tabitha and her girlfriends. His heart thwacked against his ribs.

"Please, come in and make yourselves comfortable. Philomena will be serving coffee and tea—on the house, of course."

He stepped back and the women came forward, timidly at first, and then with confidence. When Tabitha and the rest were only a few feet away, he sought out her gaze, and was a bit confused by the tender expression she sent his way. He actually glanced around to make sure she was looking at him and not someone behind his shoulder. Her laughing eyes said she knew exactly what he was thinking.

When her group reached him, she stopped at his side and let her girlfriends move inside. "Mr. Wade," she said, happiness ringing in her voice. "This is such an interesting concept you've brought to our town."

"Oh?" He was still stymied that she was here, and addressing him in such a friendly manner. The warmth of her gaze left little to wonder about. "I'm just following your lead, Miss Canterbury—you know, the readings and all."

She tipped her head and looked up at him through her lashes, a shy laugh escaping her throat.

What was going on? He'd never seen her so animated, or forward.

"I better get inside. Susanna and the rest are holding my seat." She leaned in and whispered, her fingertips resting on his forearm, "I never dreamed I'd see the inside of a saloon, or attend a show in one, for that matter. How scandalous."

Men stood in the doorways to their businesses, watching. Albert leaned against the side of the sheriff's office, his arms crossed over his chest and Thom by his side. Seemed the men were stewing. They might not understand now, but they would tomorrow night when it was their chance to attend.

Hunter gave a wave, stepped inside to the music, then pulled the door closed. His gaze went directly in search of Tabitha. He found her a few rows from the back, gazing around as if the inside of the Bright Nugget were as interesting as Niagara Falls.

By the stove, Kendall, now spit clean and shiny, waved him back. After a quick glance to the blanketed balcony, Hunter hurried over.

"Help me pour this coffee," Kendall barked. "Philomena has already gone through one pot just serving the first row. She's taking out the cookie tray while we do this."

Philomena rushed up to Hunter's side. "A woman wants to know if she can have a shot of whiskey in her coffee."

Hunter's head jerked up. "What? Who?"

"I don't know her, but the others sitting around her who heard what she'd asked for all nodded like they were going to ask for the same. When I told her all we were serving was coffee, tea, and cookies she asked what kind of a saloon we were running."

A snag he hadn't anticipated. It wouldn't be prudent for the women to return home tipsy, with the scent of whiskey on their breaths—not after he'd given his word. His plans for a packed house on Saturday night might be ruined.

"What're we gonna do, Hunter?" Kendall's voice shook with fear.

"One thing we're not going to do is anger all the men of Logan Meadows. I'll take care of this. Show me to the woman, Philomena."

Hunter hunkered down to speak quietly to the portly woman. "My waitress said you asked for something a bit stronger than coffee. I'm sorry, but today we're not serving spirits."

Her mouth pulled down. "No? Why not? Isn't this a saloon?" her voice rang out. "My man drinks whiskey here all the time. I want equal rights!" She punctuated the end of her sentence with a stomp of her sturdy black boot on the wooden floor.

A murmur went around the room and Hunter knew if he didn't do something quickly they'd have a mutiny on their hands. He just didn't know what he should do.

"Hush up!" Violet called. "Don't make trouble fer my grandson!"

Philomena appeared at his back with the cookie tray.

He stood and looked around. "Didn't think you'd want something other than coffee or tea. We didn't order extra whiskey for today, so we don't have enough to serve." *Sort of true. And your men would have my hide if I did.* "Let's see how the afternoon goes, and we'll know better for the next show. I'm sorry—but that's the best I can do."

He snatched the tray from Philomena and held it out. "Cookie?"

The hefty woman muttered angrily, then patted her moist forehead with a handkerchief she'd withdrawn from her bag. "I can't believe this!" she went on, a scowl plastered on her face. "Women always get the short end of the stick."

Tabitha stood, directing a look his way. "May I please speak, Mr. Wade?"

Relieved, Hunter nodded.

"Ladies, let's not ruin this fine chance Mr. Wade and Mr. Martin have presented us. I, for one, do not care to imbibe in anything stronger than a cup of coffee with my cookie. Your husbands and brothers are just waiting for any excuse to nix future shows. Let's not give them reason to do so. After today's performance, I'm sure Mr. Wade and Mr. Martin will appraise the situation and in the future be better equipped to serve us. As long as there is a next time. It all depends on us."

The crowd of women sat quietly, listening to Tabitha, their faces thoughtful. Some nodded, while others remained skeptical.

"I wonder who they will bring in next. A poet? Or perhaps a small play? Think about it. There are unlimited possibilities, if we don't ruin them before they get started."

"Why don't you bring a poet or play into your shop, Tabitha?" a woman asked from the last row of chairs. "Like you do for the reading?"

"For one, I don't have this kind of space." She waved her arm around. "And for another, I can't afford such an endeavor. You don't think a professional singer like Miss Bastianelli travels around for free, do you? I'm sure Mr. Wade and Mr. Martin are paying her a pretty penny to perform in the Bright Nugget. And giving us a showing for free is very generous! I don't know about the rest of you, but I'm grateful they have. If I had any menfolk in my family, I'd make sure they made the performance on Saturday night."

She looked at him and smiled, making a flash of gratitude laced with more than abundant desire snake down his spine.

"Oh, you would, would you?" an unfamiliar voice rang out from the doorway.

Hunter turned to see a tall woman who resembled Tabitha herself. Roberta Brown stood at her side.

CHAPTER FORTY-NINE

At first, Tabitha thought she was seeing things. It had been just over a year since she'd seen her mother, and having her suddenly appear in Logan Meadows, in the Bright Nugget no less, was just too much to believe. Tabitha's joy over her mother's sudden appearance was squelched the moment their gazes collided.

Her mother took a step forward, followed by Aunt Roberta. "Tabitha!" she barked out. "What on earth are you doing? Are you now a spokesperson for this . . . this . . . vile den of sin?"

All the women who'd been listening to Tabitha speak the moment before, looked from her mother to her, their heads moving in unison, waiting to see how she would respond.

"No, Mother, I'm not a spokesperson for the Bright Nugget. I just want everyone to realize what we stand to lose if they make a fuss after our first step of progress as women!"

"You call this progress?" Aunt Roberta bit out. She looked through the women until she spotted her daughter. "Hannah, you come along with Tabitha right this moment. No self-respecting woman would be caught dead in here. We're leaving at once!"

A grumble went around the room.

Hannah bolted to her feet with an expression Tabitha knew all too well. Her cousin was ready to do battle. Quickly, Tabitha raised her hand, squelching Hannah's snappy comeback. This was her war to fight.

"Mother, Aunt Roberta, where we go to watch a singer perform does *not* determine what kind of women we are." She was amazed at how steady her words sounded despite the torturous quakes that rocked her insides. Growing up, she'd never been very good at going up against her mother. Seemed things hadn't changed a bit. "If you'd like to come take a seat, I believe the show is ready to begin."

"I do *not* wish to take a seat! You are leaving with me this instant and returning to New York where your father and I can keep an eye on you! Giving you your freedom has only brought you trouble—and now shame."

Tabitha almost laughed. This crazy conversation might be funny if it weren't playing out in front of the majority of the women who lived in this town. Embarrassment that Hunter had to witness such a scene was the most disturbing of all. Since her talk with Dichelle on Wednesday, he'd pervaded her thoughts. She felt more than saw him move to her side.

"I don't have any idea what you're talking about, Mother. I'm my *own* woman. You can't *make* me do something against my will."

A soft round of applause broke out, bringing a fresh surge of humiliation to Tabitha and a frown to her mother's lips.

Her mother, used to winning all her arguments with her husband, and a majority with Tabitha, straightened to her full height, her back straight, her chin jutted. Once she set her mind on something, there was no changing it. "I most certainly can! You're my daughter. I gave you life. Mr. Brackstead has yet to marry. He's forgiven you for running off, and will go ahead and marry you even though you embarrassed him fully three years ago with your outright refusal. He's a good match for you, Tabitha! Established and strong. You're twenty-nine! Hardly the girl you once were, so stop this foolishness this instant!" She sighed heavily, her hands gripped at her sides. "I've purchased your train ticket and Frank has agreed to handle your shop until somebody buys it. You're a spinster, honey. I didn't intend to be mean, but I didn't expect to find you speaking on the behalf of a tavern." She shook her head as if in shame. "Your options have evaporated away just like your youth that you so foolishly wasted in libraries, bookstores, and reading in your room!"

Tabitha couldn't believe this was happening. Mortification paralyzed her tongue. She'd never live this down. She could hear Hunter beside her, his breathing shivering with anger.

Her mother took a step forward, her hand outstretched. "I love you, Tabitha. That's the only reason why I even considered making the grueling trip here. I only want what's best. Be assured, I will not leave Logan Meadows without you by my side."

How could anyone be so heartless! Her mother, besmirching her in front of everyone? She'd done just fine since moving here. Her mother was delusional to think otherwise. Tabitha felt her back straighten and could hardly hear for the blood pounding in her ears.

"You're wrong! I've made a good life here in Logan Meadows. I'll never return to New York. I've built my shop. I've handled my own finances. And if you must know, I'm not a spinster anymore! Or soon not to be; I'm-I'm—engaged!"

"What?" Aunt Roberta cried.

"Yes, Mr. Wade and I are getting married. We were saving the surprise until after the show today, but now it's out."

At her side, Hunter sputtered out a surprised cough. It felt as if the floor had given way and she was tumbling uncontrollably into a black bottomless pit she'd never crawl out of. Why had her mother wrecked everything? She couldn't look at Hunter, or anyone else for that matter.

"No!" her mother barked. "You can't be serious!"

"I'm totally serious, Mother! You couldn't have planned this visit any better. You'll be here for the wedding—tomorrow."

Her mother inhaled sharply and Aunt Roberta had to grasp her arm to keep her from sinking to the floor.

Tabitha glanced at Hunter and was taken aback by the anger in his eyes. He was furious with her for trapping him, but his noble nature wouldn't let him expose her falsehood. For that, she was grateful.

More than a few surprised gasps were followed by soft, embarrassed murmurs. Then whispers behind hands above wide, shocked eyes. The crowd looked from him to her and then her mother and aunt still standing at the door. If the town was looking for fodder, she'd just filled their troughs for years to come.

Mrs. Hollyhock clapped her hands together in delight. *At least someone is happy.*

Hunter remained quiet, strong, and resolute at her side, and that alone gave her courage. The depth of what he was doing for her by going along with her outrageous falsehood, even for a few minutes until she could figure out how to fix the mess she'd just made, was astounding. He'd delivered babies, helped widows, saved Violet from a stampeding Clementine and her from an angry skunk. Who knew how many countless other times he'd rushed in to the rescue. His character was to stand up for the downtrodden—and that was exactly how she felt after her mother's brazen attack. Of course, really going through with it wasn't an option. After tonight, when things calmed down, she'd tell her mother the truth and send her home. Then Tabitha would live the rest of her days here in semi-shame for making up such an outrageous lie.

Hunter laid his arm across her shoulders. "I guess the secret is out, Tabby," he said with a crooked smile, his voice deeper than she'd ever heard it. When she looked up, he looped a stray lock of her hair behind her ear. "Personally, I'm glad. I've had a difficult time keeping the good news quiet."

Her mother's face went deadly white. "Tell me you're not really meant to marry this Western ruffian. This saloon owner . . . This, this . . . You've been raised properly. Think about the consequences.

You have a perfectly good suitor waiting for your return . . ." Her voice trailed away.

Tabitha felt a moment of pity for her mother. Her ashen face stark against the dark wooden wall of the saloon brought a round of disappointment that Tabitha couldn't be what her mother wanted.

She turned to Hunter, a tangle of emotions inside. "You best go on with the show, Hunter," she said softly, only for his ears. "If I don't leave with her, she won't go either. All the women will be disappointed."

He searched her eyes. He didn't look angry, he looked concerned. "You sure?"

She nodded and turned, but he caught her arm. "I'll see you later."

"Yes, we'll talk later," she replied, knowing at that time he'd decline, and she'd have to admit her wrongdoing. At least he'd saved her the embarrassment of doing so in front of everyone.

Kendall loudly cleared his throat.

Before she knew what he was up to, Hunter kissed her cheek. "Okay, I'll see you directly after the show. In the bookstore."

Hunter looked over and smiled at her mother, a look of devilment behind his grin. "You sure you'd not like to hear Miss Bastianelli, Mother? She puts on a good show."

Her mother's mouth flapped open and closed like a fish out of water, no sound coming forth. Tabitha realized she'd never before had a handsome man doing battle for her. Just like a novel—a love story, that always ended well. Too bad reality would turn out much differently.

CHAPTER FIFTY

For Hunter, the women's show went by in the blink of an eye. The hefty woman made no more trouble about the whiskey, and the talk quieted down as soon as Tabitha left with her mother and aunt.

As always, Dichelle gave a wonderful performance that kept the ladies spellbound for almost forty minutes. Her clear voice resonated around the room as Farley accompanied her on the piano. The height of the ceiling acted to amplify her voice. Along with her singing, the women seemed fascinated with her red velvet gown, covered in rhinestones and pearls. Hunter had seen this one before, as well as most of her wardrobe. He'd helped her buy a few gewgaws in Soda Springs. He felt protective over her, and would just as soon see her fall in love with a good man and stop her traveling. But to her, that was a death sentence.

Dichelle gave one more deep bow, turned, and elegantly descended the stairs to the delight of the spectators. Seemed she'd won the crowd over as Hunter knew she would.

"That was beautiful!" Jessie gushed, her face still alight in wonder. "I've never heard such a beautiful voice. You're brilliant. I wish Sarah had been here to hear you. She loves to sing. You would be an inspiration to her."

"Yes," Brenna agreed. "As well as my girls."

"They's too young to come into a saloon," Mrs. Hollyhock scolded. "But that don't mean they can't hear Miss Dichelle sing them a little song someplace else." She gazed expectantly at the singer.

"*Sì!* That's true," Dichelle replied. "I'd be more than happy to meet them sometime and sing a few songs."

Hunter strode over to Philomena and Kendall. "You two hang around and smile until the women leave, I have to get over to the bookstore. Be sure to escort Dichelle to the hotel through the back door as soon as possible—before you let any men inside. There're some out front on the boardwalk waiting to get in. We want to keep an illusion of mystery about our secret weapon. It'll bring in more tickets. Don't forget to retrieve the whiskey bottles out of the storeroom before you get busy."

"Any more orders, sir?" Kendall asked. "Ain't you coming back?"

"Just as soon as I can. But I don't know what I'll be walking into at Storybook Lodge."

He went up a couple of steps to get everyone's attention. "My partner and I would like to thank everyone for being brave enough to try something different. It's been our pleasure having you. And now, I'm off . . ."

As he stepped away, someone called, "Go get her, Mr. Wade! Don't let her mother run you off."

"That's my adopted grandson," he heard Violet reply with pride as he went out the door. "When he sees something he wants, nothing stands in his way. No, sir. He knows his own mind."

Laughter ripped around. "I'll see what I can do, ladies," he called back, feeling the heat in his face. "I won't let you down."

With only the sheriff's office between the two buildings, Hunter was halfway to the bookstore when Albert stepped out of his office and stopped him. "So, how did it go?" he asked, a little of the sourness that had been in his voice when he'd first learned of the show still there.

The last thing Hunter wanted to do at this moment was stop and speak with Albert. "Everyone had a good time." He glanced at the bookstore, then back at Albert. "You coming tomorrow night?"

"Thought I would, you know, keep an eye out so no one gets too drunk."

"Good, I'll see you then."

He tried to move away but Albert caught his arm. "What's the rush?"

He looked down at Albert's hand on his arm. "You wouldn't believe me if I told you. Business with Tabitha. In the bookshop. I need to go."

"Yeah, seems like big things are brewing over there. Saw her and Roberta, as well as Frank and some unknown woman going—"

"Her mother," Hunter supplied.

Albert's brows shot up, but he held his tongue. His hand fell away.

In three seconds, Hunter had crossed the alley between the buildings and pulled open the door. He stopped the second he saw Tabitha, her face red with anger, Frank Lloyd, a distressed expression on his face, and Mrs. Canterbury as well as Mrs. Brown, jabbering like two hungry crows fighting over corn.

"There he is!" Tabitha's mother bit out. "How dare he walk in here as if he owns the place already. They aren't married yet!"

Frank huffed out an exasperated breath. "It's a store, Marigold, anyone can walk in."

Hunter went to Tabitha's side and took her cold hand into his own. "So what's all this fuss about?" he said looking between the two women. "A twenty-nine-year-old woman is capable of making her own decisions." He glanced at Tabitha, then leveled his gaze on the two sisters. "Especially this one. What's the problem?" When neither woman answered, he looked to the banker. "Frank? You didn't offer to sell Tabitha's business out from under her, did you? Because if you did,

I have a bone to pick with you. I don't like the sound of that at all." He tried to keep his tone pleasant, but that wasn't happening today. Her mother was trying to railroad her home against her will. The Tabitha he knew would not stand for such treatment.

"Of course not," Frank said. "I'm here to help. I'll assist my niece any way I can."

Hannah stepped through the door with Thom at her side. She gave Tabitha a meaningful look and then widened her eyes at her aunt. "Aunt Marigold," she said stiffly. After the scene the woman had made in the saloon, her tone was none too friendly. "You should have stayed for the show. It was wonderful. You would have enjoyed yourself. You too, Mother."

Roberta huffed and rolled her eyes. "Thank goodness I decided a letter wasn't fast enough and sent a telegram begging Marigold to catch the next train out. All this talk of a wedding has my poor sister almost in vapors. And I don't blame her in the least. I'm beside myself as well. I'm just wondering if Tabitha and Mr. Wade aren't bluffing."

Thom folded his arms over his chest and leaned one shoulder against a sturdy bookshelf, probably happy this didn't involve him.

"It's no bluff, Mrs. Brown," Hunter said. "If you remember, you caught us kissing in this very spot. Our feelings have been growing for some time." Tabitha glanced up into his face.

Roberta's chin angled. "I remember it well, Mr. Wade. I also remember Tabitha slapped you a good one. And you said she had no part in it. Are you pressuring her in some way? Pushing yourself on her to get your hands on your second business in Logan Meadows in an unscrupulous way?"

"Aunt Roberta!" Tabitha gasped. "Please think before you speak. Once your words are out, it's impossible to call them back."

"I don't want to call them back."

Frank held up a hand. "Stay calm, everyone. I think Tabitha is plenty capable of sorting this out without any help from us. And that means you, Marigold. And you, Roberta. I say we give her and Hunter some private time to talk. We'll go over to Hannah's house and wait there until they're through." His gaze traced between Tabitha and Hunter. "When they're ready, they can come over and let us know what *they've* decided."

"Thank you, Uncle," Tabitha said. "I appreciate your confidence in me."

The door opened again and Gabe and Julia stepped through the door, totally unaware of the dilemma playing out in the shop. They must have felt the tension in the air, because their smiles ebbed away.

"We saw everyone inside and thought you were open," Gabe said. "Should we come back later?"

"No!" Tabitha practically shouted, releasing Hunter's hand and hurrying over to the young couple.

"Fine," Frank said. "Let's go." He took both his sisters by the arm, ushering them toward the door. "Once you're ready, we'll have a calm, collected conversation."

Hunter watched them leave. The store felt quiet. Tabitha's voice filtered into his thoughts as she questioned her customers about what they were looking for. He ambled closer, seeing her in a whole new light. Was he crazy, agreeing to marry her? His heart said not at all.

"Have you heard from Jake?" Tabitha asked, looking at Gabe as Julia fingered her way through a picture book of animal sketches. "I've been wondering. Daisy looks a little lost with him gone."

"Just a telegram a few days ago. He's met his father, who is very sick. Jake's not sure how long he'll hold on."

"I'll take this." Julia handed the book back to Tabitha. "Can you please hold it for me? I don't want Nell to see it before her birthday. As you all know, she really likes animals—as well as horses."

That was an extravagant gift, Hunter thought.

"Nell has done a lot for me," she explained, as if she knew what the others must be thinking. "Mr. Axelrose too. They took me on when

I had nowhere else to go. Gave me a job"—she glanced at Gabe and smiled—"and a future. I'm indebted."

"Of course I can." Tabitha said quickly.

She nervously glanced at Hunter as Julia pulled the sides of her coat together, preparing to leave. Soon they would be all alone. And they had some decisions to make. He understood her reaching for straws after the scene her mother created, but them jumping into marriage might not be the best avenue of escape. He wouldn't lie to himself and say he wasn't tempted. He just wondered how long it would be until they killed each other.

CHAPTER FIFTY-ONE

The bells sounded as Gabe and Julia closed the door. Self-conscious of what was about to transpire, Tabitha watched them go as silence prevailed in the room. Gathering her courage, she turned to the tall, broad-of-chest wagon master standing only a few feet away.

"How did it go?" she asked, needing to start out slowly.

"Go?"

"The concert? Dichelle? Did the town's ladies love her?"

Hunter shifted his weight, a smile growing on his lips. "Sure. She has a way of winning everyone over." His eyes narrowed momentarily when he noticed Dichelle's unfinished painting leaning against the back wall.

"I hope you didn't rush out on my account."

Hunter came closer, reached out, and took her hands into his own. "Of course I rushed on your account. We have important business to discuss. I can't think of anything more pressing than that."

"Business?"

"You know what I mean."

She held his gaze. "I guess I do. Hunter, I can't possibly explain why I blurted out that we were getting married. I'm sorry. A buzzing began in my head and I just couldn't stand to hear her say those things one more time. You were right there and I—"

"You're right, I *was* right there, so you don't have to explain the whole thing to me. She's lucky that's all you did. What if you told her the truth? We weren't getting married, but that you aren't going back to New York? How would—"

"You don't know her the way I do. She'll *never* give up. She'll make my life miserable. If she said she won't leave without me, she won't. She'll end up staying here for years. I'm not leaving, and she can't possibly stay."

His hands on hers were growing all the more warm. She dropped them, and took a step away. *Why can't a marriage with Hunter work? I've been thinking about him every moment of every day. He makes my blood thrum through my veins.*

"Dichelle and I had a talk."

His eyebrow peaked.

"She shared some of the things that you've shared with her. How you delivered a baby, for starters. I was hoping you might help me out now."

His lips pulled up mischievously. "Getting married is a mighty big help."

"I agree. But it would only be a business arrangement. We're both business people, right?"

His smile ebbed away.

The thought of leaving Logan Meadows sliced her through. She'd miss so many people. Hunter the most of all. "Logan Meadows is now my home. I can't imagine living anywhere else. I feel sad saying this, but my life has been so peaceful since moving here. My mother isn't the easiest person to live with. As much as I wish she could change, and accept me for who I am, she won't. I know that from past experience."

He searched her eyes as if he could see her heart. "Logan Meadows is now my home, too," he slowly said. "I'm not going anywhere. Do you agree with your mother, that I'm an uncouth heathen with no real education?"

Tabitha couldn't stop a small smile. "She didn't quite say all that."

"Close enough. She plans to either haul you with her back to New York, or remain here—and make your life miserable. I'm not going to change my ways, Miss Hoity-Toity. Can you live with that?"

"Miss who?"

His crooked grin was back. "Miss Hoity-Toity. Your nickname."

His voice had turned soft.

"I can. I like who you are. If you agree to marry me, all I have is one stipulation."

His frown was back. "I'm the one who should be making the rules since you roped me into your problems. What now?"

"The marriage will be in name only. In case one of us has second thoughts." *You have second thoughts.* "A person can get an annulment for up to two years if they haven't consummated the marriage. I have two bedrooms upstairs that will work fine. We can sign a paper with our intentions and seal it, so the reverend will know we had this planned from the beginning and why. I'm sure he won't like it, but sometimes extreme circumstances call for drastic measures. What do you think?"

"How do you know all that . . . about two years? You sure?"

"I read it once."

"You read about annulments?"

"I read about everything."

He nodded. "That I can believe. Another thing you can believe is I'm not going to wait for two years for you to decide if I'm a keeper or you're throwing me back into the stream." He'd pulled back and his face had gone serious. Even with him staring bullets through her, she was beginning to feel giddy. This might actually work.

"No, I wouldn't expect you to. Does the sound of a month, or whenever my mother leaves, whichever comes first, sound acceptable to you? You're free to do as you please after that, and I promise I won't try to influence you either way."

He rubbed his chin and gave her a good looking over—long enough to make her face flame with heat. "That sounds fair enough. What if one of us wants an annulment, but the other decides they don't? What happens then?"

"I guess we cross that stream when we get to it," she said. Was she really going to go through with this?

"Fine then. Should we go tell your family the news?"

"I think we should," she replied. "The sooner the better." When he took her hand in his and headed for the door, the realization of what they were contemplating hit her full force. A business agreement instead of a marriage? She just might lose her heart in such a deal and regret it for the rest of her life.

CHAPTER FIFTY-TWO

Reverend Wilbrand cleared his throat calling everyone to attention. Hunter stood next to Tabitha at the altar of the small church, ready to become Tabitha's husband. He'd had the whole night to wrap his head around what was happening. When they'd first met, he'd had the distinct impression she thought him beneath her, and yesterday she'd made it perfectly clear that today was nothing more than a business arrangement. One to correct as soon as her mother went home to New York.

Glancing over his shoulder, he took in the few people in the two front pews. Tabitha's mother, her aunt, her uncle, and Markus. Thom stood next to him and Hannah next to his bride-to-be. On the other pew, the groom's side, sat Violet, a sentimental grin pulling her face.

"Are we ready?" the reverend asked.

Hunter and Tabitha both nodded. Her mother hadn't stopped crying since they broke the news yesterday. The woman had talked faster than an auctioneer, trying to change their minds, but Tabitha was having none of that, which made him proud of her gumption, even if he was a bit put out. They had set their course, and now they would see it through.

"Ladies and gentlemen, we're gathered today to witness the marriage of Hunter Wade to Tabitha Canterbury. First Corinthians says that love is patient and kind. It's not jealous, not pompous, not inflated, not rude. It doesn't seek its own interest, is not quick-tempered, it doesn't brood over injury, it doesn't rejoice over wrongdoing, but rejoices with the truth. It bears all things, believes all things, hopes all things, endures all things." He searched both of their faces. "Love never fails. If you both keep this simple scripture in mind, this will be a long, prosperous marriage."

Hunter snuck a glimpse at Tabitha, who in turn glanced at him. Did she feel the weight of those words as well?

"If anyone here is in opposition to this marriage, let them speak now or forever hold their peace."

The reverend waited so long, Hunter wondered if the man was waiting for Tabitha's mother to voice her objection. A soft sob was his only reply.

"Get on with it!" Violet huffed.

"Hunter, do you take Tabitha to be your lawfully wedded wife? To have and to hold from this day forward as long as you both shall live?"

"I do."

"Tabitha, do you take Hunter to be your lawfully wedded husband? To have and to hold from this day forward as long as you both shall live?"

Hunter felt her quiver. He waited.

"I do."

That's it. He had a wife! She may think this a business agreement, but she was still his wife. What would Thorp have thought of their shenanigans? He'd not like it at all.

"Do you have a ring?"

Hunter shook his head. "Sorry, I don't."

"Fine then," Wilbrand said. "I now pronounce you man and wife. You may kiss the bride."

Ignoring the hostility he felt drilling into his back, Hunter gathered Miss Hoity-Toity into his arms and kissed her soundly. A strange feeling of belonging began to register. This was *his* wife, and Logan

Meadows was *his* town, not just some place he was passing through. It was heady, and happy, making him kiss her much longer than he probably should have.

Mrs. Hollyhock whooped loudly, bringing Hunter to his senses. When he let Tabitha go, her cheeks were two scalding red patches.

With a hand to their shoulders, Wilbrand turned them to face their guests. "I present you, Mr. and Mrs. Hunter Wade."

Thom grasped his hand in congratulations. From the corner of his eye he saw Hannah envelop Tabitha in a hug. "Short, sweet, and beautiful, Tabitha," he heard her friend whisper.

Frank Lloyd came forward with Violet at his side. Behind him came the sisters.

"Congratulations," Frank said, and seemed to sincerely mean his words.

Holding Marigold's arm as if the woman were too weak to stand on her own, Roberta watched silently until all the chatter faded away. "Everyone is invited back to Hannah's house for a late lunch." She released Mrs. Canterbury's arm and pulled her kerchief from her bag, then patted her brow. "Marigold and I will go set things out. Be along when you're ready."

Tabitha's mother followed Roberta out the door without one word to her daughter. Hunter had seen her kind many times on the wagon train. Couldn't see past the noses on their faces if it went against their belief. Sour as week-old milk. Disgusting.

Tabitha hid her feelings well, but her mother's attitude hurt her. Her usually soft lips were a stiff pink line. Couldn't the shrew have been nice for one minute of one day?

Lifting Tabitha's hand, he kissed the back. She looked up at him in question. "Sorry I didn't have a ring."

"That's all right. I hardly expected you to."

"Let's give Mother and Aunt Marigold a few moments to get the food out," Hannah suggested. "I don't know about you, but it feels nice to have someone else doing the preparations for once. Let's take a walk down Main Street. This has all happened so quickly, I'm sure the announcement will take most by surprise."

"I don't know." Tabitha fingered the lace on the front of her soft blue dress. "Hunter has the big show tonight. He must have things that need doing at the Bright Nugget."

"Everything is in order. We made sure of that yesterday."

"That settles it," Thom said. "Let's get a move on. I'm hungry."

A few minutes later, after the four of them had said their goodbyes to the reverend, and the small group had descended the slight hill, Tabitha felt much like Cinderella the night of the ball. Hunter's arm was strong beneath her fingers. She was his wife, as well as his business partner, and spinster no more. Feeling too shy to glance up into his face, she kept her gaze trained ahead on the path. Thank goodness Hannah and Thom were doing most of the talking.

On the boardwalk, they stopped to wait for Frank and Violet, who were bringing up the rear.

"You young'uns go on," Violet said, with a sniff and a nod. She'd had ahold of Frank's arm as they'd come down the slight rise. "I have things ta do." She glanced at Tabitha. "It was a ceremony fittin' a princess, dearie. I'm so happy."

"You sure, Violet?" She let go of Hunter's arm to close the distance between them.

"I'm sure. It's time fer my nap. You all go on."

"We'll walk you," Hunter quickly said.

"Oh, pooh. I don't need no escort. You all go on now."

"I'm not going for lunch either, Violet," Frank said. "And I don't get out of the bank near enough. I'll walk you back to the Red Rooster. Think of it as doing me a favor by helping my constitution. And then these young'uns, as you call them, can go celebrate the day away."

Violet straightened her spectacles with a shaky hand. "When ya put it like that, then fine."

Uncle Frank leaned in and kissed Tabitha's cheek. "I'm so happy you picked Logan Meadows to make your home. You brought a sense of excitement to town when you arrived, with your shop and your books, and it hasn't let up since. And now you've gone and tied the knot. I know you won't be going anywhere anytime soon. Congratulations."

His words brought a soft cozy glow. The words and acceptances she wished she felt from her mother and the rest of her family. At least Uncle Frank was on her side. "Thank you, Uncle. Your words mean the world to me." She chanced a look at Hunter, who was watching the exchange.

He smiled, seemingly pleased by what her uncle had just said. "She's not going anywhere now, Frank. I'll make sure of that."

This was all so new—and strange. Hunter was her husband—in a business sort of way. That thought pricked the bubble of happiness she'd been experiencing for the last hour. She could so easily forget he'd just done this to help her with her mother. Remembering that would be the true challenge.

CHAPTER FIFTY-THREE

Hunter watched from the back wall of the Bright Nugget, a sea of men in front of him, waiting impatiently for Dichelle to take her final bow. The crowd of men pushed back on him in the standing-room-only saloon. Even though this was his and Kendall's big moment, all Hunter had been able to think about all night was Tabitha. After the ceremony, they'd spent time with her mother and aunt at the small, quiet reception, struggling to make small talk as her mother looked down her nose at him disdainfully. After about an hour of torture, he and Tabitha had gone to his apartment and collected his few belongings, bringing them over to the bookstore.

Tonight was his wedding night, but he'd not be sharing a bed with Tabitha. She'd shown him to the guest room. It had been less than a day, and he was already confused about what he should do and how he should act when it came to her.

"You done good, Wade," Albert said, squeezing in at his side. "I've never seen this many men in here at one time. Pretty amazing. And everyone is on their best behavior."

"And I hope they stay that way," he replied, able to see past a shorter man in front of him. He was glad he'd taken the time and money to build the stage. It had worked out well.

"At a dollar a ticket, you and Kendall have made a boatload of money tonight. And that's not counting the whiskey and beer you'll sell."

"I hope so. We've spent a tidy sum bringing this venture together."

Albert nodded. "I'll bet."

There was a murmur from the men up front just as Dichelle took her final bow, and the crush of men leaned to the left, shuffling in the extremely tight space. He and Albert exchanged a look.

This may be good for business, but Hunter felt wary. He didn't really know why. Caution flashed through him again when the crowd leaned unexpectedly to the right forcing him to catch his balance when he was shoved on the shoulder. Someone shouted out in pain. Kendall, behind the bar, was pouring whiskey into several tumblers on Philomena's tray, unaware of anything unusual.

Earlier, when the crowd had begun to fill faster than he'd expected, Hunter removed the chairs, stacking them in the alley to make room for more men. Seemed waiting a few days after Dichelle had arrived had given time for the word to spread. The locals were few and far between in a sea of unknown faces. He and Kendall had recruited one of the young locals to help behind the bar so Hunter could remain free, to keep an eye on the fellas. Make sure their merrymaking stayed at that. Dichelle's safety was his utmost concern. Philomena's too.

A man grasped the side of the stage and pulled himself up. He yanked Dichelle into his arms. She screamed, struggling to get free as he tried to kiss her. Alarmed, Hunter pushed forward, but was hampered by the crowd.

Gabe, who'd arrived early, claiming a prime spot in front of the stage, climbed up behind the fellow and put a choke hold around his neck, pulling him away.

Dichelle took that moment to dash away, up the stairs.

Albert shouted for everyone to be still, but the pushing had begun. The man who'd started the fuss, plainly inebriated by the way he had trouble standing, was shoved to the platform by Gabe, to a round of applause.

Below, on the floor, a few more punches were thrown amid heated cursing, and shattering glass rent the air. Hunter knew if he didn't get ahold of the situation quickly, they would have a full-blown brawl on their hands. Reaching the stairs, he took them two at a time until he was on the stage. He pulled his gun and shot into the rafters, being careful to keep his aim away from the second-story bedrooms.

At the deafening roar of his .45 Colt, the crowd fell back and the fighting stopped.

"Hold up!" Hunter shouted. "One man took liberties who shouldn't have, and now he's going to jail. Just settle down!" He really didn't want to break up the party just yet.

Albert pushed in next to him, hardly room with four men on the small stage. Once the handcuffs were set, Gabe hopped off and Albert pushed the offender toward the steps. "I'll be back just as soon as I lock him up. I'd hate to close this down, but I will if it gets further out of hand." He paused and looked back at Hunter. "And if you want to be enjoying your wedding night tonight, I'd not shoot your weapon again. That's against the law in Logan Meadows and I'll have to lock you up alongside this fellow. Consider yourself warned."

Hunter nodded and holstered his gun. "Everyone just settle down! Now that the show is over, I'll bring in a few tables for poker. Farley," he called. "Get playing!"

Grumbles turned into laughter as the music returned. Hunter watched Albert push his prisoner through the crowd. He wondered if Tabitha had heard the gunshot and was frightened. Was she waiting for him to come home? With this motley group of men, that wouldn't be for hours.

It was five in the morning, and the sun was about to lighten the sky, when Tabitha heard Hunter use the key in the front door. She'd known last night was the big show, the one he and Kendall had been planning for days. Their wedding was business, so she shouldn't feel hurt that he'd stayed out all night. That's what saloon owners did. When the gunshot had gone off around eleven last night, she'd about jumped out of her skin. Then hours had passed without any bad news. She'd finally put down her book and blown out her lamp knowing the counterpane on Hunter's bed in the guest room was turned down, but sleep eluded her. He'd be in when he was in, and not a moment before.

At four she'd risen and made a cup of tea, bringing it upstairs, and had been reading by the light of her lantern in her bedroom chair ever since. At Hunter's slow, heavy footsteps on the stairs, she pulled tight her robe sash, listening, wondering.

His door clicked closed.

He'd gone to bed.

She sat for a good ten minutes to be sure he was settled, and then quietly made her way to the first floor. It was a strange feeling having someone else here. Besides the one night Susanna had stayed over when Albert was guarding the million dollars in the bank, he was her only guest. She'd gone to sleep and awoken to her own company every night since she'd moved in. What should she do? Today was Sunday, and they were closed, so she didn't have to worry about opening the store and making noise that might disturb Hunter.

Gathering a few logs from the basket she kept next to the stove, she put them inside, and then stirred the coals. Rolling paper into balls, she soon had them smoking. Making breakfast for Hunter now would be silly. She was eager, but she'd not be wasteful. Taking the bread she kept in her breadbox, she sliced two large pieces and spread them with butter and jam. She took them to the chair by the shade-covered window and tried to relax. After eating, she cuddled back into the chair with her soft throw to keep her warm. The quiet shop was a blessing. Her lids grew heavy from her lack of sleep the night before. Closing them felt so good.

CHAPTER FIFTY-FOUR

A rapping sound brought Hunter out of a deep sleep. Not recognizing the ceiling above his head, he sat up, letting the covers fall to his hips. He'd been dreaming, but he couldn't remember about what.

The sound came again. He was in the bookstore's upstairs bedroom. Where was Tabitha? Standing, he tugged on his pants and went to the door, pushing the hair from his eyes. He was halfway down the stairs before he realized he was shirtless and being stared at by Tabitha and, at the front door, her mother.

"When you didn't show up to Sunday service I got worried," Mrs. Canterbury stated, not taking her gaze off him. "I thought this heathen might have hurt you."

"Mother, can you please come back later?" Tabitha said from behind her hand. "As you can see, now's not the best of times."

"I should say not!"

This woman was really getting on his nerves. "What did you expect, *Mother*? Last night was our wedding night."

Her eyes bulged. He didn't know if it was his familiarity or the subject matter. Either one, he couldn't stop himself and laughed heartily. A smile appeared on his wife's face as well. Marigold turned on her heel and was gone.

Closing the door, Tabitha took the throw from her chair and held it out. Feeling a mite shy, he wrapped it around his shoulders.

"Good morning," she said first, her face flushed. Her dark hair hung loose down her back. Her prim and proper robe was cinched tight, just exactly as he'd expect it to be.

"Good morning."

"I'm sorry about my mother. I know you came in very late. I'm sure you can use a few more hours of rest."

"No, I'm fine, I'm fine." The shop was warm. She must have been up for hours. From the looks of it, she hadn't gotten much sleep herself last night. "What time is it, anyway?"

"Just past eleven."

"Six hours of sleep is plenty for me. How about coffee? Have any?"

"I do. I'll go put some on. I can't believe I fell asleep in the chair by the window. Stayed asleep, too, even with people walking by on the boardwalk. I've never done that before."

"I'm sure you haven't, Miss Hoity-Toity. You're by the book with everything you do. Sleeping in is probably a sin."

She laughed again as he followed her to the curtained-off kitchen. He stood back and let her fill the pot with water and then grind the coffee beans. The heady aroma reminded him of mornings out on the trail.

"How was the show last night?" she asked as she worked. "The last time I looked, men were streaming in from everywhere. Did you pack the house?"

"Packed doesn't do it justice. I'm anticipating the take. We made a bucketload of money. Hope to do the same next weekend."

"Oh? Dichelle's staying on? I don't know why, but I sort of figured she'd be going home."

"I hope she'll stay. Can't say for sure. She's a free spirit, comes and goes on a whim." He appreciated her interest in the saloon. A man couldn't ask for more than that from his—*partner*.

"Will you bring in more shows?"

He smiled and rubbed a hand over his whiskered chin. "I don't see why not, after the great turnout—and the stage we now have."

"I agree wholeheartedly. I heard a gunshot. Was anyone hurt? I worry about Dichelle and Philomena in such a raucous atmosphere."

"Raucous?"

"Wild. Loud. Disorderly."

He'd remember that word and use it on Kendall. "Some fella hopped on the stage and tried to kiss Dichelle."

Tabitha whipped around from what she was doing. "Is she all right?"

"Shaken up, but fine. She ran into *raucous* behavior in Soda Springs as well. A room full of men is unpredictable. The gunshot was me firing a warning to settle the crowd. That got *me* a warning from Albert. But, we'll be ready next time. No one else will be climbing onto the stage."

Tabitha smiled, catching his use of *raucous*. "Especially when imbibing."

Now she was just showing off.

"After the show, I walked her back to the hotel. That was around ten thirty. From there, the men commenced to play poker and drink themselves senseless." He rubbed a hand across his stubbled chin again, not quite understanding why men so freely threw away their hard-earned money.

Someone outside shouted, then the clomping of horse hooves echoed as it crossed the bridge. Laughter. More talking. A dog barking, people walking by. The place was not big on privacy.

"I feel like I'm in a fishbowl."

"It's not much different than above the sheriff's office," she said, looking at him over her shoulder, the length of her hair flowing down her back drawing his gaze.

"It's much different. The height of being over the jail and the door being around back and up a staircase help. Here, anyone walking by might knock on your door." He pulled the throw more securely around his shoulders, clearly making his point.

She blushed.

Knock knock knock.

Tabitha's eyes grew wide and she sputtered a laugh.

When she started for the door, he caught her by her arm. "It's Sunday. You're closed. Besides, it's probably your mother having thought of another stupid question. Let it go."

"You sure? It might be Kendall?"

"It better not be Kendall. He knows better."

When whoever was there went away without knocking again, she released a breath. It must be difficult to be a woman, doing and saying all the right things, or else being looked down upon. He couldn't do it. No sir, not for a minute.

Without asking, he stepped past her to a loaf of bread and pulled off a chunk and put it in his mouth.

"Would you like me to cook some breakfast? I still have some bacon and eggs in my cold box."

"I sure wouldn't." He chuckled at the look of dismay on her face. "When you're ready, I'd like to take you out to breakfast. Nana's Place or the Silky Hen. Whichever you prefer."

She stared at him so long he thought she'd decline.

"Hunter, you don't need to do that. This is business, remember? I don't mind cooking."

I'm not forgetting you're miles above me, and I don't need a reminder of how you feel. "Business or not, I'd like to go out. Make a showing. Is that all right with you, Partner?"

She glanced away, and he saw her swallow. "Sure it is. I can be ready in twenty minutes."

"Good, time enough for me to have a cup of coffee and shave."

She started for the stairs, her color high. "I'll meet you down here then. Everything you need is in your room."

"I've seen it all, Miss Hoity—"

"—Toity," she finished for him over her shoulder. "I'll have to think up a name for you. Perhaps something that captures your wildness."

"Wildness?" That made him puff out his chest and smile.

"That's the first thing I thought when I saw you ride over the bridge and into town. That you were an untamed mountain man, windblown and hard." Her laughter followed her up the stairs. "Little did I know you were really as sweet as a pup."

"Let's not get carried away!" he called out just as he heard her door click shut. "I liked the wild mountain man much better."

Too late—she was gone.

CHAPTER FIFTY-FIVE

Sunday afternoon Tabitha sat at her desk looking over her bookwork, a stab of melancholy trying to burst her bubble of happiness. The last day and a half married to Hunter had been exciting. She recalled how handsome he'd looked on the stairs this morning, shirtless, while he'd addressed her mother as if he didn't have a care in the world. She wished she weren't so susceptible to her mother, and could just brush off her words as easily as Hunter seemed to. It was true what she'd told him about being happiest here the last year, living on her own. Now, he'd come along to make things even better.

It's only pretend. Don't lose your heart to him.

At Hunter's bidding, she'd left her shades pulled down on all the windows, and because she had, the shop had stayed quiet. Cozy. She liked it. Two lamps burned in the shadowy room. It was Sunday, and everyone deserved a real day of rest.

In the past, she'd never really wanted one. She'd been here to do her friends' bidding on a whim. She'd open up and let them look through the books. Now, she waited on Hunter to return from the saloon. The quiet seclusion felt good. What would they talk about? What would they do? Friends were staying away because they thought it was her honeymoon. She appreciated that.

The key rattled in the lock, and the door opened. Hunter came in looking a little self-conscious. He shrugged out of his coat, then hooked it by the door. He rubbed a hand over his soft leather shirt, and still wore the gun he never left behind. Did living in a town change a man?

"Are you going to take a shift tonight at the saloon?"

"I offered, but Kendall insists on doing it. Says a man only gets one honeymoon, and to take tonight off since I had to work yesterday." He glanced around nervously. "At least the disorder from last night is all cleaned up." He stretched his back and worked the muscles of his neck with one hand. He yawned and briefly closed his eyes, all the while standing by the front door.

"Sleepy? You haven't had much rest."

"I am." He seemed to jump on that. Did he regret tying himself to her for even one month?

"Why don't you go to bed early, since you have the night off?" she suggested, disappointment weighing her shoulders.

When he glanced at the kitchen, she realized that without even a small supper table, the place wasn't very conducive to relaxation. She took most of her meals upstairs to eat in her bedroom chair. She'd need to find a small table that wouldn't take up much room. Make a spot near the kitchen where he could have coffee, relax, read the newspaper.

He shrugged. Ambled over to the chair by the shaded window and lowered his large frame down slowly. "It's only five. Much too early for that." He sucked in a deep breath, and slowly let it out. "But soon. I do feel a bit worn around the edges."

"Are you hungry? You haven't eaten since our late breakfast. I can make you something, if you'd like."

"No need. Philomena made some beans and meat at the saloon. I'm good, thanks anyway."

She glanced away from his face to the ledger open on the desk. Hurt swirled inside. This was business. Nothing more. It was apparent he didn't want her hovering, feeding, or suggesting things for him to do. Perhaps he was just tired, like he said. She shouldn't read more into his grumpy mood.

The charming feel of the room had changed, and now she felt trapped. Conscious of her every thought or action, she stood. "I'm going to warm a cup of milk for myself. There are a couple butter cookies left, if you'd like."

"No, thanks."

His eyes were closed and his arms were crossed over his chest. Perhaps the planning of Dichelle's performance had taken more out of him than he or she thought. He was tired. And should go to bed. But she'd not suggest it again. Really, what did she know of him? Not all that much. Not all that much at all.

She moved around the kitchen trying not to make noise, which was difficult when one was working the heavy iron door of the stove. All the anticipation of his return whooshed out of her in one great exhalation. What to do on a long Sunday afternoon when the one you wanted to be with didn't want to be with you? That was the question. What had possessed her to make such a request to marry? Her pride. The dressing down in front of all the women. She shuddered and pushed the hurtful memory away. Her life had been going along so well before Hunter had come to town. And even after the walk, the kiss, and the slap. The two of them were on even footing then. At least she'd been her own woman and could hold up her head.

Not now. Would she ever again?

CHAPTER FIFTY-SIX

Tabitha sat bolt upright in bed when a loud clanging and banging sounded somewhere close outside. Had a late hibernating bear come into town, upsetting things in his path? Had she left her trash out again? She'd heard tell before that this time of year bears could make pests of themselves before settling in for winter, as they hunted for last-minute food.

With a pounding heart, she swung her legs over the bed and pulled her arms through her wrapper, the coolness of the air bringing gooseflesh to her arms. Searching her bedside table for some matches, she carefully lit her lamp. The sound outside was not moving along. Sometimes she thought she heard laughter, but mostly metal banging against metal. When she opened her bedroom door, she found Hunter at the top of the stairs, a sour look on his face.

"What is it? Do you know?"

"A shivaree."

His tone was none too pleased. His long hair hung around his face and his eyes were red.

The banging increased and moved around the building to her bedroom balcony.

"What do we do?"

"I suppose we'll have to make some kind of appearance or they might stay all night. I was getting some teasing in the saloon earlier—I suppose that's when they were making their plans. I should have guessed."

Was it the teasing that had him so grumpy when he came in? "We can go out on my balcony and tell them goodnight. Will that do?"

He gave a wry smile and shrugged. "I'd think. Let's get this over with."

In her bedroom, she was about to pull her curtain aside, and then open the door, but Hunter stopped her. The cries and hollering below grew all the louder, as well as the pounding of noisemakers.

"Wait," he said, looking her up and down. He reached out and with both hands mussed her hair until it felt like a tumbleweed and a good portion hung in her face. That brought a small smile to his lips. "One more thing."

She stood like a docile lamb as he reached for the sash that kept her robe together. He loosened the knot, then pulled one side open a bit, and slipped it to the edge of her shoulder. The action brought a cascading tidal wave of desire crashing through Tabitha. Warmth pooled in her abdomen and she had to stay her impulse to look into his eyes. To quiet her knee-jerk response, she bit down on her lower lip.

His brow arched. "Do you want to make this convincing or not? It's up to you. I know thoughts of being with me must be repulsive to your Hoity-Toityness, but just play along. It'll save my pride."

Why the big ox! How dare he misconstrue her reactions. Two could play at this game.

Outside, the crowd was yelling at the top of their lungs for them to get out of bed and make a showing. The lantern light must have signaled that they were now awake.

"You need some fixing, too," she said, keeping a firm hold on her quavering voice. Having him so near, in her bedroom while she was in her nightgown, was totally unnerving.

With hands as steady as she could muster, she unbuttoned his shirt and pulled it wide to expose his muscled chest. It was almost impossible to tug her gaze away from the light sprinkling of hair covering his bronzed skin. Throwing caution to the wind, she went up on tiptoe and mussed his already-tangled hair. The only thing left were his pants, which she figured he'd pulled on when he heard the racket outside, and she wasn't daring enough to go there.

"There! That's better. You look good and tousled. What's good for the goose is good for the gander."

"You're a goose, all right."

His crankiness seemed to have abated, and she thought she heard a small chuckle. She lifted her chin. "Go ahead and open the door, I'm ready."

Hunter took Tabitha's hand and stepped out, a *wild* clamor rending the air from below. Buckskin Jack, unsteady on his feet, gave a whoop of victory. He held up a triangle and striker, rounding it so quickly Hunter couldn't believe the drunk could move that fast. Beside him, Clyde plugged the ear closest to his friend and plopped to the earth, a silly smile stretching his face. Kendall was there, Mr. Hatfield from the train depot, Farley, and Mr. Harrell. And a bunch of other saloon regulars, all smiling and laughing, and calling out for a kiss.

Hunter held up his hand until they quieted. "Howdy, men," he said with as much good humor as he could muster. "Good to see you all here so late. My lovely bride and I appreciate your thoughtfulness."

That brought a round of laughter.

He looked down at Tabitha, her eyes bright with excitement as she searched his face and waited to hear what he would say next. He realized this was probably the most daring thing she'd ever done.

"Kiss, kiss!" the men shouted in unison.

Tabitha, who was nestled under his arm as if they really had just rolled out of a warm bed together, straightened her spine, probably dreading the intimacy.

"Kiss yer bride!" Buckskin shouted. "We ain't going away until ya do!" He rounded the triangle with renewed energy.

If something wasn't done fast, the whole town would come to see what was happening. As it was, lanterns at Thom and Hannah's house across the bridge and up the road had been lit just since they'd stepped out. The last people he wanted to attract were Roberta Brown and Marigold Canterbury.

He glanced down into Tabitha's sleep-soft face, his heart giving a hurtful twinge. She looked so beautiful in the light of the moon.

"What're you waiting for?" Kendall called, waving his hat. "An invitation? Get on with it! I'd think you're afraid of her or something. She's not the town spinster anymore!"

He was the only one who'd heard the small sound of distress that escaped Tabitha's throat. *Damn, Kendall.* Without waiting another second, Hunter wrapped her in his arms and found her mouth. The noise from below ratcheted up a few more notches. But that's not what had his attention. It was his wife's warm mouth, the feel of her body, void of any corset or other female thingamabob, tight next to his. Her arms circled his neck and pulled him close. Seemed she was just as eager as he was to make this look good.

"Whooeee, look at 'em!"

"Thatta boy, Hunter! Give her one for the saloon!"

"Let 'er come up for air afore she faints!"

The catcalls swirled around, but Hunter only knew the feel of Tabitha's lips on his, the curve of her back beneath his palm, and the way her ragged breathing made him feel. Lord, this was more than a kiss for show, it had stolen his soul. He'd been trying to convince himself he was just doing her a favor by marrying her, but now he had to face the facts. He'd wanted to. Had dreamed of waking by her side and gazing into her deep green eyes.

They broke apart.

She avoided his gaze.

Rocked by the kiss, Hunter glanced at the men needing to direct his attention at anything but her. "There you go, gentlemen! Will that do?"

"Darn tootin'!" Buckskin called.

Farley put on his hat and pulled Clyde up by the arm. "Let's go men. Fun's over. Let's let the lovebirds get some sleep—our whiskey awaits."

"Sleep! Pooh. We know what they'll be up to." Clyde was so busy talking and grinning up at them that he almost fell off the bank of Sandy Creek. He righted himself, gave them one last wave, and followed the rest of the men around the corner of the building and back to the saloon.

The night was once again quiet. Except for the pounding of Hunter's heart. He followed Tabitha back inside.

"I guess we did it now," she whispered much to herself.

Hunter was busy buttoning his shirt. "What do you mean?"

"The letter we wrote, sealed, and mailed to Reverend Wilbrand with a note not to open until instructed. He'll have a hard time believing our vow of chastity after he hears about the show we put on tonight."

Hunter couldn't stop a harrumph. "I don't like vowing anything. Too hard to know what's coming down the trail. That was your idea, not mine."

She was chewing her lip again. "I know. I've pretty much messed things up."

Glancing around her very feminine room, he rubbed the back of his neck. She was right. He didn't have any comforting words. "Well, good night," he said, avoiding her gaze. He disliked being so gruff, but his insides were in a knot and the feel of her lips had been too enjoyable. He needed some space. Turning, he returned to his own room, wondering how things had gotten so confusing so quickly. Without lighting his lamp, he stripped out of his clothes and got back under the covers, all the while thinking about Tabitha alone one room over.

Why was her mother so set against him? So what if he hadn't been educated in a fancy school and didn't have loads of money sitting in the bank. He was honest, and worked harder than most. He was who he was and he'd not be sorry for it.

Out of the blue, his old leg wound began to ache. He reached under the covers and pressed on his knee, remembering all he'd lived through. His life had had its ups and downs, but he'd always been in control of things. Except for now. This time, he couldn't say the same.

CHAPTER FIFTY-SEVEN

Tabitha jerked around when somebody tapped on her window. Susanna stood waiting, a basket over her arm. Ready for some company after her semiquiet Sunday, Tabitha hurried to unlock the door.

"Happy Monday morning," Susanna said, her face full of questions. "I was thrilled to see your shades rolled up even if it's only eight. I haven't gotten a chance to speak with you alone since the wedding." She glanced around. "Is Hunter here?"

"No. He was gone when I got up. The place was warm and he'd made a pot of coffee."

Susanna came in and closed the door. "Very nice. How is married life treating you? Do you have any questions?" She searched Tabitha's face so long Tabitha knew her cheeks must be red from their tingling warmth. "Well?"

"You're still a newlywed, Susanna. If I had questions, I'd ask Hannah, or Brenna, or Jessie." What else could she say? Her friends might not like the bargain she'd struck with her groom.

Susanna winked. "Believe me, you most certainly *can* ask me as well. But—I can see you're too shy to talk right now. All things in their time." She looked around, smiled. "Come with me over to the sheriff's office. This business with Rock Springs has Albert on edge. He left for the office without eating. I want to drop this by."

"I'm surprised you're not already at the restaurant."

"I traded shifts with Roberta, so she opened for me. Nate's been struggling with some of his schooling, so I wanted to help him study for a test today."

Girl time sounded good. Tabitha could get back to poster making after she took a little walk, even if it was just next door. "I'd like that. Let me get my shawl from upstairs."

A minute later, Albert looked up from his desk when she and Susanna stepped through the door. He smiled and stood, circling his desk to greet his wife with a kiss. He gave Tabitha a smile and a nod.

"I'm glad you stopped in," Albert said, his voice serious. "Telegram arrived this morning. Thom and I need to go to Rock Springs. Tensions have boiled over with the whites and Chinese. A man's been killed. Sheriff over there doesn't know if he'll be able to hold off a full-fledged riot, but would like to try. He's calling in as much law enforcement as he can."

"Albert," Susanna said, placing the basket of food on his desk to take his arm as if that would keep him safe. "I don't like the sound of that. Do you have to go? It's so dangerous."

Tabitha didn't like the sound of it either. Men dying for nothing. Why couldn't the locals and the migrants all just get along?

"I'm sorry, darlin', but I do. It's my job. Thom's, too. We'll be as careful as we can. Don't know when we'll be back, though. I hope in a day or two."

Thom came through the door.

"We all set?" Albert asked.

Thom nodded.

Susanna slipped into Albert's arms and laid her head on his chest.

"It'll be fine, honey. I'll send a telegram as soon as I can if we're going to be longer." His hands rubbed up and down her back, and Tabitha couldn't help but feel warmth behind her eyes herself.

Albert and Thom were so brave to go off, knowing what might lie ahead. And poor Susanna and Hannah. Tabitha didn't know how they could stand having their men in such danger. Hunter entered her mind, and the rumors about his past. The gunslinging and killing. That *couldn't* be true. She didn't believe a word, and nothing anyone could say would change her mind.

Tabitha returned to her shop to find her mother standing at the locked door. "Mother?"

"Good morning, Tabitha."

Alarm bells went off when she saw her mother's carpetbag sitting on the ground by her feet. "Good morning," she responded, wondering what that might mean. Was her mother finally giving up and heading back to New York?

"I've come for a visit. Do you have time?"

It was still only nine. A visit? Perhaps to say goodbye. "Yes, a whole hour before I open. Come in and we can talk. Have you eaten?"

"Oh, yes. Hours ago."

Sneaking another peek at the bag, Tabitha unlocked the door and went inside, holding it for her mother to follow. "I'll stoke the fire and put water on for tea."

"Actually, daughter, there's something I need to request from you. I'd like to get it out of the way first. So I can relax."

Tabitha halted in her tracks. Slowly turned around. She hadn't seen her mother since Sunday morning when Hunter had spoken to her from the stairway. "Yes?"

"I was wondering if I could stay with you for a day or two."

She's not going home? "Why?"

Her mother's face crumpled. She looked away and her nostrils flared. "I can't stay with Roberta any longer. We don't see eye to eye on anything. She challenges everything I say. It's not good for either of us. You have an extra bedroom. I'd be ever so grateful if I could have a nice visit with my only child."

Stunned, Tabitha thought of the extra room laden with all of Hunter's belongings. "What about Uncle Frank? He has a guest room."

Her mother's lips wobbled and she cast her gaze to the floor. "Please don't ask me to go there. He mentioned that he'd recently had an infestation of mice, more than his cats could contain. You know how I can't abide those critters. My skin crawls just thinking about them."

"What about the El Dorado? The rooms are beautiful. I know you'd be very comfortable."

"I knew I should have went there first and not bothered you."

"It's because of Hunter. We're just married."

Her mother walked to the window chair and lowered herself down. "I guess I won't be too humiliated to stay in the hotel even when everyone knows my daughter has a perfectly fine guest room. I understand, Tabitha. I do. And I don't hold it against you at all."

Tabitha's mind warred with reality and guilt. It wasn't right to ask this of Hunter. Not after all he'd already done for her. Sacrificed for her. Her mother's shoulders began to quiver. She was getting on in age. "How long would you be staying?"

"Just a handful of days. Since there isn't anything I can do now that you've gone and married that mountain man, I'll be leaving at the end of the week."

What to do? In the large scheme of things, it was only a few days, and then she'd be gone. Maybe they could make up, mend their relationship. That was doubtful, but Tabitha would like to try. It was the right thing to do. She just prayed Hunter would see it the same.

CHAPTER FIFTY-EIGHT

Hunter dipped the last bar glass into the rinse water and set it upside down on a dishrag that looked as if it could use a good scrubbing. He straightened. Stretched his aching back muscles, then dried his hands. Three men stood at the bar and two occupied one table. Dichelle had brought in a boatload of men Saturday night, and he and Kendall had cleared a hundred and fifty-eight dollars after all was said and done. Tonight was a different story. No spillover whatsoever. Perhaps growing the Bright Nugget's earning ability was a losing battle. Or maybe he was just tired. He'd stayed away from Storybook Lodge all day. Soon, though, he'd have to face Tabitha. She'd see the difference in him. She'd be able to tell that he longed to hold her again, kiss her lips. His troubling thoughts about his new wife had him skeptical he'd ever again find firm footing.

Kendall clomped down the stairs. "Morning!"

"You loco? It's after supper," Buckskin shouted back.

Kendall stopped at the bottom of the stairs and rubbed a hand over his face, clearing away the sleep cobwebs. "That all-day nap sure felt good. I highly recommend it to everyone." He smiled at Hunter. "I guess having a partner has a few advantages."

Going to the end of the bar, Hunter untied his apron and set the wadded cloth on the top of the countertop. He reached for his coat but didn't put it on for the short walk home. "Good night, gentlemen." *I wonder if there'll be supper of any kind to speak of? We never discussed any topics of importance.* He gave a mental shrug. *If not, I guess my earnings can buy another meal at the Silky Hen.*

"Good night, lover boy," Clyde replied. "Sleep tight."

Buckskin laughed and slapped his leg. He picked up his empty glass in anticipation of the change in shift. Hunter had asked Kendall not to keep feeding Buckskin and Clyde until they were cross-eyed drunk, but Hunter had the sneaking suspicion Kendall did whatever he wanted when he wasn't around.

"Hold up," Kendall called when he was about to leave. He hurried over.

"What is it, Kendall, I'm tired."

Kendall stared at him for a long time.

"You got something to say, say it."

The bartender cleared his throat, then began softly so no one else could hear. "It ain't been so bad having a partner. The boon last Saturday night was due to you thinkin' it up."

"And my hard work."

He nodded. "That's right. And now, today, I haven't had time off like that since I don't remember when . . ."

"Do you have a point you're trying to make here, Kendall, or is this some way to keep me—"

The man's mouth flattened out. "What I'm trying to say is I'm sorry."

Hunter pulled back. What was this about? "What are you talking about?"

"I," he began, then looked at the floor. "I spread some lies about you. When you first come to town and I was fit to be tied. I told a few loose lips around town that you were a gunman, a killer. I'd sent a telegram to Soda Springs, to my friend, but he said you had a reputation of being hard, but fair. That men were scared of you because you were fast, but he didn't know of any wrongdoing."

And now everything makes sense. The looks. The apprehension.

"Say something, will ya?"

"Nothin' to say, Kendall," he responded slowly. He set his hand on Kendall's shoulder, and smiled into the bartender's remorse-etched face. "People will have to judge me for themselves. Decide what to believe. Don't lose too much sleep over it. What's done is done."

It took less than a minute to reach Storybook Lodge. The shades were pulled and the signs were turned or brought in an hour ago. He thought back to the morning when he'd first come by, helping Miss Hoity-Toity out with the heavy sign. Her smile had done funny things to his insides even then. His comments had turned her face a pretty pink. He should have turned tail and run for the hills. Things sure would be a lot easier.

Tabitha looked up from the kitchen when he stepped inside. She was stirring something on the stove.

"Beef stew," she said, a nervous smile on her lips.

It annoyed Hunter that he could read her expressions so well.

"Hungry?"

"I am," he replied, unstrapping his gun belt and laying the weapon on the small table by the front door. He stared at the Colt for several long moments, understanding Roberta's narrow-eyed gaze in the bookstore. She would have made sure her niece had heard the juicy news about him, Hunter had no doubt. He started for the stairs still holding his coat.

Tabitha hurried over and extracted the garment from his grasp. "I'll take that for you."

"No need. I can do—"

"You go sit by the window and I'll serve up your supper just as soon as I get back. I'm sure your feet must be tired, standing all day in the saloon." When he hesitated, she gave his arm a nudge. "Go on, Hunter. I'll be right down."

Feeling the hair on the back of his neck prickle, he glanced up.

Halfway down the staircase, Marigold eyed him warily. Seeing her expression, he felt the same. He looked back at Tabitha.

"It's only for a few days. You don't mind, do you?"

What did Tabitha do with my belongings in the extra bedroom?

He felt his ire raise its ugly head, but Tabitha's beseeching gaze kept him quiet.

"Mr. Wade. Home from a long day of salooning?"

Again, his gaze snared his wife's.

"Mother, please keep your comments to yourself, unless they're nice."

"What's not nice about what I said?"

Without another word, Hunter went to the one and only comfortable chair in the room, but as he was about to sit, he realized he should save it for Tabitha's mother. He turned and went to Tabitha's desk, pulled out her straight-backed chair, and sat. Marigold followed him and took the flowered chair with a satisfied grin.

"Ah, this is enjoyable," she said. "I'll have a chance to get to know my son-in-law. I didn't think that was going to happen. How are you, Hunter? May I call you that?"

He nodded. "You can call me anything you like. Is Marigold fine with you? Or do you prefer Mother?"

"Anything at all. I'm just pleased to be here."

That's a switch.

She smiled.

He accepted a large bowl of stew from Tabitha, and held it on his lap until she'd served her mother. When she went back for her own, he realized there wasn't a chair for her. Standing, he went to the stool Nate had used and slid it through his legs.

"No, Hunter, you needn't—"

"This is fine. You sit at your desk. Tomorrow I'll see what I might be able to rig up for a small table."

They ate in silence, after which he followed Tabitha into the kitchen to help with the dishes. "What did you do with my belongings?" he asked quietly as her mother dozed in the chair.

"After the decision was made that she would stay, I sent her to the mercantile for a few things for supper. Thank goodness I own an extra set of sheets. I've never changed a bed so quickly in my life. Don't be angry with me, Hunter. Please."

"I just don't understand why she's here. I thought she couldn't stand me. I'd think this was the last place she'd want to stay."

"She and my aunt can't get along for more than a few days at a time."

"What about your uncle? Wouldn't she be more comfortable there?"

"She won't stay with Uncle Frank, because he's having some problems with mice. She all but broke down when I suggested the hotel. I can promise you I tried to avoid this. For your sake . . ." *For our sake.* "Hunter?"

"When you put it like that, I guess a few days won't hurt. What about tonight?"

A stain rose up in her cheeks. "We'll cross that bridge when we get—"

"We're pretty well there, Miss Hoity-Toity. You better start thinking. That note we wrote to the preacher won't be worth squat after one week. This whole charade has gotten involved."

The warm stew had mellowed him considerably. His crankiness was replaced with a feeling of home. The evening sounds of the night. How pretty Tabitha looked with her hands in a dishpan of water and wisps of her hair stuck to her moist forehead. Even with Marigold out in the chair snoring away like she were sawing a wood pile, reminding him of Clyde, there was something special about tonight.

Finished wiping down the boards, Tabitha folded the dish towel she'd used to dry her hands and set it in its place. What were they going to do to pass the time until it was time to turn in?

"How about if you help me with a little of my reading?"

Her eyes widened, and a smile blossomed on her lips. "Wonderful. Do you know where your book is?"

"Somewhere with my belongings."

"Then it's in my room now. Wait here and I'll get it."

Hunter quietly brought the stool over to the desk thinking how awkward it was going to be on the stool while trying to sound out words, but they didn't have much choice. The only other chair was occupied by her mother, or they could go upstairs and sit together on the bed. He wasn't going to chance that with all these warm family feelings rumbling around in his chest. No sir, not at the moment.

CHAPTER FIFTY-NINE

"Tom pre-presented himself before Aunt Polly, who was sitting by an open window in a p-pleasant rearward apartment, which was bedroom, breakfast-room, dining-room, and library, combined," Hunter read softly, his back aching from sitting on the high stool next to Tabitha, as he bent forward.

His wife sat at his side, looking at her own book, while he read quietly aloud, so as not to wake her mother. When he'd balked at reading aloud, she'd said it was good practice to hear his own voice as well as let his mouth form the unfamiliar words. He wondered how she knew so much about reading, but he *was* getting better, so he dare not argue. From her wide selection of books, she came up with a heck of a lot of facts he'd never heard. Best not to question her unless he wanted to be proven wrong.

He smiled inwardly. There were a few things he could teach her, if she were so inclined. He lifted his palm to his cheek as if the sting of her slap had just happened. Unfortunately, he knew exactly where his wife stood on such matters.

"I guess I shouldn't have chosen this book," she whispered, leaning in close, her light scent distracting his concentration. "I forgot about all the slang and hyphenated words. I can choose another if you'd like. Something that will flow more easily."

"What? And give this up now?" Hunter lifted his head, pretending horror, all the while taking in her soft beauty, alight with the conviction to help. "After I've struggled through three whole chapters? Nothin' doing. Besides, I want to know what happens. The story has caught my interest."

"All right. Other than the chopped-up dialect, you're doing a fine job. I must say, I've enjoyed listening to you." She glanced to the darkened town just past her rolled-down shades. "Logan Meadows sure is quiet tonight."

"Yeah, no gunshots from the saloon."

"Which makes me very happy."

He cocked a brow. "I know it does, Miss Hoity-Toity. I could go over and shoot off my Colt since Albert is away. That would liven things up a bit."

She laughed. "You're teasing, I know."

"Guess I am."

She didn't flinch when he reached over and fingered a wisp of her hair that had fallen into her face. It hurt that she thought him a killer. He didn't care about anyone else—let them think what they would. It was her opinion that mattered. "I learned something tonight."

"Oh?"

"Kendall confessed to me that he'd slandered my name. He's sorry now, and I've forgiven him, just didn't want you to—"

Her eyes widened. She knew exactly what he was referring to. "Kendall! I felt in my heart those rumors were false." She swallowed and glanced away for a moment, then slowly turned back to his gaze. "I'll admit at first, I didn't know what to think exactly, but as time went on I knew they couldn't be true. I should have told you right away."

Her sincerity healed a part of the wound. "Yes, you should have."

"I'm sorry," she whispered.

"Nothin' to be sorry for. I'm just glad the truth came out." The warm stew had made him drowsy. Her mother slept on in the chair by the window. He looked at the clock. Seven twenty-five. With the little sleep he'd gotten the night before, the soft bed was sounding better than ever. Too bad he didn't have a soft bed to his name anymore.

Hunter yawned, stretched back, and rubbed a hand across his face. What on earth was Tabitha going to do with him tonight? It wasn't right to ask him to sleep on the floor. Not after all he'd sacrificed for her.

"Oh, my," a wobbly voice said.

Mother. Tabitha glanced over. Her mother's eyes were open and she was watching them with a curious expression.

"I must have fallen asleep," she admitted.

"You did," Tabitha said. "Over an hour ago. It's almost seven thirty."

"Then I shall turn in." She grimaced as she tried to raise her head off the back of the cushion. "Ow . . . I'm as stiff as an old scarecrow. This knee is getting worse with each passing year."

Without being asked, Hunter stood and went over to the chair. He held out both his hands. Her mother hesitated for a couple of heartbeats, and then placed her own inside of his. Tabitha watched in stunned silence. Waiting patiently until her mother was stable on her feet, Hunter helped her climb the stairs to her bedroom.

"Good night, Tabitha," she called. "Sweet dreams."

Sadness at hearing the old sentiment made Tabitha drop her gaze back to her book. "Good night, Mother," she called back. "You sleep well, too."

Her mother's familiar chuckle floated down the staircase. Hunter must have said something. In a moment he was back.

"That was kind of you."

"What?"

He honestly didn't seem to know. "You helping my mother after the trouble she's caused."

He shrugged. "Holding a grudge only hurts the grudge holder."

"Thorp?"

He nodded. "I'm mighty tired myself. Have you decided where I'm going to sleep? I could take a blanket to Win's hayloft. I don't mind."

"I can't ask that of you! It's October. Besides, someone might see you. That would be pretty difficult to explain away."

"Well? What else do you have in mind?"

"I've read lots of stories where unmarried couples roll up a blanket and put it between them to separate the—"

"Roll up a blanket? That's ridiculous. That wouldn't stop an amorous prairie dog. It certainly wouldn't stop me."

The way his gaze lingered on her lips had her thinking of the kiss. The second kiss. The one last night at the shivaree. The kiss that had brought a barrage of wayward thoughts, and even tingles in places she didn't know she had. "No? Well, then, I'll take my chair in the corner of my bedroom. It's very comfortable. Then you can have the bed."

"I didn't say I was going to take advantage of you. I said a rolled-up blanket wouldn't stop me if I wanted to—" He clamped his mouth closed. "Go get yourself ready for bed, and put up the blockade if it'll make you feel better. I'll undress after you're safely tucked away under the covers. You can trust me. You have *nothing* to worry about."

He made it sound like taking advantage of her was the very last thing he'd ever want. Hurt, she headed to the back door. Taking a lantern, she used the privy, then proceeded up the stairs. How had everything gotten so mixed up? She went quietly past her mother's room and then to the armoire on the far wall, still chilled from being outside. Pulling out both her extra blankets, she dropped them on her bed. She was twenty-nine years old and more than a little curious about the marriage act. If Hunter was still interested in her, he would have said something when they'd gotten married. Wouldn't he? Surely, he wasn't that insecure about being turned down again, not at his age.

Nothing had been the same since the slap. It was almost as if he'd been expecting it.

Confused, and riddled with wanton desires, she stripped out of her dress and donned her nightgown. As quickly as she could in the chilly room, she rolled up the extra blankets, placed them down the center of the bed, and crawled under the quilts, the cold sheet chilling her further.

Tired from a long day on her feet, Daisy removed her apron, her muscles aching from leaning over the sink at the Silky Hen. She stretched and then arched her back.

"I didn't think we'd ever finish up," Susanna said, watching her over her shoulder as she spread out the coals of the stove. "Thank you for doing the majority of the pots and pans. I promise I'll do them all tomorrow."

Daisy smiled. "That's no problem. I'm taking my dirty apron, and the others in the hamper, over to the Lings. Does yours need washing?"

Susanna stood and inspected her apron. "No, ma'am. It's good for another day. You sure you want to go over now? It's dark. And besides, the front door will be locked."

"It's not that I want to, but there aren't any clean aprons left. Hannah dropped off five last week. They should be ready. The Lings don't mind if I use the back door."

"Daisy . . ."

"It's just across the street." She unfolded her normally white apron, which was spotted with gravy. "I can't wear this another day. It's disgraceful. We need clean and fresh for the morning. I'm waitressing."

Susanna's eyes went wide. "Oh, I see what you mean."

"Won't take more than four minutes. From there I'll go home. Is Win coming to walk you home since Albert's away?"

Susanna nodded. "You come back and he'll walk you as well."

"That's silly. I'm just behind the hotel, you're much farther away down the street and across the bridge. Stop worrying."

The two women went to the front door, Daisy's hands filled with soiled aprons and a few tablecloths. Susanna watched her cross the street. A warm glow shone from inside the laundry house. When Daisy got to the alley, she turned and waved her friend back inside. From where she was, she heard the click of the restaurant's front lock.

She pushed ahead in the darkened alley. Light from Main Street illumined the passage halfway through. Fifteen feet past the end was the Lings' shanty, a light burning inside. Bao would be home putting Lan to bed, but Tap would still be hard at work, and maybe Jake's mother as well. Daisy hadn't met the woman, but as each day passed, and as her lonesomeness at missing Jake mounted, she'd wondered if she should arrange a chance.

With a breath of relief, she rounded the corner of the brick building and pulled open the back door. A mouse, or something else, skittered away from under Daisy's foot, causing Daisy to yelp in fright.

Mr. Ling jerked up from his ironing board. The woman who must be Jake's mother scrambled to her feet from the wash tub where she'd been working.

Tap Ling started her way. "Miss Daisy! You hurt?"

Embarrassed, Daisy came forward. "No, I'm sorry. A mouse startled me." She glanced at Jake's mother. "I have the dirty laundry and wondered if I could pick up the clean. We don't have anything for tomorrow."

"Yes, yes, of course. I will show—"

"I know where they are, Mr. Ling," the woman said. "I put them away this morning. Please follow me, miss."

Mr. Ling nodded and went back to his ironing.

At a table of folded linen, Jake's mother took the dirty linen from Daisy and replaced them with a stack of tablecloths topped with several aprons. They were all nicely pressed.

"This should be all of it," she said. Strands of hair had come loose from her bun and wafted in front of her face.

Compassion moved through Daisy. "I'm Daisy," she said, not knowing if Jake had said anything to her about them.

"I know. I've seen you come and go in the restaurant across the street. You're Jake's girl."

They stood silently in the dim interior for several awkward moments.

"That's right." No one had spoken outright about the horrible way she'd treated Jake, but Daisy had put the pieces together. "I love Jake. I'll take good care of him."

She nodded, and in the shadowy room, Daisy thought she saw the woman's lips pull down in sorrow. The heart was capable of so much love and so much pain, and yet Daisy didn't have the words to bridge the expanse between the two. Instead, she turned with the linens, eager to be home. "Thank you."

The back door in the dark room squeaked closed. Daisy darted her gaze to see Mr. Ling still at his work, then over to Jake's mother. "Did you see somebody go out the door?"

"No. But I'm not surprised if you thought you did. This place is haunted. Always feels like I'm being watched. Have to say, it stands my hair on end."

She was relieved when Jake's mother continued with her to the back door. Just as she was about to exit, the woman laid a hand on her arm, stopping her.

"Mr. Ling," she called over her shoulder. "I'm walking Daisy home. I'll be back directly."

"You go home, too," came the reply. "You work enough today."

Relief eased Daisy's mind, though she was still disconcerted by what she'd thought she'd seen. Perhaps now she'd have a chance to voice a few of the things she'd been feeling a moment before. For better or for worse, this was Jake's mother. That alone made her want to heal the wound. Would Jake's ma be receptive to her? Only one way to find out.

Hunter waited a half hour before he proceeded up the stairs. He wanted to make sure Tabitha was good and asleep. Thinking back, her bed hadn't been all that large. By the time she added the divider, it would be even worse. At the top of the stairs, he crossed the landing, then paused at Tabitha's closed bedroom door. Too tired to think much about anything, he quietly stepped inside. A lone candle flickered on his side table and Tabitha had her back to the rolled blanket—blankets!

He smiled, even at a prick of irritation. There was so much about Miss Hoity-Toity that he admired. Her bravery was at the top of the list. Here she was, a twenty-nine-year-old maiden, trusting him to be honorable all night in the same bed as her.

In the cramped quarters, he awkwardly pulled off his left boot while balancing on one foot, and then did the same for the other. He stripped down to his flesh on the upper portion of his body but, to make her more comfortable, left on his pants.

The bed squeaked loudly when he sat on the edge. He swung his legs in. Leaning over to the table, he cupped the flame of the candle, and blew, then settled back on the pillow.

All was good until a gun blast rent the air. Tabitha stirred, half turned on her side and then jerked to a stop as if remembering he was there.

"It's just the saloon, Tabby," he whispered. He could tell she was awake. "Nothin's gonna get ya."

"I know. Gunshots just make me jumpy. I've yet to get used to them."

Knock knock knock.

Wishing he could transport himself to some lonesome prairie under the stars, he stifled a grumble. "Yes?"

"I think somebody just got shot. Do you think they need a doctor?"

"No, I don't Mrs. Canterbury. Go back to sleep."

"How thick are these walls? Can a bullet come through?"

He swung his legs off the mattress and sat on the edge of the bed holding his forehead in his hands.

"I'm sorry," Tabitha whispered. "She's not used to the noise. Back in New York, our home is in a quiet part of town. Only houses . . ."

"Mr. Wade?"

"A bullet can come through the wall, but before it does, it'd have to pass through the saloon first, and then the sheriff's office. You're safe, *Mother*. I assure you, nothing is going to happen to you in your own bed. My bed, actually," he added under his breath.

A loud indignant sniff sounded on the other side of the door. "If you're sure?"

"I'm sure. Now go back to bed before it's time to get up. My wife and I would like a little privacy."

"Oh!"

He chuckled and they heard her hurry away. Her door clicked closed. After a moment, he lay back down.

Tabitha lit a candle on her side of the bed. "You do like to scandalize, don't you?" she said, humor reverberating in her voice. "You're very naughty."

"She had it coming."

Tabitha rolled to her side facing him, a small smile pulling at her lips. He gave her another mental medal for her boldness. Intrigued, he arranged himself in the same position, leveraged up on his elbow, his head resting in the palm of his hand.

They stared at each other for several seconds, the silence heavy on the air.

"You didn't come up for a long time," she whispered. "How come?"

"I wanted to give you plenty of time to get settled." *And fall asleep.*

"And fall asleep?"

He narrowed his eyes but that only made her smile grow. "Did you just read my mind?"

She giggled. A sound that he hadn't yet heard from her. She sounded young, and unencumbered of all the social restrictions that usually weighted her mind. Her loose hair flowed temptingly over her shoulder. Didn't women usually plait it, or put it up in a cap, or something? It was awfully tempting, reminding him of melted caramel candy right before an apple was dipped. She was under the covers, but a frilly piece of lace poked out around her neck, looking mighty appealing. Her gaze softened. Invited his touch. He reached out.

CHAPTER SIXTY

Tabitha couldn't believe this was happening. Alone in bed with Hunter. Closed off in a room for hours. Just the two of them.

He stretched forward and stroked her cheek with the back of his fingers, his eyes roaming her face. She thought she'd die of the pleasure. She tried not to move, but controlling her breathing was impossible. The sheet moved in response to her pounding heart and lifting chest.

"You're beautiful, Mrs. Wade," he whispered, a crooked smile pulling his lips.

She wanted him to kiss her. Chase away all her uncertainties. Was he teasing again? In a minute would he lean back and laugh? She didn't care what anyone thought of Hunter. She loved him with all her heart. His eyes had the power to render her speechless, like they were doing now.

When she didn't respond, he leaned forward and pressed his lips to hers, his woodsy scent fogging her mind. He inched forward, and as he did, they rolled together until she was half beneath him, his arms around her, the blankets and sheets still acting as chaperone. If he wanted to make this a real marriage, she wouldn't stop him. Like Dichelle had said, she'd be the luckiest woman on earth. His mouth moved on hers in a slow perusal that made her yearn for so much more.

When he began to pull away, she tightened her hold. She prayed this wasn't a dream.

"Hunter," she whispered against his lips. "Make love to me."

He stilled, and she was frightened that she'd been too forward. Gone too far. He probably felt awkward with her mother in the next room.

He nuzzled her neck, then put his lips to her ear, sending a torrent of hot tingles racing down her back. "You sure?" he whispered. "I don't want you to do anything you don't want to do. Remember the letter we sent. What we do tonight can't get undone."

She was committed. There wasn't anything she wanted more in her life. "I'm sure."

"You deserve a whole hell of a lot better than me, Miss Hoity-Toity. I can't give you much."

"There is no better than you, Hunter. I've known it since our walk under the stars . . ."

That was all the encouragement he needed. He took claim of her mouth again, her person. She was transported to the stars and back, but never left his arms.

"Tabitha? I hate to intrude, but it's very late. I'm worried something has happened to you. That man has a reputation . . ."

Mother! Just outside her door.

Tabitha glanced over at Hunter, who'd failed to awaken at four, like he'd promised her. Love flooded her heart. She reached out and touched his bare shoulder, for a moment reliving the ecstasy they'd shared last night. How she loved him. Her wagon-train boss.

"Tabitha? *Please*, answer me."

Tabitha scrambled out of the covers and quickly slipped her night-gown over her head, finger-combed her hair, and then wrapped herself in the divider blanket that had ended up on the floor moments after Hunter had come to bed. The thought made her smile. Carefully opening the door so as not to wake her husband, she stepped out onto the landing and closed the door behind her.

Her mother's eyes popped open wide.

Had she and Father never been young?

"Tabitha!" Censure turned her mother's voice to steel.

"What?"

Her mother stammered for words, and finally waved them away, unable to voice her dismay.

"What?" Tabitha asked again. Her mother had been at the wedding. That she looked a tousled mess shouldn't be surprising.

"Look at you! I never thought . . ."

She took her mother's arm and walked her away from her door to the top of the steps. "Well, in that lies the problem. Maybe you should have. Hunter and I are married. Only three days ago. You invited yourself here. Don't make me feel ashamed for something I shouldn't. Don't do that to me ever again. I won't allow it. And while we're clearing the air, please don't imply anything about Hunter again. Everything you've heard has been lies. He's a good man and deserves your respect."

Marigold's mouth snapped closed. She looked like a chastised child.

"What time is it?" Tabitha asked.

"Ten. I've been downstairs for hours. The street is already busy. If I'd known you were going to, to, ah well—I could have opened the store for you."

Ten! It *was* late. She had the reading this evening and had more baking to do.

"Thank you for waking me then. I had no idea of the time. Why don't you go out for some breakfast at the restaurant? It will give you a chance to mend fences with Aunt Roberta. She usually works Tuesday mornings."

"What about the store?"

"I'll put a note in the window that we are opening at eleven today. Mornings are usually very slow. No one will mind."

"I already ate some—"

Tabitha crooked one brow.

"All right. Give me two minutes and I'll be gone. I've already warmed a kettle of water on the stove. You can use it to . . ." She swished a hand in front of Tabitha.

"Thank you. That was very kind." At her mother's befuddled expression she had to smile. "Everything is going to be fine, Mother," she said softly. "Go on to breakfast, and I'll see you in a little while. Don't forget we have the reading tonight, and I have to prepare the store and bake some goodies. You can help me with that."

Wonder passed over Marigold's face. "Yes, I'll be happy to." She leaned forward and kissed Tabitha on the cheek. "I'll see you later."

Tabitha smiled and gently shook her head in astonishment as she watched her mother go down the stairs. She listened as her mother gathered her things and opened the door. "I'll lock the door behind me, daughter," she said. "Don't forget to put up the sign."

Five thirty arrived like a speeding bullet. After waking late, then doing some morning chores at the Bright Nugget, Hunter had spent the day helping his wife prepare for her big day. Miss Hoity-Toity no longer, whenever Tabby came close, every sense he owned sprang to life. She'd surprised him last night, and he had to struggle to keep his thoughts on what he was supposed to be doing. At the moment, after he'd cleaned up for the second time in one day, he was putting the finishing touches on the room. He'd already pushed the standing shelves to the walls, making room for the benches she'd already had and adding five more. It was tight, but he hoped the crowd would fill them.

Susanna came in dressed for tonight, two platefuls of cookies in her hands. She smiled and took them to the kitchen. "More goodies." She glanced around. "Where's Tabitha?"

"Upstairs getting ready. She should be down any time." At that moment, Marigold started down the stairs dressed to the hilt in a blue velvet gown, and quite fancy for any doings in Logan Meadows. "What's the news from Rock Springs?" he asked. "Has Albert returned?"

A frown appeared on Susanna's face. "No. Neither he nor Thom. I did receive a telegram this morning. More tension, and one more killing. A white man this time. They can't tell if he fell or was pushed off a twenty-foot-high ledge in the mine. That's amplified the tensions. It's one thing if a Chinese man is murdered, but if a white man dies . . ." She shook her head. "Anyway, it's a mess. I'll be so relieved when they both come home."

Marigold went to the kitchen counter and surveyed the cookies Susanna had just placed there and the cakes and other baked goods she and Tabby had made. She came into the room where they were and stopped next to Hunter.

Susanna nodded politely at the same time the door flew open and Nate barreled into the shop, his color high. "Ma," he gasped for air. "Mrs. Donovan is coming down the street with Markus. Can him and me go froggin' during the reading? We'd rather do that than sit in here."

Susanna patted down his damp hair that looked as if it had been combed at one time. "No, you may not. Hannah expects Markus to sit quietly and listen. I expect the same from you. You know Sunday after church is your frogging time. Listening to literature is one way of learning."

"That's very good advice, young man," Marigold said, her fingers twined together in front of her skirt.

Nate shrugged, disappointment on his face, and exited the shop.

A buggy pulled up outside, the first of the guests to arrive. Hunter recognized the women from New Meringue, with two new faces. His wife was a darn good marketer. If this kept up, her book sales would grow handily each week, and her mortgage wouldn't be a worry.

At the sound of light footsteps on the staircase, he turned, his breath catching in his throat at the beautiful sight. Tabitha wore a creamy-yellow dress made of a fabric that looked soft and inviting. A light, matching shawl covered her perfectly straight shoulders. Part of her hair had been pulled back and done up at the crown with a matching ribbon, and the rest cascaded down her back.

Last night rushed back with a vengeance. As much as he'd felt her devotion to him, she'd never actually said that she loved him. He hadn't said it either, but he had married her when she'd needed him. She must realize that. At the troubling thoughts, he glanced away. Maybe it was only her curiosity about the ways between a man and a woman that had her invite his touch. He couldn't blame her, for the proof of her innocence had been evident. She'd waited until she married and he'd been her only man. His heart squeezed with ardent love, knowing he'd lost himself to her fully. If she still wanted to separate after her mother left town, he'd never be the same.

Tabby breezed over to their group and gave Suzanna a warm hug, her gaze finding his over her friend's shoulder. There was something different in the back of her eyes that warmed his face and brought a smile to his lips. For now, he'd enjoy his time with her, this feeling of home and belonging.

"Hello," the four women from New Meringue said as they stepped inside. "Are we too early? We wanted to get a better seat than we had last week."

Tabby put out her hands, and the first woman through the door took them in her own.

"Not at all, Mrs. Johnson," Tabitha said. "Please, come in. Save a spot and then feel free to browse. The shelves are somewhat out of order, but if you need help finding something just let me"—she glanced at

Hunter and smiled—"or my husband know, and we can assist you. Or my mother, as well. We're so happy you've made the trip."

The man who'd been driving the buggy and tending to the horse stepped in and took off his hat. "Hello," he said, looking around. He'd not been here last week. "I heard so much about your shop from my wife, I just had to come see it for myself, Miss Canterbury."

"It's Mrs. Wade now," Tabitha's mother surprised Hunter by saying. She nodded at him, a ghost of a smile playing at the corner of her lips.

Another buggy pulled up outside with faces he'd never seen before, and Brenna and Gregory, along with their children, arrived, too. It looked like tonight would be another sellout crowd, the only difference this time, he was part of the group. Last week he'd stood at the doors of the saloon wishing he were here, and now he was. His gaze sought out his wife, finding her welcoming Brenna and then going to the new arrivals and meeting them. Pride warmed him. He was surprised when he felt a hand on his arm, and looked down.

"You're a lucky man, Mr. Wade," Marigold said, as she pulled her gaze away from her daughter. "And I'm a lucky mother. I guess I never really knew her strengths before. Never opened my eyes to her value. I have to say, I'm enjoying my time here in Logan Meadows. Perhaps I'll stay longer than I planned."

Her gaze challenged him as she waited for his reaction.

He gave a wink. "You can stay as long as you like, *Mother*. You won't hear a complaint out of me."

CHAPTER SIXTY-ONE

"Thank you for coming," Tabitha said as she waved to the second to last person out the door. She hugged her shawl around her shoulders. "Please come back next week, weather permitting. Yes, Etta," she called to the buggy as it was pulling away. "Your copy should be here by then. Goodbye, thank you!"

The evening had been another success, and they'd sold nine books! Nine! That thrilling thought almost made her giggle. Her terrific Tuesdays were beginning to make up for the slow sales during the rest of the week.

She felt Hunter's hand on her back. "Are we ready to walk Dichelle back to the hotel? Everyone's gone."

"Absolutely." She beamed at her new friend. "I'm so happy you came, Dichelle. Only, at first, seeing you, such a great actress and singer at my event, made me more than a bit nervous. But, that went away as soon as I read the first paragraph. I hope you had fun."

"Oh, *sì, sì*! Tonight was a treat. I so seldom get to sit back and enjoy someone else's performance. You did a beautiful job, Tabby. *Bravo!*"

"You're just being kind. But let's get you back to the hotel. I'm worn out after our preparations today and think I'd like to turn in right away. Mother's already gone up to her room, and since we ate so many sweets, there is no need of supper. Unless you're hungry, Hunter." She quickly looked at her husband. "I can easily heat something for you."

Hunter chuckled. "I'm sure you can," he replied, slowly looking her up and down. "But I've eaten enough cookies to last a lifetime." His yawn was melodramatic.

Dichelle's eyes danced in merriment.

As Dichelle shrugged into her coat, Hunter went up the stairs, returning with Tabby's coat as well as his. "It's brisk out tonight, you're going to need more than that shawl."

A few minutes later, after they'd dropped Dichelle into her room, she and Hunter started back the way they'd come when a sound from the other side of the street made Tabitha glance across. The Lings' place was dark for the first time ever. Had the lamp run out of fluid? No. Something felt amiss. She pulled Hunter's arm to get him to stop.

"What is it?"

"I don't know. I think I heard a strange sound, and now I don't see any light at the laundry house." She shivered and looked up into his face. "They always leave a light on. I've never seen their shop dark before. Something's not right."

She peered across the expanse, trying to see. "Hunter, look! I think the door is ajar!" Without waiting for his response, she darted across the deserted street. Fear curled inside her, and a dark, evil feeling swirled in her mind.

Hunter beat her to the door, his gun drawn.

Tabby cried out when she saw a limp hand protruding from the two-inch gap of the opened door.

"Jake's mother!" Dropping to her knees, Tabitha waited as Hunter turned her over and checked for a pulse.

"She's still alive."

"Ma'am," Tabitha said softly, rubbing her arm. "Wake up. Please. What happened?"

"I . . ."

Hunter was on one knee beside them. "She's coming around. We need to get her to Dr. Thorn's." When he went to pick her up, her eyes opened despite a large bruise on the side of her face as well as cuts and scratches.

"Wait," she said, in a garbled voice. She tried to lift her arm, but was unable. Tabitha found a paper clenched in her fist, but it was too dark to read.

"Man . . . surprised Mr. Ling. I tried to fight him off. Found this paper yesterday in the back of the shop . . ."

Tabitha gasped. "Where is Mr. Ling?"

"Inside, I think. Hurt or . . ."

"Bao and Lan?"

"The man took Bao." Tears leaked from the corner of the woman's eyes, mixing with blood from several cuts and scrapes. "I tried to fight, I tried . . ."

"Come on," Hunter said, lifting her and striding toward the doctor's office. "Let's get her to Dr. Thorn's. I need to go after Mrs. Ling."

Dr. Thorn opened up after several moments of pounding.

"What?" He blinked in astonishment. He was still dressed in the dapper trousers and wool vest he'd worn to the reading.

"Jake's mother. She's been hurt and says that Mrs. Ling has been abducted," Tabitha said, her voice trembling.

Dr. Thorn lit several additional lamps. "Lay her on the table." He went to his water pitcher and washed his hands. Tabitha took the note to the lantern and quickly read the message.

"Someone is offering a reward for deportable immigrants! How disgusting! That would be Bao! Dr. Thorn, what will this do to her baby?"

"Don't know." He shook his head. "If she makes it that far. I've heard that takes too much time and money and they kill and scalp for the reward—"

Tabitha blanched. "No! That can't happen! Lan too? Whoever did this struck on a night they knew everyone would be in my shop all the way down the street. So their struggle wouldn't be heard." She glanced at Jake's poor mother, who'd put up a good fight. "We have to find them, Hunter!"

"Right now, I have to look for Mr. Ling," Hunter said. "We think he's in the shop unconscious." He picked up a lantern and rushed out the door. She turned for the door but Hunter caught her arm. "You wait here."

A minute later Hunter was back with the small man in his arms. He'd been badly beaten, very much like Jake's mother. Tabitha cleared a space on a sofa against the wall, and Hunter laid the unconscious man down.

"Let's go, Tabby," Hunter said. "I'm taking you back to the shop and you're staying put. I don't like that this has happened with Albert and Thom out of town." He looked at the doctor and then at Jake's mother, who lay silently, her eyes closed and her breathing shallow. "Can we do anything for her? Or Mr. Ling?"

"No." The doctor had stripped out of his vest and put on an apron. He was busy gathering his antiseptics.

They argued all the way back to the shop. But he'd put his husbandly foot down. When that hadn't sat well, he asked her nicely, saying he could ride faster and cover more ground if he knew she was safely locked inside Storybook Lodge with her mother. They were in their bedroom, where he hastily filled his saddlebag with more ammunition.

"But no one is after me, Hunter. I can be another set of eyes for you."

"I'll round up Win, and Charlie when I go for my horse at the Axelrose ranch. It's dark, so riding will be dangerous. If we don't strike fast—"

She'll be killed, is what he's not saying.

"I'm worried, Hunter! What if something happens to Bao's baby? What if they both die?" She was unable to keep a frightened sob from her throat. "And I'm worried about you. I don't want to lose you. Those men are ruthless. To hurt Jake's mom, a pregnant woman, and a little girl they'd have to be pure evil." She reached out and grasped his arm.

"Don't worry." He slipped his gun into its holster. "I can take care of myself."

"I'm worried about that deportation law. If you kill the man, you might be the one in trouble. It's crazy when it comes to the Chinese."

"Kidnapping is against the law, so rest easy." He caught her face between his palms and took a moment to study it. Then he leaned down and kissed her, tenderly at first, and then with passion. "I won't kill anyone if I don't have to. I'll leave it to the law," he said, pulling away.

Tabitha wrapped her arms around herself, but couldn't stop a violent shiver from racking her body. "I know you'll save them, Hunter. It's what you do. You're a hero through and through. That's why I knew you'd marry me when I needed a husband fast. It's in your blood . . ." Realizing she was rambling, she glanced up at Hunter, who was looking at her with the strangest expression she'd ever seen. She couldn't make it out. "What?"

He shook his head, and shrugged into his coat. "I need to get moving. I've already squandered too much time."

She blinked at his curt tone. "You're right." She had to run to keep up with him as he bounded down the stairs. Her mother, in her dressing gown and nightcap, opened her bedroom door.

"Keep this door locked at all times," he said without looking back.

Before she could get any more words out, he was gone.

CHAPTER SIXTY-TWO

Hunter cursed himself the whole way to the livery. "Win!" he yelled. "You here?" He didn't wait for an answer but strode angrily down the dirt aisle toward the back of the large barn. Why should he feel upset? Tabitha had needed a husband and he'd stepped in. That was plain. Their marriage was no more to her than business. Like one of the romances she liked to read. *So what!*

Winthrop came through the back barn doors leading a horse. "Hunter, what's wrong? I heard you call. You sound upset."

"I am! Mrs. Ling and her daughter have been kidnapped for bounty. Seems someone, most likely someone from Rock Springs, has put bounty money on any Chinese that can be legally deported. Whoever did it beat up Mr. Ling and their work woman."

Win stood speechless, his face stoic.

"I'd planned to get my horse from Charlie's, but that'll take too long. I need a horse now."

"I have one right here." Win tossed the lead rope to Hunter and reached for the saddle pad and saddle hanging on the top rail of the stall. Within moments, the gelding was ready.

"I'll go with you!"

"I'm ready to ride now. Heading toward Rock Springs. With Albert and Thom out of town, we're shorthanded. You ride out and get Charlie and whomever else you can find, and I'll get moving. With Bao in the family way, we don't have a minute to lose."

"The tea is ready," Tabitha called over her shoulder to her mother, who'd come down after Hunter had left. "Would you like a cookie with your tea? By some miracle, we have a few left over." The troubling look in Hunter's eyes still had Tabitha anxious. What had she said, or done? She couldn't figure it out.

"Yes, please. Can you get it all?"

"I have a tray. Stay put."

Carrying the tray into the large room, Tabitha settled the fare on the small table beside the flowered chair, and pulled up her desk chair. Her mother took a cookie and offered her the plate.

"I couldn't. My insides are knotted. This tea is all I want." She picked up her cup and gently blew on the steaming brew.

"What you told me is horrible. I met that nice woman just yesterday. And her little girl. I'm very worried about them, Tabitha."

She nodded. She wished she could make sense out of the situation, but she had nothing. "Some people are lawless. And evil. How could anyone harm Mr. Ling, or Jake's mother?" She didn't want to consider what might be happening to Bao and Lan.

"I wish your sheriff was back. Or the deputy."

So do I.

At a scuffling noise, her mother's cup rattled. "What was that?"

"I don't know." Tabitha set her cup on the table and went to the front door. Pulling back the lowered blind just an inch, she gazed out into the very dark, deserted street. She wondered about Hunter, where he was and if he was safe.

"Tabitha? Do you see anything?"

"No. Nothing. Must have been . . ."

A distinct scratching sounded—this time at her back door. Her mother bolted to her feet. Leaning over, she blew out the lantern, leaving only one by the staircase burning.

". . . the wind. Mother, what are you doing?" *It doesn't sound like the wind.*

"Someone is scratching on the back door! What kind of a person scratches on a back door? A bad one, that's who."

"It's probably just the skunk that was here two weeks ago. Must be back for more of my trash."

This time when the sound came, Tabitha crossed to the middle of the room, stopped, and stared at the back door. It definitely sounded like someone scratching. Or knocking softly. Her heart pounded. Hunter had said not to open the door. What or who was out there?

Rock Springs was a fair piece away and Hunter's mount was already lathered as he galloped down the road. Hunter had never been this way before so he had to concentrate in the dark not to take a wrong turn and get lost. As he'd been doing approximately every quarter mile, he reined his mount to a halt. When his horse quieted, he listened for the sounds of wagon wheels, or a whimpering child. Anything. Surely, transporting the young girl and Mrs. Ling, they must have a wagon. Which would mean slower going and more noise. He didn't want to ride up on them and give himself away.

Then again, they might already be dead, divested of their scalps, and bodies hidden.

He wouldn't think that.

His horse pulled at the reins and pawed the ground. Seemed he was as agitated as Hunter.

"All right, we're going," Hunter mumbled. Just as he was about to give the gelding his head, a whimper sounded in the bushes to his left.

Hunter cleared leather fast, pointing his gun in the general direction he'd heard the noise. A deep gasp sounded, then a low curse.

"Don't move!" Hunter called out. "Or I'll blow your head clear into Rock Springs!"

"P-Please d-don't shoot!"

He knew that voice, but couldn't put a name on it.

"Throw down your guns—all of 'em! Before my finger gets itchy."

He heard one weapon clatter into some rocks, and surprise washed through him. This was the easiest outlaw he'd ever encountered.

"Bring the wagon out slow and easy." This was another guess, but so far he'd been right. Why stop now?

Coming in his direction, a team of horses emerged from the brush-lined roadside. By the light of the moon, he recognized Clyde, the drunk, sitting in the driver's seat and holding the lines.

"What the hell, Clyde? What're you doing?"

Riding forward, with his gun trained on Clyde's head, Hunter saw Mrs. Ling sitting in the bed of the wagon next to a Chinese man he didn't recognize. Their hands were tied behind their backs and their mouths gagged. Lan wasn't there.

"Spill your guts, Clyde!"

Clyde's hands began to shake.

"Clyde," he gritted out through his clenched jaw. Mrs. Ling's eyes were wide over a bandanna tied around her mouth.

"I . . . I—"

"I saw what you did to Mr. Ling and the other woman. I should shoot you right now, you cowardly scum—" He clamped his lips closed out of respect for Mrs. Ling.

"I didn't do that. I was waitin' with the wagon. He never said he was gonna hurt no one! Said Mrs. Ling would have a better life back in

China. I seen how hard she works all the time. He said they gave 'em a hefty grubstake to get started once they was off the ship. He said she'd be happy to go home."

Revulsion washed through Hunter. "Was that before or after you're paid for their scalp?"

"What? He never said nothin' about killin'!"

"Who?"

"Mr. Sundstrom, that fella hanging around with Dwight."

"He tell ya he was a bounty hunter?"

Clyde's eyes went wide and he shook his head.

"Is Dwight involved?"

"Don't think so. Sundstrom would shut up whenever we was talkin' when Dwight come around."

Hunter growled. "Wanted to keep all the bounty for himself, never intending to pay you."

"Honest to Pete, Hunter," Clyde babbled through his tears. "I couldn't go through with it. I was bringin' 'em back, that's why the wagon's pointed in this direction. I ain't lying!"

Confident Clyde didn't have the guts to shoot him even if he did have another gun hidden somewhere, Hunter rode to the far side of the wagon where he climbed inside and freed the captives.

Finished, he jabbed his gun into Clyde's side. "Where's Sundstrom now?"

"B-Back in Logan Meadows. When we was almost out of town, the girl jumped out and ran off. He went after her and told me to head to Rock Springs. I hid in these bushes because I thought you was Sundstrom. I'm gonna lock myself in jail just as soon as I take Mrs. Ling home. I figure I should probably hang."

Logan Meadows!

He had to get back, but what about Mrs. Ling? "How do you feel, Mrs. Ling? Are you hurt in any way?"

She took a deep breath. "I fine. Worry about Lan! And Mr. Ling!"

"I am, too, ma'am. Your husband is with Dr. Thorn now. I need to get back to Logan Meadows."

The Chinese man, now unfettered, jumped out and picked up the guns. "No worry. I make sure she get back to Logan Meadows." He pointed the gun at Clyde. Hunter had to trust him. That was the only way he'd get back before something terrible happened.

CHAPTER SIXTY-THREE

At the whimpering cry, Tabitha yanked open the back door to something huddled at her feet. She recognized the black hair instantly and hoisted Lan into her arms, relief surging into her heart. *Thank you, God! Thank you for bringing her here.*

Stepping inside, Tabitha slammed the door, and threw the lock.

"Who is it?" her mother whispered, as if there were others around they had to be careful of alerting. "Is it the little girl?"

Tabitha nodded, the icy-cold child shivering in her arms. No telling how long she'd been hiding outside afraid to go for help. She carried her to the chair and picked up the throw, wrapping it around Lan's shoulders and tucking it in. Holding her like a baby, she gently rocked back and forth. Lan fisted her reddened hands into the blanket. Frostbite could be deadly. "Mother, fix another cup of tea, so we can warm her insides. She's half-frozen. Her teeth are chattering."

Marigold hurried away. "I'm stoking the fire as well and will heat some of the leftover stew."

"Lan," Tabitha said quietly, some of the girl's hair tickling Tabitha's face. "Do you know where they've taken your mother?"

"Wagon," she sobbed. "Going out of town."

Please God, help Hunter find Bao—before it's too late. Is she even still alive?

"Which way, Lan? Which way did it go?"

"Over bridge."

Marigold hurried from the kitchen alcove with a cup, stirring the contents with a spoon. "Here we are. Nice and hot. Set her in the chair and wrap her up, then she can hold the cup. It's weak, but will warm her fingers."

We need to get this information about the direction of the wagon to Hunter. I wish Albert were here. Or Thom. Surely Win went with Hunter. Dr. Thorn is all the way down the street with his hands full. What to do, what to do . . .

Lan was reluctant to release Tabitha when she tried to set her in the chair. "It's all right, sweetie. Nothing is going to hurt you now. You need to drink this. To warm up."

Finally nestled back into the seat, Tabitha raised the cup to Lan's lips when pounding on the front door made her hands fumble.

"What in God's name?" her mother screeched from the other room. Whoever it was pounded again. Lan jumped to her feet.

Tabitha scooped her up. "Mother!" she called in a frantic whisper. "Stall! I'm taking Lan upstairs. I have a very bad feeling."

Their gazes locked. *"Go!"*

"Open this door!" a man's voice demanded from outside. "I see your shadows in there. Open up! I need to speak with you."

"I have no authority to do so, sir," she heard her mother argue back. "I don't live in Logan Meadows, although I'm coming to find the town quite charming. Do you live here? Where are you from? Have you seen how bright the stars are at night?"

It felt like ages before Tabitha ran back down the stairs. Her mother stood in the dim room at the door, the heavy iron teakettle still in her hands. "I'll *not* do as you demand, so you can just go away this instant. You're bothering me!"

When Tabitha arrived, relief and fear swept over her mother's face. She stepped aside as if very thankful to hand the problem over to her.

Bolstering her courage, Tabitha took ahold of the pull and rolled up the blind with no intention of opening the door. The sinister eyes that glared back at her had to belong to the perpetrator of this horrible crime, searching for the one who'd gotten away. "My husband will be down in one second!" she barked, making the angriest face she could. "He's known to shoot first and ask questions later! You'd better run while the gettin's good. How dare you bother us at this time of night! Now get!"

An ugly sneer spread across his mouth. Slowly, he raised one hand until she saw a shiny revolver pointed right at the glass. "Open up or I'll start shooting. You'll be dead before you hit the floor. Then I'll kill the other woman."

She'd hidden Lan in her bedroom armoire. She pictured the silent tears streaming down the child's face. She thought of Jake's poor mother, her face battered and bruised. Mr. Ling and poor Bao. From somewhere she got the courage to laugh in his face. When she quieted, she stated flatly, "Go ahead, you filthy animal! Every man in this town will be on you like flies on the dung you are! How dare you threaten us like that!"

Her mother gasped.

"What's wrong?" Tabitha called. "Why aren't you shooting? Scared to hang?"

Tabitha opened her hand and the shade dropped down with a snap. She marched over to the lamp by the stairs and extinguished the flame, casting them into darkness. Black fear burned her insides. She wished she owned a gun. That would at least optimize their chances. If nothing else, she could shoot into the air in hopes of drawing someone's attention.

"What are we going to do?" Her mother's voice wobbled. "If he gets in, we'll be dead before anyone can come to our rescue. I really don't want to die just yet."

"Maybe he took my words to heart and thinks Hunter is upstairs. Maybe he went away."

"And maybe he didn't."

A startled screech burst from her mother's mouth when the back door reverberated loudly. The man must have rammed it with something hard. She jumped into Tabitha's arms, shivering like a puppy in a thunderstorm. He struck again. *He's found the woodpile.* How long would it take until he broke through? What should they do? She'd not lie down like a lamb to slaughter.

She set her mother away with a firm hold on her shoulders. "We can't let him get to Lan. The poor child has already been traumatized enough. I'm sure she can hear everything that's going on."

Crack!

"Do you have a gun?"

"No. But I do have a fire poker." She hurried to the kitchen, and hefted the iron rod, which was not as long as she remembered. He'd have to be awfully close for her to be able to use the weapon on his head. She swallowed down her fear.

Crack!

Her mother skittered over. "The door's weakening. What should we do? It won't be long before he's inside! Let's scream for help from an upstairs window."

"No one will hear us! Shady Creek is on one side making noise, on the other, the abandoned sheriff's office, and next to that, the Bright Nugget where Farley is sure to be playing the piano. It's up to us . . ."

Her mother nodded.

Crack!

"Go upstairs, into my room," Tabatha commanded. "Shut the door and barricade—"

An idea struck her and she clamped her mouth closed. "Yes. I think it'll work. Come on, Mother, we don't have a moment to lose!" With the iron poker clutched in her fist, she bolted up the stairs and into her room. She threw back the covers, ignoring the embarrassing stains of her virginity and ripped off the sheet. "Sorry, Mother. I meant to change them before Hunter returned . . ."

"No need to explain, daughter," her mother replied. "What can I do?"

Crack!

"Go to your room and bring me your sheet, quickly!"

Tabitha had never seen her mother move so fast. While she was gone, Tabitha quietly opened the door to her balcony. She lowered to her tummy and scooted out on the small deck, and tied one end of the sheet to the post, double and triple knotting the anchor.

Crack. Crackle. *Time is almost up.*

Her mother was back. "What on earth are you planning? I'm not going down—"

"You will. He's almost inside. Like you said, he'll shoot us and take Lan. It's her only chance. *Our* only chance." She took the end of her mother's sheet and tied it to the corner of hers, making sure it was secure. "It's not all that far down. If you end up falling halfway, it won't kill you. We'll be down and he'll be in here, trying to get into the bedroom. "Once we're down, we'll avoid the back of the shop and run across the bridge. Uncle Frank's is only a couple of houses down. He owns several guns!"

"Yes. That's a good plan."

The splintering of wood made Tabitha bolt to the armoire and pull Lan from her hiding spot. "Here, sweetie," she crooned into the child's face, her eyes black with fear. With the starry night above, Tabitha scooped the girl up and held her over the bannister until Lan took ahold of the sheet. "Don't worry, it won't break. Now scurry down and we'll be right behind you. Go on," she prodded when Lan just hung there, looking down at the ground. "Go on, honey, we all need to get down." *In time.*

Crack. Boom. Crack.

"You better watch out, because here I come!" the nasty man bellowed, his crazed voice shooting up Tabitha's spine. He wasn't even trying to be quiet any longer. He must be deranged.

"Mother, go!"

"You go!"

Tabitha pointed. "I can hold him off better. Get to Uncle Frank's!"

She didn't have to say it twice. Her mother put her leg over the bannister and swung over. Pulling aside her skirt, she wrapped one leg around the sheet and began her slide. That was all Tabitha saw. When she heard boots on the stairway, she bolted to her bedroom door and tried to slam it closed, but the man had stuck one arm inside. Wedging her shoulder against the pulsating door, the weight of the iron poker in her slick palm filled her with frantic determination.

CHAPTER SIXTY-FOUR

Hunter leaned over the neck of his mount, riding for all he was worth. The rhythmic blows of the horse's hooves beating into the ground as the gelding galloped back toward Logan Meadows was the mantra pounding into his brain. *Hold on. Hold on. Hold on. I'm coming, Tabby, hold on.*

How much time had passed? Hunter wasn't sure. He did know that Sundstrom had no regard for life and couldn't care less if someone lived or died. The thought of him in town with Tabitha turned his blood to ice. Still, the bounty hunter might not be there at all, or have anything to do with his wife, he tried to reason with himself. This ride could be all for naught.

Something in his gut told him that was not the case.

To get there as soon as he could.

From the corner of his eye, Hunter recognized an old barn he'd passed on the way out of town. He was almost there! Soon he'd pass Albert and Susanna's house, across from Brenna and Greg's. Then he'd cross the bridge to his destination.

Hold on, Tabby! Hold on!

Rounding the corner, the bridge came into sight. Across that was the bookshop, which was uncommonly dark. He thundered across the bridge. On a sheet hanging out from Tabitha's balcony hung Marigold, her skirts flying like a flag. Lan stood nearby.

Sliding his mount to a halt, Hunter swung out of the saddle, letting the horse trot off toward the livery.

He ran beneath the woman. "Where's Tabby?" he shouted up to her.

"Inside! Hurry! Go round back!"

That was all Hunter needed to hear. The broken-down door caused black fear to clamp his gut. He couldn't lose her now, not now. Not when they'd finally found each other. These past three weeks had been the best of his life, and he knew Thorp wouldn't even mind his saying that. Tabby might think of him only as a hero for now, but he'd win her love, someway, somehow.

Halfway up the stairs, he saw Sundstrom, pounding on Tabitha's door, screaming through the one-inch gap that held his arm, so angry and mad with killing lust he didn't hear Hunter's approach.

Hunter heard the sickening snap of the man's arm bone when, somehow, Tabitha must have struck it with some weapon. Sundstrom's animalistic roar of pain was deafening.

"Get away from the door!" Hunter shouted.

Sundstrom turned in surprise, his broken arm dangling uselessly. With his good arm, he went for the gun holstered on his hip.

Hunter was fast. He killed the man with a single bullet to the heart.

"Tabby!" he shouted. He took the last few steps two at a time, then stepped over Sundstrom's lifeless body and entered the room.

Tabitha, when he'd shouted for her to get away from the door, had flattened herself on the other side of the room by her reading chair. He was there in two strides and pulled her into his embrace, so thankful she was still alive.

"Hunter," she breathed. "Hunter," she said again, her voice thick with emotion.

He had no words, so he sought her mouth with his. He ran his hands down her back as she pressed closer. This room that had held such ecstasy last night had almost been her death chamber. The realization was too horrible to contemplate.

"Lan? My mother?"

"Outside and safe." He pulled back to gaze into her eyes. "I found Mrs. Ling. She's safe too and on her way back to Logan Meadows. I can't believe you were—"

"Shh, I wasn't. Because of you. Only because of you. I love you so much, Hunter. All I could think about as I was holding the door against that horrible man was that I was going to die and never be able to tell you that. That you'd never know. You're everything to me! I love you so much it hurts."

That was all he needed to hear. He kissed her again, passionately. "And I love you, Miss Hoity-Toity. I don't know how I lived until I met you." He chuckled even though the question was between them. "But, what about the letter we sent to the preacher, about calling the marriage quits after your mother leaves? What should we do about that? If he reads it, he may be mighty confused."

"That's easy. We'll just ask for it back unopened."

"What's this I hear?"

They turned. Marigold, tousled from her climb down the sheets, had come back in and was standing only a few feet away.

"Where's Lan?" Tabitha asked, still standing in Hunter's embrace.

"She's waiting outside. Susanna saw Hunter gallop by her house. She, Greg, and Brenna all ran down here to see what was wrong. Lan is with them. But I was worried about you, Tabitha. I figured it was safe to return since Mr. Wade was in here shooting his gun. He wouldn't let that horrible man get the best of him, I was sure." She glanced for a moment at the body on the landing. "But don't try to change the subject on me. I don't know what you meant about splitting up after I leave, but whatever it is, I'll not stand for it! The two of you are perfect for each other. I couldn't have made a better match myself, and that is saying something. I just want you to get busy and give me some grandchildren."

She turned slowly to leave, but looked back around. "Oh, I guess you'd like to know I've decided to stay on until after Christmas. No use spending all that money on travel and not visiting for a good long time." She smiled knowingly, and then quietly went out, stepping over Mr. Sundstrom to descend the stairs.

"Well?" Hunter asked.

"You heard her." Tabitha's smile reminded him of a mischievous fairy. "She rules the roost. I guess we best get busy making her happy."

Never having enough, he kissed her again. "My thoughts exactly."

CHAPTER SIXTY-FIVE

Three days later, with a firm hold of Hunter's hand, Tabitha stepped out of the Silky Hen in a haze of happiness. All the trouble that had turned Logan Meadows on its ear had calmed, and for that she was thankful. They stood for a moment in the crisp morning sunshine, taking in the scene.

"It was nice of your mother to move out for a few days," Hunter said as he nodded to Dr. Thorn going by in his buggy.

"Yes, it was. I'm glad she made the first move to make up with Aunt Roberta. More than anything, I think her motivation was to give us some privacy. Every newly wedded couple deserves some time alone."

Hunter smiled down into her face. She took that time to memorize every detail about him. They'd both come so close to losing each other. "More likely, it was the memory of Sundstrom charging up the stairs to kill you." He chuckled. "Still, it's awfully good of her. And I appreciate it, whatever the reason. I'm anxious to make new memories and chase the old away."

"Hunter, you're so romantic!"

"You haven't seen nothing yet, Miss—"

She cocked her brow.

"If you'd let me finish, I was going to say, *Miss Hotty-Body.*" He ran his hand down her back, and she moved closer. "I'm glad you didn't change your straitlaced ways until you married me."

Tabitha laughed, enjoying Hunter's playful side very much.

"Tabitha, Hunter," a soft voice called out. *"Ciao."*

Dichelle hurried their way, having come out of the mercantile. She looked stunning, as usual, a cheerful smile on her face, and her eyes bright with excitement.

"Have you heard?" she asked, looking straight at Tabitha. "Your *madre*, she is an *angelo*!"

"What? I don't know what an *angelo* is, Dichelle." She and the Italian singer had become very close, and she adored this little songbird. She understood now how Hunter could call her that. "I have no idea what you're talking about."

"Your mother! She is an angel. She's offered to take me back to New York with her when she goes, using the ticket she purchased for you! She will also try to open some doors for me once we arrive. I am speechless. Beyond words." She dashed at a tear that had slipped from her eye.

"Well, I'll be," Hunter said. "That's pretty nice. That leaves us some time to have a few more shows."

Dichelle laughed. "That is exactly right, my *amico*. That's precisely what we will do. A few more golden eggs for the Bright Nugget."

Gabe Garrison rode down the street with a ranch hand from the Broken Horn, a sack tied to the back of his saddle. The two stopped in front of the laundry house, dismounted, and untied the sack. They disappeared inside.

Tabitha tugged on Hunter's arm and gestured to Dichelle. "Let's go see Bao. I want to check on Lan, too. That girl is always in my thoughts. I hope someday she will be able to forget what happened."

Dichelle leaned in and kissed both of Tabitha's cheeks, then did the same for Hunter. "*Arrivederci*, my dear friends," she said. "I must go and write to Ned, tell him I won't be returning to Soda Springs after all. *Fate i bravi.*"

"Fate i bravi?" Tabitha hadn't heard that before.

"Be good," she said over her shoulder as she hurried away.

Entering the shop, they found Gabe and Tyler Weston waiting in the foyer. Tap Ling, his face bruised and a cut healing above his eye, stood behind the counter listening to the cowboys. His eyes brightened when he saw Tabitha, but he kept his attention on what the cowboy was saying.

"I need ta apologize to your wife, Mr. Ling," Tyler Weston said, his hat gripped firmly in his fingertips. "May I please speak to her?"

Mr. Ling gave a small bow. "One moment, please," he said and hurried away. The front door opened and Daisy stepped inside, coming to stand with Tabitha and Hunter.

Tabitha ran her hand down Daisy's arm. Jake's fiancée hadn't been in the restaurant when they'd eaten. She looked drawn and tired. When she looked up, Tabitha couldn't help but notice her red eyes. "How is Jake's mother?"

"I've just come from the Red Rooster. Marlene is healing, but isn't yet ready to come back to work just yet." A shadow crossed over her face, and Tabitha wondered if she was thinking about Jake.

"Any word?"

She shook her head. "None since the first telegram. I'm worried. I pray he's all right."

"I'm sure he is, Daisy. It's only been a little over two weeks. Who knows what circumstances he's been thrust into. Jake's smart, and loyal. You have nothing to worry about."

She hoped she wasn't setting Daisy up with false hope. In truth, she and Hunter had had the same conversation over their meal. Seemed everyone was worried over Jake and what was happening.

Bao appeared at the dividing door, with Mr. Ling at her back.

"Ma'am," Tyler said softly. "I have ta apologize for giving you such a scare the other day when I was—" He paused, and glanced at Tabitha, Daisy, and Hunter as if embarrassed to go on. He swallowed. "Looking in your alley window. Especially now, after what happened."

Bao stood quietly, her own bruises still visible on her face.

"You see, Jake's my good friend. It was the day he left and I was on my way to the saloon. I just wanted to see his ma. I was curious over something that was none of my business. Jake said she'd come to town and was working for you. I didn't mean any harm."

For the size and breadth of the handsome young man, he seemed as skittish as a bunny.

"No harm done," Tap Ling said firmly, surprising Tabitha. He turned and exchanged a few words in Chinese with his wife, then she disappeared into the back of the shop.

Gabe, quiet all this time, set the bag of laundry on the counter. When he turned, he caught Daisy's eye. "Jessie expects you for dinner Sunday night. I'll come pick you up around four."

Daisy nodded. "Thank you, Gabe. I'll be happy to come."

Her voice didn't carry much cheerfulness.

Gabe and Tyler said their goodbyes, as did Daisy. Now that it was just Tabitha and Hunter, she asked, "How is Lan, Mr. Ling? Is she recovering?" *As much as a child can from such a frightening experience.*

"She exceedingly resilient," Mr. Ling said softly. "She okay. Bao and I thankful to you for your help. Both you."

Tabitha felt Hunter's arm around her back. Thank God worse hadn't happened.

Mr. Ling's head tipped to the side. "Sheriff and deputy back in town. Say man who pay bounty hunter killed in riots."

"If you can be glad over a killing, he'd be the one," Hunter said. "You can be sure we'll all be keeping a closer eye on your place. I'd like to say all danger is completely gone, but I can't. But with the ringleader dead, that's more than half the battle."

Lan peeked her head out from the work area.

Tabitha waved. "Lan! I'd like to speak with you."

Lan came out slowly, looked around, and when she saw it was just them, she ran into Tabitha's arms. They stayed that way for several seconds.

Tabitha picked her up and rocked her to her chest. "I'm so happy to see you," Tabitha said, stroking her hair and holding her tight. The warmth in Hunter's gaze made Tabitha's eyes sting with emotion.

Lan whispered something against her neck.

"What, honey? I didn't catch what you said." She looked down into the child's sweet face.

"I will change the way people think."

It took a moment for what she'd just heard to register, then she sucked in a deep breath at the child's perception. This time she wasn't able to hold in her tears. "Yes, Lan, I think you will. We *all* will."

Lan squirmed to get down and ran off, Tabitha watching her go.

"Come on, wife. Let's let Mr. Ling get back to business. He has other things to do besides watch you get emotional."

Hunter's soft tone belied his words, and his love wrapped around her heart. She may be twenty-nine, but after the peril they'd just lived through, she realized how young that really was. She had plenty of years to show Hunter just how much she loved him. And she wasn't going to wait one more second before she set her hand to that course.

ACKNOWLEDGMENTS

With a grateful heart, I reach out to all the wonderful people who have helped make *Whispers on the Wind* a reality. First, to every single person on the Montlake team that has made this author's journey so special—thank you. To Maria Gomez, my editor at Montlake, for her never-ending interest and support—what would I do without you? To Jessica Poore, Author Relations, you rock! Your humorous and witty e-mail responses and FB posts keep me smiling! To Caitlin Alexander, my developmental editor extraordinaire. Working on a book with you is painless and fun. You have taught me *so* much. I'm indebted! To my husband, Michael, and grown sons, Matthew and Adam, and their wife, girlfriend, and daughter, Misti, Rachel . . . *and* Evelyn, I cherish each and every one of you with all my heart. Your creative ideas keep me writing. To Shelly, Sherry, Jenny, Mary, and Lauren, my sisters—you know the inner workings of my soul. I love you. To my dear friend, author Kit Morgan, for your help brainstorming my hero on the ride back from the Women Writing the West Conference. If you read Mrs. Hollyhock and Hunter's buffalo scene, you will see I took your words to heart. Thank you. To my dear readers who keep calling for more Logan Meadows and asking whose story is next. You have no idea how much your concern that each of my characters have their own HEA touches my heart. And, of course, to our magnificent God. His dreams are always better than anything we can think up on our own. Thank you for everything!

ABOUT THE AUTHOR

Photo © 2009 Family Gallery

U*SA Today* bestselling author Caroline Fyffe was born in Waco, Texas, though her father's career in the US Air Force took her all over. After earning a bachelor of arts in communications from California State University, Chico, she embarked on a twenty-year career as an equine photographer. During long days at the show arena, she began to write fiction, blending her love of horses and the Wild West to create the award-winning Prairie Hearts series. *Where the Wind Blows*, the first book in the series, won the prestigious Golden Heart Award from the Romance Writers of America. Fyffe and her husband have two grown sons. They currently live in the Pacific Northwest.

Made in the USA
Charleston, SC
06 July 2016